THE POISONED CLERGYMAN

The Perfect Poison Murders, Book 2
A Georgian Mystery

E.L. Johnson

ARE YOU SIGNED UP FOR DRAGONBLADE'S BLOG?

You'll get the latest news and information on exclusive giveaways, exclusive excerpts, coming releases, sales, free books, cover reveals and more.

Check out our complete list of authors, too!

No spam, no junk. That's a promise!

Sign Up Here

www.dragonbladepublishing.com

Dearest Reader;

Thank you for your support of a small press. At Dragonblade Publishing, we strive to bring you the highest quality Historical Romance from some of the best authors in the business. Without your support, there is no 'us', so we sincerely hope you adore these stories and find some new favorite authors along the way.

Happy Reading!

CEO, Dragonblade Publishing

Additional Dragonblade books by Author E.L. Johnson

The Perfect Poison Murders
The Strangled Servant (Book 1)
The Poisoned Clergyman (Book 2)

Acknowledgments

I am grateful to my family for their constant support, and to my husband for pointing out all the plot holes along the way. He adds that he has also kept me in regular supply of chocolate cake, so I suppose that is a suitable trade-off.

I am also thankful to the staff at the Hertfordshire county archives for answering my questions about Regency-era hospitals, my critique partner Melanie, as well as the staff of BITC for their regular questions, requests for updates on the status of this novel, and just generally making me feel loved as a resident author.

CHAPTER ONE

Hertford, 1806

I T WAS A beastly hot summer day when Poppy reflected that she wouldn't mind another murder. Not causing one, of course, but solving one. A few months ago she had solved what she mentally called "her first murder" and it had opened her eyes to a world of heartache and betrayal. A public misunderstanding had upended her sterling reputation overnight, and in her need to restore her good name, Poppy had discovered enemies masquerading as friends, neighbors who weren't what they seemed, and loved ones who showed their true colors.

She had loved it. For her part in unmasking a killer, she had been praised for her intelligence rather than her feminine charms. But now that the excitement was over, her life had returned to a steady and unremarkable routine of neighborhood dinners, visiting the sick, household chores, and wishing for something extraordinary to happen that never did.

July had ushered in a regular series of hot, uncomfortable days for the ladies of the parsonage, and despite sitting in the shade of the blue sitting room downstairs, Poppy wished she could be somewhere cooler. The open windows offered no welcoming breeze, and her aunt fought a desperate battle against the heat, fanning herself vigorously with a delicate wooden fan that added to rather than detracted from the heat in the room.

Poppy smiled as she heard her aunt sigh. Hertford was a pretty market town with lush green hills and rich countryside, but the winters were cold, the summers were hot, and despite its trim brickwork, the parsonage was not well-insulated.

At that moment, Poppy felt beastly and out of sorts. She looked up from her uncle's day-old newspaper and met her aunt's gaze, which had taken on a dreamy quality.

"Remind me, when did you last hear from him, Poppy?"

There was no doubt in Poppy's mind who her aunt meant. Only one man in her life held such consequence as to deserve the familiar reference "him."

"Whoever do you mean, Aunt?" Poppy asked.

Her aunt paused her fanning. "You know full well who I mean. Constable Dyngley, of course!"

"I have not heard from Constable Dyngley for some time now." Poppy cast her eyes down at the newspaper's pages, ignoring the tremble in her hands.

"I do not mean to bring up unpleasant memories, my dear. I only wish to see you happily wedded, like any girl of sixteen to thirty should be."

Poppy let out a little snort at that. It had been months ago, but she still remembered the details vividly, for it had been the last time she and Dyngley had seen each other. During her first murder, in which Poppy's close friend had gone missing and was presumed dead the night after a fight with Poppy at the Assembly Rooms, Constable Dyngley was one of the few people who believed in her innocence.

Constable Dyngley had sensed she was a kindred spirit and since then they had often talked together, resulting in more than one society matron wondering at Poppy's marriage prospects. Indeed, despite it being months ago, she could remember their last conversation as if it was yesterday.

Dyngley and Poppy had taken a turn around her aunt's small flower garden, using the chance to speak privately. It was an astute move, for her aunt was no doubt watching through the parsonage windows and hoping for a proposal or at the very least a declaration of love, Poppy reflected.

Dyngley had beamed at her with a dashing smile, marked by two dimples that sprang to life in the corners of his cheeks when he smiled. His dark hair had a perpetual unruly look as if he had just raked his fingers through it, giving him a boyish appeal. He looked into her brown eyes and said, "I wonder if I might call on you from time to time?"

"Whatever for?" She raised an eyebrow.

"You help me think about things, more than I would care to admit. Even if you are infuriating at times." He grinned.

"You say that like it's a compliment."

"It is. My life was easy and uncomplicated before you entered into it."

The memory of his warm smile faded as her aunt interrupted, "But did he not take your hand in his, and press it against his heart? I am sure he did."

Poppy laughed. "No, Aunt."

"Are you sure? I thought for certain I saw him take your hand—"

"Were you watching us?"

Aunt Rachel's ruddy cheeks reddened more, and she set down her fan with a snap. "Only as much as is appropriate. You may be nineteen, but you are still a young woman, and it is not so very long ago that you came out."

"Other girls come out when they are fifteen and sixteen."

"And they often end up making very bad marriages, unless they have their relations to look after them." She sniffed. "But that is not the point. It is my duty to look after you and that includes when you're walking around the garden with young men. But never mind that, did he not say when he would write or see you again?"

"He did not."

"Pooh. And now so many men gone to fight, I don't know

what we shall do."

It was true. For three years men had honored Britain by pounding French ships, courtesy of the British navy. A most worthwhile occupation, in her mind; Poppy fancied that it must take nerves of steel to man one of his majesty's ships and face cannon fire from a foreign enemy.

Indeed, the newspaper she held boasted of an incredible naval victory, calling the Battle of Trafalgar to be the greatest British victory yet.

There came a quiet knock at the door of their blue sitting room, and the family's maid, Betsey, walked in looking as meek as a church mouse. With a clean white apron and wispy fine blonde hair askew, she curtseyed and said, "I have news from town, Mrs. Greene."

"Oh? And what is it?" Aunt Rachel asked.

"I saw my sister in Hertford center and she said there was a carriage accident outside town on the main road."

"Goodness. Was anyone hurt?"

Betsey shrugged. "I couldn't say. Oh, and there's to be a dance at the assembly rooms in a fortnight, on Saturday. Will you and Miss Morton be going?"

"Aha! That is just the thing." Aunt Rachel clapped her hands in delight. "Yes, Betsey, we will. A dance is just what we need to lift our spirits. What do you say, Poppy?"

Poppy's smile faltered. In the warm weather, her limbs felt heavy and dull, her serviceable white linen gown stuck to her back, and she felt a droplet of sweat trickle down her neck. She set down her uncle's newspaper on the overstuffed pale green sofa. "One dance at the assembly rooms is much like another."

"Hah. Spoken like a bored ingenue if I ever heard one," Aunt Rachel said.

Poppy's uncle entered the room. A short, rotund man with a balding pate and kind eyes, Reverend Reginald Greene's mouth was set in a frown, his gray bushy eyebrows knit together unhappily. He held in his hand a letter and sat in the stiff high back chair facing them. "Rachel, Terrence is sick."

Poppy spied a myriad of emotions flit over her aunt's face: worry, concern, then anger and snideness. Aunt Rachel chose worry and said, "Oh dear. I shall write to that wife of his and send along a recipe of mine. Is it gout? They do make things out to be worse than they are, you know."

"No, it's something worse. He caught yellow fever on his trip coming back from Antigua. Hilda has written, asking me to come," Uncle Reginald said.

Poppy's eyebrows rose. "Is he all right?"

"Hilda fears it is very serious," her uncle said.

"Oh, that Hilda, always overdramatizing things. She could have had success on the stage," Aunt Rachel said.

Uncle Reginald quelled her with a look. "Hilda does not think he has long, Rachel."

"Oh, pish tosh. Do you actually think—"

"I had better go. I'll leave within the hour," he said.

"What? An hour? But what about us? What should we bring? And Poppy? We were going to go to a dance in a fortnight." Aunt Rachel took up her fan again, waving violently at her thin brown locks. "And what of the journey? You know I cannot abide long trips and your brother lives some hundred miles away. I shall fall sick from the constant motion and my embroidery will be nothing to speak of." She picked up a round wooden embroidery hoop from the side table next to her, presenting a sorry mishmash of string and color.

From what Poppy could see, her aunt hardly needed the excuse of a bumpy carriage ride to declare her embroidery a work of many hours' toil but no beauty.

"My dear, the invitation is for me alone," Uncle Reginald said gently.

The delicate wooden fan slipped from her aunt's fingers and tumbled to the floor. "Hilda would have you abandon us? At a time like this?" Aunt Rachel said.

"It will be easier with just me. I can travel by post. It will be faster and save you both the journey. There is no reason to tax yourself," he said.

Before Aunt Rachel could reply, he was up and out of his seat, faster than Poppy would have expected of a man his age. He quit the comfortable sitting room, calling for Betsey to attend him.

True to his word, Poppy's uncle was gone within the hour, much to her aunt's dismay. From her sour expression, Poppy knew how much Aunt Rachel disliked it when her life of comfortable routine became disrupted by sudden demands on her or her husband's time.

"I do not know what we shall do with ourselves while he is gone." Aunt Rachel picked up her fan from the floor and opened it, waving away a light sheen of unladylike sweat from her forehead.

Poppy wondered aloud, "Lucky for us that today is Sunday. Who will give the sermon next week?"

Within three days a letter came, addressed to Poppy's uncle. The ladies did not open it, but held it up to the lamplight and wondered at its contents.

"Perhaps it is from Aunt Hilda, to say that Uncle Terrence is better," Poppy said.

"I doubt that. Hilda will want your uncle there, all the more to give her attention where none is due."

Poppy glanced at her aunt, who set down the unopened letter on a side table. "Why do you dislike her?"

"Hilda?" Aunt Rachel colored for a moment. "You know me, I would not speak rudely of anyone, especially our relations."

Poppy coughed to hide her smile. "And yet?"

Her aunt scratched her hair beneath her white, frilly mob cap. "Well, Hilda has always struck me as a selfish sort of person."

Poppy listened, waiting for more.

"She always made it understood that she came from a very wealthy family and that she was marrying for love, rather than for money or position. She made it clear in no uncertain terms that by marrying your uncle Terrence, she was marrying beneath her.

But never a word to Reginald or Terrence, of course, only to me," Aunt Rachel said quietly, smoothing down sweaty curls that had escaped her mob cap. "Reginald refused to believe me when I told him. He so wanted Terrence to be happy, to this day he won't hear a word against her. And then he revealed that she had called me common and expressly told Reginald he should not have married me."

"She did?" Poppy's eyes widened.

"Oh yes. She makes a point of it every time we meet, making me feel inferior as if it weren't enough that we live in a small town with little enough to live on. I've often told Reginald that if it weren't for your dear Mama we would have very little…" Aunt Rachel's hand flew to her mouth.

"What do you mean?" Poppy said.

"Oh. Never mind. Nothing. My tongue runs away with me sometimes."

"Aunt, what did you mean? What about my mother?"

"She's dead, child. You know that. She's been dead since you were a babe." Her voice was dull.

Poppy looked down, pained by the burden of having lost a parent she had never known, then raised her head. "Why did she come to your mind?"

"Oh. Only that Celeste wouldn't have cared what a silly woman like Hilda thought. She'd have told Hilda what was good for her, and not cared if she never received another invitation to their house or not. A striking woman, your mama."

"What was she like? Was she pretty?" Poppy asked.

"Hah. Tall. Very strong-willed. Put off a good number of gentlemen callers, I daresay. Like you, lots of opinions."

She said no more on the matter, despite how much Poppy coaxed her.

But the matter of Hilda and ailing Uncle Terrence was soon forgotten, for the question of who would give Sunday's sermon remained unresolved and with each passing hour, it weighed upon them. By Thursday, they began to get nervous. Then on

Friday afternoon, the sound of a horse's hooves striking the ground and the arrival of a carriage came from outside.

Aunt Rachel popped up off the faded green sofa in the sitting room, pushed aside the thick curtains, and glanced through the paned glass window. "That's a lovely carriage. Could it be the constable?"

Poppy came up beside her and looked out, her heart thumping in her chest. "No, it isn't."

She would recognize Dyngley's steady gait anywhere, but the round, blond-haired gentleman strolling up the walk and trampling on her aunt's flowers was most definitely not the handsome, serious, dark-haired constable she knew.

"It is a young man though."

Aunt Rachel peered closer, pressing her face against the windowpane. "I've never seen him before."

"No, nor I," Poppy agreed, stepping back.

A short knock came at the door. As Betsey went to answer it, Aunt Rachel sprang into action, flinging stray ribbons at Poppy and sending sofa cushions into disarray. "Quick, sit! Perhaps he might do for you, Poppy, if your manners are to his liking," she instructed, as Poppy dutifully sat on the green sofa and picked up her needlepoint, nudging her uncle's newspaper beneath the sofa with her foot.

A moment later Betsey came to the blue sitting room and announced, "Begging your pardon, ma'am, but there's a Reverend Charles Ingleby to see you." Betsey scarcely had time to step aside before the young man strode into the sitting room, like a hunter on the chase. Upon first glance, he reminded Poppy of an egg, with a round seat stuffed into light beige trousers, a white waistcoat embroidered with white thread that shone like silk in the light, and a smart tan traveling coat. He looked a trifle disheveled, but stood at attention in the doorway and eyed them both with a glassy expression, and a small mouth pursed as if he'd eaten a lemon. He had light gray eyes and bright blond hair artfully disarranged close to his head.

"Hello. This is the county parish for Hertford? The parsonage?"

"Yes. I am Mrs. Greene. This is my niece, Poppy," Aunt Rachel introduced, and the ladies dutifully curtseyed.

This went unnoticed by the young man, who instead devoted his attention to the room, observing its humble furnishings. Decorated with a handful of amateur family portraits and a framed needlepoint of a rose, he observed the smoky stains from candles marring the blue walls a darker color and frowned at the overstuffed pale green sofa, its array of mismatching cushions, and the small but serviceable fireplace. "Well, this is not what I expected. Are you the housekeeper?"

"I beg your pardon?" Aunt Rachel asked, "I—"

He cut her off. "Where is Mr. Greene?"

She laid her fan down with a snap. "I am Mr. Greene's wife. He is away, visiting his brother."

"Already? I should have thought he would have at least paid me the compliment of seeing me before he left. It could be thought that it is his charitable duty to see me settled in." He frowned, eyeing a bit of dirt on his boot, and shook his foot, sending the dirt flying onto the thin threadbare carpet. "When will he return?"

"Not for some time I suppose," Aunt Rachel said, "Was he expecting you?"

"Yes. He should have received a letter about my arrival. Has the post been delayed?" His mouth twisted unhappily.

"I'm sorry, but who are you?" Aunt Rachel's cheeks flamed red, a sure sign of her annoyance. Her sharp tone made him pause.

"Forgive me, madam, but the journey has been long and I am tired. I should like to retire to my room. Where is it?"

"Your room?" Aunt Rachel sputtered. "Perhaps you'd better explain the nature of your visit."

His expression darkened. "Very well. I see I shall receive no hospitality until I explain myself, even though this is most untoward." He sighed. "I have lately graduated from Oxford Divinity College, where I took orders. I have since been assisting Rector Jones and his patron, Lord Ryder. Do you know him?"

"Rector Jones?"

"Lord Ryder."

"No."

His mouth curved into an arrogant smile. "I thought not. He is a leader amongst his peers and if I may say so, one of the very best of men. He lives in Foxglove Park, in Oxfordshire, and has dozens of servants. When I attended tea there I had my very own footman, just to look after my person." He sighed happily.

"Indeed," Aunt Rachel said.

"Oh yes. Foxglove Park has over four hundred acres of woodlands." He clasped his hands, pleased with himself. "Rector Jones's family and I dine there once a week. They were very sorry to see me go."

"Ah. And you came here?"

"Yes. Your husband wrote to him and begged for help. I gather his brother is ill? As Mr. Greene needed someone capable and worthy to look after the people of this parish and Rector Jones could not possibly leave his flock, I was the obvious choice."

"And you will be replacing my husband?" Aunt Rachel asked.

"Temporarily. Just for his absence, until he returns."

"You look very young to be a rector."

"I am twenty-seven and have just taken orders a year ago." He began peering at the portraits on the walls, sniffing at one and ignoring the rest.

Poppy's polite smile fell as she watched him swipe a finger across the mantel above the fireplace, frowning as his finger came away soiled with dust. "I am surprised you allow the servants such laxity in their chores. You must run a very generous household. I will bring some necessary changes, I can see."

"Forgive me, but are you planning to stay here?" Poppy asked.

It drew a look of horror from Aunt Rachel and a glance from

Mr. Ingleby. "Yes," he said, as if noticing her for the first time. "Sorry, who are you again?"

"Poppy Morton. I'm Mr. Greene's niece."

He looked at her unfashionably tall height, her uncurled hair that hung in sweaty waves around her shoulders, and her thin body that boasted few feminine curves to tempt a man. With an uninterested flick of his eyes, he dismissed her as a poor relation. "Do you live here too?"

"Yes," she said.

"Oh." Disappointment crossed his face as he turned to Aunt Rachel. "Well, now that I have explained my reasons for coming, where is my room?"

"I didn't know you were coming to stay. I'll have Betsey make up one for you. Betsey!" Aunt Rachel called.

Betsey must have been listening, for there was a muffled sound behind the door and she appeared immediately. "Yes, ma'am?"

"Make up a room for Mr. Ingleby. He's going to stay awhile."

Betsey bobbed a curtsey and left.

Mr. Ingleby said, "Oh, and I have two traveling trunks outside." He called, "Be a dear and bring them in."

He turned to Aunt Rachel and Poppy. "In the meantime, I'll have tea." He sat down in the reverend's high back chair and stretched out his legs.

Aunt Rachel and Poppy exchanged a look. "I'm sure Betsey will fetch some tea as soon as she's done preparing your room."

He gave her a stunned look. "Do you mean to say you have just one servant?"

"Yes." Aunt Rachel's mouth withered.

He blinked and ran a hand through his blond hair, then tried patting it down. "I see."

Betsey came downstairs and said, "Mr. Ingleby's room is ready. If you'll follow me, sir."

Mr. Ingleby rose with a sniff and followed her upstairs.

Once the door to the blue sitting room closed, Aunt Rachel

let out a sigh of relief. "Well, what are we to do with him? Imagine sending a boy barely out of divinity school to do a man's job."

"He did say he was twenty-seven," Poppy said with a smile.

"That makes no difference. Your uncle and I were married by then. And did you see the way he minced about the room as if he owned the place? Such airs in a man, I've never seen their like before." Aunt Rachel tutted.

"It is strangely unholy," Poppy wondered.

"Unseemly, more like. Let us hope he shows a more amiable attitude at dinner."

BUT AS THEY sat down to a meal of mutton, peas, and boiled potatoes that evening, Poppy felt decidedly ungracious. She rubbed her sore lower back and shot a dirty look at their guest, who took no notice as he sliced into his mutton.

Earlier that afternoon, it had fallen upon Betsey and Poppy to drag and lift Mr. Ingleby's two traveling trunks upstairs to his room. He informed them that he had suffered a sore back from the journey and couldn't possibly lift a thing, he said, reclining on his bed. That didn't stop him, however, from ordering Betsey to unpack his trunks.

Dinner was a quiet affair, with Mr. Ingleby picking at his mutton and boiled potatoes. Like a child, he moved his peas around the simple plate with his fork and sliced into a potato, his utensils screeching against the plate. He took no notice of the smart dining room they sat in, preferring to drink heavily from a bottle of red wine.

Aunt Rachel studied him in silence, while Poppy took pains to make him feel welcome. "Your rector's patron must feel lucky to have two clergymen at his disposal. He must be very generous to allow you to go."

"Oh yes, Lord Ryder prides himself on being a most support-ive patron. Does your uncle have a patron?" he asked.

"Yes. Lady Cameron," Poppy said.

At the mention of a title, he raised his head, his light gray eyes alert. "Ah. And does she visit often?"

"No. But we are invited to dine with her often, and usually take tea with her once a month," Poppy added.

He stuffed some boiled potato into his mouth, chewing. "And when will your next visit be?"

"I do not know. Whenever her ladyship condescends to invite us, I suppose."

He drank some red wine and swallowed, wiping his mouth with a cloth napkin. "I should meet her. Make her acquaintance. It wouldn't do for her not to be aware of the situation."

Aunt Rachel and Poppy exchanged a look. Despite it being the first instance of him taking an interest in anything aside from his dinner, the ladies knew from their long acquaintance that Lady Cameron considered it an obligation, rather than a pleasure, to involve herself in society. Now in her late sixties, she was becoming more of a recluse, and couldn't be bothered to care who gave the sermon on Sundays.

"I say, you look done. Are you going to finish that?" He nodded at Poppy's plate of peas.

"I—No," she answered.

He took her plate and swiped her peas off her plate and onto his with his knife, then set her plate to the side and resumed eating.

Aunt Rachel cleared her throat. "I expect you'll want to get started soon. You have parish duties and you'll need time to plan out your sermon."

He blinked. "My sermon?"

"For Sunday services? You will be able to lead the service, won't you?" Aunt Rachel asked.

"Of course I will. What a ridiculous question." He scoffed and drank more wine.

"And you'll need to visit the families of the neighborhood. They'll all want to meet you," Poppy said.

He brightened at this.

"And then there are a few villagers who are sick. You'll want to visit them, of course," she added.

His smile fell. "I find that I am not able to offer comfort to those who are sick. I have a weak constitution and can fall ill at the slightest provocation. Besides, it is a womanly duty and Mrs. Jones would always visit the poor and sick herself. She has such a way with them."

"Indeed. And what did Rector Jones do instead?" Aunt Rachel asked.

He colored. "He devoted himself to his congregation and to spiritual matters."

"I see." Aunt Rachel quietly finished her peas.

Mr. Ingleby pushed aside his plate and dabbed his napkin at the corner of his mouth. "What is for dessert?"

"Why, nothing." Aunt Rachel and Mr. Ingleby stared at each other with equal confusion.

In that instant, Poppy realized that it would no more occur to Mr. Ingleby not to have dessert, than it would occur to her aunt to dine on jam tarts on a regular basis.

She said, "We do not usually have dessert, Mr. Ingleby. It is more of an extravagance. But whenever we dine out, we are often treated to a bit of cake or cream tart after dinner."

His expression was dark. "Can the household not afford it?" he asked bluntly.

"I beg your pardon—" Aunt Rachel started.

"How much is the living per annum?" he asked.

Aunt Rachel was speechless. He had spoken out of turn, and it was a question that a young man in the reverend's tutelage might delicately ask after years of being in the family. For a guest, a stranger, to ask so boldly was beyond the pale.

"In truth, I do not know," Poppy said, stepping on her aunt's foot beneath the table. "But we have cake and tarts a few times a year, for Christmas and Easter, and birthdays. My uncle says we don't need such extravagances when there are people going hungry in town."

"Hmph." Mr. Ingleby returned to his wine, draining one glass and filling up another. "I had been led to believe that the living in Hertfordshire was very profitable."

"It is a beautiful place, but the living is humble," Poppy said.

Their eyes met, and for the first time, he took the trouble to properly look at her. He observed her round face, thin brown eyebrows, and spotty chin. His gaze flickered to her dress, a simple white linen hand-me-down from their neighbor, who had three grown-up girls. The dress was two years out of date, had faded into more of a dull gray color, and needed washing, especially after hours in the heat.

"I see," he said. To Aunt Rachel, he asked, "Perhaps tomorrow you might introduce me to some of your neighbors. It would be good for me to meet your husband's flock."

Mr. Ingleby went to bed shortly after dinner, leaving Poppy and Aunt Rachel to clear the dishes away and spend the time sewing together in the blue sitting room by the fire.

"But what were you on about earlier, Poppy? Telling him we could hardly afford dessert. You'll have him think we are paupers," Aunt Rachel chided.

"I suspect something in his character. I have the feeling he is used to a grander style of living than we have here, and I suspect somewhat more frequent tarts. Do you still think he might do for me, Aunt? Were my manners pleasing enough?" Poppy teased.

"Him? Do for you? Absolutely not. What an absurd notion." Aunt Rachel sniffed and returned to her sewing. "You just keep an eye out for that constable. Oh, pooh." She tossed aside her embroidery.

"What?"

"I've just realized. He means to stay with us a few days, at least. Maybe a week."

"Yes. And?"

Her aunt shot her a look. "That means we shall have to bring him along with us to the dance on Saturday."

"Perhaps he doesn't dance." Poppy stifled a giggle.

As Poppy found out, Mr. Ingleby was delighted to accept the invitation to accompany the ladies to the assembly rooms for the following week. "It will give me the chance to make a greater acquaintance in the town." He rubbed his hands together.

That afternoon at the proper hour, Poppy and Aunt Rachel dutifully took Mr. Ingleby calling at their neighbors, repeating the tale of Uncle Terrence's yellow fever and Reverend Greene's subsequent departure until it became a dull subject. In contrast, Mr. Ingleby seemed to enjoy relaying his part in the sorry news, positioning himself as the hero of the day, coming to the rescue of the poor souls of the people in Hertford.

This tale was told at the Alleyns', the Grants', and around the neighborhood until they had drunk enough tea and eaten enough little cakes to ruin their dinner. From the way Mr. Ingleby helped himself, Poppy wondered if that was his aim. But he did rise to the occasion, discussing her uncle in the best light, with the due respect a junior clergyman should.

When it came to seeing the Blooms, however, he stopped short outside the humble dwelling. "I would rather rest," he said, eyeing the poor condition of the house and the wild state of the family's overgrown garden.

"What is it? Are you unwell?" Aunt Rachel asked, looking at him from the shadow of her bonnet.

He removed a handkerchief from his sleeve and dabbed at his forehead, exuding an air of men's cologne. "I confess I am rather tired and would like to return to the parsonage."

"But you haven't met the Blooms yet."

"I am too tired. My feet are killing me, I did not realize you had such a busy neighborhood. So many calls to make. Another time, I will see them at church." He gazed down at Aunt Rachel. "I am very tired."

It was as if the sun itself glared at her, for she wilted beneath his stern gaze. "Very well." She turned and led the way home. They were a quiet trio on the way back, but Mr. Ingleby perked up when he saw a letter had arrived, addressed to him. He snatched it and went upstairs into Mr. Greene's study, closing the door behind him.

Betsey entered the corridor where the ladies began to hang up their bonnets and walking coats and asked, "Excuse me, ma'am, but did you finish the oatcakes?"

"I beg your pardon?" Aunt Rachel asked.

"The oatcakes, Mrs. Greene. I made them two days ago and set a plate out in the kitchen. I couldn't find it this morning and wondered if you'd seen it or served them at dinner. I need the plate is all."

Aunt Rachel glanced at Poppy, who was just untying the strings of her straw bonnet. "Poppy, did you eat them?"

"No. But I can hazard a guess that I know where they disappeared to."

The ladies looked toward the ceiling as they heard Mr. Ingleby's muffled footsteps walk back and forth in his room. They heard him bustle about a few minutes before he came down and ordered Betsey to make tea. He then sailed into the comfortable blue sitting room, sinking into Reverend Greene's favorite high-backed chair, stretched out his legs, and let out a happy sigh.

Poppy did not look up from her novel, but Aunt Rachel was quick to react. "Who wrote you?"

He smiled. "I have had an invitation to dine with the Grants this evening."

"Oh, excellent. We can put off having mutton another day. Poppy, you'll want to wear something nicer than what you have on," Aunt Rachel said.

Mr. Ingleby coughed delicately. "I beg your pardon, but the invitation was addressed to me alone."

Aunt Rachel froze. "Do you mean to say we are not invited too?"

"I'm afraid not. The invitation expressly said I was to dine with them. I suspect they wish to consult me on spiritual matters and it wouldn't be appropriate to have you there as well. They wouldn't feel comfortable." Seeing Aunt Rachel's mutinous face, he said, "If you prefer, I can beg off..."

"No, no, you must go. I wouldn't dream of keeping you from the Grants," she said.

"That is very good of you, Mrs. Greene." He rose, took a brimming teacup from Betsey, and quit the room.

Aunt Rachel turned to Poppy. "Well, what do you make of that? I've never known the Grants to be so ungenerous."

Poppy shrugged. "Perhaps he is right, and they do want to discuss things of a spiritual nature with him. I daresay we will be more comfortable at dinner."

"That is beside the point. It's not seemly, for the family to only invite one member of our household and not us as well." She stabbed her steel needle into her embroidery cloth. "You know, I think he is becoming quite popular in our neighborhood."

"Whether that lasts is another matter. What do you think of his sermon tomorrow? Have you read it?"

Aunt Rachel shook her head. "I haven't. Reginald normally takes hours to prepare, and I've read most of them. I will be curious to know what the young man has to say."

THAT EVENING, MR. Ingleby headed off and the ladies were treated to a quiet evening at home, just to themselves. In truth, they were relieved to be rid of their guest, if only for a few hours.

But much later, Poppy woke up at the sound of a clatter. She sat up in bed, eyes open wide in the darkness. She wondered if it had been a dream, but then heard a man laugh and close a carriage door with a slam. A minute later a carriage rattled down the road, making Poppy wonder who was out so late. Then she realized, *of course, Mr. Ingleby. He's back.*

She got out of bed, put on a robe, and raced out of her room, across the corridor, and down the stairs, her bare feet creaking against the wooden floorboards. With Betsey gone it was just the two of them in the house, and she didn't want her aunt awakened at this late hour. She reached the front door just as there was a loud knock on its wooden frame, and she fumbled with the thick iron key and the catch, flinging the door open.

Any concern she had over the state of her undress was unfounded, as Mr. Ingleby lurched, half tripping, half swaying as he slumped inside the house.

"Mr. Ingleby," Poppy said.

He burped in reply and staggered on his feet.

She squared her shoulders and hefted him to a standing position before he looked at her with glazed eyes.

"Did you enjoy yourself, Mr. Ingleby?" she asked.

"Oh yesh." He proceeded to march forward, expecting her to get out of the way. She did, and shut the door hurriedly, twisting the thick iron key into the lock with a hard twist, and closing the iron latch on the door.

He swayed on his feet, narrowly missing knocking a painting of flowers off the wall. He ignored her offer of help and marched into the blue sitting room, and plonked himself down in Mr. Greene's chair which groaned beneath him. The fire in the hearth had mostly dimmed to a few coals, which offered a tiny light. In the darkness, she spied his dark gray coat and plain white shirt that strained against a light waistcoat and wondered at him.

He fixed a bleary-eyed gaze at Poppy, traveling up her plain white nightdress and up to her face. "You are uncommonly tall," he commented.

"Yes, I know." Her mouth pursed in displeasure. He may have a peer for a patron, but she found his manners decidedly ungenteel. "How was your evening?"

He relaxed in the chair. "Wonderful. Such excellent food. We had wood pigeon and partridge, with rosemary potatoes and claret, and fruit tarts for dessert. The Grants are so nice. A very animated family. So hospitable."

"Oh? And did they have spiritual matters to discuss?"

"What? No, they just fancied entertaining me for dinner. They asked all about me and my travels. They were so attentive and asked many questions about my patron, Lord Ryder."

"You mean your rector's patron."

"What?" He fixed an unsteady gaze on her.

"You mean your rector's patron, surely."

"Oh. Yesh, of course, I do. Most gratifying dinner. Do you know he has one of the most coveted estates in all of Cambridge-shire?"

"I thought you said Foxglove Park was in Oxfordshire."

"It is. Haven't you been listening to a word I've said?" He wagged a finger at her.

"Mr. Ingleby," Poppy said, gritting her teeth.

"Yes?"

"My aunt takes to her bed early and is trying to sleep. You do realize that it is late?" She looked pointedly at the small wooden clock that sat above the fireplace on the mantel. Its hands reached 11.36 pm. "It is after eleven at night," she said.

"Is it? My word. Time does fly, doesn't it?"

"Yes. But you are also aware that tomorrow is Sunday?"

"What of it?" He scratched his head.

"Is your sermon ready?"

"What? Oh. Yes, of course!" he nodded, his chin wagging.

"Excellent," she said, not believing a word of it. "I shall see you tomorrow then."

"Good night, Miss Morton." He burped.

THE NEXT MORNING Poppy awoke again to a loud crash. This time she had the presence of mind to throw on a shawl and some house slippers and hurried downstairs. As she entered the blue sitting room, she beheld a curious sight; there sat Mr. Ingleby on the floor, wearing the same gray coat and suit he wore the night before, and standing over him was Betsey, her hands on her hips. On seeing Poppy, she straightened and said, "I found him asleep on the sofa, Miss. But church is in an hour."

"Uh... I must have just fallen. Yes. That's it." Mr. Ingleby muttered and held out a hand. "Help me up."

Poppy crossed her arms beneath her chest. "Mr. Ingleby, did

you sleep there?"

He looked up at her, with bloodshot eyes, craning his neck to meet her gaze. "I was just resting my eyes after that delightful supper at the Grants. Such kind, God-fearing people. So hospitable." He burped. "They served wood pigeon you know."

"I trust you will be ready for church?"

"Of course I will! What kind of question is that? For a young woman, you ask a lot of impertinent questions."

Poppy drew herself up. "Forgive me, Mr. Ingleby, but when I found you on the floor, my thoughts instantly went to your health. The town depends on you."

"Yes, well." He ignored Betsey's outstretched hand and got to his feet, leaning heavily on the sofa cushions to stay upright. He stumbled from the room and clambered up the stairs with all the grace and noise of a lumbering warthog, gasping as he reached the top step.

FORTY MINUTES LATER Poppy stood at the parsonage's entrance with her aunt and Betsey, waiting. They all exchanged a look in the silence, when Aunt Rachel asked, "You're sure he is awake? Perhaps you should go check on him."

At that moment, Mr. Ingleby thundered down the stairs, dressed in a clergyman's black habit and carrying one of Mr. Greene's hats and a portfolio of paper. His shined shoes creaked loudly on the steps as he joined them. He clapped on the black wide-brimmed hat and said, "Let's be off. I cannot stand people who are late." He moved swiftly and every few steps he turned and urged, "Come along. Don't dawdle."

As they approached the church, there was a queue of people waiting to enter. Heads turned as Mr. Ingleby called out, "Make way! Let me through." With his head held high, he cut a path through the crowd of parishioners and brandishing an old iron key, unlocked the church doors.

The drafty old building had once boasted beautiful stained glass but since the dissolution of the monasteries by King Henry

VIII, the church's shattered glass had been replaced with plain ordinary windows, and any semblance of the Papist trappings of Rome had disappeared. Now its wooden rafters had darkened with age, its pews creaked, and its one remnant of former beauty was an impressive wooden pulpit, carved with ornate curves and lines, as to depict flowers, vines, and expressive angels cut into the wood.

Two young assistants came forward and one asked, "Where's Mr. Greene?"

Mr. Ingleby gave the youth an unfriendly look and adjusted his hat. "I am Mr. Ingleby and will be replacing him for the present." He followed the youths to an area behind the altar and a short while later came out dressed in clerical robes. The church bell rang and people began to file inside. Poppy, Aunt Rachel, and Betsey sat together in the second row, as was their custom.

Mr. Ingleby introduced himself to the congregation and explained the circumstances of his arrival. He graciously thanked the Greene family for their hospitality, before in the same breath thanking the Grants for their very Christian charity and generosity.

Aunt Rachel nudged Poppy's side with her elbow and whispered, "He makes it sound like we aren't very generous at all."

"I was just thinking the same thing." Poppy replied. She looked over her shoulder and spied Mrs. Grant in her Sunday finest, looking very pleased with herself. She beamed at Poppy and nodded, to which Poppy inclined her head and turned back.

Soon it came time for the sermon and Mr. Ingleby settled into a comfortable rhythm, beginning a warm, kindly written piece that lulled the congregation. All except Aunt Rachel, who beside Poppy, sat staring at Mr. Ingleby with an open mouth.

"Aunt Rachel? What is it? Are you all right?" Poppy asked.

"I... That bastard," she swore with murder in her eyes. "He's stolen Reginald's sermon!"

CHAPTER TWO

P OPPY STARED AT her aunt. "What are you talking about?"
"That's not his sermon. He didn't write it. Reginald did."
Her face twisted in anger.

"What are you saying?" Betsey asked on the other side of
Poppy.

"I'd know those lines anywhere. Reginald wrote it last Mon-
day, and he read it out to me, just like he does so many of his
sermons." She looked at Poppy, her eyes wide. "Mr. Ingleby stole
your uncle's sermon."

The three of them looked at Mr. Ingleby with a new realiza-
tion.

The rest of the service passed quickly and once it ended,
Poppy and her aunt prepared to follow the congregation outside.
Betsey curtseyed and hurried away to prepare Sunday luncheon.

But just as Aunt Rachel began to make her way to the head of
the queue to speak with Mr. Ingleby, she was forced back by a
series of parishioners who were keen to be the first to chat to the
charming newcomer.

Mr. Ingleby was in his element, flattering and laughing,
throwing his head back to reveal fine white teeth as his golden
hair caught the sun. Like a lord holding court, he charmed young
women and society matrons alike, who fawned over his every
word and admired his shining hair and pleasant expression. He

laughed and bowed deeply to those who Poppy inwardly dismissed as social climbers, who only attended church as a means to catch up on the latest gossip, or to be seen in their newest frocks. He stood in his church robes, beaming at each parishioner who stopped to chat.

Beside her, Aunt Rachel fumed quietly and crossed her arms beneath her chest. They entered the queue, no longer receiving pride of place as the close relations of the reverend, and followed the congregation outside into the midday sun. More than one came up to them and complimented them on their charming houseguest, like Mrs. Alleyn and her eldest daughter Louisa, who upon seeing Aunt Rachel's sour expression, added a wish for the Reverend Greene's swift return. Mrs. Grant, however, did not notice them, for she stood by Mr. Ingleby, as proud as if he were her own son, and Poppy heard her remark, "I've never seen such happy manners in a member of the clergy. I hope he stays forever!"

Aunt Rachel shot her a baleful look and walked past with her head held high, leaving Poppy to hurry after. Once they were out of earshot, Aunt Rachel muttered, "What a ridiculous man. Is there anything more insipid than newcomers? I can't abide them. And especially those who fawn over them. You'd think he was a visiting prince the way he goes on." She sped down the stone walkway away from the church in a flurry of skirts.

Poppy hurried to keep up. "Aunt—"

"Is there anything more odious than a man who steals sermons? I wonder if he even attended Oxford Divinity. I can't stand it. After all the hard work Reginald put in, only to have it taken by this upstart." Her hands trembled with anger. "I shall write to Reginald immediately and tell him what has occurred. He deserves to know. I—"

"Aunt," Poppy interjected, "let us see what Mr. Ingleby says. It may be he has a good explanation for why he—"

"Stole Reginald's sermon? He'd better have a bloody good reason. And the way he fawned over Mrs. Grant as if she were

Lady Cameron herself. He wouldn't know a person of quality if they smacked him in the face. He only likes Mrs. Grant because she gives him a good dinner. It makes me sick." She kicked a rock with her boot and sent it flying.

By the time they had returned to the parsonage and finished a quiet luncheon, Poppy had left her aunt's company to weed the vegetable garden out in the back of the house. Once the heat had gotten to her and she felt she could weed no more, she attended to the chickens they kept out back, tossing them leftover peels, seeds, and meal. Five chickens scurried around the back garden, pecking at the flying food. Once she had fed them, Poppy went back inside the house, sat at her small writing desk in her room, where she pushed aside her small looking glass and pulled out a quill and ink. With a fresh sheet of paper, she wrote,

Dear Constable Dyngley,

I hope you are well and in good health. It has been several months since our last conversation, and I am keen to hear from you.

She scratched it out and tossed the letter aside.

Dear Constable,

I have not heard from you in some months, and I wondered how you were faring. Do tell me of your–

She crumpled up that letter too and shook her head. She would not be the first to write. It was his place to write first. He had said he would call on her, and she would simply have to be patient and wait. But it was intolerable, this waiting. What if she waited for words that never came?

IT WAS NOT until the late evening that Mr. Ingleby returned to the parsonage. Poppy sat with her aunt in the sitting room by the fire, and Poppy had just risen to stoke the wood with an iron poker when she heard the front door of the house open and shut.

Poppy made eye contact with her aunt and heard the first stair on the staircase creak, when Aunt Rachel called, "Mr. Ingleby, is that you?"

He entered the sitting room, which was warmly lit by a comfortable fire in the hearth. "Mrs. Greene, Miss Morton." He nodded hello. "I am surprised to see you both still awake."

"We were waiting for you. We didn't see you after church." Aunt Rachel's mouth quirked as if she was trying to hold her tongue, then she blurted, "And that sermon you read, it was my husband's."

Mr. Ingleby's eyes narrowed and he opened his mouth to speak.

"Don't try to deny it, I recognized it right away. Reginald read it to me earlier this week." Aunt Rachel looked at him accusingly.

Mr. Ingleby squared his shoulders as if preparing for a chore, then pasted a smile on his face. "My dear Mrs. Greene, if you thought I had taken your husband's spiritual sermon as my own, I would be mortified." He took the hardback chair that Aunt Rachel reserved for visitors and sat, stretching out his feet. "Let me explain. Although we are not personally acquainted, I have found your husband to be one of the most well-meaning of men. He left the sermon out for me to use with his warm wishes. I suspected he knew that a young clergyman such as myself would feel adrift in a parish like this, with such a variety of society and souls to look after. I believe he meant it as a kindness, to ease my settling in."

Aunt Rachel gave an unladylike snort.

Poppy set the poker aside and pushed the thin metal grate back against the fireplace, taking the chance to resume her seat beside her aunt and study the now sweating Mr. Ingleby. It could have been the warm night that caused beads of sweat to form on his forehead, but she thought not.

He looked at her fleetingly and swallowed, returning his gaze to Aunt Rachel. "Dear madam, I am mortified, truly. I would never have touched that sermon if Mr. Greene had not laid it out for me."

"I know every word of that sermon," Aunt Rachel told him.

"I should hope so. You're the perfect audience."

"I beg your pardon?" Her embroidery fell to the floor.

He picked it up and handed it to her. "You are attentive, honest, and a good listener. I am sure Mr. Greene could not find a better audience to inspire and improve his sermons than you, and they are the better for it."

"Well…" Aunt Rachel accepted the embroidery and set it aside. She looked mollified, for he had flattered her vanity.

"It is unfortunate I was unable to return straight after church, but you see, Mrs. Alleyn came to me asking a matter of importance and I spent the afternoon counseling her on a serious theological issue. Then the hour grew late and she begged me to stay to dine with her family. It seemed like the least I could do."

Poppy's mouth quirked into a smile.

"I see," Aunt Rachel said.

"I felt it necessary to accept the invitation to stay for dinner and I was sure you would approve. I want to build trust with the townspeople like your husband would have done. He is so respected by the people of Hertford, he has set a high standard to live up to. I could not dream of filling his shoes, but I can only try my best."

"Well that is very kind of you, I'm sure. But please do send a messenger or a note and let us know, so that we don't worry. The roads are not always safe at night," Aunt Rachel said, "There was a carriage accident on the high road just a few days ago."

"Yes, I heard about that. Of course, I will try to remember for next time." He bid them goodnight and left them to the quiet of the sitting room.

"Hah. If there is a next time," Poppy said.

BUT THERE WAS, and the very next day he sent two notes to say he was having luncheon with the Alleyns and later that evening, dinner with another family.

"My word, he is certainly popular," Aunt Rachel commented, turning over the second note.

"He has very pleasing manners," Poppy agreed. "I wonder how long it will last."

"Whatever do you mean?"

"Just a notion. Mr. Ingleby seems to act all well and good, but that didn't stop him from filching the oatcakes or taking Uncle Reginald's sermon. Do you not think him deceptive? He plays court to you and all the neighbors, while filling his stomach at their expense."

"Don't be uncharitable, Poppy, there's many a person who would pay more than a few tarts in order to have a clergyman at their table. Don't you know? It gives them something to talk about. Something to be proud of, and to congratulate themselves on, having a clergyman to dine. He should offer spiritual comfort and guidance as well, but it is no small thing. Almost like an accomplishment," Aunt Rachel said.

"I just wonder about him." Poppy gazed at the crackling flames.

"Oh no. I see that look in your eye. You are in want of some diversion to occupy your mind. If I didn't know better, I'd say you're thinking about solving another murder with that constable."

Poppy snorted.

"None of that, Poppy, put it out of your head. Mr. Ingleby may have his faults but that's no need to think he's better off dead."

THE FOLLOWING AFTERNOON, Betsey ushered a young lady into the sitting room: "A Miss Jane Heyworth to see you, ma'am."

In a glance, Aunt Rachel and Poppy ascertained that neither knew the young woman, who was immediately shown in and said, "Hello."

The ladies curtsied and Aunt Rachel invited her to sit. Jane was a pretty young woman, about eighteen years old, with light brown hair, freckles, and a pert nose. She wore a serviceable white dress with a smart blue pelisse, along with a straw bonnet and a matching blue ribbon.

She fashioned a polite smile and said, "Forgive me for interrupting your solitude. Is Mr. Greene here?"

"No, he has been called away. But there is Mr. Ingleby upstairs who might speak with you. He is Mr. Greene's temporary replacement. What is the matter?"

"Oh. It is no great thing. It's just… My father is laying abed with an injury. His horse fell on him, you see, and he broke his leg. The doctor said he must keep to his bed to rest. But he is bored, and we wondered if Mr. Greene might visit him to offer some guidance? It is just my mother, myself and our maid to look after him and I know he would appreciate a visit from the Reverend. I'm positive it would do him some good."

Mr. Ingleby stepped into the room. "I thought I heard voices. Do we have visitors?" He saw their guest and gave her a warm smile. "Good afternoon, Miss…?"

"Jane Heyworth."

"And here I thought I had been introduced to all the families in town," he said, shooting the ladies a sharp look. "Pray, tell me about yourself." He leaned against the doorframe, there being no other comfortable chair in sight aside from the sofa.

"Oh, we are but newly arrived. Papa is an architect and he came here for a new assignment, but I should think that will fall through now that he has broken his leg. He is stuck in bed, you see."

Now Mr. Ingleby's gray eyes glazed over and he straightened, brushing down his mustard yellow waistcoat. "I am sorry I cannot be of service, Miss Heyworth, but I have a sermon I must attend to."

"But—"

"I have no doubt that Mrs. Greene and Miss Morton will be

able to help. They have such a way with the people in this town. I shall leave you in their capable hands." He left without another word and hurried up the stairs. They heard the door to Mr. Greene's study slam shut.

"Well," Aunt Rachel said.

"I don't understand. Was it something I said?" Miss Heyworth blushed. "It is not because my father is in trade, is it?"

"Perish the thought, my dear. Mr. Ingleby takes no notice of such things and neither do we. Do we, Poppy?"

"Not at all. Mr. Ingleby is newly ordained and so spends a great deal of time in religious study and preparing his next sermon. He will be upstairs for some hours, I should think."

"Oh. Papa was so looking forward to the idea of a visit." Jane looked at her shoes.

"No matter, Miss Heyworth. Poppy and I would be glad to accompany you," Aunt Rachel said.

"You would?"

"Yes. I often visit the sick when my husband is on church errands, and Poppy too. I shall meet your mother and welcome her to the neighborhood properly."

"Oh, that is very kind of you, thank you. Our society is a bit limited at the moment, on account of my father's injury. We were going to attend a dance at the assembly rooms this week, but Mama felt it a bit rude, what with Papa being unwell."

There was very little Aunt Rachel loved more than a country dance. "Nonsense, you must go. Your father would want you to attend, surely."

And so it was decided, they would pay the Heyworths a visit that very afternoon. It was a process of donning bonnets and matching pelisses and then walking through town in thick boots to the Red Lion Inn, where the Heyworths were staying.

Aunt Rachel formed a firm ally in Mrs. Heyworth almost immediately, and Mrs. Heyworth gave the girls some pin money to go and amuse themselves, while she and Aunt Rachel became acquainted over tea.

IN THE CENTER of town, the girls had perused the millinery, admired and discussed the merits of new bonnets and ribbons, and now sat by the window of a little confectioner's shop sharing jam tarts when Jane brushed away flaky golden crumbs and declared, "Mama is determined to find me a husband. But I don't see what the rush is. I'm only eighteen."

"I've heard of girls getting married younger than that. What do you want?" Poppy asked, feeling all of her nineteen years.

"I don't know. I don't have many accomplishments, we couldn't afford much. I can dance and sketch but I can't sing. Ohhh, who is that? He's handsome."

Poppy followed Jane's gaze out the window. There walked a young man she had never laid eyes on before.

Jane was right, he was handsome. He had a long face, but it suited him. His chestnut hair was artfully disheveled, his off-white cravat tied just so, his tan trousers and dark boots suitable for the dusty road and his brown waistcoat and overcoat looked smart without being too fine for the high street. He also carried a silver-topped walking stick that winked in the light. Poppy's discerning eye could tell he was young, handsome, and came from wealth.

The shop's bell dinged, announcing his entry. He turned and scanned those inside, his gaze resting on Jane. From her companion's straightening of her shoulders and bloom to her cheeks, Poppy knew a flirtation had begun.

How wondrous these things were, these chance meetings where one might lock eyes with a stranger and feel as if struck by lightning. In seconds a look could pass between two unacquainted people and yet both would be in perfect understanding with the other. She felt a pang in her chest as she thought of Constable Dyngley, and wished he would enter the shop as well.

But he didn't. The young stranger's eyes lit up at the sight of Jane and he drank in the look of her sitting there so prettily.

Jane leaned forward in her seat. Poppy could tell her companion longed to speak to him, but they had not been introduced, and so would remain perfect strangers.

Jane whispered, "Do you know that gentleman?"

"No. I have never seen him before."

"Nor I. But I daresay he is very handsome. Don't you think?" Jane asked, holding a very full cup of tea to her lips.

Poppy grinned and nibbled at her jam tart. The young man in question loitered before a display table of finely decorated cakes and pastries before settling on one decadent-looking confection. He offered Jane a slight smile and left with his purchase, glancing back at her through the shop window as he parted.

Jane let out a sigh worthy of the stage. "So handsome. I wonder what his name is. Something perfect, no doubt."

"It could be something like Ebenezer or Cornelius."

Jane giggled. "Or Fortescue."

"Would you still like him then?"

"I suppose I'd have to." They dissolved into giggles and Jane asked, "What about you, Poppy? Do you have a young man? Any beaus?"

Poppy blushed. She'd half-expected this question. "Not as such. Just a good friend."

"And is this a handsome friend?" Jane teased, when the shop door opened and shut, the bell rang and a young man's voice said, "Jane!"

"Robert!" Jane waved from her seat.

A charming-looking man who looked to be the male mirror image of Jane strode toward them, a pleasant smile on his face. He dressed smart enough but his gray waistcoat and jacket were of a coarser quality, much like Jane's serviceable blue pelisse. He had a head full of light brown hair that fell into his eyes and greeted them like old chums. "Dash it all, Jane. I thought I saw you in the street. And here I find you stuffing your face with cakes again? What would mother say?"

Jane turned red and turned to Poppy. "Miss Morton, meet my brother, Robert. Robert, I have just made a new friend, Miss Poppy Morton."

Poppy rose and curtseyed, rising to see Robert give her a

cheeky wink and bow. He said, "Don't believe anything Jane tells you, my sister has a flair for dramatics. She could have been on the stage."

Jane threw her napkin at him and laughed, "Pray do not pay him any attention, Miss Morton, he does not think before he talks, and thinks too highly of himself to think of anyone else."

Robert clapped a hand to his heart as if mortally wounded, and staggered over to an empty seat. "And what of you, Miss Morton? Have you any siblings to be equally ashamed of?" he asked with a smile.

Poppy shook her head. "I do not. I live with my aunt and uncle at the parsonage."

"Good God, your uncle's a clergyman? How dull," Robert said, helping himself to some of Jane's tea.

"Robert!" Jane smacked him on the arm. "Ignore him, Miss Morton, he's just saying that to get a rise out of you."

And so it went on. Poppy found herself passing an enjoyable afternoon laughing in the company of her new friends. That is until Mr. Ingleby entered the shop, gazing at all its wares.

"Who is that?" Robert asked.

"Mr. Charles Ingleby. He is looking after the parish while my uncle is away."

"He's very fond of cake, isn't he?"

It was true, Mr. Ingleby had already helped himself to the tray of free samples, of tiny cut squares of vanilla sponge, and now licked icing sugar off of his fingers.

Poppy drank more of their rose-flavored tea and ignored him, until Jane whispered, "Miss Morton, he's looking at you."

Poppy looked over and met the wandering gaze of Mr. Ingleby. He had purchased a series of iced buns and watched as the shopkeeper wrapped them into a secure box. They locked eyes and both nodded hellos. Mr. Ingleby did not say a word in greeting but walked out with the box.

"That is very good of him. It looks like you'll be enjoying some iced desserts after your dinner tonight," Robert said.

Poppy wasn't so sure.

THAT EVENING, THERE were no iced buns to be found. At dinner, Aunt Rachel asked over a bowl of green watercress soup, "Mr. Ingleby, I hope you haven't forgotten about the dance at the assembly rooms this Saturday. Would you still like to go or will you be too busy?"

"Oh yes, indeed, I love a country dance. So provincial. Quite different from what we have in London, I imagine. I will join you. There are some who have said I am very light on my feet."

"Oh good," Mrs. Greene declared, sipping her soup.

CHAPTER THREE

D ANCING FOR POPPY was a pleasure, but was not to be that Saturday evening.

From the moment they entered the assembly rooms, Poppy could see that Mr. Ingleby dearly loved to dance. He fidgeted like a child as they paid the admission fee, rolling up on the balls of his feet as he looked around the general assembly.

Poppy smiled and introduced Mr. Ingleby to all whom he wished to make the acquaintance of. She soon grew tired of making so many introductions but felt it was her duty to socialize with their guest, particularly since her aunt was not up to the task.

Aunt Rachel had promptly escorted Poppy and Mr. Ingleby into the assembly rooms and then sought out her friends, fellow society matrons and mothers with young people to monitor and survey. That left Poppy alone with Mr. Ingleby at an early stage in the evening, but she did not mind and looked forward to when she could be alone in her thoughts.

Bedecked prettily in a pale muslin gown, trimmed with a pink ribbon around the high waist, Poppy was grateful for its lightness and short cap sleeves. As it was only a local country dance, she wore no gloves or headdress, nor any greater ornament than a thin, slippery necklace of finely beaten gold chain around her neck.

True to his word, Mr. Ingleby was light on his feet but had little concept of timing. Dressed in a fine blue overcoat, a light cream-colored waistcoat that encased his plump form and tight-fitting tan trousers, he danced every dance and laughed gaily at the witticisms of those he believed were the fashionable set.

He did Poppy the honor of asking her to dance, but as soon as they took their places in the set, he fixed her with a severe look, ignoring all others, except to admire their dress and search for signs of wealth. His observations caused him to step out of turn with the others, causing Poppy to blush with embarrassment, but he made up for his shortcomings with friendly smiles and laughter toward their partners in the set.

Mr. Ingleby was in his element, trotting alongside young girls who laughed and thought him very silly, earning the benevolent smiles of matrons, and bowing deeply to those who dressed very fine and held themselves apart from the general assembly, for these were the very persons he wished to court.

Poppy danced one dance with Mr. Ingleby before he left her in search of more attractive company, abandoning her to stand on the sidelines beside gossiping matrons and young people. It was a young female voice at her shoulder that said, "Intolerable, aren't they? There must be at least twenty young women standing without a partner and not a man to care for any of them."

Poppy smiled. Even though it wasn't suitable to converse with those to whom she had not been introduced, the voice was so cutting in its observation of the company present, she couldn't help but agree. "It's true. Perhaps it's that the men here don't feel up to the challenge of dancing with better partners than themselves."

"Aha!" the young woman laughed aloud. "I knew I was not alone in my thoughts. You must be Miss Morton, are you not?"

Poppy turned. Standing before her was a young woman of eye-catching beauty. She stood a few inches below her, with fashionably long hair that was mostly up, with coils of auburn hair that rested at her bosom. She was overdressed for a simple country dance, which pegged her as either a stranger to the town or a cut above the rest. Judging from her smart rust-colored dress with cap sleeves and modest neckline, Poppy deemed her as both. Her eyes were shining, light freckles dotted her nose and cheeks, and when she laughed, as she did now, dimples adorned her smile. She wore a set of pearl earrings and a charming strand of pearls around her neck that blushed pink in the candlelight.

Poppy felt plain and ugly compared to this young woman's beauty but decided to make the best of her own arsenal, namely a sweet temperament and polite manners. She curtseyed and said, "I'm afraid you have the best of me. I don't believe we've been introduced."

"What a joy you are. Do people still care for that these days? I am Caroline Everly. You are Miss Poppy Morton if I'm not mistaken."

"Yes, but how do you know me?" Poppy's eyebrows knit in confusion.

"I have heard so much about you, I feel as though we are already good friends." Caroline gave her hand a warm squeeze.

Constable Dyngley stepped into her view and Poppy's breath caught. Here was the man she had spent many hours thinking about, waiting for a letter that had never come, and preparing the sitting room into a welcoming state for a guest who had never arrived. Now he was here, in Hertford, standing before her.

He bowed. "Hello, Miss Morton. It is a pleasure to see you again." He looked handsome as ever in a dark suit jacket, navy silken waistcoat that shone in the candlelight, and a snowy white cravat, tied expertly at his throat.

Poppy curtseyed and rose, "Constable. It has been some months, I think."

"Since you solved that mystery together, oh how delightful!" Caroline said, clapping her hands together. "And now that we three are here I am sure we will have some exciting adventures. Tell me, is all of Hertfordshire so—"

Constable Dyngley smiled and put a hand on the young lady's

shoulder. "Caroline, a minute, if you would."

"Oh very well. I see a footman nearby with wine and I am parched. I shall leave you two to catch up, but I demand to spend the evening at your side, Miss Morton. I cannot wait to make the better acquaintance of the young woman who solved a murder." She left in a cheerful flurry of skirts and Poppy felt like she had been speaking with a whirlwind.

Dyngley laughed, seeing her dazed expression. "You look a bit subdued. Caroline has that way with people. You have met, I see."

"Yes, just now." Poppy looked into his eyes, admiring the warm brown gaze he gave her.

"Would you care to dance?" He held out a hand.

"I would be delighted." She blushed, casting a backward glance at her Aunt Rachel, who stood watching with some of the other matrons in attendance. Her eyes widened at the sight of Poppy and Dyngley, and she hurriedly grabbed her neighbor's elbow and began whispering.

Dyngley took Poppy's hand, as gently as one might hold a rosebud, and led her out to join the queue of dancers waiting for the start of the next dance. The music picked up, with strings heralding the start of a new country dance. They faced each other in a long line of dancers, and as the music filled her ears, she began, "I have not seen you for some time, Constable."

"That is entirely my fault. I have been occupied elsewhere," he explained, as they walked around each other in formation. "But surely you have not been so bored as to notice my absence?"

She smiled. For all their friendship, he had a limited understanding of the long hours and tediousness of a young woman's average day. With little to do, she had felt his absence very much, but determined not to say so.

"Miss Everly is very lively," she commented.

"Yes, I thought you would like her. Your minds are much alike."

As dancing partners, they rose like the swells of an ocean

lapping at the shore. The dancers moved and glided together seamlessly, clasping delicate gloved hands and releasing with the barest of touches. Poppy did her partner the honor of moving in step with him, so as to present a more pleasing picture to those present, and perhaps seem like a suitable dance partner for any other young gentlemen watching.

This was an elegant country dance with graceful, slow movements, best suited for those of an easy temperament or those who wished to be seen, rather than risk exerting themselves with excessive exercise.

"Will you both be staying long in Hertfordshire, Constable?"

"A little. Miss Everly wanted to visit the area. She will buy her wedding dress in Town, I believe. She has a favorite modiste in London."

"Oh, she is engaged? I shall offer her my congratulations."

"I will tell her myself if you like," he offered.

"And who is the lucky man?" Poppy asked, smiling.

Constable Dyngley stopped and cleared his throat. "She is my fiancée, Miss Morton."

Poppy missed a step. "You are engaged?"

"Yes."

She continued to step in time with the dance, but her movements were wooden. She stepped in the right formation but her dancing had little grace and no feeling, unlike her heart which felt heavy with emotion.

"Poppy, I—" he started.

"Please do pass on my congratulations. I hope you will be very happy together." Her face was a mask of pleasantness, but he knew better.

"I thought you knew. My father is too infirm to look after the estate properly, and my older brother fell ill when I left here a few months ago. He is not well. They depend on me."

"I'm sorry," Poppy said, feeling for him. "And Miss Everly?"

"Is a lovely young woman with a kind heart. I had hoped to introduce you so that you might be friends. She was in raptures at the story of our finding a murderer together and was keen to meet you."

Poppy let out a breath, and let him guide her into the final steps of the dance. "She is very sweet. I like her already."

"I thought you would. Poppy…." he started, but the dance had ended.

In seconds, they were interrupted by Caroline and Aunt Rachel, who clasped Dyngley's hands and shook them vigorously. "Constable Dyngley, I do declare, you have been a stranger around these parts for months now! It is a pleasure to see you again and to see you two dancing, what a pretty sight you make."

Poppy felt rather than saw Constable Dyngley's strained smile, as he received her aunt warmly and bowed. "Mrs. Greene. I could not return to Hertfordshire without calling on you. May I call on you tomorrow afternoon, after church?"

"Of course, I shall save the best plum tarts for you," she promised and turned to see Caroline beaming at her. "And who is this young lady?"

Constable Dyngley coughed. "May I present Miss Caroline Everly, of Enfield."

The ladies curtseyed, and Caroline playfully dug an affectionate elbow into Dyngley's stomach. "You have not told them the news, Dyngley."

"And what is that?" Aunt Rachel asked.

"Why, we are engaged to be married this autumn. He is my fiancé," she said pleasantly.

Aunt Rachel's smile could have cut glass. "How wonderful. Our congratulations, I'm sure." She turned to her niece. "Poppy, come, I must speak with you about Mr. Ingleby's sermon for tomorrow…" She dragged Poppy away from the happy couple with an iron grip.

Poppy let herself be led away, grateful for her aunt's intervention.

Once across the room and safely situated away from prying eyes and listening ears, Aunt Rachel released Poppy's arm. "Are you all right?"

"Yes, I'm fine."

"I must admit, you seem in fine humor about it. I was sure he had come back to make you an offer, and when I saw you both dancing together, well, I thought..."

Poppy shook her head. "No, aunt. We were always just good friends."

"Yes, I see that now. Did you know about this fiancée of his?"

"No, but she seems very nice. I like her already," Poppy lied, "I'm sure they will be very happy together."

"Hmmm, yes. Fine words, Poppy." Aunt Rachel appraised her niece. "A fine match, indeed. Are you sure you're all right?"

"Yes, of course. Why wouldn't I be?" She aimed for lightness in her tone.

"Very well. Oh, I see Lady Cameron decided to grace us with her presence. Do make sure you say hello to her tonight. I am going to see what I can find out about Miss Everly." Aunt Rachel disappeared into the crowd.

Lady Cameron was attending the dance, but due to her advanced age, did little aside from standing in one place and holding court. Sensing they were in the presence of a lady far more genteel than themselves, many people kept a polite distance, as much as was possible in a fairly crowded room. Lady Cameron stood alone, looking very smart in a white and black striped silk dress, with a white ostrich feather adorning her gray hair. From her pursed lips to her darting eyes, she presented a stern countenance to the average observer, but Poppy had dined at her park for years now and greeted her with the easy familiarity one might welcome a very wealthy aunt.

Poppy curtseyed and said, "Hullo Lady Cameron."

"Good evening, Miss Morton." The lady inclined her head.

"Are you enjoying the assembly?"

"Somewhat. I saw you dancing just now with a handsome young gentleman. Is he your beau?"

Poppy flushed. "No, ma'am. That is Constable Dyngley, and

he is newly engaged to Miss Caroline Everly."

"Ah." The woman held up a small monocle that dangled from her wrist. "Charming. Do you know, Miss Morton, I should like to meet her. She looks like a pretty sort of girl."

"Yes, ma'am." Poppy curtseyed and a short while later brought a beaming Caroline over to Lady Cameron. "May I introduce Miss Caroline Everly."

Caroline curtseyed and said, "It is ever so good to meet you, your ladyship. Your dress is very... striped."

Lady Cameron laughed. "The pleasure is all mine. And is it true that you are engaged to the local constable?"

Caroline's eyes danced as she glanced over to where Constable Dyngley stood, conversing with another gentleman. "Yes. We were much thrown together in London you see, and it's a funny story actually, for he was on the search for a set of pearls."

"Oh? For whom?"

"A close friend, he said, who had hers ruined. Anyway, he was at a loss so I instructed him on what to buy, and we became close confidantes ever since. But then he played a trick on me, and gave me the pearls himself!" She touched a set of dainty white pearls at her neck. "It took my breath away when he proposed a month later, but here we are! I so wanted to come to Hertford and meet the people in his acquaintance." She turned to Poppy and squeezed her hand again. "Especially you, Miss Morton. Dyngley tells me that you are his special friend, and I know he looks upon you quite as his own sister."

Poppy smiled at Miss Caroline, even though her words sliced into her heart.

Caroline said, "I know we will be the best of friends, I can already tell. And when we are married, you must come visit us at the estate. Although I suppose you will have to call me Lady Dyngley, won't you?" She laughed. "I think that's what the wife of a baronet is called."

Poppy blinked. A baronet? She excused herself, pleading lightheadedness, and wandered out through a set of glass doors to one of the balconies, where she took in a breath of fresh night air. The cool air chilled her, and small baby-fine hairs stood up on the back of her neck, but she didn't care. She relished the chance to be away from all the noise, just for a moment.

The glass door opened and closed behind her. A familiar voice said, "I didn't expect to find you out here."

She looked to her left. There leaning against the stone balcony was Constable Dyngley. "Constable," she said, turning to go.

"No, don't leave. I'm sorry if I startled you. I needed some fresh air."

"So did I."

He started toward her. "Miss Morton…"

"Do excuse me, Constable. I don't wish to keep you from your fiancée. I am sure the future Lady Dyngley is wondering where you are." She quit the balcony and opened the thin glass door, stopping at the sudden cacophony of warmth, light, noise, and drunken laughter that threatened to overwhelm her senses.

She was soon joined by Mr. Ingleby, who nodded to her. "Ah, Miss Morton."

"Mr. Ingleby. How are you enjoying the dance?" she asked.

"It is very entertaining. A fine way to spend an evening," he said.

The glass door opened behind them and Dyngley said, "Miss Morton, I–" he stopped short.

Mr. Ingleby sniffed. "Miss Morton, are you acquainted with this gentleman?"

"Yes. Mr. Ingleby, may I present Constable Dyngley. He is a friend of the family. He and Mr. Jenkins keep order in Hertford."

"How do you do, sir?" Constable Dyngley said.

"How do you do?" Mr. Ingleby was ready to dismiss him and return his attention to Poppy when something caught his eye.

Poppy wondered what it was. Perhaps it was the fine cut of Dyngley's dark suit, the crisp white cravat that graced his neck, or the navy silken waistcoat that caught the light as he moved. It could have been the fashionable tailoring of his pantaloons that cut to the knee and or the shape of his calves in white dress stockings that hinted at a slim athleticism. Whatever it was, Mr. Ingleby was curious and nodded to him.

But before he could say a word, Dyngley bowed and excused himself, crossing the room to lead Caroline into the next set for a dance.

Poppy stood beside Mr. Ingleby, and after a moment he stiffened, the blood slowly draining from his face.

"Mr. Ingleby? Are you unwell?" she asked.

"I am very well. There are so many people. I didn't know there were so many new friends to be met." He watched as Dyngley began dancing with Caroline. "Who is that?" he asked.

"That is Constable Dyngley's fiancé, Miss Caroline Everly. I made her acquaintance earlier. Do you wish to meet her?"

"She does not look very ladylike to me," he muttered.

"Pardon?"

"They do not look very well suited as a couple," Mr. Ingleby said.

Poppy stared at him.

"Forgive me. I have had too much wine. Shall we go?" He offered her his arm.

She took it and allowed him to escort her in a turn around the room. The air was warm and heady, the floorboards moved with the weight of many dancers upon it, and the sound of chatter, laughter, and gossip filled their ears.

"Miss Morton, who is that fine-looking woman over there, in the striped dress? She looks like a very prominent sort of person."

"That is Lady Cameron, my uncle's patroness. She owns Blackgate Park." Appreciating the company beside her, she added, "It has some two hundred acres I believe."

She could practically hear the man's mind turning over. "I must meet her at once." He strode toward the lady, cutting a swath through the chatting people on the sidelines.

"Mr. Ingleby, wait! She will think it rude if you address her when you're not introduced!" She moved after him but was cornered by her aunt. "That man is insufferable, I tell you."

"Pardon me, aunt." Poppy moved aside but it was too late. Mr. Ingleby had approached Lady Cameron and swept her a wide bow.

"Oh my," Poppy breathed, watching the scene unfold.

Lady Cameron stared at the man, then turned and walked away. When Mr. Ingleby rose, he found himself all alone and turned red in the face.

Aunt Rachel snickered beside her, holding up a fan to hide her laughter.

Poppy came to him and said, "Mr. Ingleby…"

"Pardon me, my dear girl, but I need a drink. The company here is… an acquired taste." He left her standing there as he went in search of wine.

Poppy was soon greeted by Jane and Robert, who asked, "I say, did Mr. Ingleby just try to speak to that grand lady? It looked like she cut him dead."

Poppy winced.

Jane said, "Never mind that. Robert, you must dance with Miss Morton."

Poppy tensed. She offered a polite smile and said, "That's all right, there's no need to–"

"It would be my honor," Robert said.

A little fissure of embarrassment ran through Poppy. Jane was trying to do her a kindness, but it was not needed. "Honestly, I don't mind standing on the sidelines," she said. She was used to it.

"Now I must insist. I would be a poor friend if I did not whisk you away for a dance." Robert extended his hand.

Poppy laughed and gave Robert a bright smile as she accepted his hand. Determined to be a good and amiable dance partner, she graced him with cheerful looks as they danced a quadrille with another couple. As the dance ended, she curtseyed and moved to leave when he took her hand.

She looked at him. "Mr. Heyworth?"

"Miss Morton, I wondered if you might like to dance another?" he asked, his eyes bright.

Surprise filled her. "I would be delighted."

They were partners for the next dance, and it flew by as he charmed her with cheeky quips and witticisms. She found herself laughing out loud, even catching the eye of the partners around them. Then the dance ended, and she looked up into his warm brown eyes. They hinted at mischief.

"Do you fancy another?" he asked.

"Another dance? No, it wouldn't be proper." She curtseyed and joined Jane.

"He's a joy, isn't he?" Jane said.

"A very good dancer," Poppy agreed. "There was no need to ask him to dance with me though, I don't mind being without a partner."

Jane laughed aloud. "Is that what you thought? Miss Morton, he has been wanting to dance with you all evening and has been too shy to say so. I thought I would put him out of his misery, otherwise he'll be a bore the entire way home."

Poppy stared, stunned.

THE FESTIVITIES ENDED shortly thereafter, much to her relief. On the carriage ride home, Mr. Ingleby looked displeased and refused to speak to anyone, and Aunt Rachel whispered to Poppy, "Who was that young man you danced with?"

"Mr. Robert Heyworth, Miss Heyworth's brother."

"Indeed? And is he single?"

That earned her a sharp look from Mr. Ingleby, and Poppy bit her tongue not to laugh.

Aunt Rachel said, "It was very smart of you to only dance two dances with him. You can dance with whomever you wish, of course, but... a little caution might be wise. More than two dances could suggest you two have an understanding, you know."

"Yes, Aunt." Poppy nodded.

"Constable Dyngley was looking well, was he not? And his

new bride has very pleasing manners."

Seeing as Poppy was loath to reply, Aunt Rachel added, "But I cannot believe he would be so mercenary."

"What do you mean?" Poppy asked.

"Why, I heard that Miss Everly has a dowry of £10,000. Your constable must need the money for her to be such an attractive marriage partner. But why would her family sanction the match? I thought him just a lowly constable. Handsome to be sure, but I never thought he was mercenary."

"Aunt, his family has an estate to look after," Poppy started, but her aunt continued as if she hadn't spoken.

"It is a sorry business, but all men fall victim to it one way or another. I married for love, of course, but not all people can. Some people make it their business to try and marry well, or for money. You, my dear, I am sure will find love." Aunt Rachel smiled at her.

Poppy tried to return her warmth but failed and settled for looking out into the night. A baronet? Could Miss Everly be right? Why would he need to work for his living if he came from such a high-ranking family? Why had he never told her of this connection? How could he have fallen in love with a young woman so very quickly, even if she did have £10,000? And worse, how could she face them both once they were married?

CHAPTER FOUR

T HE NEXT DAY was Sunday, which for Poppy, meant another morning at church. Poppy and her aunt sat in the second row and listened to another of her uncle's sermons, this one having been delivered a few months ago. But perhaps it wasn't the best choice, what with it being late July at the same moment as Mr. Ingleby spoke of spreading goodwill toward men that winter season. After a few curious looks were exchanged and at least one giggle was heard, Mr. Ingleby tugged at his clerical collar, reshuffled his notes, and cleared his throat. "As I was saying…"

After church, a letter awaited the ladies, addressed on a fine card with a smart red wax seal. "I'd recognize that anywhere," Aunt Rachel said, tearing it open.

"Who is it from?"

"Lady Cameron." She began reading and her face fell. "We are invited to take tea with her. I suppose we will have to bring along Mr. Ingleby. No doubt she will be wondering where my Reginald is."

"Have there been no notes from him?" Poppy asked.

"Just a short one to say he'd arrived at his brother's, nothing more," Aunt Rachel said primly, as Mr. Ingleby entered the parsonage.

Having recovered from his embarrassment the previous

night, Mr. Ingleby was delighted at the invitation from Lady Cameron. He took the invite from Aunt Rachel and broke into a smile as he stroked the fine card, turning it over in his pudgy hands. "Capital. I shall finally meet the esteemed owner of Blackgate Park. I will dress in my very best. Will she provide a good luncheon?"

TEA AT LADY Cameron's was always a pleasant affair, and Mr. Ingleby declared himself delighted with everything he saw, from the grand weeping willow trees that overshadowed the park's entrance, to the wild purple freesia flowers that dotted the sides of the road. Large rose bushes offered pink blossoms that perfumed the air, and Mr. Ingleby's blue eyes grew wide as her ladyship's carriage delivered them to the courtyard outside Blackgate House.

It was a large, white, stately building, boasting high columns and many windows to take in the view of the manicured lawns. A pair of footmen walked out and opened the carriage door, helping the ladies out onto the hard gravel walk.

Mr. Ingleby was again delighted, this time by the sight of footmen in livery, and followed pompously, hurrying ahead of the ladies as he took in the sight of the stately building's foyer. They stood upon a floor of intersecting squares of black and white checked marble, facing a large staircase. The head footman, a slim fellow with a prim white powdered wig, led the way, his shoes striking the smooth floor.

They were led through the foyer into a resplendent sitting room, which reminded Poppy of a forest. Mr. Ingleby let out a contented sigh at the surroundings, admiring the dark forest green walls and thick velvet green curtains, pinned back by braided gold rope.

There at the head of two fragile sofas, trimmed in sea-green silk, sat Lady Cameron in an olive-green high-backed chair. Today she wore a prim dress of dark gray silk, and white lace framed her neck. She smiled and said, "Hullo there, you are very welcome."

Aunt Rachel stepped forward, followed by Poppy. "It is a pleasure to see you again so soon, Lady Cameron." They curtseyed and were rewarded with a warm smile.

"And who is this young man?" Lady Cameron asked.

Mr. Ingleby stepped forward and gave their hostess an elaborate bow worthy of the stage. "Mr. Charles Ingleby, at your service, your ladyship."

Lady Cameron's mouth curled in amusement and she said, "Do sit down."

Mr. Ingleby sat by her right on a curved settee, upholstered in sea-green silk. He admired the family portraits that hung on the walls, including that of Lady Cameron in her youth. He stroked the silk cushions and reclined on the settee.

"Shall I ring for some tea?" Lady Cameron asked.

"Oh, yes, please," he said, "Do you know, I do think this rivals the grounds at Foxglove Park? My patron, Lord Ryder, has his estate there and it is very grand."

"How charming," Lady Cameron said, eyeing a footman, who disappeared. She added, "Speaking of charming, I met Miss Caroline Everly last night at the dance. Such pleasing manners in a young woman. I take it she is to marry soon?"

"Yes, your ladyship. She and Constable Dyngley will marry in the autumn, I believe," Poppy replied, looking down at her lap.

"Lovely girl. And what is her family like?"

"I do not know. I only made her acquaintance last night. But she is very kind and has a pleasant way of speaking," Poppy said, thinking of the small whirlwind of animation that was Caroline.

"Hah. What Poppy is too delicate to say is that the girl has an inheritance of £10,000. That will make her an attractive marriage partner to any young man in want of a wife," Aunt Rachel said.

Lady Cameron smiled. "I do enjoy hearing the latest gossip, Mrs. Greene. Ah, here is tea."

She paused as two footmen entered the room carrying large trays. One set down a silver tray on a side table with a steaming silver teapot on it, as well as four gold-rimmed white china teacups and saucers, decorated with flowers.

Mr. Ingleby's face lit up as he eyed the teacups, admiring their gold handles and gold-rimmed saucers. He sat patiently as Lady Cameron poured tea for everyone and they passed the small dainty cups around, adding sugar or milk as desired. The second footman put down a platter of mini scones and tarts, where the guests helped themselves. The ladies each took a tart, whereas Mr. Ingleby piled his small china plate with two of each.

He munched on the first golden flaked pastry and said, purple blackberry juice dribbling down his chin, "These tarts are wonderful."

"Thank you. My cook makes a wonderful blackberry tart. Although I prefer a good plum pudding, do try the rhubarb and apple tarts, they are excellent too."

Mr. Ingleby responded by putting an entire tart into his mouth and chewing, much to Lady Cameron's amusement. Once he finished and swallowed his mouthful, he wiped his mouth and said, "You are such a kind and generous hostess, your ladyship. But I suspect you didn't know there is a lot of good you could do for the town."

"What do you mean?" Lady Cameron asked.

"Well, I suspect it escaped your notice that the church roof is in a sorry state, and needs fixing."

Aunt Rachel looked askance. "I beg your pardon?"

Mr. Ingleby ignored her. "I made an inspection of it today before I returned from church, and it is in dire need of repair. I daresay it will be very hard for the parishioners to pay attention to my sermons when the roof is leaking above their heads."

"Is it actually that bad?" she asked, sipping her tea.

"Oh yes," he said, "Mrs. Greene is far too polite to say anything, but it's true. I have looked into the Reverend Greene's accounts and found that he has been saving funds out of his own pocket to pay for its repairs. It is why the ladies have a supper more suitable for paupers, with no pudding."

"No pudding? None at all?"

Aunt Rachel looked at Poppy in dismay, her face red.

"It is true. I for one love a good tart, and these are wonderful," he added, biting into another, shedding golden crumbs all over himself and the silk cushion.

Poppy shot Mr. Ingleby a hard glance. "We do have pudding, for birthdays and holidays. It is not as sparse as you might think, your ladyship."

Mr. Ingleby talked over her. "I for one am going to start asking for collection during the services, to help pay for the roof's repair. It is unfair that the good reverend's family must suffer in this way."

Aunt Rachel sputtered, "We are hardly suff—"

"Tut, tut, Mrs. Greene. You are too good-natured to admit it, so I will plead for you. She is too modest, you see," he told Lady Cameron.

"But this is news to me. Pray, why haven't I heard about this before?" She glanced at Poppy and her aunt.

Poppy opened her mouth when Mr. Ingleby stepped on her foot and said, "The good ladies would never dream of being so gauche as to ask for money, especially from a personage they hold in such high esteem. I think Mr. Greene rather considered it a point of pride to save the money and solve the problem on his own, at his family's expense, rather than ask for help. These two women are so devoted to Mr. Greene and the church, they would hardly say no."

"I see. And here I have been wondering what I could do to become more involved with the town." She raised a cup of tea to her lips.

"This is fortuitous then. Perhaps one might even call it providential." He popped another mouthful of blackberry tart into his mouth, chewing furiously. "If you were to donate funds, I am sure the townspeople would follow your example and be very grateful, not to mention Mr. Greene's pleasure at your generosity."

"Well…" she started to think, sipping her tea. "I could donate some, I suppose…"

"Capital." He rubbed his crumbly hands together.

"But there is something so impersonal about just donating money."

"These tarts are delicious," Poppy said, biting into one. It was a bit tart, but she was being nice. It didn't come close to her aunt's baking.

"That's it. You've just given me the most brilliant idea." Lady Cameron clapped her hands. "Come. I should like to show you where the berries came from," Lady Cameron said, a mischievous smile on her features.

"But your ladyship, what about the church roof? Your donation?" Mr. Ingleby said.

"Tut tut, Mr. Ingleby, all in good time. No more discussion until I have shown you my idea."

They followed her into another room and outside to a large open balcony, which led down to the ground level. She took the lead and walked confidently along the lush green grass, leading them back behind the stately home to where there were finely planted and arranged orchards. It was acres upon acres.

"My lord. I've never seen so many…What sorts of trees are they?" Aunt Rachel asked.

"Apple, plum, quince. Over there are the berries." She showed them to tall rows where brambles had seemingly overgrown, but Poppy could see the early fruits of raspberries, strawberries, and blackberries. In a week or two, Lady Cameron's garden would have hundreds of berries.

"This is where we get all our berries for the year. My cook makes them into fruit tarts, cakes, and jellies, and we have fruit jam all year round. I was thinking I would host a small get-together here at Blackgate Park, and we can charge people for a slice of the tarts. All the money will go toward the church."

"Excellent idea," Mr. Ingleby said, pulling out a crumbling tart from his pocket.

"You could always make it a competition, and award a prize to the best baker," Aunt Rachel said.

"You are such a smart woman," Mr. Ingleby told her, "But I doubt anyone could come close to her ladyship's cook's baking."

"Oh Mr. Ingleby, you are too kind. I think that is a wonderful idea. I'm sure if we told the shopkeepers in town, they too would want to exhibit their own creations. And it's for charity."

"Where would you hold it?" Poppy asked.

"Inside the house, surely," Mr. Ingleby said.

"And have the entire town traipsing through my sitting room? I think not," Lady Cameron laughed. "No, I have a better idea. I will host a berry-picking picnic at my home. Then I will speak to the mayor and see about organizing a little fete in the center of town, and we'll hold a baking contest there. What do you think?"

"Lovely. Provided the sun is out, this would be wonderful. I cannot thank you enough, your ladyship," Aunt Rachel said.

"Yes, thank you, Lady Cameron."

"Oh, it is nothing. I have wanted to do more for the town. And for those people who don't wish to bake, they can buy some of the tarts available, so all the money collected can fund the church roof."

"With this competition, what will be the prize?" Mr. Ingleby asked, wiping his hands on his trousers.

"You and I shall be the judges, Mr. Ingleby, and I will award a suitable prize for the best dessert. It will be something very good indeed." She smiled. "Oh. That does mean we will have to try all the entries. You don't mind, do you?"

Mr. Ingleby clapped in delight.

On the carriage ride home, Mr. Ingleby sat back against the comfortable cushions with a happy sigh and fixed the ladies with a serious look. "You both must bake something spectacular. Your family cannot be outdone by these townspeople."

Aunt Rachel laughed, "Mr. Ingleby, where is your competitive spirit? Although I suppose as a judge, you're not allowed to enter a dessert."

"I will be too busy to bake anything. But Lady Cameron is bound to award a large monetary prize. She is a wealthy woman. Money means nothing to her," he pointed out, "that would be an attractive object to many people."

Poppy snorted.

"Do you bake, Miss Morton?" Mr. Ingleby asked sharply.

"No."

"Then I suggest you learn."

CHAPTER FIVE

THE NEXT FEW weeks heralded more social calls for Mr. Ingleby to make (alone, he informed them), more evenings of him dining out, as more people of the neighborhood were flattered by his attentions and welcomed his company at their dinner table. Poppy wouldn't have minded, but she could see her aunt felt slighted by the invitations that came just for him. What Poppy couldn't figure out was: were they truly such poor company, or did he have a hidden charm that she and her aunt just could not see?

Poppy sat in her room reading when her aunt tapped on the door. "Poppy, have you seen my bracelet? You know, the silver one your uncle gave me for my birthday. I cannot find it anywhere. I must have left it laying around."

"When did you last see it?" Poppy asked.

The day of the dance, I think. I brought it downstairs for Betsey to polish and can't remember what happened to it."

"Did you wear it to the dance?"

"I don't think so. But I can't recall," Aunt Rachel said.

"Then it must still be in the house. Have you asked Betsey?"

"Not yet. Betsey!" She and Poppy went downstairs and found their maid in the kitchen, making bread.

Her wispy blonde hair was tied back beneath a kerchief and her sleeves were rolled up as she kneaded the dough on a worktable. At their entrance to the warm airy kitchen, Betsey stopped. "Yes, ma'am?"

"I am missing a bracelet. The silver one that Reginald gave me for Christmas. Do you know where it is?" Aunt Rachel asked.

"No ma'am."

"But I told you I wanted it polished for the dance that night. I left it out on the table in the sitting room for you."

Betsey shook her head. "I didn't see it, ma'am. I thought you'd changed your mind."

"No, I didn't."

Betsey's forehead wrinkled. "I don't know where it is, Mrs. Greene."

"Please do look for it when you clean. It's very dear to me."

Betsey bobbed a curtsey and returned to her kneading, a nervous expression on her face.

Poppy ushered Aunt Rachel into the sitting room and whispered, "I don't like this. I believe her, but if we keep on like this, she'll think we're accusing her of stealing."

"Good servants have been lost for less," Aunt Rachel agreed.

"Could you have left it somewhere else? Or forgotten to give it to her?"

"No, I remember distinctly setting it on that table. It's so strange," Aunt Rachel said. "She wouldn't steal. She's been with us for at least five years."

Poppy agreed. "Could you have worn it to the dance after all? Or could it have fallen onto the floor?"

The ladies moved the sofa back and got on their hands and knees to look. They upturned sofa cushions, looked beneath tables, and peered on the floor, but the bracelet was not to be found.

"Aunt Rachel, I think we both can guess where it's gone." She looked up at the ceiling in the direction of Mr. Ingleby's room."

"You don't think... No, I can't believe it. You don't think he would take it, do you? It wouldn't suit him," she deadpanned.

Poppy laughed. "I can't imagine why he would want it unless

to sell it for money. And if he did truly take Uncle's sermon earlier... I think we may have a thief in our house."

"I think we can believe Mr. Ingleby when he says that Reginald left the sermons for him. My Reginald would be kind like that. But to learn of my missing bracelet..." Aunt Rachel sat on the sofa again with a sad poof and held a small cushion in her hands. "Reginald won't be pleased when he hears about this. What do we do? Confront him?"

"Not yet. I want to gather proof before I accuse him of anything."

"Oh, Poppy, are you sure about this? It could all be one big misunderstanding. Are you sure it's not just you... you know," Aunt Rachel said, smoothing the now rumpled cushion.

"What?" Poppy asked.

"Well, since you and the constable dealt with that unpleasantness before with the murdered servant, I gather you are a bit fatigued with our way of life. Do you not think this seeing Mr. Ingleby as a thief could not just be you wanting a crime, as an excuse to see Constable Dyngley again?"

Poppy frowned. "No. I mean, I may be suffering from some ennui, but I don't think I'm creating villains out of misunderstandings."

"Well it's like you say, until we have proof, there's nothing more to be said."

"But what about your bracelet?" Poppy asked.

"I'm sure it will turn up. But let's say no more on the matter, I feel guilty suspecting a man we've only known for a short time. Perhaps we are doing him an injustice. Besides, I have received a letter from your uncle that needs answering. I'm sure he would say you should devote yourself more to your studies, Poppy." Aunt Rachel left the room.

THE NEXT WEEK, Lady Cameron sent around invitations to a picnic at her estate. She had recently opened the grounds to the public for berry picking, and for one day only, people from the town were welcome to come and enjoy themselves. Mr. Ingleby was pleased and brought his own basket, taken from Mr. Greene's study.

Not having a carriage of their own, they took their cart to Blackgate Park, much to Mr. Ingleby's disgust, especially as he discovered he was expected to drive the horse all the way there. He flicked the reins angrily and said, "When I win the prize, I shall buy the parsonage a carriage. Traveling in a cart is noble but also very humbling. Surely the living can afford an appropriate mode of travel. What does Mr. Greene do for long distances?"

"He travels by post," Aunt Rachel said, "But that is very kind of you, Mr. Ingleby."

"Yes, well," came the answer.

They were not the first to arrive, and their cart joined a queue of carriages, curricles, and a phaeton, all pulling into Lady Cameron's open courtyard. Mr. Ingleby's manner changed, and he waved hello and was all smiles as they pulled up behind a curricle, to see Jane and Robert turn around and wave. "Hullo there!"

Once everyone had disembarked and their horses seen to, it was a merry party that was greeted by Lady Cameron. Many townspeople had come laden with baskets to do the picking, and Lady Cameron had ordered her footmen to provide baskets, tables of refreshments, and chilled drinks for everyone.

As Poppy stood with her aunt and Mr. Ingleby, she could hear her ladyship encouraging guests to tour the grounds and walk through the many acres of orchards devoted to fruit trees, and to avail themselves of the many rows of orderly planted berries, boasting hundreds of raspberries and blackberries.

Jane immediately took Poppy's arm and took her to stroll through the orchards, admiring the finely tended rows of raspberry bushes and blackberry brambles. "I have a secret," Jane said.

"What's that?"

"You have an admirer." Jane giggled, her blue eyes dancing.

"You're teasing me," Poppy said, "I don't believe you."

"Believe me or not, it's true." Jane grinned, then pulled Poppy to a stop. "Look at that."

"What? Poppy looked around.

"He's here."

"Who?"

"The man of my dreams, silly, that's who. Don't you remember? The young man from the sweet shop. He's here!" Jane hissed. "He's coming. Act natural."

Poppy snorted as they purposely looked at the wall of raspberries before them when the young man entered her peripheral view. He wore a light green coat and tan trousers, with an ornate silver-topped walking stick. He strolled alongside the wall and touched his top hat as he passed by. Poppy nodded while Jane kept her eyes fixed straight ahead at the berries.

"He's gone," Poppy told her a minute later.

Jane sighed. "Did he look at me?"

"Yes. Although he probably wondered why you were staring at the berries and not at him," Poppy teased.

An unwelcome voice said, "Shouldn't your attention be better spent in some useful employment rather than lurking in the bushes and watching innocent men?"

Poppy and Jane turned around. "Mr. Ingleby." They did not curtsey.

He rounded on them, hefting a basket laden with raspberries. "Miss Morton. I had thought you would have a better influence on your friend, being a clergyman's niece. Perhaps this evening I shall lecture to you on Fordyce's Sermons for an hour or three."

Poppy and Jane exchanged horrified looks. "That is very kind of you, Mr. Ingleby, but—"

"I am sure it would be a much better use of your time than eyeing men who are of a different station than yourselves."

Jane gasped and Poppy's nostrils flared. "I'm sure I don't know what you mean."

His upper lip curled back into a sneer as he eyed Jane's simple gray dress, light walking coat, and frayed straw bonnet. "You are too good to speak of such things, Miss Morton, but I saw the way your friend eyed that young man. As a clergyman, it is my solemn duty to remind you young people—"

"You are only eight years older, sir." Poppy pointed out.

Mr. Ingleby glared at her. "As I was saying, it does not do to encourage romantic entanglements outside of one's station. I have seen it before and it only ends in heartbreak or worse, children born out of wedlock."

"We were simply picking berries and he happened to walk by," Jane said.

"I know what I saw. Take it from me, that young man has more interesting things to do than dally with young ladies from a humbler situation than he."

"Mr. Ingleby," Poppy started, her face turning pink.

"Just a word of advice, Miss Morton. Now if you'll excuse me, I see Mrs. Grant and her husband." He walked off, swinging his basket with purpose, unaware of the trail of raspberries he left in his wake.

"What a nuisance," Poppy said. "Are you all right?"

"I'm fine. I just feel sorry that you have to live with him. I'm glad he didn't come to see my father. Broken leg or not, he would've kicked Mr. Ingleby out of his house."

"I would have loved to see that." Poppy grinned.

The girls walked on, with Poppy observing all the men they passed by. Finally, Jane asked, "Who are you looking for?"

"No one. Just admiring the grounds. It's all so pretty."

"I don't like it," Jane said.

"Why ever not? These are beautiful grounds." Miss Caroline Everly approached, walking beside Constable Dyngley. Today Miss Everly wore a pretty pink linen dress, embroidered at the hem with purple flowers and tied back at the waist with a light pink ribbon. She wore a light green overcoat that was so light it was almost yellow, and a fashionable bonnet with a pink ribbon. Beside her, Constable Dyngley looked very fine in a pale gray jacket, silk gray waistcoat, and light tan trousers.

Poppy avoided his eyes and made the introductions. The ladies curtseyed, and Caroline said, "Forgive me for interrupting your conversation, but I couldn't help overhearing. I find these orchards delightful. How easy it is to pick the berries without tearing your clothing. I am glad Lady Cameron had such forethought in her planting."

Miss Heyworth was not to be deterred. "Easy, yes, but not so wild as I would like. What worth does a treasure have when it is given to you on a silver platter? I prefer to earn my rewards, and if my troubles cost me a torn sleeve, so be it."

Miss Everly simpered. "No doubt your tailor would agree."

"Miss Morton, what do you say?" Constable Dyngley asked.

Poppy looked fleetingly into his warm brown eyes, then at Caroline. "I appreciate both. I don't mind working for berries, but sometimes it can be tiring and I like the easy way of it too. I don't think either way is better, just different."

"Hear, hear," Dyngley said.

"Hmmm." Miss Everly eyed Poppy and placed a proprietary hand on Constable Dyngley's arm. She told him, "I am parched. Let us see if there is anything to drink, although I hope it is not too much trouble to get. Or would you have us trek up mountains and swim in rivers to get our water as well?" She turned and smiled at Jane.

The constable, seeing as he was immersed in a tete-a-tete between the ladies, decided to remove himself from it as quickly as possible. "Let us see what Lady Cameron has in store for her guests." He nodded to Poppy and Jane and led Miss Everly away.

"Ooh, she's a spiteful one. What a rude creature," Jane said, watching them go. She saw Poppy's face and said with a flash of intuition, "That's the man you fancy, isn't it? The constable."

Poppy shook her head. "Not at all. He's just a friend."

"But you wish he was more."

Poppy snorted. "I'm happy for him and Miss Everly."

"I wouldn't be."

Poppy glanced at Jane. "Why ever not?"

"Because he seems like a genteel sort, and she seems spiteful. It's clear he's only marrying her for her dowry. I heard she has £10,000, is that right?"

"I heard that, yes," Poppy said.

"Even so, did you see the way she put her hand on his arm after he asked you your opinion? He values what you think, and she noticed."

"Miss Heyworth…"

"Oh for heaven's sake, Miss Morton, we are friendly enough to be sisters. Call me Jane and I shall call you Poppy. Besides, I know of at least one person who will be happy to know you are single." She touched her nose. "But I shan't tell. I say we leave Miss Everly and her constable to her £10,000 and we start picking berries. I am sure we will pick enough for a dozen sweet pies and desserts."

They began filling their baskets with blackberries that stained their fingers when pulled too roughly, ruby-red raspberries and strawberries, more than enough to fill a number of fruit tarts and pies. As they made their way back to the entrance of the grounds, they heard Lady Cameron say, "Pick as many berries as you like, for this time next week I shall host a small competition, to see which one of Hertford's residents is a prize baker among us."

Murmurs and chatter began amongst the people there. Jane said, "My lord, a baking contest! That is exciting."

Lady Cameron added, "Next week I shall host a fete in the town center. Anyone who wishes to submit a dessert for the competition is welcome to do so, and I shall be the judge, along with Mr. Ingleby, our local rector. Everyone can come and purchase a slice of pie for a small sum, and the profits will go toward repairs of the church roof."

There was a small smattering of applause. Lady Cameron added, "Oh, and I will be awarding a prize to the best dessert. So whether it is a family recipe for a cake or a new culinary creation for a pie or tart, anyone could win."

More conversation and whispers began as the people chatted amongst themselves. Poppy joined Lady Cameron and Aunt Rachel at the refreshment tables and helped herself to a cup of fizzy ginger beer. Its slightly spicy taste was refreshing as the chilled drink trickled down her throat.

Jane came to Poppy, all excited. "Can you believe it? A prize for the best dessert. I can make a blackberry tart."

Caroline appeared by Poppy's other side. "I have been told I make an excellent apple pie."

The ladies locked gazes and Poppy realized she stood between two fierce competitors. "I for one am looking forward to trying the desserts."

Caroline laughed. "Wouldn't you rather try your hand at baking and earn the prize? I daresay your servant could teach you."

Poppy smiled. "I could, but I am sure my aunt will want to bake something for the contest. I think it would be unfair for us both to compete." She didn't mention that she was hopeless at baking and would no doubt need their maid's help in producing an edible cake.

Aunt Rachel approached them and said, "But where is Mr. Ingleby? I was sure he would want to be here for her ladyship's announcement."

"Maybe he is touring the grounds?" Poppy said.

"I did see him walking toward the blackberry patch," Lady Cameron said, "perhaps you might find him there."

Poppy smiled at this. What Lady Cameron called the blackberry patch were rows upon rows of meticulously trimmed and cultivated blackberries, grown so tall and sprawling to be considered hedges, and stretching out to cover almost an acre.

"I'll walk with you." Jane took Poppy's arm and they walked together through the rows, past tall walls of raspberry plants and blackberry brambles.

"Mr. Ingleby," they called, "Mr. Ingleby."

They passed rows of berry bushes, more than one happy

couple picking fruits, and even the handsome man that Jane fancied, who tipped his hat to them. Jane paused for a moment before Poppy tugged her along.

Jane said, "Let's split up, we'll cover more ground that way."

"All right." The girls parted ways and wandered in separate directions. Poppy walked for a bit until she heard a cry, and rounded the corner. "Jane, what is it?"

Jane stood alone and pointed at the ground. There behind a wall of blackberry vines, lay Mr. Ingleby. His basket of berries was scattered across the freshly cut grass, his small eyes were closed and his face was pale as death.

"Is he…Is he dead?" Jane asked.

Poppy stared. There stuffed into his mouth, were dozens of blackberries, purple juice staining his cravat like blood.

CHAPTER SIX

P OPPY KNELT TO his side. "Jane, go get help. Quickly, run!"
Jane fled, dropping her basket.

Poppy dug some of the blackberries out of his mouth, grazing her knuckles on his teeth. She scooped them out until his mouth was empty, then shook him. "Mr. Ingleby? Sir?"

He lay there, his face pale, his mouth open. Cuts and slices of blood marked his cheeks as if he'd run face-first into the blackberry bushes. She slapped his cheeks and called his name, but he lay unconscious. She called out, "Somebody help! He's hurt!"

In minutes, townspeople crowded around. Running toward them came Jane, Caroline, and Constable Dyngley. "Move aside!" he ordered, and a few townspeople shuffled back. "Is there a doctor? A physician?"

A smartly dressed man who Poppy recognized as Mr. Grant spoke up. "No. Dr. Wilson is back in town. It's at least a twenty-minute ride into town to fetch him."

Poppy exchanged a knowing look with Dyngley. That meant another few minutes to notify the doctor of what happened and then bring him back. There simply wasn't time.

Constable Dyngley asked Poppy. "What happened?"

"I don't know. We were looking for him and found him like this, but with berries in his mouth." She leaned her fingers against his cheek and said, "He's still warm."

Constable Dyngley laid his ear against the man's chest and put his hand flat beneath Mr. Ingleby's nose.

"What are you doing?" Caroline asked. "Dyngley, you shouldn't touch a body. Who knows what could have killed him?"

Dyngley ignored her, waited a few seconds, then said, "He is breathing. He's alive."

He opened Mr. Ingleby's mouth and peered down. "I can't see anything. Do you think he choked?"

"I can't tell. I scooped out the berries as best I could," Poppy said.

"He needs a doctor. Surely we could take him to the village?" Caroline asked.

"Look, he's waking up." Jane pointed.

Mr. Ingleby's eyelids fluttered and he coughed. His eyes opened wide and he jolted awake, turning to retch and vomit on the grass. He coughed up berries and bile, much to the embarrassment of all present.

"Move away, give us some air," Constable Dyngley ordered. "He'll be fine, just leave us be."

People walked away until it was just Caroline, Poppy, and the constable left with Mr. Ingleby. Constable Dyngley said, "Caroline, fetch one of Lady Cameron's footmen. Mr. Ingleby will be needing a carriage home."

Poppy got to her feet as Mr. Ingleby took a perfumed handkerchief from within his waistcoat and wiped his mouth with it. The strong scent filled the air, which was an improvement from the small bit of bile that stained the grass next to him. He sat up with Constable Dyngley's help, and asked, "What happened?"

"That's what we want to know. Did you choke on some berries?" the constable asked.

"No. I was walking and then I… woke up here. I must have fallen. Perhaps the grass is wet and I slipped." His face was pale.

Poppy and the constable looked at the ground. The well-trodden yellowish-green grass was very dry, indeed, for it had been a hot July so far.

"Do you remember nothing?" Constable Dyngley asked.

"Nothing at all." He gave a weak smile at Dyngley and Caroline. "I am clumsy sometimes; I must have had an accident."

"Something you ate perhaps," Poppy said.

"What makes you say that?" Mr. Ingleby asked.

"Miss Heyworth and I found you with a lot of blackberries stuffed in your mouth. We thought you had choked."

"Me? I never choke. I may like my food, but I always take a bite of what is perfectly modest and proper, as befitting a clergyman," Mr. Ingleby said, wiping his mouth again. He put his hand down on the grass and touched something soft. "Ugh." He lifted his hand to find it covered in blackberry remnants and purple berry juice.

"Mr. Ingleby, your hand," Poppy said.

"Yes, I know, I've just planted it in blackberries thank you very much," he snapped.

"No, I mean there's spots on your skin. Are you all right?"

He fixed her with a dirty look and wiped his hands on the grass. "I am fine. Too much sun, perhaps."

Constable Dyngley helped Mr. Ingleby to his feet. "I have ordered you a carriage. I think it is best if you rest at home."

Mr. Ingleby at first brushed him off, then wavered on his feet. "Oh. Perhaps a brief rest would be good." He turned to Poppy. "I feel weak. Carry my basket back for me?"

She nodded.

"Oh, and I seem to have dropped some berries. Be a dear and pick them up for me. It would displease her ladyship to learn we had squandered her generosity toward us today."

Poppy waited until the constable and Mr. Ingleby were out of sight, then snorted. "If he didn't choke, I'll eat my bonnet." She scooped a few handfuls of the berries into his basket, then stopped. A pair of men's boots stood before her.

"That would be a shame. There are too few pretty girls in the world, I'd hate to see one lost due to death by bonnet."

Poppy glanced up. It was Jane's mysterious man. If only Jane could be there at that moment. And yet, he looked into her eyes with a flirtatious smile. He had a long face, wavy chestnut hair tied back in a ribbon, a skewed white cravat, tan trousers, and a light green waistcoat over his arm with white shirt sleeves pushed up to his elbows. He carried a smart walking stick, topped with a silver handle that he leaned on as he surveyed her for a second. He set down a basket and said, "A definite shame. Can I help you with that? I didn't think her ladyship allowed people to carry two baskets."

Poppy smiled. "I'm filling this back up for Mr. Ingleby. He fell but didn't want to come away empty-handed."

He met her smile with his own. "Allow me." He set down his walking stick and scooped large handfuls of berries from the grass back into Mr. Ingleby's basket, avoiding the mess. "I have seen you before, I am sure of it. In town, perhaps?"

Poppy nodded. As polite as he was, it would not do to converse with a gentleman when they hadn't been introduced. What would her aunt say?

"Your pretty friend was walking with you earlier. Where is she now?"

"Poppy, there you are!" Jane turned the corner and came back, coming to a stop. "Oh, forgive me. I did not mean to interrupt."

"Not at all, we were just collecting berries for Mr. Ingleby." The man rose to his feet and handed Poppy the clergyman's basket. He bowed and said, "Forgive me for speaking out of turn when we have not been properly introduced." He gave Jane a sly smile and walked away.

The young women waited until he left, then Jane flew to Poppy's side. "Oh my goodness, you have to tell me everything. Who is he? Did he give his name? What did he say? Tell me right now before I go mad!"

Poppy laughed and picked up her own basket. "Come, let's go."

They walked back to the garden entrance as Poppy relayed the conversation. They carried the baskets and curtseyed as Lady Cameron expressed her well wishes for Mr. Ingleby's fast recovery. He had already been sent home in her ladyship's carriage, so all that was left was for Poppy to load up their humble cart and mule and drive home.

POPPY REFLECTED THE following early afternoon that all was not to be well. However peaceful the parsonage was, its gentle comforts were disrupted by the most innocent of visitors. There was a knock at the front door, and Betsey ushered in a youth, one of the altar boys that helped Mr. Greene each week. "Master Geoffrey Sutton," Betsey announced.

Poppy looked up from her reading, and Aunt Rachel paused from her embroidery. "Hello, Geoffrey."

The boy bowed a bit awkwardly and hung his head. Once Betsey had gone, he mumbled something, his eyes focused on the floor.

"What is it, boy? Speak up, I can't hear you," Aunt Rachel said.

The boy's face screwed up as he blinked away tears.

"What is it, Geoffrey?" Poppy asked gently.

"Um…"

Aunt Rachel rose and set her embroidery aside. "I think we have some sweet biscuits in the kitchen. Would you like some?"

Geoffrey didn't speak, but only stood twisting a small cap in his hands.

Aunt Rachel disappeared from the room, leaving Poppy and Geoffrey alone. "Come, sit down," Poppy said kindly.

In a minute, Aunt Rachel returned with a plate of biscuits and offered them to the boy. He took the plate and held it in his lap as he sat on the hardback chair facing them. He took one biscuit and bit into it, his attention diverted by the crunch of a ginger biscuit.

"Now then. What's the matter?" Aunt Rachel asked.

Geoffrey looked up, glanced from Poppy to Aunt Rachel, and

mumbled, "The money. The church collection money. It's all gone."

Aunt Rachel asked, "What do you mean, gone?"

"After church, Cornelius and me, we take the money from the church plates and put it in the box in the sacristy for safekeeping."

"Right, go on."

He bit into another biscuit, shedding dark brown crumbs onto his shirt. "I went around to clean after service and I was putting my things away when I saw that the collection box was unlocked. I opened it up and it was empty." He teared up. "I swear I didn't take it. I'm no thief, honest."

Poppy said, "No one thinks you are, Geoffrey."

"But what will Mr. Ingleby say? He locked it up and said it had to be kept safe. Now he'll think I stole it, but I didn't." He wiped his eyes, his face red. "Will I be sent to prison?"

"No one is going to prison, Geoffrey," Aunt Rachel said, "Do you know how much money was taken?"

Geoffrey shrugged and wiped his eyes on his sleeve. "I didn't count it, but when Cornelius asked how much it was, Mr. Ingleby said it was more than forty shillings."

Poppy's eyebrows rose. That was more than double what her uncle normally counted in the weekly church donations. "Such a sum. Do you remember who was in charge of it last?"

"No. Last I saw it was locked away by Mr. Ingleby while me and Cornelius swept the church after service. The reverend said it was fine, that he would lock up after us. My mum was pleased cause I was home early."

Mr. Ingleby appeared in the doorway. "What's this I hear about the church?"

Geoffrey rose, scattering biscuit crumbs on the floor. "Pardon, sir. But..." He stopped and set the plate on the chair. "The money, sir. The church money's gone."

Mr. Ingleby's face clouded.

Geoffrey spoke woodenly as if reciting a text at school. "The church collection plate money, it's gone. Somebody stole it." He looked up. "It weren't me!"

"But you were in charge of cleaning the church while I was speaking to the parishioners." Mr. Ingleby pointed out and looked at the youth's scruffy appearance. "Boy, did you take the money? I understand life is hard, but that's no reason to steal."

"I didn't take it! I swear," Geoffrey said, "I swear to God I didn't."

"Do not take the Lord's name in vain, boy. He looks down upon those who steal, and so do I."

Geoffrey's face screwed up again and he wiped his nose on his sleeve.

"Mr. Ingleby," Poppy started, "We have known this boy for years and have no reason to believe he would start to steal now. He has always been a good and honest helper to my uncle. I cannot believe he would do something so uncharacteristic as stealing."

Mr. Ingleby's face was grave. "Then what are we to do about the missing funds? Just assume it will reappear? The church roof needs repair, Miss Morton, or would you perhaps have the townspeople attend service in the rain?" Seeing her face, he said, "I thought not. No, what the boy needs is discipline. He cannot go through life assuming his actions are without consequence."

"We have no reason to believe he would do such a thing," Aunt Rachel said.

"And who else would? The only people in the church after services were myself and the two boys, and I happen to know that Cornelius Alleyn's family is very comfortable. The Alleyn boy would have no need to steal, whereas this boy... well."

Big fat tears rolled down the boy's cheeks. He looked up into Mr. Ingleby's eyes, his face red. "I didn't steal. I'm no thief."

"The law will decide that, my boy."

"I hate you!" he pushed past Mr. Ingleby and ran outside. The front door opened and closed with a slam, making the ladies jump.

"How could you say that to him? He's just a boy," Poppy said, "and besides, surely it would be foolish of him to report the theft if he's a suspect. Surely he would have created a fictitious person or persons and blamed it on them instead, if he was guilty."

Mr. Ingleby gave her a knowing smile and eyed the book in her hands. "I think you read too many novels. He may be just a boy now, but you wait, soon he'll be stealing more and then pilfering. In a few years' time when he demands your coin-purse and aims a pistol at your face, will you be so forgiving then?" He snorted. "No. You will instead report him to the authorities and attend his hanging. These boys need to learn rules and discipline, Miss Morton. Encouraging their wickedness with a soft heart and forgiveness will not help them."

Aunt Rachel stared at him. "Sir. We are not in the habit of—"

"I am not in the habit of entertaining young criminals, but here we are. If you two exercised a greater degree of caution and I daresay decorum, these ne'er do wells would know better than to come here and ply you with a sob story. His family is poor, he was in the right place when no one else could have done it, and that's it. I will report him to the local magistrate immediately."

"You will do no such thing," Aunt Rachel snapped.

Mr. Ingleby glared at her. "You forget yourself, madam."

"I do not. You forget yourself, Mr. Ingleby. Your patron would be ashamed of the unhappy manners you have shown toward that boy. I myself am ashamed for you, and if you were not our guest, I would ask that you remove yourself from the house this instant."

He gasped, eyes wide. "How dare you talk to me like that. Do you know who I am?"

"A greedy, self-righteous prig who dares call himself a man."

"Well. I never. Take care when you speak to me, Mrs. Greene. I should hate for you to be found wanting as a clergyman's wife. When I tell your husband of your unwomanly behavior, well…"

"Is that a threat?" Poppy said.

"It is a warning, and it goes for you too, Miss Morton." He stormed off and spoke to Betsey in the kitchen before stomping up the stairs.

"Well." Aunt Rachel sagged on the sofa. "What a miserable man. I cannot believe anyone would accept him as a clergyman. He is too unkind, too unfeeling, too…"

"Unchristian," Poppy said.

"Exactly. There's not a charitable bone in his body, the self-righteous sod."

Poppy's eyebrows rose.

"Sorry, dear." Aunt Rachel apologized. "He just winds me up. When I think about poor Geoffrey in tears…" She rose. "I'd better go visit Mrs. Sutton and reassure her. No harm will come to that boy. And if Mr. Ingleby does speak to the magistrate, I'll tell him that the man is foolish and doesn't know what he's talking about. That boy didn't steal a penny."

POPPY WAS LEFT to her own devices and felt better for it. She took up a spare dress that needed hemming and set to work, thinking as her needle dipped swiftly in and out of the fabric. She believed in Geoffrey's innocence, but what if Mr. Ingleby was right, and the boy had taken the money? And why was Mr. Ingleby so quick to believe in his guilt, when he himself may have taken the plate of oatcakes and her aunt's bracelet? He could be forgiven a touch of greediness, but with her aunt's bracelet missing and now this? Was he in dire need of funds or was her mind running away with her? She penned a note for Betsey to take to the constable, asking him to come see her straight away. She could explain what had happened about the missing church money. She trusted that when presented with facts, Dyngley would act with a calm demeanor and not rush to any conclusions.

LATER THAT AFTERNOON Betsey shared that Mr. Ingleby had

requested a tray be brought up to him for his dinner, as he had hours of spiritual meditation to focus on. Poppy smirked and consulted the family's recipe book in the kitchen. Perhaps she could bake something for the competition. Baking wasn't too hard to learn, was it?

Taking pleasure in the coolness of the wide-open space, she took the book down from its place in a corner of a worktable and pulled up a chair at the square wooden table, brushing it clear of crumbs. It served as the workspace for Betsey and was mainly her domain, but in the summer it was blessedly cool. She sat down in one of the sturdy wooden chairs by the kitchen table and made herself comfortable. The book was a thick volume that had been passed down for years, and as she opened the aged brown leather cover, she noticed a drawn family tree dating back decades. Unfortunately, it was all along her uncle's line, so there was little mention of her family except at the bottom, where there lay written:

Reginald Greene + Hannah – ~~Celeste Morton~~

Poppy Morton

Poppy stared at the faded spidery writing. From the looks of it, Hannah's sister was Celeste and her biological mother. That made sense, but it didn't give her a clue beyond the name. She flipped through the recipes, noting a number of receipts for medical conditions including gout, cough, sore throat, as well as recipes for biscuits, cakes, and even a cheesecake, which required no cheese at all, but eggs and ground almonds. That looked easy enough to do, especially as they had a surplus of eggs, thanks to their chickens.

An hour or so later, Aunt Rachel came back, weary from her visit to the Suttons. "Well that's that," she said, tugging her bonnet ribbons loose. "I've told Mrs. Sutton it was all a big misunderstanding. He's still nervous but I said just keep on doing what he's told and not put the reverend's nose out of joint." She sat down at the table and helped herself to one of the leftover ginger biscuits. "Still. You should have heard the things that woman said. I had thought Mrs. Sutton such a quiet creature but when her boy came home in tears, she was ready to fight a bear." She looked at Poppy. "I wonder if Mr. Ingleby is starting to rub people the wrong way."

"If he isn't careful, someone is going to do something about it," Poppy said, "Aunt, you don't think what happened to him at Lady's Cameron's picnic was…"

"What? An accident?"

"What if it wasn't? What if he went too far and someone reacted?"

Aunt Rachel shook her head. "The man's right about one thing, you have been reading too many novels. Your imagination is running away with you, Poppy. Let's say no more about it, it's over and there's baking to be done." She looked pointedly at the recipe book Poppy held.

A FEW DAYS later Poppy stood in the warm kitchen, covered with flour. Her attempts at oatcakes had left her and the kitchen a mess. The mixture had split and then when she attempted to cook the mixture, it turned into more of a dark oaty sheet rock. She was just inspecting the hard brick of oatcake on a plate when Mr. Ingleby stuck his head through the door of the kitchen. "This smells promising," he said.

"Thank you. I'm trying to bake oatcakes but without much success," she admitted, wiping her floury hands on her apron.

He approached the worktable and said, "May I?"

"Be my guest." She gestured toward the hard brick of oat-cake, freshly removed from its tin.

He took a thick knife and inserted it into the mix, then tried to smoothly cut a piece. Unfortunately for him, the knife didn't move.

"Oh." Mr. Ingleby wiggled the blade, but it hoisted the entire brick-hard loaf of oatcake in the air. He dropped it back on the plate with a loud thud and wrinkled his nose at the sight. "It is very good that you are baking something to help raise money for the church roof. I have no doubt you will improve with practice. And what of your aunt, is she baking as well?"

Poppy didn't like the hard glint in his eyes. "Yes, I think she'll bake a tart. We have many plums out back, so her plum tart will be popular, I'm sure."

"Ah, excellent." A loud gurgle escaped him. His forehead glistened with a light sheen of sweat and he clutched his stomach.

"Mr. Ingleby, are you all right?"

"Yes. Just something I ate. Forgive me, I need the privy." His face turned pasty as he hurried from the room.

Poppy glanced at the rock-hard brick on the plate before her, the knife still standing up inside it. "At least it wasn't one of my oatcakes."

CHAPTER SEVEN

C ONSTABLE DYNGLEY DIDN'T come in response to Poppy's note about the missing church collection money. Instead, Mr. Arnold Jenkins arrived, a round, pugnacious fellow with short-cropped dark hair under a hat, with a large brown waistcoat that strained to contain his bulk, dark brown breeches the color of mud, and a temperament that would rile a saint. When he listened to Poppy's account of what happened, he only scratched his head and said he'd look into it.

When Poppy asked why the constable himself didn't come, Jenkins grinned. "He's engaged elsewhere. Busy with the wedding plans, I hear. Nothing to concern you."

Poppy gave him a polite smile through gritted teeth as Betsey showed him out, then rolled up her sleeves and entered the kitchen, determined to bake her frustrations away.

But after two days of baking, failing, and producing far too many miniature cheesecakes, Poppy gave up. Her cheesecakes were small, the pastry was far too crumbly, and the fake 'cheese' element, in fact a wet almond mixture, had an unfortunate tendency to run over one's hands. However, she was just in time for the competition, and that week had seen many flyers and broadsheets posted about the town. The day was very fine out, with light blue skies and a dusting of white clouds that flitted by.

The air was warm, as befitting late July, and the trees hung heavy with branches overloaded with green leaves. In the town square, a large tent had been set up, with tables and chairs. It was like a small village fete had come to Hertford, and to Poppy's surprise, Lady Cameron had been in touch with the local shops ahead of time. As a result, when Poppy, Betsey, and Aunt Rachel entered the town center carrying a plate of Aunt Rachel's plum tarts, it was like walking into a fairground. Small food stalls had been set up and Poppy heard a bookie calling out bets for which pie would take the prize.

Aunt Rachel led the way like a duck through water, passing through the milling crowds of people. Children ran about and more than one young couple took the opportunity to sneak away for a private stroll.

Clutching a very securely wrapped dessert, they were stopped by Mrs. Alleyn, who said, "Hello there Mrs. Greene, Miss Morton. What a nice occasion this is."

Aunt Rachel smiled politely.

"You must be so delighted with all the good works Mr. Ingleby is doing. I've never met a man so devoted to charity."

Aunt Rachel's eyes narrowed.

"That is, of course, aside from your own dear husband." Mrs. Alleyn said, blushing. "I have, of course, baked a little something for the contest, but I wanted you to know that we have also made a donation toward the church roof. There's no reason why Mr. Greene should pay for it all himself."

Poppy's face warmed. Mrs. Alleyn had just confirmed that Mr. Ingleby had been gossiping about the reason for the contest, at their expense.

She looked at Poppy and Aunt Rachel and allowed herself a sly smile. "Well, I must be off. Good luck to you both. May the best pie win."

Aunt Rachel waited until Mrs. Alleyn had left before turning to Poppy. "Good works indeed. The only good work Mr. Ingleby has done is fill his stomach at the table of every good household in town," Aunt Rachel snorted.

They walked up to the long table full of entries and gave Aunt Rachel's name to a footman, who penned her name down on a little card and set it behind her plate of tarts. As they parted ways to explore the stalls on the village green, Poppy spied Dyngley walking with Caroline and ducked behind a stall, bumping into a person.

"Oh, I'm sorry." She turned around. "Mr. Heyworth."

"Hello there. Are you hiding from a lover or hoping to see me?" Robert teased. Today he looked smart in a dark green overcoat and light linen waistcoat, white shirt, and tan trousers. He tore off the overcoat and said, "It's too hot for this," and slung it over his shoulder. "So what are you about today? I was hoping to run into you."

Poppy blushed. "I am here with my aunt; we are delivering her plum tart for the contest."

Robert laughed. "I should have known. Good luck to you, although if you tell my sister I'll deny it. She is determined to win with her raspberry trifle."

Poppy's eyes lit up. "I love a trifle."

"Me too." He grinned. "I must admit, I am lost in this place. Walk with me a little?"

"I…" She paused. It wouldn't be proper to walk with a single man, alone, unescorted. They were neither related nor courting and without a guardian or young woman to keep them company, tongues would wag. "I shouldn't…"

"That's a shame. Do you always do what's expected of you?"

"Ooh, there you are, Poppy, I've been looking everywhere for you." Jane came by and took her arm. "Come, come, the contest is about to begin."

Together the trio walked through the aisles and past the food stalls, as well as merchants selling cloth, ribbons, hats, gloves, as well as toys for children. There were also sellers of cookware, boasting fine plates, silver forks and other cutlery, along with tablecloths, tea sets, and glassware. A large bell rang, and Jane said, "Ooh, it's about to start. I can't wait. I entered a trifle made with raspberries. I hope it wins. Did you enter anything?"

"No, my cheesecake failed miserably," Poppy told her.

"A shame. What about that Miss Everly, did she enter?" Jane asked, glancing around.

The opportunity came to ask Caroline herself, as they came face to face with her and Constable Dyngley. The ladies curtseyed and the men bowed politely. Caroline smiled sweetly at Jane, "I hope you did not go to too much trouble to make your dessert, Miss Heyworth."

"Not at all, Miss Everly. The raspberries from Lady Cameron's party made an excellent trifle."

"How charming. I have made an apple pie. Humble, I know. But ever so sweet and Dyngley loves apples, don't you?" She smiled at him.

He gave a curt nod. "Are you entering the contest, Miss Morton?"

"No. But my aunt is. She's got a plum tart that should go down well."

"Best of luck." He nodded and led Caroline away.

Jane tugged at Poppy's arm. "Look. So many people are taking slices of the cakes and tarts."

Poppy realized it was true. Aside from a slice of each entry that had been set aside for the judges, the bakery was proving very popular, and some of the entries had already disappeared. She didn't mind, however, as each person who took a slice also dropped coins into the wooden collections box in the center of the table, which was guarded by Geoffrey Sutton. "Have a slice of cake and help the church! Give money for the church roof!" another altar boy called.

People crowded around the tent as two footmen and Lady Cameron entered, walking behind the tables laden with desserts. There were more than twenty available, ranging from humble tea cakes and muffins to more ornate-looking cakes and tarts, as well as a pie or two.

"Where is Mr. Ingleby?" Lady Cameron asked, looking

around.

"Coming!" a voice called. Mr. Ingleby walked fussily past people, brushing by others and not so gently knocking against some in his haste to reach the tent. He wore a blue overcoat over beige pantaloons and polished boots, a patterned light blue waistcoat, with a white shirt and fussily tied cravat around his throat. His face was pale as he mopped his brow with a perfumed handkerchief.

"He looks a bit peaky. Is he all right?" Jane whispered to her.

"I have thought the same the past few days. He does look a bit unwell. But when I have asked him, he has always assured me he was fine. Perhaps it's the heat." She watched with concern as Mr. Ingleby approached the tent and bowed to Lady Cameron deeply, then rose, standing beside her as he gazed around at the people gathered there. "Forgive me, your ladyship, I had a headache."

Lady Cameron nodded and gave a short speech, calling on the townspeople to donate funds by purchasing slices of the wonderful desserts on sale, with all the proceeds going to repair the church roof. At the mention of a prize to be awarded for the best pie, people clapped, and the contest began.

A forward-thinking footman had cut small slices of the tarts and passed them on plates to Lady Cameron and Mr. Ingleby, the latter of whom dug in with gusto. At the second tart, Lady Cameron made a face and beckoned a footman over with a glass of lemonade. "Too much salt instead of sugar," she gasped, taking a large swallow of her lemonade. "An easy mistake to make."

As they reached another tart, Lady Cameron took a tiny bite, smiled, and chatted with the young clergyman. All of a sudden Mr. Ingleby crowed, "Stop."

Silence followed.

"What is it?" Lady Cameron asked.

"This entry is disqualified," he announced, holding up an offending plate of plum tart.

"What for?"

"It is baked by Mrs. Greene, the wife of the good reverend. As she is my hostess, it would be inappropriate to allow this entry into the contest. People would believe I was playing favorites, or… what's the word? Nepotism!" he declared.

"But Mr. Ingleby…" Lady Cameron started, seeing Aunt Rachel's shocked face.

"No, no, we cannot have favorites here. This is a fair contest, and I won't be accused of nepotism just because someone loses. No. I am sorry, Mrs. Greene, but it is only fair." He smiled at Aunt Rachel, and his mouth had a curling sneer to it.

Poppy's mouth dropped open. She remembered the hard glint in his eyes when Mr. Ingleby had pointedly asked her if her aunt was baking. For him to disqualify her wasn't just a matter of circumstance, it was cruel. Anger bloomed within her, and her fists clenched.

Poppy disengaged herself from the party and went to her aunt, who stood stiff as a statue, her face bright red. "Are you all right?" Poppy whispered.

"I could kill him," Aunt Rachel's voice shook, "I spent hours baking that tart and now to be disqualified. That man…"

"I am so sorry, Mrs. Greene, but he has a point." Lady Cameron said apologetically. She took a bite of her plum tart and said loudly, "Oh well done, Mrs. Greene, this is delicious. I would like the recipe for this."

People looked at Aunt Rachel, whose grim expression softened.

"Well, that is one consolation," Poppy said.

"That is very kind of her ladyship," Aunt Rachel sniffed.

The crowd watched as the two judges tasted one dessert after another, with Lady Cameron only managing small bites, "Eats like a bird, she does," Aunt Rachel remarked, while Mr. Ingleby shoved forkfuls of cake, tart, and trifle into his mouth.

"That man eats like there's no tomorrow," Caroline said by Poppy's ear.

Then all of a sudden, he stopped. Mr. Ingleby froze, chewing.

"Mr. Ingleby? Are you all right?" Lady Cameron asked.

His eyes grew wide, and he tugged at his stiffly tied cravat. He burped, coughed, and hiccupped. Then his face turned red, then white, and his lips turned blue. He stumbled and clawed at the table, causing plates and dishes to fall onto the ground.

"Oh my lord," Caroline said, "Is he choking?"

Mr. Ingleby coughed, a dry gasping sound, pointed at Aunt Rachel, and fell over, vomiting copiously on the ground, much to the horror of the onlookers.

"Mr. Ingleby, Mr. Ingleby!" Lady Cameron fretted. "Someone call a doctor! Where is the doctor?"

People stared, frozen in place. Voices called for a doctor, and within moments, a young red-haired man pushed through the crowd. "I'm a doctor. What happened?"

"There." Lady Cameron pointed to Mr. Ingleby's fallen form. "He was sick a moment ago. Has he fainted?"

The red-haired doctor hurried around the table and knelt by Mr. Ingleby, his ginger eyebrows knit in concentration.

Poppy and her aunt moved closer to see, but Mr. Ingleby and the doctor were hidden from sight by the table. Seconds later the doctor's voice rang out, "This man isn't sick. He's dead."

CHAPTER EIGHT

Poppy stood like a statue. "Dead?" she repeated.

There were a few seconds of silence, then all was in an uproar. Women screamed, men argued, babies howled, and more than one young debutante fainted. Whether this was a case of too tightly laced stays or the late July heat, Poppy didn't know. But the effect was impressive.

"Everyone stop. Stay where you are," Constable Dyngley ordered, but no one stayed to hear him. Poppy and her aunt stood, stunned as people around them weren't sure whether to run or stay. No one liked being near a dead body.

Constable Dyngley left Caroline with the crowd and strode over to the doctor, crossing around the table. "How did he die, Doctor?"

"If I had to guess, he choked." The young doctor examined Mr. Ingleby's cooling corpse. "But the vomiting is odd."

"Why did he point at that woman?" Caroline asked, pushing her way through the crowd of people.

"Who?" Dyngley asked.

"Her." She pointed at Aunt Rachel.

Dyngley cleared his throat. "Are you certain he pointed?"

"Yes, he did." Robert came up, nodding. "The lady beside Miss Morton."

Dyngley's face shifted into a blank expression. "That lady is

Miss Morton's aunt."

Aunt Rachel came up to the group with Poppy. "Did he actually choke?"

"Yes, and he was pointing at you." Caroline said, "Why would he do that?"

Aunt Rachel tensed and tugged at her russet bonnet strings. "I don't know. Maybe he was asking for help?"

"But you're more than five feet away. Why wouldn't he ask Lady Cameron for aid instead? She was standing next to him." Robert pointed out.

"Well I'm sure I don't know, but whatever the reason, the man is dead. It can't have been important," Aunt Rachel said.

"On the contrary, I think the man's last actions to be very important." The young doctor rose to his feet. "Constable, we need to remove this man to my surgery. Will you watch him while I hire a cart?"

"Yes, of course," Constable Dyngley nodded and turned to Lady Cameron. "Your ladyship, might I spare a moment of your time?"

Lady Cameron stood staring at Mr. Ingleby's body, her face pale. "What?"

"Your ladyship," Constable Dyngley said, "I need to ask you a few questions."

"Oh. Right. Why?" She could hardly tear her gaze away from the body.

"I need to learn more about the circumstances of this man's death. Seeing as you were next to him, I wondered if you could answer a few questions of mine?"

"Uh, yes. Certainly. But not now. I am tired, and I wish to return home. You may call on me later. Tomorrow, at the proper time," she decided, gaining her resolve.

"Yes, your ladyship," Constable Dyngley bowed as Lady Cameron removed herself from the scene. She was a tall, grand lady, who swept through the crowd of people like a ship.

Constable Dyngley looked at the others standing there. "You

can all go home. There is no need for you to stay."

Poppy said, "It doesn't seem right to leave him. He was our houseguest."

"And he was doing so much to raise money for the church roof," Aunt Rachel said, "Actually, has anyone seen the donations for the church roof?"

"They were collected in a box, I think." Caroline pointed to the center of the long table, then did a double-take. "It was there. The box I mean. It's gone. The money's gone."

"What do you mean it's gone?" Poppy said.

"The collection money was in a box, but it's gone," Caroline said.

"Someone took the baking competition money?" Aunt Rachel's face fell.

"So now we have a thief on our hands," Robert said, his expression glum.

"All that for nothing. I cannot believe someone would be so uncharitable as to steal. This is horrible. And poor Mr. Ingleby…" Aunt Rachel's chin trembled.

"Constable, I think–" Poppy started.

"Not now, Miss Morton. Another time." He brushed her off, turning to the doctor.

Poppy stared after him, her face turning pink. She turned away and saw her aunt standing there tearfully. "Let's get you home," Poppy said to her aunt. But her mind went wild as she led her aunt from the green. First the church donation money goes missing and now this. Was Robert right? Was there a thief?

THE NEXT DAY, Constable Dyngley called at the parsonage, his strong face set in a frown. He nodded to Aunt Rachel and accepted her offer of tea, oblivious to her not-so-subtle attempt to leave them alone for a moment.

Poppy set aside her book. "Hello, Constable."

"Miss Morton." He removed his hat and sat down in the high wingback chair they saved for visitors, holding his dark top hat in his hands. "I am sorry for your loss. Mr. Ingleby's death must have been very trying for you."

"Yes, it is sad." She tried to keep her face solemn, but since he had passed out of their lives, a welcome peace had re-entered the household. "But we did not know him very well."

He looked up. "I find that hard to believe. The man was your houseguest for some weeks and during that time you didn't get to know him well?"

"Not at all, Constable," Aunt Rachel re-entered the room, carrying a tea tray. "The fact is, the man barely set foot in the parsonage. He didn't like it here."

Constable Dyngley's face clouded. "I did hear something about that."

"What? What did you hear?" Aunt Rachel set the tray down with a hard thump on a small table between them.

Constable Dyngley's smile was kind. "Your neighbors gossip, Mrs. Greene. It did not go unnoticed that Mr. Ingleby took many of his meals elsewhere, but no one seems to know why. Did he feel unwelcome here?"

"Unwelcome? In my house?" Aunt Rachel frowned as she held an old teapot aloft over the tray. Its spout dipped perilously close to the constable's knee. "Certainly not. We did everything we could to make him welcome here, didn't we Poppy?"

Poppy helped herself to a rote cake that Betsey had baked that afternoon. "We did try. I think he wanted to get to know the neighborhood."

"And their kitchens, more like. He spent more hours dining out than he did with us, and that's a fact. But I don't have to tell you that. If Mrs. Grant and Mrs. Alleyn are saying what I think they are, you'll know everything." Aunt Rachel poured hot water through a strainer on the tea leaves, handed him a fresh cup brimming with black tea, and set the teapot down hard on the tray, taking a seat beside Poppy.

Poppy cleared her throat. "Is it certain then, that Mr. Ingleby died from choking on one of the desserts at the competition?"

"Heavens, Poppy. What a thing to say," Aunt Rachel chided her.

"But Aunt Rachel, it's true. We all saw it." She looked at the constable.

"This is not a subject suitable for ladies." Aunt Rachel gave her a hard look.

"And when have I ever cared about that?" Poppy said, too excited to hold her tongue.

Aunt Rachel and the constable looked at her. The constable tugged at his cravat and cleared his throat as Aunt Rachel said, "Poppy, mind your tongue. The constable will think you don't care for ladylike pursuits at all." She gave a little laugh. "I assure you, Poppy is just excited over what's happened to us the past few days. It's not every day one of your houseguests... you know."

Poppy looked down into her lap, blushing.

The constable took a sip of tea and burnt his tongue, but did not say so. "I completely understand. My fiancée won't talk about anything else." He smiled at Poppy. "On that note, it would not be surprising, for a man who was known to be fond of his food, to choke by eating too hastily... But I wonder, for he did not look well on the day of the picnic, and at the baking contest, my fiancée mentioned to me that he seemed pale. Did you notice any complaints from him?"

Aunt Rachel sniffed. "Aside from the fact that he found our company rude and our meals too humble? No, none at all."

"I see. And did he have any enemies? Anyone he disagreed with? Anyone who might have wanted to hurt him?"

Poppy and her aunt exchanged a look. How much had their neighbors gossiped, and what had Mr. Ingleby said about them while dining at their tables?

"I don't know, Constable. Why are you asking these sorts of questions? I thought he choked. Do you suspect it was something more?" Poppy asked.

"No, but something doesn't feel right. When a person chokes, you will find a piece of food stuck in their throat, blocking their airway. With Mr. Ingleby, there was nothing. He had either swallowed the food, or vomited it all up, so either way, he would have continued breathing. I'm not sure why he died."

Poppy sensed he was thinking aloud, rather than making polite conversation. Aunt Rachel said, "I'm sure the young doctor will know."

"Yes. I wonder, have you met Doctor Wilson? He is very smart," Constable Dyngley said.

"No, I have not."

"Did Mr. Ingleby complain of any stomach pains in the last few days?" he asked.

"Not at all, but then we've not seen him much. What are you thinking?"

"Only that perhaps this was an ongoing illness. If he was already unwell, perhaps whatever he ate at the competition made his condition worse."

"His condition? Forgive me, Constable, but this sounds rather farfetched. Surely the good doctor will say whether there is anything amiss about Mr. Ingleby's death," Aunt Rachel said.

"Yes, he will. I will go there shortly to hear his report. It's just… Mr. Ingleby did not hide the fact that he has a very wealthy patron. My superior, Magistrate Tomlinson, has asked me to look into the matter and to make sure there is nothing untoward." Seeing Aunt Rachel's expression he added, "I don't expect to find anything amiss. But I do need to make sure, just in case."

"In case of what? You don't believe anyone wished to hurt him, do you?" Aunt Rachel asked.

"That is what I am trying to find out." He sipped his tea, which was cooler now. "You don't know if he complained of any foul humor or any physical distress?"

"No, Constable. If he did, he did not share any of these pains with us," Aunt Rachel said, and that put an end to the tea.

Poppy felt at odds and bit into another rote cake, barely tasting the hard crumbly pastry and sultanas on her tongue. She wanted to discuss Mr. Ingleby's death with the constable, but couldn't within the bounds of propriety. Going over the details of a man's death was not polite conversation to be had over tea.

As the constable left, Poppy thought back to that fateful afternoon. She got up, ran out the door, her house slippers slapping the dusty approach to the parsonage, pebbles biting into the soft flats of her shoes. "Constable." Poppy hurried after his retreating form.

"Miss Morton." He turned and bowed.

"I forgot something," she said, slightly out of breath. "About Mr. Ingleby, on the day he died."

"Yes?" His dark eyes lit up with intelligence.

"I think he hadn't been feeling well. When I saw him before, he looked a bit sick, and the day of the contest he looked very pale as if he'd been ill. It wasn't like him."

His smile was kind. "Thank you, Miss Morton. But I'll need hard evidence to take action on this case if it even was suspicious. I'm starting to think the man may have died from indigestion, especially as if you say, he was slightly unwell beforehand and the day of his death." He bowed, walked a few steps toward his horse, when he turned around.

Poppy brightened as he came back to her. "Constable?" Her eyebrows rose.

"Dash it, Miss Morton, but there's something about this situation which doesn't feel right. I will go to see the doctor tomorrow afternoon. Will you come with me?"

She felt light as a bird, then weighed down by propriety. "Constable, it wouldn't be proper."

"I know. And I don't know this doctor very well. We need to find a reason for you to be there, in case he is uncomfortable with…"

"What?"

"You know. He may be averse to the idea of a woman being in the presence of a body."

"Oh." She knew it would be inappropriate for them to be

seen together, but hadn't considered that reason. "What if I were to call and wish to visit him? Mr. Ingleby was our guest, and the closest he had to family in this town."

"Yes. That's an excellent idea. You could go and pay your respects. Perfect. Tomorrow morning? Say ten o'clock?"

"I will be there." They shared a smile, and it filled her with warmth. She returned to the parsonage with a lighter step, filled with purpose. They would work together again, and it felt right.

She walked around the back of the house, past chickens running around and the vegetable patch, over to the plum tree that had provided the bounty for her aunt's disqualified plum tart. As she reached up and plucked one of the ripe dark purple fruits from its branches, she bit into the fruit and thought about what she knew.

Her aunt's bracelet had gone missing, only a short while after a plate of oatcakes had disappeared. Knowing Mr. Ingleby's penchant for cakes, it was hard not to imagine he had something to do with their disappearance.

But to the facts. Not long after he began presiding over the church services, the weekly church donation money had gone missing. Mr. Ingleby may have been hard on the altar boy who relayed this news, but what if it was a parishioner down on their luck, who thought to take advantage of Mr. Greene's absence by stealing the funds? It could be someone who needed the money and was too proud to say so. Mr. Greene would never begrudge someone who truly needed it. And if that was the case, was it worth investigating at all?

Poppy ate more of the ripe plum, licking the juice off of her fingers. And then there was the matter of Mr. Ingleby's death. He could have choked, but something was odd. Did he just happen to be sick in the days preceding his death, or was it more serious than that? The fact he had been found unconscious at the berry picking with berries in his mouth suggested either he had eaten too many or perhaps had stumbled and knocked himself out.

Poppy tossed the small plum stone off into the foliage, away from the chickens. No matter which way she thought about it, Mr. Ingleby was at the core of this activity. Now if she could just convince the constable.

CHAPTER NINE

T HE NEXT MORNING, Poppy stopped by the doctor's surgery in town. The former town doctor, Dr. Howlett, an ornery, crotchety fellow, was more apt to spend his hours in one of the village taverns self-medicating than attending patients. He was, however, very fond of giving advice after having had a few drinks, and more than once had fallen asleep on his bar stool. It came as a great relief to the townspeople of Hertford when the young (and single) Dr. Jeremiah Wilson arrived to take up residency, having just finished a stint in London.

Poppy picked up the heavy iron door knocker and rapped three times. In a minute, the door was opened by Dr. Wilson, who looked at her with a head of wild red hair and said, "Yes? What is it?"

"Um…I'm here to…This is…"

"What? You need a midwife?" he asked.

"No. I'm here to see Mr. Ingleby. The clergyman," she said.

"I'm sorry miss, but he died the other day. Did you not hear of it?"

"Yes, I did. I've come to pay my respects."

"That's a bit irregular. You do not wish to wait for the funeral?"

Poppy shook her head.

The doctor scratched his chin, which bore a slight trace of

unshaven fuzz. "Very well, come in. Although I warn you, it is not a fair sight. You should prepare yourself."

Poppy walked in after him, prepared to give a further explanation of the nature of her call when she found it wasn't needed. In fact, she barely needed to have spoken much at all, before she was shown into a back room where there on a long, wide wooden table lay a body, covered with a bedsheet.

"Goodness," Poppy said.

"I warn you, it is not for the faint of heart." He fixed a curious gaze at her. "Why are you here? Was he a sweetheart of yours?"

Poppy gave an unladylike snort. "No. He was our houseguest, and I was there when he died. It doesn't seem right not to see him."

Doctor Wilson nodded. "Quite right. But are you sure? I wouldn't normally let a lady see a dead man like this unless she were family."

"We are the closest thing he had to family in this town," she said.

"Ah, very well. You'll be wanting to sort the funeral arrangements then. I warn you, it is not a pretty sight." He whisked the tablecloth off and Poppy gasped.

The body smelled. She should have expected it, being late July, but she hadn't expected the smell to be that strong.

"Here." He handed her a few sprigs of lavender. "Smell them."

She held them to her nose, and it was bearable then. The man who was Mr. Ingleby now looked very sad and pathetic, with his limbs splayed out for all to see. He was clothed and his abdomen was distended like a large egg. He wore the same blue overcoat, light blue patterned waistcoat, and white shirt and cravat he'd worn the day of the contest, and Poppy swallowed, realizing that when he had dressed that morning, he would have had no idea that would be the last outfit he would ever wear.

She spied the stains of vomit down his shirt front, his golden hair now faded to a dull yellow, and his mouth hung open in a stiff grimace. His final moments had been in pain, she was sure of it.

There was a knock at the door, and Dr. Wilson said, "Do excuse me. I'll just be a moment. You'll be all right with him alone, won't you?"

"Yes, I'll be fine."

The doctor left, and a few minutes later re-entered with the constable. Their eyes met, and Constable Dyngley bowed and said, "Hello, Miss Morton."

"Constable." She curtseyed and tried to ignore the little thrill seeing him brought her. Today he wore brown, but brown clothes on him looked so different than on any other man. She noticed him. He wore a deep brown double-breasted tailcoat over a white shirt with a high collar and smartly tied cravat. His waistcoat looked to be of a fine stiff material with vertical yellow and white stripes, and below that he wore brown breeches over smart black boots and brown gloves that matched a brown top hat. As she eyed his clothes, their eyes met, and she looked away.

"Doctor, I've come to view the body," he glanced at Poppy, "If that doesn't disturb Miss Morton."

Poppy shook her head as the doctor said, "Join the queue. I don't mind saying but who is this man? Why is he so popular?"

"He was the town reverend, temporarily. Do you not attend church, doctor?" Poppy asked.

"Not as often as I should. There are too many people needing care that I find when I do carve out the time, there's usually someone at my door asking for help." He shrugged. "Constable, I appreciate you're tying up loose ends, but why all this interest in the body? He died."

Constable Dyngley cleared his throat. "My superior wants to make sure there was nothing untoward about his death. We have to write to his patron, you see, who will be surprised at his dying, especially for one so young."

"Ah. Well, do have a look." He turned to Poppy. "I assume you'll be speaking with the carpenter in town."

"I'm sorry?"

"For the coffin. It's Ambrose Parker, just up the road." Seeing her face, he added, "It shouldn't cost more than a few shillings."

"Right. Of course." She peered down at the body and walked around it, avoiding looking at Mr. Ingleby's face. Upon closer inspection, she stopped.

"Have you seen something?" Constable Dyngley asked.

"It's strange. He was only in his twenties, but he was already losing his hair." Poppy pointed at his head, where clumps of dull yellow hair had fallen from his scalp onto the table.

"That is odd," Dyngley said, "Doctor, what do you make of it?"

"I'm not sure." He leaned closer to Mr. Ingleby's body and recoiled at the man's breath. "This man's breath is foul, worse than normal. Did he eat a lot of garlic at your house?"

"No." Poppy shook her head. She wished to say, *he took pains not to eat with us at all*, but thought better of it.

"What's that? There's a spot on his wrist." She pointed to his left glove. "You can see it peeking out."

Dyngley came around and looked beside her. "So there is. Doctor, do you mind?"

"I'll remove it." Dr. Wilson gently tugged the glove free, revealing a pale waxy hand, covered in dark splotches and lesions.

"Good God." Dyngley breathed. "What is it? The pox?"

Poppy and the doctor peered closer, eyeing the lesions that marred Mr. Ingleby's skin.

"Miss Morton, get away from there." Dyngley took her by the arm and pulled her away. "Don't go near it," he said.

"Fiddlesticks," Poppy said, pulling her arm free. "I want to see."

"Not until we know it's safe. Stay back," he said.

She glared and walked past him, around the body to Mr. Ingleby's other hand. "What is it, Doctor?"

The doctor pulled a large magnifying glass from a side table and held it close, along with a candle. The flame lit his young features. Poppy judged he couldn't have been more than twenty-five, and the warm candlelight shone on his dark ginger hair.

"Is it the pox?" Dyngley asked.

"No, I don't think so. Miss Morton, remove his other glove, if you would."

Poppy did so, revealing another lesion and spot-covered hand. "I've seen these before on his hand, at the picnic. But not so many. He said it was from too much sun. Was he right? What does it mean?"

"Hmmm. Was he sick before he died? I mean aside from the vomiting. You say he choked. Was he at all ill before?" Dr. Wilson asked.

Poppy thought hard. "He seemed a little unwell that morning, and when I spoke with him a few days ago, he looked pale. I asked if he was all right and he assured me he was, but now I'm not so certain."

"What do you think, doctor?" Constable Dyngley asked.

"I'll need to check my books." Dr. Wilson set down the candle and disappeared into another room.

Alone, Poppy and Dyngley looked at each other. "Miss Morton, I don't like you being here. You have a strong nerve to be near a body, stronger than many women I know, but this is different."

"Constable–" she began.

"I mean it, Miss Morton. I don't like you being near this man when he could carry the pox, or who knows what else."

"I want to know what happened to him, just as much as you."

They exchanged a frown when Dr. Wilson returned, holding aloft a thick tome. He set it down on a side table with a heavy thud and took the candle to read, turning the pages. After a moment he said, "Aha. Just as I thought. This man has been poisoned."

"Poisoned?" Poppy and Dyngley exchanged a look.

"Yes. Those spots on his hands? I suspect we'll find them elsewhere. If I'm right, and I usually am, then this man has died from arsenicosis. He has been poisoned with arsenic trioxide."

"Arsenic?" Poppy repeated, "But arsenic is so common. I could purchase some from the druggist in town."

"I have some in my storeroom," Dr. Wilson admitted.

"Every household will have some," Constable Dyngley said, his face glum.

"Still, I think you should be pleased, Constable," Dr. Wilson said, "You have a mystery to solve."

"Be serious, man," Dyngley chided.

"Oh, I am. This is the most exciting thing to happen to me since I left London. Most of what I treat are broken bones, coughs, and colds. This is novel." His blue eyes lit up with excitement.

Poppy flashed the doctor a smile, for she well understood the thrill that ran through his veins. A murder. Just like before. While this wasn't the first dead body she had seen, it still shocked and thrilled her at the same time. She gave a little shake of her head. This man's body deserved respect, not to be gawked at for a cheap thrill.

"Miss Morton, are you quite well?" Constable Dyngley asked.

"Yes, I'm fine, thank you," she said, taking in the sight of Mr. Ingleby's pale spotted skin. It had a dull yellow, waxy look that threatened to turn her stomach. She swallowed and held the lavender sprigs closer to her nose. "What else can you tell us, Doctor?"

"I think it is what you can tell me, Miss Morton. Did you notice anything odd about his person the last few days? Or on the day of his death?" the doctor asked.

"He did complain of a headache at the start of the contest. And he looked pale. He had a stomachache a few days before that, but beyond that, nothing."

"I see." Dr. Wilson set down his magnifying glass and began undoing Mr. Ingleby's cravat. What had once been fussily tied with care now lay limp and soiled with dried vomit. Dr. Wilson carefully untied the cravat and loosened the man's shirt, unbuttoning the stiff waistcoat and opening the shirt up to Mr. Ingleby's chest. Now uncovered, the smell of unwashed corpse rose to meet their noses, and Poppy breathed in the lavender quickly, taking short breaths.

"Look at that," Dr. Wilson said.

Like his hands, Mr. Ingleby's chest bore traces of black spots and lesions. Dr. Wilson picked up one of the dead man's hands and said, "There are hard patches on his skin." He nodded. "This is arsenic poisoning, for sure."

"How was he poisoned?"

"It would have been something he ate." He peered closer. "Yes. He most likely ingested it. It is easy to mistake it for flour or even sugar. Especially icing sugar."

Dyngley and Poppy shared a look. "The baking contest."

Poppy asked, "But would he have died so quickly? It seemed like he hardly took a bite of the dessert before he started to choke."

"You are thinking it was the last dessert he ate that killed him, but what if it was one of the others? It could have been the first, the third, or the second to last one he ate. What if it only started to take effect once he had reached that last dessert?" Dr Wilson asked.

Constable Dyngley groaned. "We have to speak to the bakers. Everyone is a suspect." His shoulders slumped. "The magistrate will not be pleased."

"Then you will start an investigation?" Poppy asked.

"We'll have to, Mr. Jenkins and I. Doctor, would you say some poisoned food could cause death to happen quickly?" Dyngley asked.

"If you mean within the space of a few minutes, no, not unless it was a highly concentrated amount. But the lesions on his body tell me this poisoning is in an advanced stage. He was being poisoned slowly, for some time. Then say, a large amount of arsenic, ingested, would have resulted in rapid death."

"Miss Morton, how many cakes had he eaten before he collapsed?" Dyngley asked.

"Five or eight, I think. Yes, eight. I'm certain he had taken eight large pieces of the tarts and cakes before he died," Poppy said. "He and... Oh my God. Lady Cameron. She ate the tarts too."

There came a loud knocking. "Doctor! Doctor!" A man called, thumping on the front door.

"Yes, yes, I'm coming." Doctor Wilson called, shooing Poppy and the constable away from the body as he pulled a sheet over Mr. Ingleby and opened the door. "What is it?"

Dread grew in the pit of Poppy's stomach as she recognized the man wearing the formal livery of Lady Cameron's footmen.

"You must come immediately. Lady Cameron is sick."

CHAPTER TEN

C ONSTABLE DYNGLEY LATER came by the parsonage and told Poppy what had occurred after they had so urgently parted ways at the surgery. He explained that by the time they reached Lady Cameron, she lay in bed, being attended by her companion, Miss Sugg, who sat by, dabbing at her forehead with a damp towel. Dyngley and Dr. Wilson were ushered into the room and announced by a footman, and passed by a maid removing a porcelain dish of bile from her ladyship's bedside. Constable Dyngley observed that Lady Cameron laid back against a mountain of pillows in one of the grandest wooden four-poster beds he had ever seen.

"Oh, Constable. I regret that I am unable to properly receive you." Lady Cameron's eyes fluttered and she gave a heavy breath, resting against her pillows.

Dr. Wilson sprang into action and shuffled Lady Cameron's companion aside, as he felt along the inside of her wrist and then her neck for a pulse. He asked Miss Sugg, "What happened?"

"She felt ill yesterday eve and this morning when she didn't come down, I came to see what happened. She…" Miss Sugg, a middle-aged spinster approaching her later years, patted her graying hair and said, "Her bed clothes were soiled, and when I went to check on her today, she vomited. At first, she said it was nothing, just a slight illness, but then she fainted and we called for you. Will she be all right, Doctor?"

"Has she eaten anything since the contest yesterday afternoon?"

"No, I don't think so. Her ladyship never eats very much, but she didn't want to touch any food since she came home. Not even a breakfast tray." Her lower lip trembled. "Constable, is it true what they're saying? That the town clergyman fell ill after eating one of the pastries?"

"I can't comment on that," Dyngley told her and turned to the doctor. "What do you need?"

"If she's had vomiting and diarrhea, she's likely already purged the toxins from her body, but we'll need to be sure," he said, "Forgive me, but I need to examine her person."

Miss Sugg bit her lip. "Are you sure that's proper? What will you do?"

"Would you remove her hands from beneath the blanket?" Dr. Wilson asked.

"Yes." She gently took Lady Cameron's left hand from beneath the covers, and held it out for the doctor to see. It was clear of spots.

He sighed with relief. "That is good. And her other hand?"

"All right." Miss Sugg leaned over the bed and pulled Lady Cameron's other hand into view. "I don't understand, why do you need to see her hands?"

"I'm checking for something. Could you please loosen the strings of her nightdress?"

"I beg your pardon?" Miss Sugg stared at him.

"Please, just a little. I need to see if she's come down with an illness," Dr. Wilson said.

Giving him a strong look of disapproval, the companion loosened the high ruffled collar of Lady Cameron's white nightdress, revealing a neck and chest that was pale and aged, as befitting a woman of older years, but free of spots.

"Very good. You can stop now," he said, standing aside. "It is probable she was poisoned as well but has likely gotten rid of it. I would hazard a guess she only ingested a small amount. Enough to make her sick, but nothing too serious."

"Poisoned!" Miss Sugg's eyes widened. "Who would want to hurt her ladyship?"

"We don't know. For now, let her rest, and give her lots of fluids. Wine, and a light broth. No pastries or desserts. Only fortifying liquids," Dr. Wilson said.

"And medicines? What medicines shall I give her? We stock laudanum, castor oil, camphor essence, syrup of ipecac…"

"No medicines. Do not prescribe her anything without my consent. She needs rest. And I don't need to tell you this, but we need to keep this quiet. Please don't tell the servants."

From Miss Sugg's wry expression, Constable Dyngley knew she was already preparing the choicest gossip to share with the maids.

At Dyngley's retelling, Poppy's eyes widened. "It sounds like Miss Sugg had a whole medicine cabinet ready for her."

"Indeed. I can well understand her companion for being so concerned," he said.

"For the loss of her close friend, you mean."

"No. I was thinking more critically. If her ladyship were to die, and Miss Sugg is also advanced in her years, what situation is left to her? She has been a lady's companion for quite some time, I would guess, and so would be accustomed to a certain way of living. I'm sure she feared what would happen if her current situation were to be disturbed. We don't know the particulars of Lady Cameron's will, so it could be that Miss Sugg would have a motive in either case for wanting to do her ladyship harm, or not. There are not many options open to a woman, especially unmarried," he said.

Poppy stiffened. "You make it sound like marriage is the only option for a woman to have a comfortable situation in life."

He laughed. "I did not mean it to be quite so harsh, but there is some truth to it. Young women are easily persuaded and their mothers are like hunters. With many properties entailed to male heirs, it is understandable. Your situation I am sure will not be so dire. I suspect your mother's wasn't if she is anything like you."

"My mother is dead." Poppy's smile was fleeting. "I never knew her."

"I am sorry. I didn't mean to speak so plainly." Dyngley's pleasant expression disappeared.

"No, please. What are friends but those who can speak honestly to one another?" She looked at him then, and he blushed.

"Miss Morton, I… About my engagement to Caroline." He paused. "I honestly was going to tell you…"

"Never mind that," Poppy said graciously. In the comfort of the parsonage's blue sitting room, she observed him fidget on the hard-backed chair across from her and knew he was uncomfortable. She wouldn't push him to discuss his private affairs. She just enjoyed spending time with him. "Now, about this poisoning. We know that Lady Cameron and Mr. Ingleby both tried eight of the desserts before he died."

"And we suspect that one of them was poisoned with arsenic," he said, "we'll have to talk to each of the bakers," he said, sipping tea.

"We?" she smiled.

"No, I mean I. Myself and Jenkins. Although I could use your help in thinking about it. And in speaking to these people. Some people dislike talking to a constable or magistrate, especially if they think we are looking for someone to blame."

"Aren't you?"

"Yes, but the right person. Not the first person who seems suspicious. That's why I need your help."

"Wouldn't you rather take Caroline along?" she pointed out.

"Be serious, Poppy." His decorum slipped, "Murder investigations are no place for ladies."

Seeing her wounded expression, he said, "That's not what I mean. I meant that Jenkins and I will need to follow every lead. And as much as I dislike the idea, Miss Sugg may be right in that someone may have tried to hurt Lady Cameron."

"But why? She is just a sweet old lady," Poppy said, "No, I can't believe that."

"Then you would rather think that someone attempted to kill Mr. Ingleby? Or worse, both?"

"Could it not have been an accident?" she asked.

There was a knock at the door.

Poppy rose when Betsey hurried to answer it, returning shortly with Mr. Jenkins and Dr. Wilson.

"Doctor. Mr. Jenkins." Poppy curtseyed, her hands brushing against the folds of her light blue linen dress.

Mr. Jenkins strode into the parsonage's blue sitting room. He brushed crumbs off his dirty brown waistcoat and gazed at her with dislike. "Miss Morton. I thought we'd find the constable here."

"What is it, Jenkins?" Dyngley rose, his face coloring. "Doctor. What brings you here?"

"My surgery was broken into. Someone has rifled through my things, and has tampered with Mr. Ingleby," Dr. Wilson said from the doorway, running a hand through his red hair.

"What did they take? Were you robbed?" Dyngley asked.

"I'm not sure. It happened while we had gone to see Lady Cameron," Dr. Wilson said, "When I came back, the front door was open and Mr. Ingleby's body was partially undressed and on the floor."

"He came to me, and I knew right where to find you. Now that we've got a murder on our hands, I trust you won't be wasting your time drinking tea," Jenkins said, smirking at Poppy.

"Do excuse me, Miss Morton," Constable Dyngley bowed to her and left.

Poppy bid them goodbye and sat back to finish her tea. Who would have broken into the surgery, and why? What could they have been looking for? And why disturb Mr. Ingleby's body?

CHAPTER ELEVEN

P OPPY WAS DISSATISFIED. Not only had she and her aunt felt like social pariahs for the past few weeks thanks to Mr. Ingleby's avoidance of their company, but now the man had died. Poppy wondered if his death worsened their situation, making them very much talked about, but not very talked to. And she couldn't voice her views on the subject, for her aunt had given her very strict instructions on the matter.

"Investigating murders is not for young ladies, Poppy," she had said, biting into a rote cake. "I know that young constable has favored you now and then in asking your opinion, but you should be focusing your attention on how to attract a man, not figuring out how one died. Leave it to the constables, dear girl."

"But Aunt, I know I–"

"I do not care, and neither would your uncle if he were here. We had enough trouble with you getting involved in an investigation before. I hate to think of what Mr. Ingleby's death has done to your marriage prospects."

Poppy wanted to respond, to argue, but she could think of no fresh quip or witticism to plead her case. Instead, she frowned, read, and attended to her household chores in a bad temper.

Fortunately, these negative thoughts ended when a cheerful knock came at the parsonage door, and she answered it to find two welcome distractions. "Miss Heyworth. Mr. Heyworth, how good to see you. Do come in." She showed them into the blue sitting room and bade them sit on the overstuffed green sofa. "Shall I ask Betsey for some tea?"

"No, no. We've come to tell you the news. Mr. Ingleby is dead, but do you know how he died?" Jane practically kicked her heels in delight. "He was poisoned."

Poppy sat straight in her seat. How should she react? Play dumb? Or be honest?

She had to do neither as Jane said, "It is altogether too shocking."

"How are you?" Robert asked, looking calm in a light russet-colored overcoat, cream waistcoat, and tan trousers. He shot her a winning smile. "You seem very poised, considering."

Poppy smiled. "I did hear the news already, actually."

"Oh, pooh." Jane pouted. "Well, we have come to take you on a walk. I can't stand still doing nothing for very long, and it's so dull inside our house. Will you come?"

She barely had to ask. In minutes Poppy joined them at the entrance of the parsonage, dressed in a light blue spencer over her gray walking dress, along with a straw bonnet and light blue ribbon.

Jane declared, "Very pretty, wouldn't you agree, Robert?"

Robert coughed and looked at his boots, a light flush blooming on his cheeks. "Very nice."

Jane shot Poppy a smile, who shook her head. "Where shall we go?" Poppy asked.

"I have heard there is a tree nearby, planted by Her Majesty Queen Elizabeth. Is that true?" Robert asked.

"Yes, it's in Panshanger Park," Poppy said.

"Can you show us the sight?"

"It would be my pleasure." Poppy smiled at him. Their eyes met, and at his warm gaze, she felt a slight flicker between them, but she did not know what.

They began walking through town, when Jane said, "I heard that Mr. Ingleby died from eating a poisoned tart."

"Who did you hear it from?" Poppy asked.

"One of our maids, Mary. Her sister is a kitchen maid at Blackgate Park, and she said that her ladyship was sick because of it."

"I wonder which tart it was," Poppy thought aloud.

"I have no idea. It couldn't have been mine, of course," Jane said.

"Remind me, what did you bake?" Poppy asked.

"A raspberry trifle. Actually, my mother supervised, otherwise I would have added salt instead of sugar." Jane laughed. "It's happened before."

Poppy grinned. "That's better than my attempts. I tried to make a cheesecake, but every time I baked one it either sank, spilled out, or the mixture split. I'm not sure why."

They walked on, and took a path through Panshanger Park, a cool shaded wooded area newly landscaped by the eminent landscape designer Humphry Repton. It boasted lush green fields dotted with sheep, grazing cows, lakes, and even a handsome brick orangery farther along. They passed other groups walking along the dirt paths, and crossed the top of a large expanse of green fields, where the trio admired the view of the blue lakes below that glittered in the sun.

As they passed a stone quarry under construction and an impressive orangery, Jane said, "Oh, I think I see it. The tree, up ahead." She hurried forward, leaving Poppy alone with Robert.

They walked along in companionable silence, until Poppy said, "You are very quiet, Mr. Heyworth."

He coughed and turned red. "I hope you will not look upon me too harshly, Miss Morton. On the day of the contest, I spoke in haste. I felt caught up in the moment and I spoke out of turn. I hope you don't think me unkind."

"What do you mean? What did you say?" she asked.

"Why… When Mr. Ingleby collapsed at the contest, I pointed out that he had pointed at your aunt. I didn't realize she was your relation, I thought she was just one of the townspeople. If I had known, I would never—"

Poppy smiled. "You would never have hinted she had something to do with his death?"

He fell silent.

"You have nothing to fear, Mr. Heyworth. Think no more of it. I do not hold grudges and it was just a pointed finger. I have no more reason to believe that my aunt would poison Mr. Ingleby than you would."

He frowned. "That's good of you to say. But I must admit, I am not sorry to see him gone."

"Oh?" Her eyebrows rose.

He picked up a long stick and began swatting at the bushes as they walked, his gaze firmly on the ground. "Miss Morton, I hope you will not think me forward, but I feel I can talk to you about things. And I know you were not close to him, so I don't think I need to speak with false modesty when I say I have my own reasons for disliking the man."

She blinked and remained silent, waiting for him to continue.

"Mr. Ingleby refused to visit my father, who spends his days at home with a broken leg. I work where I can, but I don't have his skills or his reputation. When Jane asked Mr. Ingleby to visit and he refused, my father took it badly. We tried to convince him that Mr. Ingleby was busy, but I was inclined to think less of the clergyman at that point. Who would consciously avoid the company of a sick man, when it is his duty to visit and tend the sick?" He looked at her. "I hope this doesn't change your feelings toward me. Or our friendship."

"Not at all, Mr. Heyworth. Let us be friends and say no more on the matter. Come now, your sister has found the tree." She led him to a wide heavily shaded area, where the giant tree had been enclosed by a wide circle of iron railings. The tree's grayish-brown trunk spanned wider than two people side by side and looked thicker than anything Poppy could compare it to. It had long, thick outstretched branches that bore miniature branches and boughs of green leaves, so close that Poppy could reach over the railing and touch them.

"That's impressive," Robert said, joining Poppy and Jane by the iron fencing.

Poppy made a circuit around the wide fencing, and admired the healthy tree when a person came up to her.

"Miss Morton, there you are." Caroline came up to her. To-day she wore a light linen walking dress embroidered with flowers, a short purple spencer of lavender-colored silk, and a matching dark purple bonnet with lavender ribbon. It framed her dark hair and petite face prettily, and she smiled at Poppy. "I was on my way to see you and I saw you walking ahead with those two. I hope you don't mind the interruption."

"Not at all. How do you like the tree?" Poppy asked.

"It's beautiful. I've never seen one so big. It is old, is it not?" Caroline asked.

"Yes, it's around three hundred years old." Poppy smiled back. "Why did you wish to see me?"

"Oh, I've come to bring you my troubles. It's a horrible mess. Have you encountered Mr. Jenkins?" She walked alongside Poppy, shading her eyes from the rays of sunlight peeking through the leafy green boughs of the tree.

"Yes, why?"

"He's a character all of his own. Do you know, he came by my cousin's house and demanded to see me? When I came down, he began interrogating me about the contest. And my apple pie. Can you imagine?"

"What did he ask?" Poppy asked.

"He wanted to know if I disliked Mr. Ingleby. I told him, 'We all dislike him, he's rude and frightfully common,' and then that deputy laughed at me and asked how did I know so well if I wasn't common myself. I swear, I would have kicked him out on his arse if I hadn't been in polite company. It's why I came to find you."

"Me? Why?"

Caroline gave her a firm look. "That deputy accused me of killing Mr. Ingleby and I want you to find out who did it. If you don't, I could hang."

CHAPTER TWELVE

"WHAT?" POPPY SAID. "Me? Why would you want my help? Surely the constable can do it. It's his job."

"Dyngley? No, he's blind where I'm concerned. He'd slay dragons for me but said he must stay impartial in an investigation." Caroline scoffed and kicked at a rock, sending it flying at the tree. "Can you believe it? The man proposes, but he can't be bothered to believe me when it comes to a dead man. I mean, honestly."

Poppy smiled. "I'm happy to help, but I don't know what you think I can do that the constable can't."

"Oh, you're so modest. That's exactly why I like you. Dyngley said that you had a sharp and enquiring mind, as intelligent as any man's, but that you could slip into social settings unnoticed whereas him going around asking questions would put people's backs up." She frowned. "He's like Jenkins in that way, although much more handsome."

"And less obnoxious," Poppy said.

The young women matched gazes and knew they were in complete agreement.

"Will you do it? I can't very well marry Dyngley with a murder charge hanging over my head. His family would never allow it. And it was hard enough convincing mine. They're convinced he's marrying me for my dowry, but I told them I don't care, I love him, and he loves me," Caroline said.

Poppy smiled through her teeth. "I'll do what I can, but why me?"

"I know we don't know each other very well but you have such an honest face, and such a sterling reputation, no one would fault you for asking a few questions. And with a good word from you, that murder accusation would disappear. Won't you do it? Dyngley speaks so highly of you. He trusts you, and that's good enough for me. I know he views you quite as his own very good friend, almost like a sister," Caroline told her.

An ill humor filled Poppy. But she rallied and said, "That is most kind."

"I will of course pay you," Caroline said.

"No, I couldn't possibly let you do that." Poppy eyed Caroline's fine walking dress, so fine and delicate compared with her own plain dress and sturdy walking boots, covered in dust from the path.

"Oh I know it's forward of me, but I think too well of you to think you harbor any ill will. And especially after I heard about your difficulties..." Caroline began.

"Our difficulties?" Poppy's voice rose.

"What with your uncle taking it upon himself to deprive your household of desserts in order to pay for the church roof, it's simply not fair for you and your aunt to have to face the burden of paying for that man's funeral, especially after what he said about you."

"What do you mean? What did he say?" Poppy asked.

"Well..." Caroline took her arm and led her away from Jane and Robert. "One evening he dined at my cousins'. They were asking him how he liked Hertford and then he said, "Hertford is very pleasant and I should like it immensely, were it not for the rude manners of my hosts."

Poppy stared and stopped in her tracks.

"I know," Caroline said, "We were shocked to hear it. But then he mentioned how your aunt thought he was stealing her husband's sermons, when Mr. Greene had only left them out to be of use to Mr. Ingleby, and then he said how your aunt flatly refused to serve any pudding and liked eating only the meanest and humblest of foods, as befitting a clergyman's wife."

"But… That is not true. Even you just said–"

"It doesn't matter now anyway, the man is dead. But I didn't like what he said about you, not at all." Caroline shook her head, her bonnet swaying prettily.

"What did he say about me?" Poppy asked, unable to resist enquiring.

"Simply that your aunt's manners were rather common and less than hospitable, and that you were a spinster in the making. He said you were the dullest creature he'd ever met, and that you and your aunt hadn't two original thoughts between you." Caroline stifled a giggle and watched to see Poppy's reaction.

"Oh." Poppy swallowed.

"I, of course, told him that was nonsense, and that I had it on good authority that you were one of the cleverest girls in all of England." Caroline beamed at her, tugging her along on a sojourn around the ring of iron fencing surrounding the tree.

"Thank you." Poppy felt a frisson of pleasure.

"No need to thank me, it was Dyngley who came to your rescue. He told Mr. Ingleby that he was mistaken in his opinions of you, and asked whether engaging in gossip was entirely appropriate for clergymen. He said that perhaps if Mr. Ingleby spent more time on religious study, he might not need Mr. Greene's sermons."

Poppy's eyebrows rose and she grinned. "That sounds like the constable."

"He's wonderful, isn't he? I couldn't have said it better myself. As you might imagine, that quieted Mr. Ingleby up instantly. He watched his tongue the rest of the evening and spent the time shooting my constable little looks as if trying to weigh him up. Dyngley ignored him entirely, of course."

"Of course," Poppy echoed.

"But now Mr. Ingleby is dead, and I am suspected of murder. I cannot believe it myself, but Dyngley explained that he must talk with everyone who baked a dessert for the contest, even me." Caroline pouted. "What I don't understand is why everyone is so keen to talk to the bakers from the competition. Mr. Ingleby ate at everyone's table in the town; any one of them could have poisoned him at any time."

"You think it wasn't one of the bakers?" Poppy asked.

"Well, I don't know. All I know is it wasn't me, and I don't think it was you. So will you help me, Miss Morton? I don't think I need to say how important this is, to me and to Dyngley." She disengaged her arm and squeezed Poppy's left hand. "It would mean so much to us, were you to find a way to prove my innocence. Dyngley is so caught up in catching whoever did this and that Jenkins just wants a person to arrest. I think he dislikes me and wants to force us apart, that's why he thinks I did it."

Poppy looked away. Her aunt had warned her away from involving herself. And as much as she wanted to help, it also bothered her that he hadn't told her about his engagement to Caroline. It rankled her still more, but she did not want to look further into her own feelings as to why. She just knew that she had to act.

"What say you, Miss Morton? Will you help me?" Caroline asked. "Please?"

Poppy met her gaze. "All right. I'll do it."

"Ah!" Caroline clapped her hands. "I knew you would. Dyngley is right, you are a generous person."

"But I'll ask for one thing in return," Poppy said.

"What is that?"

"That you help me find my mother," Poppy said.

"Your mother?" Caroline repeated, "do tell."

Poppy and Caroline walked around the tree, which took longer than one might think. "I think my mother died giving birth to me."

"Oh, how sad." Caroline's face fell.

"But my aunt, her sister, will sometimes mention her. I would like to know anything about her, but my aunt and uncle won't speak of it and when I ask, they refuse. If you could help in any way, I would be most grateful," Poppy said.

"What a mystery! I should be glad to help, but I don't know what I could possibly do."

"You have connections in London, I think, do you not?" Poppy asked.

"Yes, I do. That's where I met Dyngley, you know. I will write a letter to my mother and see if she can make any enquiries. If your mother is anyone, my mother will know of her." Caroline gave a decisive nod.

"Thank you. Her name is Celeste Morton, but that's all I know. She would have died in 1787."

"Was she in trade? A gentlewoman?" Caroline asked.

"I don't know. I didn't think to ask."

"Well, never mind. My mother has a stunning memory. She'll know most people and if she doesn't know her, she'll know people who will."

"Thank you." Poppy and Caroline shared a smile.

"Miss Morton, I hope you do not mind if I ask, but what are you hoping to find?" Caroline asked, her dark brown eyes curious.

"I'm not sure. I never knew her. But it feels wrong not knowing anything about my mother." Poppy gazed at the tree.

"But why this interest now?"

"My aunt mentioned how I am like her, yet she won't tell me about her. I don't know where to start looking and I'm sick of not knowing about my own mother," Poppy said.

"So that's where I can help. I understand. But are you sure there is nothing more I can do for you? It hardly feels fair."

Poppy shook her head. "Let us shake hands on it."

The ladies shook hands, and a deal was struck. Like it or not, Poppy was conducting an investigation of her own. The question was, should she keep it a secret?

CHAPTER THIRTEEN

POPPY KNEW JUST where to start her investigation. She returned home that late afternoon to find her aunt waiting for her. Her aunt came into the entryway, holding a letter. "Poppy, what have you done?"

"What do you mean?" Poppy asked, hanging up her straw bonnet and light blue spencer on the coat pegs at the parsonage entrance.

"I've just had a message from the carpenter in town, who says he'll charge us for Mr. Ingleby's coffin. Can you believe it? Now we're stuck with taking care of the man's funeral." She pouted and handed the offensive note to Poppy. "And what's worse, I've received calls from the Grants, the Alleyns, the Suttons, all offering their condolences. As if we gave a whit about that man." She sat down on the stuffed green sofa with a loud poof and leaned back against the cushions.

"Aunt, I was thinking back to the day of the competition," Poppy said.

"Yes, what of it? A horrible day. I'll never forget what that man said. Disqualifying my plum tart, when he knew full well that we would be baking something. Horrible man."

"When you put your tart on the table, did you happen to see the other tarts?"

"Yes, I'd say so. Why?" She gave Poppy an even look. "What

are you up to?"

"Nothing, I was just thinking about it, and I wondered who the other bakers were."

"You mean you're trying to figure out who killed him."

"Aunt…"

"No, Poppy, no. I know what you're doing. You think that by investigating this murder that will bring Dyngley back into your company but let me tell you, it won't work. All it will do is cause trouble and wind people up, and they won't want to talk to you, especially Constable Dyngley." She gave Poppy a hard look. "He is engaged, Poppy."

"I know, Aunt Rachel." Poppy strode past her into the blue sitting room, removing her gloves with a snap.

Her aunt followed. "Then why don't you just admit it and look elsewhere? There are plenty of handsome young men around town. You're bound to fall in love with one of them. What about Mr. Heyworth who called for you with Jane? He seems very handsome."

"Mr. Heyworth is very kind," Poppy started.

"He seems very amiable and that sister of his is charm itself. Why don't you give him a chance? I think you should."

Poppy smiled thinly and looked away. She would, but there was just one small problem.

He wasn't Dyngley.

THE NEXT DAY Poppy found Jane walking into town. "Hello, Miss Morton, what a pleasure to run into you again. You must be sad not to find Robert here."

"Yes, of course," Poppy said politely.

Jane beamed. "I'll tell him you asked about him. He's busy working."

"Actually, it's you I came to see. Do you remember the desserts at the baking contest?" Poppy asked.

"What? What about them? Don't tell me you're looking into it?" Jane asked.

"Miss Everly asked me to. I've helped with investigations before, so…" Poppy briefly recounted her "first murder" to Jane, whose eyes grew wider and wider.

"My word. You're not joking."

"No. Miss Everly has asked me to help her prove her innocence, as she's been suspected of poisoning her tart," Poppy said.

"Well, I'm not surprised, considering."

"What do you mean?" Poppy asked.

"Well, it's just that she is nice toward some people and rude to others. She's never the same to anyone. And if she befriends you, well… I would be careful what I say around her. I think she would either abuse you to make herself more attractive to the opposite sex, or she would try to use you for her own ends," Jane said.

"Use me?" Poppy laughed. "The very idea that Miss Everly would *use me* is preposterous."

"Is it? You are good friends with her fiancé, are you not? I could very easily see what the benefit of having you on her side would mean for her future happiness, especially when she is so close to the altar."

"You make it sound like I'm out to ruin her engagement." Poppy shook her head.

"An engagement is only that, a temporary agreement ahead of a union. It can be broken. Watch what you say around her, mark my words," Jane said. "I would worry that her aim is to break up your friendship with the constable. Would he take kindly to the idea of your looking into Mr. Ingleby's death?"

Poppy paused. She hadn't thought the idea would bother him, but what if Jane was right, and it was a ploy by Caroline to discredit her or worse, break up their friendship? "I made Miss Everly a promise that I would. She's counting on me. Mr. Jenkins has as good as accused her of his murder."

Jane frowned. The effect was pretty. "In that case, I'll try to help. But don't forget what I said."

They walked along the path that followed the millstream,

which gradually led through a little wooded area into town. "There were loads of desserts on that table. How are we to remember each one?"

"There were little cards by each dessert. I remember that when I went up to the tent, a footman took down my name and my dessert."

"That sounds very organized," Poppy noted.

"It was! I think Lady Cameron planned this event to the smallest detail. It was very formal."

"Then I'll need to speak to Lady Cameron."

"Or her footman."

"I might be of some help there." A tall, young man stepped into view from behind a tree. It was the young man Jane had fancied through the shop window from before, and who they had encountered at Lady Cameron's berry picking event.

"Forgive me, but I couldn't help overhearing your conversation. You are trying to find out which of the bakers killed that clergyman?" The man smiled down at Jane.

"Yes, that's right," Poppy said, seeing as Jane was staring at her shoes. "I think there was a rhubarb and apple pie... or a raspberry tart..."

"I was there that day. Why are you looking into this at all? It's a bit of an irregular hobby for two young ladies."

Jane smiled at him prettily and Poppy said, "We're trying to recall how many puddings Mr. Ingleby had before he died. I'm helping a friend clear her name."

"Oho! A quest. That's very good of you." He rested his hand on the silver top of his walking stick. "If I remember correctly there were eight puddings the man got through before he toppled. There was a raspberry trifle, a rhubarb tart, a cheesecake, a plum tart, a gooseberry fool, and a blackberry tart. Oh and an apple pie."

Jane looked up. "How do you remember all of that?"

"You must have a very good memory," Poppy remarked.

The man grinned. "When it comes to good food, I do. I love a good tart." He winked at Jane, earned himself a blush, and added, "I meant to try all of them and only had a slice of the cheesecake. It was a shame about him disqualifying your mother's pudding. Very unfair."

"That was my aunt, and thank you. I'll tell her." Poppy rewarded him with a smile.

"Who is the lady under suspicion?" he asked.

"A friend of mine, Miss Caroline Everly."

"Caroline?" he laughed. "That's my cousin you're talking about. She didn't tell me she'd hired a private investigator." His tone made it sound mocking as if it were all a great joke.

Poppy opened her mouth to explain when Jane stepped on her foot. Poppy tensed and said, "Forgive me, but it seems strange to keep running into you when we don't even know your name."

"Colin Barton, at your service." He bowed. "And to whom do I have the pleasure of speaking?"

Poppy and Jane curtseyed. "I am Poppy Morton, and this is Miss Jane Heyworth."

At the mention of her name, Jane's gaze wandered up to Colin's. "How do you do, sir?"

"How do you do? Did either of you bake anything?"

"A raspberry trifle," Jane said, her cheeks turning rosy pink.

"Ah. I'd meant to try that. It looked delicious." He held her gaze for a moment. "Well, I must be on my way. Good luck in your investigations." He touched his hat and walked away.

Jane waited a moment and then grinned. "Oh, Poppy, isn't he the most handsome man you've ever seen? He is so polite, so cultured... And he's helped us with your investigation. Wonderful."

Poppy walked into the town beside Jane, listening to her extol the virtues of Mr. Barton.

After a moment, Jane asked, "Are you even listening to me? What are you thinking?"

"Sorry. It's just that we don't know him very well. Why

would Mr. Barton help us? And to speak to us when we have not been introduced?"

"Oh, don't be like that. He was just being kind. It was a very gentlemanly thing to do, especially when he overheard us talking. Besides, maybe he had another reason for wanting to help." Jane smiled, her eyes dancing.

"And that would be?"

"To get to know me, of course. He's not the first young man to talk to me when we've not been introduced." She laughed and skipped down the dirt path.

Poppy caught up with her. "Introductions aside, we've got eight puddings that we know of, one of which was poisoned."

"Right. He had a slice of cheesecake."

"He's also in perfect health, so it's unlikely that was the poisoned one."

"But we don't know. He could have been unwell and just not told us," Jane pointed out.

"You're right."

"I have it. I'll ask him, the next time we see him. It will give us something to talk about." Jane grinned.

"We also don't know who baked which pudding." They entered the town center of Hertford, just in time to see Constable Dyngley walking with Mr. Jenkins. The men stopped and parted ways, with Dyngley waiting for the young women to approach.

"Miss Morton, I was just on my way to see you. And you have a friend. I think we met at Lady Cameron's picnic, but I didn't catch your name." He bowed.

"Constable, this is Miss Jane Heyworth. Her family has recently moved here."

"A pleasure to meet you again, Constable." Jane curtseyed, eyeing him.

"Miss Heyworth." He touched his hat.

Jane rewarded him with a smile, then said, "Oh, I see Mr. Barton just popping into a shop. You don't mind if I go on ahead, do you, Poppy?"

"No, not at all." Poppy barely had time to say the words before Jane was off, leaving tiny whirls of dust in her wake as she hurried away. Now alone with the constable, Poppy felt ill at ease. What could she say?

"Caroline tells me she has asked you to look into this poisoned pie business," he said.

"Yes. She is afraid her reputation will suffer. I think she felt it better to ask me, as a friend, than to burden you with it."

"Burden me? She is no burden. She should have come to me, she should've—" he stopped. "Never mind. I was walking toward the parsonage to see you. I wanted to discuss this case with you."

Poppy felt a little frisson of pleasure. "What have you found out?"

"There were eight puddings on display before Mr. Ingleby's untimely death," he began, "I propose we team up and interview the people, then exchange notes."

"But we don't even know who to speak to."

"That's where you're wrong. We do. A footman took the name of each baker and their pudding entry so that the judges would know who to award the prize to. We have the names of each baker," he said happily.

"Excellent! Who are they? I know some but not all of them."

He pulled out a small bit of paper from his trouser pocket and handed it to her. It read:

Mrs. Alleyn – blackberry tart
Mrs. Grant – gooseberry fool
Miss Heyworth – raspberry trifle
Mrs. Greene – plum tart
Mrs. Sutton – honey cakes
Miss Everly – apple pie
Mrs. Walker – rhubarb tart
Lady Cameron – cheesecake

She looked it over and handed it back to him. "May I make a

copy of this?"

"I'll write you one. Do you know these women?" He took the paper back.

"Yes, I've met all of them before. Mrs. Grant and Mrs. Alleyn are neighbors of ours and of course Aunt Rachel and Miss Heyworth and Miss Everly. I don't know Mrs. Walker very well."

"Then that leaves Mrs. Sutton and Lady Cameron," he said.

"And Mrs. Sutton, who lives on the other side of town, I don't see her often. And Lady Cameron... But surely you don't suspect her. Especially when she was sick," she pointed out.

"I have to suspect everyone," he told her.

"But she wouldn't have eaten something she had poisoned," Poppy said.

"Wouldn't she? It's the perfect cover."

"There is no motive. She would have no reason to want to poison him. She hardly knew him."

"You are forgetting something, Miss Morton."

"What's that?"

"These grand ladies never lift a finger themselves. Her entry would have been baked by her cook, who may have intended to get her ladyship in trouble or poison her."

Poppy's shoulders slumped. "Then we're nowhere. That does however suggest that Lady Cameron is innocent. I have known her since I was a girl."

"I will still have to speak to her. Can you say the same for the others?" he asked.

"Well, my aunt certainly didn't do it, and I think we can both agree that Miss Everly and Miss Heyworth didn't poison their cakes," Poppy said.

"Are you so sure about that? Miss Heyworth is new to town. How well do you know her?"

"I could say the same thing about Miss Everly, Constable."

"Ah, but she has asked you to look into her situation. And I can vouch for her innocence," he said. His dark eyes flashed, and she understood he would brook no argument where Miss Everly was concerned.

"Then that leaves Mrs. Sutton, Mrs. Alleyn, Mrs. Grant, and Lady Cameron, or her cook."

"I will speak with Lady Cameron and Mrs. Grant," he said, "if you will call on Mrs. Sutton and Mrs. Alleyn. Mr. Jenkins will speak with Mrs. Walker."

"What reason shall I give to pay a call?"

"You're neighbors. Do you need a reason?" He gave her a familiar smile, and for an instant, she felt like they were close friends again. Then a second passed and she remembered that she had to watch her behavior. It wouldn't do to be too friendly with an engaged man. A pang of emotion went through her, but she couldn't identify it. Instead, she bid him good day and went to find Jane.

Chapter Fourteen

T HE NEXT DAY Poppy paid a visit to Mrs. Alleyn, a wealthy woman who lived on St. Andrews Street, a little way off the main road into town. Her brick home looked very comfortable and had a well-tended garden. The grass was trimmed and there was a smart stone walkway up to the entrance.

Upon calling, Poppy was ushered into a pleasant sitting room. It had ordinary white wallpaper bordered with tiny blue flowers, and large windows to let the sunlight in. Upon Poppy's arrival, she was quickly joined by Mrs. Alleyn, a middle-aged matron with light blonde hair, bright eyes, and a penchant for blue dresses. She was soon joined by her daughters, Louisa and Mary. Louisa was twenty-five, thin with a pale, limpid face, while Mary was twenty, wore spectacles, and had dark eyes to match her hair.

As Poppy sat on a comfortable sofa and accepted Mrs. Alleyn's kind offer of tea, she surveyed her hostesses. Louisa wore a light yellow day dress and looked pleased at the interruption, whereas Mary's sour expression suggested she had been dragged away from a good book.

"How good it is to see you, Miss Morton," Louisa said. "I suspect you are saddened by the death of Mr. Ingleby."

"Yes," Poppy said, taking courage. "It's why I came. I believe he liked to come here and visit."

"Oh yes, he came here very often. He liked to come read to

us many an afternoon." Mrs. Alleyn's expression was tight around the eyes. "I'll just see what the delay is with the tea. Back in a moment."

As she quit the room, that left Poppy alone with Louisa and Mary. "How are you both?"

"Tolerably well," Louisa answered her. "It is a great loss." She lifted a hand to her eyes. "He was a great man."

Mary rolled her eyes. "Louisa, if you need to…"

"No, no, I'll be fine. The fact is, Miss Morton, he often came to see me," she told Poppy.

"Oh. He was a…"

"Yes. He was a beau of mine," Louisa said.

Mary snorted, earning herself a sharp look from her sister.

"And despite not everyone believing it, I have no doubt that his intentions were true," Louisa sighed.

"His intentions? You mean you were engaged?" Poppy's eyebrows rose.

"We would have married, yes. He loved this place, our company, and—"

"Mama's cakes, you mean," Mary said.

"He had a healthy appetite, but that is no crime," Louisa said sharply.

"Only that he practically ate us out of house and home," Mary countered.

"Well, perhaps if we hadn't been so stingy with our table he might have stayed longer," Louisa snapped.

"You are deluding yourself. He only came for the cakes and once Mama got wise to him, he stopped coming. You were the only one who cared to hear his hours of endless spouting…" Mary said.

Louisa shot to her feet. "You are wrong. He was a kind, gentle soul. I won't stand here and listen to you blacken his name. Shame on you." She turned and stomped out of the room.

Poppy stared after her.

Mary sat back and crossed her legs, slouching against the seat cushions of her high-backed chair.

Poppy surveyed her for a moment, and Mary laughed. "I suspect that's why you actually came here, isn't it? You wanted to know how well we liked him. Well, I liked him not a jot, and that's the truth."

"Is it true that he and Louisa were sweethearts?" Poppy asked.

"Only in her head. They had no understanding. I love my sister, but she would spend hours gazing at him, listening to him talk. He would stay until it came time for dinner and of course we had to invite him, whereas Louisa would say anything to keep him here. It was an arrangement that suited only themselves."

"What about your mother? Did she like him?"

Mary gave her a pensive look as if judging how much to say. "She did at first, then not at all. I think she was quite relieved to see him go, to be honest."

"Why do you think that is?"

Mary pushed her spectacles higher on her nose and shrugged. "I don't know. I'm only glad to see him gone. Louisa is too ready to fall in love with any young man that gives her a second glance. I didn't like him."

"Why not? Besides the hours and the cake eating," Poppy said.

"You ask a lot of questions. Why do you want to know? He's dead, that's all that matters. Now we can go back to our lives," Mary said.

Poppy shrugged. "We didn't know him very well. He didn't spend a lot of time at the parsonage."

"Yes, I heard about that. He did make a few pointed remarks at your expense, but I simply laughed at him and told him he didn't sound very clergyman-like. Louisa and Mama were scandalized of course, but I didn't care. I don't like people who try to prop themselves up by putting down others."

"Nor do I," Poppy said.

At that moment Mrs. Alleyn returned with a tea tray and set

it down on a wide wooden table that sat between the sofa and chairs. "There we are. I hope you like green tea, Miss Morton." She poured a cup and passed it to Poppy. "What were you both discussing when I came in? And where is Louisa?"

"She left. She didn't like hearing my view of Mr. Ingleby's character," Mary told her, pouring herself a cup of tea.

Mrs. Alleyn's face darkened. "I see. Mind you keep that tongue of yours in check, Mary. It will get you into trouble if you're not careful."

Mary hid her smirk and left, taking her teacup with her.

"Well now. What will you do, what with Mr. Ingleby having passed on?" Mrs. Alleyn asked as she filled her own teacup. "Who will conduct the church services?"

"We'll write to another clergyman I suppose, or to my uncle," Poppy said, "It is sad that he died. He was doing such good work for the church, raising money for the roof."

"Oh yes, that baking contest was a nice idea. I even baked a blackberry tart for it. Such a shame about what happened."

"Yes," Poppy agreed and sipped her tea. She sat back against the sofa cushion and realized she had no clue what she was doing there. It was clear that Mrs. Alleyn had no wish to do Mr. Ingleby any harm. Indeed, one of his daughters fancied herself in love with the man, as hard as that might seem to Poppy.

"Louisa seems to have been very fond of him," Poppy said, "I'm sorry to not be able to offer you congratulations soon."

"Congratulations? Whatever for?"

"Why I thought... Louisa said that..."

"Oh, she was fond of him all right. But I wouldn't have allowed a match between them, heavens no. Not to him." Mrs. Alleyn sipped her tea and surveyed Poppy. "I did hear him say some rather far fetched remarks about you and your aunt. I dismissed them of course. You know I never listen to gossip."

"Of course not," Poppy murmured over her tea, blowing on its contents.

"And a good thing too, for I used to think he was very smart.

But the more I got to know him, the more I thought that his opinions were rather rude, and many things he said did strike me as being unchristian."

"Oh?" Poppy asked.

"Well, uncharitable at the very least. Do you know, I think the man couldn't abide sick people. When Mary came down with a cold, he stayed away for five days straight. Louisa was inconsolable. But then when she ran into him in town and said Mary had recovered, he was back for dinner that very night. I used to think he might do for one of them, but—" Spots of color rose in her cheeks, and she gripped the delicate handle of her teacup. "Why are you here, Miss Morton? Surely you knew the man well enough to form your own opinion of his character."

"Something does not sit right with me about his death, and I wished to know your thoughts about him," Poppy said.

Her hostess set her teacup down on the table with a clatter and met Poppy's eyes. "Well, I don't need to tell you not to butt into the constabulary's business, but I can't imagine that man Jenkins finding anything. He couldn't find his nose unless it was on his face," she said with a huff. "The fact is Mr. Ingleby was rude and uncharitable, particularly toward us, when we had invited him to dine with us for so many evenings. Louisa was quite taken with him, and when I hinted that perhaps there was another reason for his wanting to spend time with us, he was dumbfounded."

"Surely not," Poppy said.

Mrs. Alleyn's face twisted unhappily. "Oh, yes. He laughed in my face. Properly laughed as if I'd told him a very funny joke, and told me that the very idea was ridiculous. He said that my girls were the homeliest pair he'd ever laid eyes on. He said that Louisa was very patient, and that Mary had a fair countenance, but that he would never consider marrying a girl who was so... so..."

"What?" Poppy asked.

"Dull. He found my girls dull, both of them. Can you believe it? My girls. I told him then that we couldn't possibly have him over for dinner the following night, as we were entertaining and our table would be quite full. He shrugged and simply helped himself to another sticky cake before he left. The nerve of the man." Her voice shook as she smoothed out the folds of her blue dress on her knees. "No, I am not sorry to see him gone. And I would not see him again, not even if he were still alive and came calling."

"That is horrible," Poppy said, "I am so sorry."

"Poor Louisa had no idea. She thought she had done something to offend him, the poor girl. And what is worse, he then started befriending the Grants, and you know what they are like. Mrs. Grant is always baking some sweet confection. So he began seeking out their company and... I have heard that their daughter is to inherit £5000."

Poppy breathed in. "Very attractive indeed."

"Exactly. I had not thought him at all mercenary, but when I realized he knew that my girls would not inherit so much... It's hard not to take offense."

After a few more minutes of polite conversation, Poppy walked back to the parsonage, her mind going wild. Did Mrs. Alleyn have it in her to poison a man who had offended her and her daughters? She didn't know. But she certainly had a good reason to.

CHAPTER FIFTEEN

POPPY OPENED AND shut the door of the parsonage, about to call out a greeting when loud voices came from the sitting room. She entered the normally pleasant room to find her aunt red in the face, her plump body trembling with anger as she faced an unwelcome visitor, Mr. Jenkins.

A large, round man who was prone to sneering, Mr. Arnold Jenkins had a way of putting peoples' backs up. Today he pointed a rude finger at her aunt. "How do I know you didn't do it? It's all around town that you didn't like the man. He made no bones about the fact that you two didn't get along. What do you have to say for yerself?"

"I didn't kill him. I would never do such a thing. I'm the wife of a parson, for God's sake," Aunt Rachel said. Seeing Poppy at the entrance she said, "Oh good, you're home Poppy. Maybe you can talk some sense into this man."

Mr. Jenkins turned and spotted her in the doorway. He did not bow. "Ah, Miss Morton. Come back, eh?"

Poppy wondered at the man's ability to make such a harmless question sound so suspicious. "Yes, I was out."

"Where? With whom?" he demanded, his bushy dark eyebrows knitting into one angry brow.

"I was paying a call to Mrs. Alleyn."

"You were, were you? Sit down, Miss Morton, and tell me

about the day of the baking contest. What were you doing when it all happened?" He directed one dirty gloved finger toward the sofa.

Poppy looked at him evenly and slowly untied her ribbon and loosened her bonnet from her hair, patting at the sweaty loose brown strands. She felt like a lazy cat as she crossed the room to sit calmly beside her aunt on the sofa. She felt Mr. Jenkins' annoyed gaze on her but she cared little for his feelings just then. This man had intruded into her home, and she would not be put ill at ease. "I met with Miss Heyworth and Mr. Heyworth and joined my aunt at the tent. The competition started—"

"Ah. What were you doing before then?" he asked.

"Walking into town."

"Why didn't you walk with your aunt?"

"I did, both I and our maid, Betsey, came together. Mr. Ingleby drove our cart to save us the journey and parked the horse and cart by the post near The Crosskeys tavern. We walked the rest of the way together, just the three of us."

"Aha!" he turned a pair of piggish eyes at Aunt Rachel. "Leaving the man alone, eh? What made you want to abandon him?"

"He had people to speak to, and I needed to deliver my tart to the tent. Many people go their separate ways at a fete, deputy. That is no crime," Aunt Rachel said.

"When did you arrive?"

"I think around half-past noon. The contest was due to start at one. When I arrived at the tent it was nearing the start time. There were a lot of people and a lot of shops and stalls to walk by." Aunt Rachel sat beside Poppy on the sofa.

"Uh-huh. Why didn't you get along with Mr. Ingleby?" he asked.

Poppy and Aunt Rachel shared a look. "We disagreed about things," Aunt Rachel said.

"What sort of things?" Jenkins asked. "It's common knowledge that you two hated each other. He told half the town he couldn't stand to be under the same roof as you women. I just don't see why you'd want him dead over some idle gossip."

"Deputy, that is simply not true. He—" Poppy started.

"Oh, don't start, you're only going to lie when I know the truth of it. You both hated him, didn't you?"

"What? No. I disliked the man, but I wouldn't go so far as to say I hated him," Aunt Rachel said.

"Hated him, I'd say. For sure. You didn't like that he was so popular around town, did you? And the things he had to say, well…" Mr. Jenkins tutted. "Word is that you weren't very hospitable to the poor young man."

"Hah! That is a joke. I did try. We both did." Aunt Rachel turned up her nose.

"And yet everyone knows he couldn't stand to be here. He took his meals elsewhere. It takes a lot for a man to do that, and leave a woman's cooking. Are you that bad a cook? Were you angry at the slight and decided to poison him at the contest? Or were you jealous of his popularity in town? Maybe you thought the townspeople wouldn't want your husband back, what with Mr. Ingleby proving so popular."

"Deputy, that is nonsense," Poppy said, "we weren't jealous at all. He was rude, and made it his business to visit all the people in the neighborhood."

"But he didn't like coming back here, did he?"

"No, he did not. And the reason for it is because he found our company rude and our table not handsome enough for his tastes. There. Is that what you wanted to know?" Aunt Rachel snapped.

"It's a start," Jenkins said, crossing his arms.

There was a knock at the door. Poppy rose and answered it to find Constable Dyngley on her doorstep. "Constable," she said, "Come in."

"I wanted to discuss this situation with you," he started, following her into the sitting room. He stopped at the sight of Mr. Jenkins and Aunt Rachel. "Hello." He bowed.

Aunt Rachel said, "Hello, Constable. Could you please tell your man that I am not a murderer?"

Dyngley looked at Jenkins. "Deputy?"

Mr. Jenkins removed his stiff hat and ran a hand through his dark curly hair. "I didn't say that. I was just asking her some questions."

"And suggesting that I had something to do with Mr. Ingleby's death," Aunt Rachel said.

"Everyone knows you two didn't get along. What's to say you didn't do him in? Did anyone see you make the pie?" Mr. Jenkins said, earning a dirty look from Poppy.

"It was a tart, made from plums in our backyard. If you don't believe me, go look yourself." She crossed her arms beneath her chest.

Mr. Jenkins opened his mouth to retort when Constable Dyngley said hurriedly, "Mrs. Greene, Mr. Jenkins in no way meant to insinuate that you had anything to do with Mr. Ingleby's death. It's just that we have to speak to each of the bakers who had a dessert there that day. For all we know, Mr. Ingleby might have had a poor constitution and or have suffered from a pre-existing condition. If he had, then it might have been made worse by what he ate or drank that day."

"You mean it could have been an accident?" Aunt Rachel asked.

"He's lying to spare your feelings. We know he was poisoned by an arsenic-covered tart," Jenkins said, smirking at Poppy. "But then he would try to be kind to you."

"As a gentleman should," Aunt Rachel said.

"Not all gentlemen." Jenkins grinned at Dyngley.

"Mr. Jenkins, you can take your leave." Dyngley's expression was hard.

"I'm only asking what you would've asked."

"You've asked enough. I'd like a word with the ladies now. Wait for me outside," Dyngley said.

"You'd like a word with one of them, for sure," he muttered and leered at Poppy before walking out. The front door slammed behind him. Once Mr. Jenkins left, it was like an angry dark cloud had lifted, and they were in polite and easy company again.

"Ignore him," Dyngley said. "He likes to make trouble."

"Thank you, Constable," Aunt Rachel said.

"I'm sorry about that. Mr. Jenkins means well but his methods can be harsh at times," Dyngley said.

"It's fine, Constable. What did you want to know?" Aunt Rachel asked.

"I wished to speak with Miss Morton. And yourself, about the investigation." He colored, avoiding Poppy's gaze. "But I see that Jenkins has already spoken with you, so there is no need. Good day." He bowed and was out the front door within half a minute.

Poppy stared at the empty space he had occupied. "That's strange. What has gotten into him?"

Aunt Rachel crossed the room to peer out one of the windows. "It's not strange at all." Aunt Rachel gave Poppy a wide smile. "He'd come to see you of course."

"Aunt…"

"I know these things, Poppy, and mark my words, I will be shocked if he's not here again soon. I had no idea you were so close."

"We are friends, Aunt. Nothing more."

"For now, perhaps. But do you believe he comes all this way just to discuss his investigation with you?"

"Yes."

"Then you are fooling yourself, and he is too if he believes that. What a pair of fools, the both of you." Aunt Rachel walked out of the room, calling to Betsey about that night's dinner.

Poppy stood by the left window and watched Constable Dyngley and Mr. Jenkins mount their horses and trot away. Could her aunt be right? Did Dyngley fancy her? Or were Mr. Jenkins' sniggering glances just meant to cause trouble?

THAT NIGHT, POPPY lay in bed, staring at the ceiling. She couldn't sleep, despite the darkness that filled the room, and the wind whistling outside. Her body felt tired, but she kept thinking back to the day of Mr. Ingleby's death and seeing him collapse in front of everyone. She would never forget the expression his face held in those final moments as he struggled to breathe. His jaw hung slack, his pasty face contorted as his eyes turned glassy and stared at nothing. His arms splayed out like a forgotten doll's at his sides and a tart lay crushed beneath his right hand.

Poppy's imagination ran wild and she could almost hear a plate shatter as he fell. She opened her eyes with a start. The sound of glass breaking. Footsteps. She sat up in bed. Was someone wandering around the house?

She slipped out of bed and put on a thin white robe, tying its material around her waist with a sash. The dull thuds of footsteps hit her ears, and she wandered out of her bedroom, her bare feet cold against the hard wooden floorboards.

She padded down the corridor, walking confidently by her aunt and uncle's bedroom. Perhaps her aunt was feeling pecking and had tiptoed downstairs for a midnight snack. But as she passed by the room, she could hear her aunt's steady snores. Unladylike, yes. But a chill ran through Poppy when she realized that if it wasn't her aunt, then who?

A flicker of light shone from beneath the door of her uncle's study.

The light flickered, and muted footsteps came from inside the study. Poppy hastened forward until her hand touched the doorknob. "Betsey?" she whispered.

The movement stopped.

The floorboards creaked beneath Poppy's feet, and she turned the brass doorknob, feeling it warm beneath her hand. She opened the door, and the light went out.

"Betsey?" she whispered, "Betsey, is that you?"

She felt blind in the darkness but worse, someone was in the room with her.

"Who's there?" She breathed and then someone shoved her, knocking her against the door and out of the room. She fell on her hands and knees, skinning her right knee in the process. She cried out, "Oi!"

Whoever it was thundered down the stairs, their footsteps echoing loudly enough to wake her aunt. "Poppy? What's that noise?" she called sleepily.

Poppy scrambled to her feet and ran after the dark form, but tripped in her robe and crashed down the wooden stairs, bruising her bottom. Her feet slapped the hard wooden floor as the dark figure stopped at the front door. Finding it locked, the person kicked it in frustration.

"Stop!" Poppy said, lunging for them.

The person shoved past her and ran into the blue sitting room, bumping into furniture and howling in pain.

Poppy ran after the person and froze in the doorway. Cold night air slapped her in the face. "Stop. Who are you?"

The person hobbled to a large broken window on the left, which now bore horrible, shattered glass. The room filled with chilly night air as the stranger's shoes crunched against the glass on the floor and they jumped outside.

Poppy ran across the room and paused at the window, her feet cramping in pain. She'd walked on shards of broken glass, and they cut into her bare feet. Dozens of tiny cuts sliced into her skin. She winced and looked up just in time to see the figure disappear into the night, getting enveloped by the darkness of the trees. "Damn."

Then it was quiet, and the only sounds she heard were the quiet call of birds and the low whisper of leaves as the wind passed by. Cool air drifted into the room, making her shiver as she took stock of her injuries. Her palms and her right knee hurt, and her feet felt sore, as tiny glass shards bit into her skin with every step.

A small light appeared in the doorway of the sitting room, revealing the tired face of her aunt, holding a candle. Her frilly white mobcap hung askew on her long hair, and she wore a frillier white robe over her nightdress. "Poppy? What are you doing down there? Are you all right? Why is it so cold in here?"

"I'm fine. But I caught someone upstairs."

"What do you mean? Are you sure you saw someone? Could it have been a dream?"

"No." Poppy frowned at her bare feet. "Whoever it was broke a window and got inside."

"Good heavens. Where are they?"

"Gone. They ran past me. I think they wanted something from uncle's study."

"Oh God." Her aunt came forward, clutching a small candlestick that bore a thin smoking tallow candle. "Are you all right?"

Poppy said, "I'm a little sore but I'm all right. Stay back, there's broken glass everywhere."

"Oh no, have you stepped on it? Shall I help you walk?"

"I'll be fine."

"Very well. You take care of your feet and go on back to bed. We'll clean this mess up in the morning. I can hardly see in front of my face, it's so dark," her aunt said, and disappeared with the candle, leaving Poppy alone in the darkness.

With not much else to do, she waited a few seconds for her eyes to readjust to the darkness, then pulled a set of heavy dark blue curtains across the window, wincing as glass crunched beneath her bare feet. She bit her tongue in pain and felt blood trickle from the bottoms of her feet, and looked around for a weight. Walking on her tiptoes, she pulled the curtains in place over the broken window and pinned them against the wall by setting two heavy tomes of her uncle's on the floor. Once she was satisfied they would not move, she gingerly walked up the stairs to her room and over to the small dressing table that sat beside her writing desk.

Devoid of cosmetics but burdened with more than one book of poetry, the humble wooden table bore an ordinary looking-glass and more importantly, a basin of water and a washcloth. Poppy didn't much care for bathing as the water was always cold, and they did not have footmen to carry up pails of hot water to their large basin, and lugging up hot water herself was a chore, so she usually bathed only when she felt particularly dirty, as was their custom.

She pulled up the wooden seat from her writing-table and sat by the small table, dipping the washcloth into the water and cleaning her feet as best she could. While her eyes had adjusted to the darkness, it still was messy work, and it was still some minutes before she could no longer feel tiny shards of glass digging into her skin. Eventually, she stuck both feet in the basin and let them soak before drying them clean. By the time she tumbled back into the bed, morning light had begun to seep through the window and she fell into an exhausted asleep.

POPPY WOKE UP to a scream. Tearing her head from the pillow, she heard Betsey's voice carried up from downstairs, crying out, "Mrs. Greene? Miss Morton?"

Poppy jumped out of bed and winced as her bare feet hit the cold floor. She remembered about her feet and felt the sore flesh hurt. She hurriedly tiptoed down the corridor and stopped at the head of the stairs. "What is it, Betsey?"

Their maid stood at the foot of the stairs by the entrance of the parsonage. "There's bloody footprints everywhere." Her eyes were wide.

"Yes, umm..." Poppy wandered down the stairs as Betsey went into the other rooms and crossed herself. "The footprints come from the parlor. Why are the curtains pulled against the window?"

"We had an intruder last night," Poppy said.

Betsey glanced at Poppy's bare feet. "I thought a ghost had come in. There's bloody footprints all over the floor."

Poppy looked at the floor and realized that in the darkness, she had tracked blood from the broken window in the sitting room all the way upstairs to her room. The dark spots of blood were clear in the morning light, dotting the wooden stairs. "Sorry, that was me. I stepped on the glass and cut myself."

"I think you should see the doctor, Poppy. I had no idea

you'd hurt yourself so badly," her aunt said, coming out of her bedroom. "Oh Betsey, you'll never believe what happened to us last night."

"I can hardly believe it now. An intruder, here? What did they want?"

"I don't know. I caught them in uncle's office," Poppy said. She leaned against the wooden staircase and glanced up at her uncle's study. It felt violated somehow, as though her uncle's private sanctum had been disturbed. As much as she and her uncle disagreed at times, she missed him at that moment and wanted him back home, safe.

Aunt Rachel pulled her robe around her thick form and gave a little shiver. "It's terrifying to think a stranger came in here. He could have killed us in our beds." Her eyes grew wide and she gave her head a little shake. "I'm sure they were just after money or something. I suppose we had better call the constable and that miserable deputy of his."

A SHORT WHILE later, there was a knock at the front door. Dyngley and Mr. Jenkins arrived at the same time as the town doctor. Dyngley observed the bloody footprints and wandered upstairs while Mr. Jenkins supervised Dr. Wilson bandaging Poppy's feet. "You're lucky," the doctor said, wrapping two clean white linen bandages around her feet.

"Why is that?" Poppy asked. Now that she was dressed and it was daylight, she felt more herself. Today she wore a serviceable light gray dress that was simple and hugged her tall form, but she didn't care. In her stays and long dress, she felt secure as she sat on the sofa, watching Dr. Wilson care for her feet.

He said, "Whoever broke in here was dangerous. You're very brave to have gone after him."

"Or very stupid," Mr. Jenkins said.

"Deputy…" Dyngley warned, entering the blue sitting room.

"It's no place for ladies to be running around after strange men," Mr. Jenkins said.

Poppy gave an unladylike snort. "It's not like I invited him in. Would you have preferred me to stay back and hide while the intruder rifled through my uncle's belongings?"

"Poppy," Aunt Rachel tsked. "She is overwrought at the intrusion. We all are."

Dr. Wilson chose that moment to take the pair of plain cotton stockings and pull one up over Poppy's left foot. He tugged it over her ankle and his hands on her bare skin made her gasp. His brisk movement stilled all conversation in the room.

Poppy stiffened and blushed. "Doctor…"

"Yes?" So focused was Dr. Wilson on his work, it was clear to Poppy that he did not think of her as a woman, but as a patient, a body to be dealt with and cared for. Which in his mind, included the tying on of bandages and pulling on of stockings.

Aunt Rachel was scandalized. Her voice was strangled, "Doctor, please. You've done enough. I am sure Poppy can pull on her own stockings, thank you."

Poppy dared not raise her gaze for she feared the shocked expressions she might see. Dr. Wilson stopped, his hand still on her bare leg, and he looked up.

She said, "I can finish this. Thank you, Doctor."

Dr. Wilson slowly removed his hands and straightened, tugging at his cravat. "Of course."

Poppy glanced up and met Dyngley's eyes. He swallowed, glanced at the curve of her ankles, and looked away.

So distracted was the group, they did not hear the parsonage door open and close, nor the arrival of a new visitor until Caroline entered the sitting room. "Hello! Miss Morton, I wanted to speak to you–Oh my lord. What is going on?"

Poppy's face bloomed red, as she now had her bare feet and ankles exposed to not just her doctor, but four other people. She squawked and strove to cover herself with her bare hands.

Constable Dyngley turned to her. "Caroline, what are you doing here?"

"I've come to speak to Miss Morton, but I can see she's busy entertaining." Her eyes narrowed.

"That's not it at all. The doctor was examining her injuries when we came in," Constable Dyngley said.

"That's not what it looked like to me…" A smile crept over her face. She winked at Poppy as Dyngley hustled her out of the room. "I'll call again later!" she called, as the parsonage door opened and shut.

Aunt Rachel sank into a chair. "Heavens, are we to have the entire town call on us while Poppy's ankles are exposed?"

Dr. Wilson turned his back to Poppy and said, "Yes, well. I think it best you put your stockings back on now, Miss Morton."

Mr. Jenkins turned red as he too avoided the sight of Poppy pulling on her stockings. "A young lady has no business in this, no business at all. This wouldn't have happened if you hadn't stuck your nose in where it doesn't belong."

"Mr. Jenkins, I assure you, my niece has not been doing anything inappropriate."

"That's not what I heard. I heard Dyngley's fiancée hired her."

"My niece has done nothing of the sort. And I'll ask you to keep a civil tongue, or I must ask you to leave."

Mr. Jenkins's eyes narrowed. "I'm just staying, it's her interfering in this business that's come back to her. Investigations should be left to the constabulary." He left the house.

Aunt Rachel shook her head. "Odious man. Poppy, you haven't gone and agreed to help that young woman, have you?"

Poppy blushed. "Aunt, I've been meaning to tell you…"

"Oh heavens. I can't take much more of this. You are determined to choose these unladylike pursuits. I shan't breathe a word of this to your uncle, he'll have a fit. Speaking of, where are my smelling salts?"

Poppy rose from the sitting room's pale green sofa, crossed the room to a side table and fetched a small bottle out of a drawer, and passed it to her aunt. The men were silent as her aunt took the bottle and sniffed heavily.

"Have you looked in my uncle's office?" Poppy asked Dyngley. "Did you find what he was looking for?"

"I'm not sure. It would be better to have your eyes over it, to be honest."

"Oh." Aunt Rachel piped up, then thought better of it. "Yes, perhaps you had better go look, Poppy. Lord knows I never go in there, and my eyes are never good this time of day. It is so bright."

Dr. Wilson looked as if he might protest. "What Miss Morton needs is rest. If your eyes are troubling you, I would be happy to have a look."

"No, no, it's fine. I am very well, thank you." Aunt Rachel turned pink. "Do go on and accompany the constable, Poppy, for I am sure you will know better what is out of place than me."

Poppy tried not to smile. Her aunt's matchmaking attempts knew no bounds. "Yes, aunt."

Poppy moved past the crowd in the room and entered the corridor. She let out a breath and held onto the wooden staircase banister to support her weight.

"Are you all right, Miss Morton?" Dyngley asked.

"Well enough. I'm tired more than anything."

"We don't have to do this now. I can come by later..." he started, but she was halfway up the stairs.

Once at the top of the stairs she turned right and walked over to her uncle's study and opened the door. The small, normally sunlit room had been ransacked. Papers lay strewn on the floor and the contents of his writing desk were overturned. Drawers had been pulled out and emptied, and more than one book had been torn from its place on his bookshelf and tossed onto the floor.

Poppy stopped in the doorway. Seeing her uncle's study like this struck her, and she stiffened.

"Poppy, are you all right?" Dyngley asked.

Poppy turned her head, slightly amused at his using her familiar name. It wasn't proper.

"I am fine."

"You don't sound it." He stood at her elbow and looked past her into the room. Now lit by the angles of the morning light, it looked like a shoddy mess, with a wine glass overturned, and dust motes floating in the air. "Miss Morton, you don't need to do this. Upon reflection, I can't see how your perspective would be much help," he said.

Poppy ignored him and walked into the room, wincing at the tenderness of her feet. She vaguely noticed the missing serving plate Betsey had been hunting for, that lay on the floor, covered with crumbs. But beside it, papers were scattered in a mess. She bent down and picked up some of the papers, seeing old versions of her uncle's sermons, as well as household accounts and shopping lists. Notations for the price of candles, beef, and sugar caught her eye, and she lifted them and put them on the table.

Dyngley lurked in the doorway like a silent shadow. "What do you think he wanted?"

"Why are you calling it a *he*? Surely a woman could have broken in," Poppy said.

"Perhaps. It is surprising that the broken window did not wake either of you."

"We were asleep at the time. If they were quiet about it, and if they knew what to look for, they could have broken in and not disturbed us. But what they wanted up here I don't know. Money maybe?" She said, eyeing the papers on the desk's messy surface. She lifted one of the drawers and put it back inside the desk. There below it on the floor, lay a series of letters. Unfamiliar handwriting caught her eye, and she picked up one. It read:

I hope you are taking care of my Poppy, and let her know that her mother wishes her well—

Poppy dropped the letter. Her hands shook.

"Poppy, what is wrong?" Dyngley asked.

"It is a letter from my mother," she said, scrabbling for it. Her knees pressed against the hard floor as she reached for it, finding others.

"Oh?" he said, "Is she well?"

"My mother is dead. Or at least that's what my aunt and uncle told me. That she died in childbirth, delivering me." Poppy's hands trembled. "Was this all a lie?"

CHAPTER SIXTEEN

D YNGLEY LOOKED AT Poppy's solitary form. Too tall to suit any but the tallest or most confident of men, and too plain-faced to be a beauty, he watched Poppy's pale hands tremble as she dug carefully through the debris and dust on the floor, holding each newfound letter close like a courtesan might gather her diamonds.

"What does it mean?" he asked.

"I think they were hiding her from me. My own mother. But why?"

"Were they close, your mother and your relatives?"

"I don't know. The earliest memory I have is of my aunt and uncle. I don't even have a sketch of her. They're the only family I've ever known," she muttered. "How could they keep this from me?"

He looked around the room. Mr. Greene's study was clearly disturbed, and yet he knew from looking that it represented the soul of a very orderly man. Books lay strewn on the floor but the high bookshelves against the walls boasted neatly arranged tomes without a speck of dust in sight. That cleanliness could have been the result of diligent attention from the maid but somehow Dyngley doubted it. He glanced at the early morning beams of light that streamed in at an angle, illuminating the desk's surface.

Despite it being scattered with papers and stained by an overturned inkwell, Dyngley could see this was the man's inner sanctum and wondered why a person had come here. And yet he could see the presence of Mr. Ingleby as well, for there on the floor beside the desk sat a large serving plate littered with crumbs, as well as a two-pronged knife and fork. Crumbs lay scattered across the surface of the desk, the chair, and the floor, and he wondered at the man who had so lately disturbed the household's peace.

Outwardly he saw no reason why a person would come in here unless they fancied reading from one of the many volumes of religious texts or sermons scattered on the floor. He glanced at Poppy, "Have you found anything else?"

She looked up from her reading and held the delicate letters against her chest as if to guard them against future harm. "No. But I don't know why I would be kept in the dark. If my mother is alive then why wouldn't she want to see me? Why the charade?"

"Perhaps she wanted a better life for you. Placing you in the care of your aunt and uncle might afford you a better life, especially if your mother needed to earn a living." He delicately did not suggest some of the more unsavory reasons why this could be.

She chewed the inside of her cheek, a sure sign she was stressed.

"I will leave you, and we'll send a man for your window." He bowed and walked out, followed by Mr. Jenkins.

Once outside, Dyngley asked, "What did you find out? Anything?"

Mr. Jenkins scratched his chin. "The women are rude, but it's clear to me, the house was broken into. One of the misses couldn't do that."

"What makes you think that?"

"Glass was inside the house, on the floor. That means it was broken from the outside. And..." Mr. Jenkins sounded grumpy.

"What?" Dyngley asked.

"Unless Miss Morton or her aunt are conniving, they wouldn't have done this. I doubt Miss Morton would have gone to the trouble of injuring herself." Mr. Jenkins rubbed the side of his face.

"I agree. The girl has shown great spirit and wouldn't have knowingly injured herself. She's too smart for that."

"Unless she slipped out of the house at night and broke in to distract us. She could have made it all up," Jenkins added.

"Do you think she did? What reason would she have?"

"To distract us from investigating her aunt. Everyone knows that the aunt and the dead man hated each other. Mayhap she knows something and wants us to think someone broke in, so we wouldn't suspect her aunt of poisoning him."

"Smart, but I doubt it," Dyngley said.

The doctor caught up with them in a few moments and said, "Constable, I have a question for you."

"What's that?" Dyngley asked, turning around.

Dr. Wilson wore a white shirt and cravat loosely tied around his neck, tan trousers and a light beige overcoat to keep away the morning chill. His ginger hair stood out like a beacon and he had a thin face, but eyes that sparkled with intelligence. Dyngley liked him, for the most part. The doctor carried a leather satchel that bore the traces of hard use and raked a hand through his messy hair. "On the day of the baking contest, we all assumed that Mr. Ingleby choked to death. No one suspected any of the cakes were to blame. Now that we know it was poison, what happened to the other puddings?"

"The mayor of Hertford will know. John Evans. He's the one who allowed this contest to happen in the first place. Just as well he likes his puddings," Mr. Jenkins said.

A TRIP TO John's home found the man at the town jail, speaking with the keeper. When Dyngley approached him, John quickly excused himself and made to leave, when Dyngley said, "Mr. Evans, I wonder if I might have a word."

Mayor Evans looked surprised. A man in his mid-forties, he had thinning light blond hair, a narrow build and a thin wiry strength. But a conversation with him revealed little beyond, "Oh yes. I got rid of the pies right away."

"You did?"

"Well, if Mr. Ingleby had choked then that's unfortunate, but I didn't want the poor woman who baked the pie to suffer from the scorn of her neighbors, so I disposed of all of them. Why?"

Dyngley winced and coughed delicately. "We have reason to believe Mr. Ingleby was poisoned."

Mayor Evans paled. "Poison? Then the rumors are true. I'm glad I acted when I did. His death is a tragedy for our community. Those poor women, I wonder what Mrs. Walker will do now?"

"What do you mean?"

"Well. I gather that poor Mrs. Walker was treating Mr. Ingleby for his gout. He would have gone to the doctor but knew the old woman was hard up, so he sought her medicines. Without his coin, I don't know what will happen to her. She's a lonely widow with little to live on."

"I'll check on her. Thank you, Mayor."

"Of course, it's no secret that Mr. Ingleby and Mrs. Greene were at odds. Have you looked closely at her?"

Dyngley's expression clouded. "I have. But I don't suspect her of any wrongdoing."

"I rather thought you wouldn't." Mayor Evans tapped a finger against his lips and said, "I'm not one to gossip, Constable…"

By which Dyngley took to mean the exact opposite.

"But it seems to me that more than one person has commented on your… friendship with Miss Morton."

"My friendship?" Dyngley blinked.

"Yes. You are an engaged man, are you not?"

"I am," Dyngley said with pride.

"Then perhaps you should attend your fiancée, and instead ask your deputy to look closely at the woman who's got a motive and reason to want Mr. Ingleby harmed."

Dyngley snapped, "Mayor, you are mistaken, Miss Morton and I are just friends. I would never neglect my fiancée."

"Of course not. I wouldn't dream of suggesting such a thing. You do know that young gentleman walking with her then?" Mayor Evans looked past Dyngley's shoulder.

Dyngley turned. There across the green walked Caroline beside a young man he had seen before. His silver walking stick caught the light, and he stood very close to his fiancée, rather too close for propriety. The man's identity eluded him and Dyngley felt an angry red flush creep up his neck. "Excuse me, Mayor."

Dyngley walked away and caught Caroline's eye. He held up a hand in greeting and Caroline whispered something to her companion, who glanced at Dyngley and left, exiting through the gates of the castle green.

Dygnley wished to pursue the man, but Caroline stepped in front of him. "Dyngley, what a wonderful surprise."

The sight of her made his heart skip a beat. She wore a long white linen walking dress, with a trim white three-quarter-length coat trimmed with ruffles at the wrists, and buttoned at the bodice with a single large button. She wore pale yellow gloves and a fetching yellow bonnet that framed her round face and auburn hair. She smiled up at him and he swallowed. She looked lovely and he felt a fool for doubting her for even a moment. But he had to ask.

"Who was that young man?"

"Him? Oh, that's Colin, my cousin. Colin Barton, of Enfield. He was asking directions to the nearest tavern, that's all," she said, "I've been staying with him."

Dyngley's mouth set in a frown.

"You're not jealous, are you? What a laugh!" Caroline giggled and took his arm, steering him away from the gates and past the crumbling ruins of the 12th-century castle gate, admiring the ducks and geese that waddled by. "It is pleasant, is it not?"

"What? The ducks?"

"No, to be together, enjoying the warm weather," she said,

"Oh, you're distracted. What's on your mind? Is it that ghastly man's murder?"

"Mr. Ingleby, yes. But why should you dislike him?" Dyngley asked.

She smiled at him. "I wondered when you would get around to asking me that."

He met her gaze and she gave a little laugh. "The truth of it is I had no reason to. He was polite and civil to me in every way. I should be sad to see him dead."

"But?" he asked.

"But... I think he was only courteous to certain people. He strove to make the acquaintance of me and Lady Cameron but spoke ill of Miss Morton and her aunt in public. I heard him insult them more than once. Why would he do such a thing?"

"Perhaps he did not get along with his hosts," Dyngley said.

"That is the rumor. But having met Miss Morton and her aunt, I cannot believe they would be that odious to live with. They are smart, sensible women who would no sooner treat a stranger badly than eat their own bonnets."

Dyngley laughed. "Your words do you credit, Miss Everly." Warmth bloomed in his chest.

"It is because of this, and his behavior, that I think him a nasty person. I'm not unhappy to see him gone," she said.

He nodded in understanding.

"I'm sure the ladies at the parsonage would agree. He was quickly turning the neighborhood against them."

"How do you know that?" he asked.

"Ladies talk, Dyngley. You should have heard the things that Mrs. Grant told me. Such ungracious and unkind words he said about Poppy and her dear aunt." She shook her head. "I know you and Miss Morton are friends, but I hope—"

"I am not blind, Caroline. She and her aunt are suspects, just like everyone else."

"Good. You are honest and kind, and I know you too well to think that a friendship would cloud your judgment when murder is concerned."

She beamed up at him, and with a traitorous flutter of his heart, he wondered just how honest a man he was.

CHAPTER SEVENTEEN

POPPY WAS SEETHING. She stood in the morning light, beams of sun streaming through the window in her uncle's study, and all she wanted to do was scream. An assortment of her mother's letters sat clenched in her pale hands. She looked down and saw her hands were trembling; the letters were in danger of falling to the floor. In retrospect, she was rather grateful to the intruder for disturbing her uncle's study. Had they not, she would never have found evidence that her mother was still alive. And yet, here was a mystery all of her own.

She wanted to toss her mother's letters in her aunt's face and demand to know why. Why had she been told that her mother was dead all these years? Why had they lied to her? Why had she not been allowed to write to her? Why had they been kept apart? Unless…

The letters fell to the floor. What if her mother didn't want her? Maybe she didn't want Poppy and gave her away, so she could be rid of her. And that way she assuaged any guilt she had by paying for her upkeep. Maybe that was it. And all this time her aunt and uncle simply tried to do her a kindness by telling her a lie.

"Poppy! Come down for tea. I need you," her aunt called.

No longer trembling, Poppy gathered up the letters and gently arranged them in a pile, then tucked them away in one of her uncle's desk drawers. She would come back for them later when she had more time to think. Either way, she had to find out what had happened to her mother, and why her uncle and aunt had been hiding that she was alive.

ONCE SHE HAD sat through tea and taken most of the day to rest, Poppy felt restored and at the sociable hour, made a slow journey across town to Mrs. Sutton's home. She lived with her boy Geoffrey on the outskirts of town, in one of the poorer sections. It wasn't necessarily run down, but the buildings were of a newer, cheaper quality than others in Hertford and Bengeo, near the main road. But the front garden was well kept and the small dwelling trim and tidy.

Poppy gave a quiet knock on the front door and was greeted by Mrs. Sutton herself, whose polite expression faltered at the sight of her. "Miss Morton. My word, how nice to see you. I wasn't expecting visitors, but do come in."

Poppy was ushered into a small cottage with a thatched roof that needed rethatching, for there was a draft. She followed Mrs. Sutton into a small poky hall that offered a cozy kitchen to her right, and a humble sitting room to her left.

Mrs. Sutton all at once fretted, for she truly hadn't been expecting any visitors. "Shall I make some tea? I can bring it to you in the parlor if you care to sit."

"Oh, I'd rather join you in the kitchen if that's all right. So much warmer, I feel at home in a kitchen," Poppy said.

"I know exactly what you mean. Never mind it being August and all, it could be March judging from the weather outside," Mrs. Sutton said, eyeing the gray English skies and pale expanse of fields stretched out behind the cottage. "I'll just make tea."

Poppy began to relax as she watched Mrs. Sutton bustle about the kitchen. The space was small but warm, with a worktable on the side, covered with plates, cups, and glasses set aside in a small cupboard. The hearth for cooking dominated the space but kept the room warm, and a medium-sized window let fresh sunlight in. The walls were white and had the look of being cleaned regularly, and a round table and chairs off to the side were where the family ate. It had the appearance of being a well-used, comfortable place, and it was here that Mrs. Sutton bid Poppy sit.

As she heated a kettle over the fire and set out a cracked china teapot and cups, Mrs. Sutton said, "I expect you're here about Geoffrey. Well, I'll tell you now, it's no use trying to convince us otherwise. He's not going back. He's already found a different church."

"Mrs. Sutton, what are you talking about? What about Geoffrey?"

Mrs. Sutton stopped. "You mean you're not here about…" Mrs. Sutton colored and turned away. A minute later she poured steaming hot water from the black iron kettle into the teapot and let it steep. Poppy watched as her hostess took out a strainer and removed a pinch of tea leaves from a small wooden tea caddy, pouring the hot water onto the leaves in her cup. The scent of green tea infused the air. Mrs. Sutton set the iron kettle back on its hook and took a seat at the wooden kitchen table beside Poppy. After a moment she removed the strainer and passed the cup to Poppy, then filled a second cup for herself.

"I thought you'd come about Geoffrey. You see…" She looked at the hot steam swirling in the air from her cup. "When Geoffrey discovered that the church money was missing, he went to the parsonage to tell Mr. Ingleby straightaway. I've always taught my boy to be honest, no matter what. But he came home in tears and said that man hadn't believed him. Called him a liar to his face."

"Oh my lord," Poppy said, "I thought my aunt came to speak with you about it. Nothing will happen to Geoffrey. Don't worry."

"She did come, and I thought all was well, but then Mr. Ingleby comes across my boy in town and…Can you believe it? That man calls him a thief. Told him to come back with the money or don't come back to church at all." Mrs. Sutton's mouth twisted into a frown. "If I had been there, I would have given that man a stern talking to, but I keep odd hours. I take in washing from the neighborhood and I do for the Elliot family up on the hill. So I don't have time to attend church, not as often as I'd like." She folded a pair of rough, hard-worked hands in her lap.

"I don't blame you. But what about Geoffrey? Is he all right?" Poppy asked.

Mrs. Sutton's gaze flicked up to her eyes. "My boy is fine now, but he wasn't then. The next day I went up to church to give that man a piece of my mind, but instead, I found him at the sweets shop in town. I told him that Geoffrey is an honest boy, not a thief. He wouldn't take any money that don't rightfully belong to him. You know what he said?"

"What?"

"Mr. Ingleby took one look at me and sneered, 'Madam, from your state of dress I can only assume that you needed the money. If you were so desperate, why did you not come to me for help? There are almshouses in Hertford. There was no need to risk your boy's immortal soul for a few pennies.'"

Poppy stared at her in horror. "My God."

"I'll never forget his words until the day I die. Not so long as I have breath in my lungs. I've never met a clergyman so rude." She blew on her steaming tea and sipped it.

"What did you do?"

"I walked away. My boy helps around town doing odd jobs, so we're all right. We do just fine without anyone's help," Mrs. Sutton sniffed.

"You know that Mr. Ingleby died," Poppy said, "he won't be troubling you anymore, or anyone else for that matter."

"Aye, I heard that. Good riddance too. That man was a blight upon this town. I've never been so glad to hear about a death." Mrs. Sutton crossed herself. "He liked his sweets too much, that one. It's no surprise to me that they were the death of him."

"Yes. I wonder, did you happen to bake anything for the competition?"

Mrs. Sutton's expression became shrewd. "Aye, I did. But you'll not be thinking I had anything to do with his death."

"Of course not. I was just wondering. He died at the competition, and I just thought of it."

Mrs. Sutton shot Poppy a glance as she drank more tea. "That's a funny question to ask. Sounds to me like you're looking for information." She snorted. "I'm not stupid."

"Mrs. Sutton I wouldn't dare to suggest—"

"You don't need to say anything. I know you. You're the reverend's daughter but you're keen on that constable, so you thought you would try to help him in his investigation. I know all about it. Do you think Geoffrey doesn't hear about what goes on in this parish? He tells me everything."

Poppy's eyes widened. "Mrs. Sutton, I—"

Mrs. Sutton gripped her chipped teacup, the hot liquid threatening to spill onto the table. "Tell me I'm wrong. That you're not trying to winkle information out of me just to get in good with that man you fancy. You should be ashamed—"

"Now wait a minute," Poppy interrupted. "It's true, I am asking questions. But that is because Miss Everly has asked me to."

"Miss Everly? Who's that?"

"She is new in town. She is Constable Dyngley's fiancée."

Now Mrs. Sutton's eyes widened. "Well, well, that is news. And she's asked you to help her? Why?"

"Constable Dyngley and I believe—" Poppy paused. "The constable and his deputy believe that one of the bakers at the contest may have tried to harm Mr. Ingleby."

"Poison? With their pudding? My word. Geoffrey didn't say a thing about that."

"Where is he? How is Geoffrey doing?"

"He's fine. Helping out at St Leonard's church in Bengeo. It's a little out of town but he don't mind. He's a good lad," Mrs. Sutton said, "but what about Miss Everly? Why does she want your help?"

"Mr. Jenkins believes—"

"Jenkins? Spiteful man. He told me Geoffrey was stealing apples from his mum's orchard and if he ever caught him, he was going to send him to the jail." Mrs. Sutton shook her head. "He's horrible. Suspects everyone. But why should Miss Everly ask you? Surely her constable can speak for her."

Poppy shrugged. "I think because she is new, and knows that Constable Dyngley trusts me. She is a friend."

"Hmph. I still don't see why she should ask you."

They sipped their tea in silence. Poppy said, "I would never believe that Geoffrey would steal. He has been so helpful to my uncle. I know if he were here right now, he would tell you himself how lucky he is to have Geoffrey helping during the service."

Mrs. Sutton gave her a hard smile. "That's kind of you, but I still don't think you should be sticking your nose where it doesn't belong. Bad things come to those who nose around where they're not wanted."

Poppy paused over her teacup. "Is that a threat?"

"Just some good advice. I'd take it and leave the questions to the authorities. What you need is to find a man, although I know it will be hard, considering." She looked pointedly at Poppy's unfashionable bonnet, years out of date, her faded brown spencer and plain white walking dress that bore grass stains at the hem. "We can't all be blessed with beauty, and you should leave that constable alone. Let him and Miss Everly be happy together."

Poppy rose, unable to stand another minute in Mrs. Sutton's now stifling kitchen. "I intend to. If you'll excuse me, I have to go. Thank you for the tea."

ON HER WALK back into town, Poppy hailed Mr. Jenkins across the road. The deputy was not best pleased to see her on an average day, but Poppy didn't care.

He frowned and stood by as she crossed the dirt road. He stood in front of The Crosskeys and scratched at his chin irritably.

"Wot you want?" he asked.

"Mr. Jenkins." She gave a tiny curtsey. "I've just been to see Mrs. Sutton."

"I don't care who you call on, girl."

"But I was asking her questions. About the murder."

He ran a hand over his eyes for a second and shook his head, then removed his dark hat and ran pudgy fingers through his thick curly hair. "Why would you do that? You're not a deputy."

"Miss Everly asked me to look into this after she became a suspect."

His face twitched in anger. "She did, did she? Well, let me tell you something right now. She has no say in what we do in this investigation, and neither do you. Stop going around putting people's backs up."

"But I was only trying to—"

"Help, I know. That's all you ever try to do," he said, in a rare bit of civility. "But the fact is you're an amateur. You don't know what you're doing. You go around asking the wrong questions without any idea of the tells or knowing what to make of it or how to put it all together."

"What?" she asked. "What do you mean by tells?"

He sighed. "People will tell you they're saying the truth, but their actions might say something different. They'll 'tell' you with their body, their manners, their reactions, whether they're being honest or not. There's more to investigating than calling on people and having tea."

Poppy colored.

"Like I thought. Now I've got to go to Mrs. Sutton and try to get information out of her. You've made my job harder for me."

Poppy's mouth opened. "But I didn't. I mean, I did call on her, but I didn't make a hash of it, I promise."

"You wouldn't know, girlie. You're so ignorant, you wouldn't know even if you did."

She frowned, her eyebrows knit angrily.

"Did you learn anything?" he asked.

"Only that her son, Geoffrey, found that the church donation money was stolen and when he reported it, Mr. Ingleby blamed him. He was rude to her and drove Geoffrey away from the church."

"Did the boy do it?"

"What, steal? No. Geoffrey is an honest boy," Poppy said.

"Not when it comes to apples." He snorted. "What about the mother?"

"No. She's too busy to go to church."

Mr. Jenkins nodded. "Right, I'll see what I can find out. Did she talk about her honey cakes?"

"Uh, no. She didn't. I tried to ask about the competition and then she got all angry and told me off." She looked away.

Mr. Jenkins cocked his head at an angle and looked at her. "What else did she say?"

"She was rude, that's all. Same as you, she told me to stop asking questions." She bit the inside of her cheek. "I think I did make her defensive."

"I bet you did. Leave the questions to me, all right?"

Poppy said nothing but looked at her leather boots, damp from walking in the wet grass. "Mr. Jenkins, do you truly suspect Miss Everly of wanting to kill Mr. Ingleby? He annoyed everyone, I think."

The deputy looked this way and that and motioned for her to walk with him. Once they were safely out of earshot of shoppers and other townspeople, he said, "I've got something on my mind, but I don't want you gossiping all over town if I tell you. I know how you ladies love to gossip."

"I wouldn't–"

He laughed. "Like I said. It's private, but... I've known Dyngley only a short while, but you get a feel for the man after a while. I respect him."

Poppy nodded, staying quiet.

"But he goes to Cambridge, then London and in two or three months is engaged to a woman I've never met. Who is she? What does she want? And how did she and Dyngley get engaged so fast?"

Poppy smiled faintly. "Perhaps they fell in love."

"Maybe. But I don't trust her. Something about her. Seems common to me."

"What do you mean? She will inherit £10,000."

He spat on the ground. "Believe that when I see it. She's common. Like calls to like, Miss Morton. Can't prove it, but I can tell you she is."

Poppy laughed.

"You don't believe me, fine. Suit yourself. But Miss Everly seems too smug for her own good. And she just happens to bake a pie in a competition where a man dies?" He shook his head. "Seems too much of a coincidence to me."

"Why should you dislike her? She seems perfectly kind," Poppy said.

"She's a stranger to town. Same as him. Who's to say they didn't know each other? The only other strangers in town are the Heyworths."

"That's my friend Jane you're talking about," Poppy said.

"Aye, and how long have you known her? A few weeks? Can you truly call her a friend?" he asked.

"Yes. We haven't known each other long but I am confident that we are good friends."

Mr. Jenkins smirked. "Good luck with that. Remember what I said. Don't go around asking any more questions. Don't want to find you dead from a poisoned pie, even if it's from a friend."

CHAPTER EIGHTEEN

POPPY'S FEET BEGAN to ache as she began to walk home. She stopped to rest on a fallen tree branch when Robert and Jane met her.

"Miss Morton," Jane said, "We have been looking for you."

Jane looked very fetching in a light purple spencer and white linen walking dress trimmed with lace, lilac-colored kid gloves, and a straw bonnet with a lavender ribbon.

Beside her, Robert looked stiff and ill at ease in a slim tan jacket, yellow waistcoat, and beige trousers. His handsome face frowned at the sight of Poppy, and he kicked a stone away with his boot. "Yes, we were just on our way to see you," Robert added, "Are you all right?"

"Yes, I have just been, well…" She relayed the story of the intruder at the parsonage.

Jane started. "An intruder. Goodness. it's like you're living in one of Mrs. Radcliffe's gothic novels."

"Are you quite all right, Miss Morton?" Robert asked.

"I'm fine. It's just my feet are still a bit sore from the broken glass." Their eyes met and Poppy smiled. Two spots of color rose in his cheeks and he looked away.

Jane snorted and sat down on the branch beside Poppy. "I wanted to invite you to accompany us to a concert."

"Oh?"

"Yes. There is to be a music concert at the assembly rooms in Hertford, isn't that exciting?"

"Do you like music, Miss Morton?" Robert asked.

"Yes, I do. Very much. When is it?"

"Tuesday next. Oh, say you'll come with us. It's our treat. If you're not otherwise engaged…" Jane said with a discerning eye.

"No, I'm free. I would be happy to join you. Let me just ask my aunt," Poppy said.

"No matter, of course, she will say yes. I have read in this morning's paper that a quartet will be performing some of Hayden's new Scottish songs. They were published in London just this month. Isn't it wonderful?"

ON TUESDAY EVENING, Poppy dressed in her second best, which meant it was not her finest, but almost. For an evening concert, she wore a light pink linen dress with short puff sleeves and a high waist gathered at the bosom. Their maid, Betsey, had artfully arranged Poppy's hair in a braided bun at the top of her head and threaded a ribbon through the braid. The result looked pretty without seeming pretentious, which was just what Poppy needed, for she had no jewels of her own.

Armed with her dancing slippers and light linen gloves, she was ready to go. Downstairs she waited with her aunt in the sitting room until the Heyworths' curricle pulled up outside. Poppy saw Robert descend and turned to go.

"Will I need a shawl?" Poppy fretted.

"It's August, of course not. Go, go," her aunt said, shooing her toward the entrance.

"What about a reticule?"

Aunt Rachel pressed a half-crown into her hand. "Not that you'll need it. Now go." She surveyed Poppy. "Betsey did a marvelous job with your hair."

"Thank you," Poppy said as there was a knock at the front door. She slipped the coin into her glove and hurried to open the door.

There stood Robert, looking very comely in a dark overcoat, brown silk waistcoat, and expertly tied white cravat. His hair had been combed and freshly shaven, he looked very handsome indeed. At the sight of his smile upon her, Poppy felt a little thrill and curtseyed, her gaze falling to the floor.

As she looked up, Robert smiled at her. "Good evening, Miss Morton. You look very fine this evening." He extended an arm. "Shall we?"

Poppy took his arm and let herself be escorted to his curricle, where Jane waved. "Hello!" She scooted aside to let Poppy in. "Come, come, we can't be late. And oh, I love your hair. Did your maid fix that style?"

No sooner had Poppy sat down did Robert take a seat across from her and Jane and closed the door. The driver set off at a steady pace and they were off. Jane kept up a steady chatter as the barouche flew down the dusty road and on into town, passing by other carriages and coaches. The cool fresh air was a relief from the heat of the day and soon the barouche came to a stop before the assembly rooms. Robert alighted first, helping down Jane, then Poppy. Was it her imagination or did he hold her hand longer than was necessary?

Robert paid the entry fee and escorted Jane inside, leaving Poppy to follow them. Inside the building candlelight shone, and Poppy followed her companions through a small corridor and into a large room. Normally open for dancing, now the event space had been turned into a small theatre, with a smart pianoforte at the front, neighbored by two additional chairs and music stands.

Poppy stood observing the room as Jane and Robert made their way to the front, when she heard, "Miss Morton, what a surprise. I didn't expect to see you here."

Poppy turned around and curtseyed. "Miss Everly."

Tonight Caroline looked especially fetching in a light lavender silk gown with embroidered flowers on the sleeves and hem, with light purple silk gloves to match. Her hair was artfully arranged like a Greek muse, similar to Poppy's, except she had the benefit of snowdrop pearl earrings and a dainty strand of pearls adorning her neck. Poppy felt like a poor cousin beside her.

"You're here for the concert?" Caroline asked, eyeing Poppy's attire.

"Yes." Poppy spied Constable Dyngley approaching and nodded to him.

"Miss Morton," he bowed.

"You're not here alone, are you?" Caroline's voice carried.

"She is sitting with us." Robert appeared by Poppy's side. He ignored Caroline and said, "Shall we?"

Poppy gave him a grateful smile and took his arm, allowing him to lead her away from Caroline's watchful gaze. Jane looked behind and waved, patting at the seat next to her. Poppy sat down and realized she was now safely ensconced between the Heyworth siblings.

Robert fetched them a concert program to share, and within minutes the musicians entered the room, ignoring the audience with diva-like airs.

The concert began and Poppy felt happiness spread through her chest; she loved the lively Scottish airs. The playful tunes made her want to tap her feet to the music, and she took pleasure in the golden warmth of the room lit by dozens of candles, the polite and genteel company, and the kindness of her new friends to invite her along to a pleasant evening.

"Do you play the pianoforte, Miss Morton?" Robert whispered. "I have a particular liking for the instrument."

"I'm afraid not," Poppy whispered back, aware of how close they sat.

Thank goodness for the bounds of decorum. She could smell Robert's strong cologne and risked a glance back over her shoulder. Caroline and Dyngley sat some rows behind them, and upon meeting her gaze, Caroline smiled sweetly at her and placed a hand on Dyngley's arm.

Poppy's heart beat loudly in her chest as she returned the

smile and turned back around. She sat here, at a musical concert with her friends, dolled up in her second-best dress. What an enjoyable evening to be had!

And yet her mind would not settle. She could not help but think about the death of Mr. Ingleby. He had been a thorn in their sides, to be sure, and had certainly disrupted the peace of their household. She personally disliked him and if the rumors were to be believed, he had returned the favor and then some. But someone had killed him, and for that, she could not be at peace until she had found the guilty party.

In the soft candlelight, she felt herself get swept away by the upbeat Scottish tunes of the pianist, violinist, and bass player and began to relax. Her slippered feet rested against the floor and she felt her toes tap along to the lively beat, and before she knew it, she began to go over the facts of the investigation. So far she had spoken with Mrs. Alleyn and her scorned daughter, as well as Mrs. Sutton, while Lady Cameron, Caroline, and Jane weren't suspects. That left Mrs. Walker and Mrs. Grant.

Robert murmured something in her ear.

"Pardon?" Poppy asked, distracted.

"I said, the music is nowhere near as lovely as you." He smiled.

Poppy swallowed, feeling her cheeks warm. "Oh. Thank you. That's very kind."

"I'm not being kind. It's the truth," he said, brushing her hand with his.

Poppy frowned. That was very forward of him. It was almost taking a liberty, and with his sister present! She ignored him and looked straight ahead, focusing on the music.

He pressed his hand closer to hers and she asked, "Might I see the program?"

"Of course." Robert plucked it from his sister's hands and gave it to her.

Jane hissed, "Oi, I was reading that."

Robert replied, "Miss Morton wanted to see it."

E . L . J O H N S O N

"Thank you," Poppy whispered and poured over its double-sided page, staring at the printed words without properly seeing them. She waited for her heart to calm down, and let out a little breath. At least it gave her hands something to do.

"Do you like the music?" Robert asked.

"Oh yes, very much." Poppy replied.

"Ssshhh." A lady in the row ahead turned around and frowned at them.

Robert snorted while Poppy smiled and held the program on her lap. She was grateful when the intermission came and rose from her seat as soon as the clapping finished. As people rose and mingled out in the aisles of chairs, Robert asked, "Miss Morton, where are you going?"

"Oh just for a drink, I'm thirsty."

"I'll go with you," he said, making to follow her.

Jane shot Poppy a knowing smile. "I'll have a drink too, Robert."

Poppy smiled and with Robert fast on her heels, she joined the general assembly and helped herself to a glass of wine from a passing footman.

"It is very good, is it not?" Robert asked her, taking one himself.

"Yes," Poppy agreed, without knowing what she was agreeing to.

Their eyes met, and Poppy felt heat within his brown-eyed gaze. She looked away, at a loss as to what to do. She felt traitorous; happy to be desired and liked, but unhappy at not feeling any return affection. And worse, unkind for knowing she would have to speak to Jane and put a stop to it, which might ruin their friendship. She had few friends, and even fewer people she could count on.

"You look very pensive," Robert commented. "I hope my company hasn't put you out of sorts."

Poppy laughed. "Not at all. I was just thinking about—"

"Oh Miss Morton, just the person I was looking for." Caroline and Dyngley approached them. Caroline laid a light hand on Poppy's upper arm. "Come, I must speak with you this instant."

Poppy looked at her in surprise and gave Robert an apologetic smile. "Sorry."

Robert looked unhappy, especially when Caroline pressed Poppy's empty wine glass into his hands. She smiled sweetly at him and said, "You must forgive my selfishness, but we have womanly things to discuss."

Robert blushed and looked ill at ease, which was precisely the effect that Caroline had intended. She led Poppy away to a far-off corner of the room. Once she felt they had enough space between them and the concertgoers, Caroline turned Poppy around so her back was to the audience and said, "There, now you don't have to look at anyone you don't want to. I'm so glad I took you from him. You don't mind, do you? It's just that he had that mad look in his eye, and you looked so uncomfortable."

Poppy smiled. "Was it obvious?"

"A bit. But only because I recognized that look on your face. I've worn it myself, many times. I do hope you'll let him down gently, although I suspect he's not one to leave without good reason."

Poppy swallowed. "What was it you wished to speak with me about?"

Caroline patted her finely arranged hair. "I have made some enquiries about your mother."

Poppy froze. "And?"

"Nothing. I can't figure it out. It's annoying me now. Have you any idea where she might have lived?"

"No, no idea. But I will. I recently found some letters from her, and—"

"Oh yes, I heard about that. Dyngley told me. Such a dear, and so trustworthy. He keeps all my secrets," Caroline said.

Poppy's smile froze on her face. Dyngley had told Caroline about her mother's private letters?

Caroline said, "Oh don't worry. He knows we are good

friends. He only mentioned it because I was saying how frustrated I was, that I hadn't found anything about her."

"Ah, of course."

"Now, what are you going to do about Mr. Heyworth?"

Poppy smiled. "I don't know. I think very highly of him."

"Censure indeed," Caroline said, eyeing over her shoulder, "But why do you dislike him?"

Poppy said, "I don't dislike him. But I hold no affection for him, aside from that of a friend. And I am friends with his sister, so I don't want to ruin my relationship with her."

"You have said quite enough, madam," Robert said behind her.

Poppy whirled around. "Mr. Heyworth, I…"

Red in the face, Robert turned on his heel, marching stiffly back to his sister.

Caroline snickered as Poppy stared after him. "Caroline, why didn't you say anything? You knew he was right behind me?"

"And ruin the fun? That was the most amusement I've had in ages, and besides, he deserved it. I saw the way he was acting toward you as if he owned you. It was wrong. I was doing you a favor."

"But what I said… it wasn't intended for him to hear." Poppy blushed with embarrassment.

"He'll live. It's not like he's never been rejected before. Now you don't have to suffer the agony of breaking his heart."

"It's not how I would have wanted to tell him," Poppy said, frowning.

Caroline shrugged. "Well, now you don't have to worry about it."

Poppy left her and went after him, when she was waylaid by Jane. Jane said, "Whatever did you say to Robert? He's furious and wants to leave."

"I… he overheard me talking and I'm afraid I spoke out of turn."

Jane's face fell. "What did you say?"

"I hold much admiration for him, but I worry he has affection for me."

"Well of course he does. We are great friends," Jane said.

Poppy's face burned, if that was at all possible. "I mean as more than a friend."

"You mean you don't care for him? I thought after the picnic and the contest and seeing you walk together, you seemed so encouraging," Jane said.

"I only meant to be friendly."

"Oh," Jane looked at her shoes. "Well, he's very out of sorts at the moment. I think he must have seen or heard something that upset him, so I'll have to go. I hope you don't mind making your own way home." She left without curtseying.

Caroline appeared by her elbow. "What did she say?"

Poppy ignored the smirk tugging at Caroline's mouth. "They had to go."

"Just like that? No explanation whatsoever? How rude." Caroline's eyes danced.

"No, not at all. They received some unhappy news and needed to leave."

Caroline's mouth dropped open, and she quickly covered it with her mouth. "I cannot believe it."

Poppy looked at her miserably. Her friends, gone. And it was all her fault.

"Some friends they are, that they would leave you like that. And you in such nice dancing shoes as well. How are you supposed to get home?" Caroline asked.

"I don't know." Poppy bit the inside of her cheek.

"Who's going home?" Dyngley appeared, holding two glasses of wine.

Caroline took one and drank, leaving Dyngley to kindly offer the second to Poppy.

She waved it away, shaking her head.

"Miss Morton, is something the matter?" he asked.

"Her friends have abandoned her," Caroline said. "It's cruelly unfair. I cannot believe they would be so unkind, but then what can you expect from such people?"

Dyngley glanced at her and said, "Your friends left you here?"

"Yes, they had to go," Poppy said, avoiding his eyes.

"Dyngley, it is monstrously unfair, the way they have treated her." Caroline turned to Poppy. "How are you to get home? You can't walk. You'll be attacked by highwaymen. No, it won't do at all. Dyngley, you must take her home. Or at least see her to a carriage."

Poppy lifted her gaze and met his own enquiring one.

"May I see you home, Miss Morton?" he asked.

"I..." She looked at Miss Everly. "No, I wouldn't dream of disrupting your evening. I will be fine."

"Are you certain? It's no trouble," he said, his eyes looking into hers.

"I am fine, truly. I will just hire a carriage to take me home." She lied through her teeth.

"If you're sure," he said, his eyebrows furrowing.

"Of course I am. Now, don't let me keep you. The concert is about to start," she said lightly.

Caroline took Dyngley's arm and chatted to him as Poppy made a swift exit from the room.

Once in the corridor, she looked around. Footmen walked here and there, and well-dressed women of different ages strolled by, taking in the fine surroundings. She stood off to one side near the entrance, not sure what to do when someone bumped into her. "Oof!"

Poppy whirled around. There stood Louisa Alleyn, looking pale in a light gray dress. "Oh, I'm sorry, Miss Morton. I wasn't paying attention to where I was going."

"Miss Alleyn, are you all right?"

"I have a headache, and the room is so warm. I felt faint," she admitted, holding her right hand to the side of her head. "It is silly, is it not? I know that so many young women faint in order to get attention, but I can't stand the idea..." She fainted dead away.

Poppy stooped to catch her and said, "Help!"

People stopped and turned to stare.

Poppy struggled to keep Louisa upright; she was heavy. "She's fainted. Someone help me…"

A footman came forward when Poppy said, "Call the doctor. See if Doctor Wilson is at his surgery."

Poppy laid Louisa on the ground, and people stood around, watching them. Poppy knelt by her, holding her hand.

Miraculously, Dr. Wilson appeared at her side a minute later, dressed in finery. "What's happened here?" he asked, "Someone call for a doctor?"

"Dr. Wilson," Poppy said, "She's fainted. She said she had a headache and then collapsed."

"Right." He turned to the group of audience members standing over them. "Back up, the girl needs air."

He knelt in his charcoal gray evening suit and took Louisa's hand from Poppy, delicately feeling along the inside of her wrist. He then took out a smart silver pocket watch from within his dark waistcoat, and looked at it, counting with his lips.

"What are you doing?" Poppy asked.

"Taking her pulse. She's a little thready." He dropped her hand and looked at Poppy. "Miss… What's her name?"

"Alleyn. Louisa Alleyn," Poppy supplied.

"What's happened here?" Dyngley and Caroline pushed through the crowd and stopped, staring.

"Is she dead? Has the killer come back?" Caroline asked, "Poppy, what are you doing there?"

Dyngley shot her a look before asking, "Doctor?"

"The girl has fainted, that is all." Dr. Wilson muttered. "Please, everyone back away. Go back to your seats."

Poppy refused to budge from her spot, and said, "Louisa? Miss Alleyn? Miss Alleyn."

"Have you got any sal volatile?" Dr. Wilson asked.

"What?"

"Smelling salts," he said.

"No."

"What about perfume? Are you wearing perfume?"

"I… No." Poppy admitted.

Caroline snorted and Dyngley said, "Come away, let's give them some space."

Louisa's eyes fluttered open. "Oh. What has happened? Miss Morton?" She blinked. "Why am I on the floor?"

"Stay where you are, Miss Alleyn," Dr. Wilson said. "It's not wise to move after you've had a fall."

"I fell?" Louisa's eyes widened.

"No, you fainted," Poppy told her.

Louisa looked around and saw she had acquired an audience. She blushed and said, "Oh. Who are you?"

"Dr. Wilson, at your service," he said, "how are you feeling?"

"I'm all right." She lifted a hand to her hair. Her finely coiled hair had now tumbled and strands hung askew.

"Is she sick?" Caroline asked.

Dr. Wilson said loudly, "She's fine, you can all return to the concert," he told the people standing there. He took Louisa by the hand and supported her back, helping her sit up when her mother came running from the main room.

She pushed past the footmen and men and women standing there and said, "Oh, Louisa!"

Louisa swallowed. "It is all right, Mama, I am fine." She reddened, seeing the impropriety of the good doctor's hands on her person. "I am perfectly well, thanks to Dr. Wilson." She smiled at him.

Mrs. Alleyn was no fool; she took one look at the doctor and Louisa and said, "Thank you, doctor. I don't know what we would have done without you here."

Dr. Wilson blushed. "Yes, well." He tugged nervously at his cravat. "I'm glad I was here. To help, I mean."

"Thank you," Louisa said, holding out her hand to him.

Dr. Wilson helped her to her feet, and tangles of her brown

hair fell into her face. She mumbled, "Oh, my hair."

"That's all right. Allow me." He pulled a hairpin out of her messy style and her long locks tumbled down her back.

"Oh no, he's ruined your lovely hair," Mrs. Alleyn said.

"On the contrary, I think it looks rather pretty," Dr. Wilson said, oblivious to the beaming smile Louisa cast on him. Seeing the predatory look of Mrs. Alleyn however, he coughed and said, "Excuse me. I should return to my surgery. Do call on me tomorrow and I'll check your head. Make sure there are no more fainting spells." He bowed. "Good evening." He bowed again, earning amused glances from the people there.

Poppy said, "Are you all right, Miss Alleyn?"

Louisa watched the good doctor disappear out the front door. "Oh yes, I'm fine. I don't know what came over me." She wandered back to the concert with her mother, looking back from time to time.

Poppy met Dr. Wilson outside, where he was taking a pinch of snuff. He shut the small silver snuffbox and rubbed his nose. "Ah, Miss Morton. Needed some fresh air too? You're not feeling faint, are you?"

Poppy grinned. "No, doctor." She looked around, but only recognized footmen and attendants, without a free carriage in sight.

"Are you waiting for someone?" he asked.

"No, not exactly."

He gave her a curious look, then his young face broke into a smile. "Let me guess. You're waiting for your beau. He's promised to meet you here and you've slipped away from your party to see him. Am I right?"

Poppy laughed. "Not at all. I have no beau."

He smiled. "Well, then, if you are not waiting for a beau, what are you doing outside?"

"Umm… that is, you see… I was…"

"Miss Morton," he said, "It's not safe for a young woman to go about unchaperoned. Is your aunt inside?"

"No, that is... "She looked down at her shoes. "I need a ride home. My party had to leave unexpectedly..."

"And they left you here? Alone? That is... unfortunate. Allow me to see you home."

"No it's fine, I am perfectly happy to walk."

Dr. Wilson laughed. "Miss Morton, you forget that I know where you live. Do you honestly mean to walk across town in your best dress? Your shoes alone would get ruined. Please, let me escort you back to the parsonage. Your party may be ungracious, but I promise I won't be."

Poppy appraised him.

He ran a hand through his ginger hair. "Please allow me the honor, Miss Morton. I don't see any free carriages about for hire, and it is too far to walk. Besides, you wouldn't want to get carried away by a highwayman, would you?"

"No, but you are teasing me and that's very unfair." She smiled.

He grinned and called a footman to bring his cart around. Once it arrived, he climbed into the driver's seat and offered a hand down to Poppy. She accepted it and took the seat next to him.

"I know it's probably not the carriage you were expecting, but..." He shrugged.

"I didn't expect anything. To be honest I rather thought the evening would end differently."

"Oh? How so?" he asked, but Poppy was distracted.

At the assembly rooms' entrance stood Louisa Alleyn, who watched her and Dr Wilson, her face a picture of ill-temper. Her pretty eyes narrowed at the sight of them together, and as she locked gazes with Poppy, her expression soured. Poppy tried to smile kindly at her and wave, but her attempts at friendliness went unrewarded.

"Come on," Dr. Wilson said as he gently flicked the reins and the dark horse started off, its strong hooves striking the ground. As they turned around the corner of the building, Poppy stared.

Either her eyes were deceiving her or there stood Caroline Everly, locked in an embrace with a man who was not Constable Dyngley.

CHAPTER NINETEEN

P OPPY SAT QUIETLY through the carriage ride as Dr. Wilson took her home, the cool night breeze offering a welcome respite from her heated thoughts. As he drove the carriage with a deft hand, he occasionally glanced at her but didn't speak. Neither spoke of what had happened. Upon dropping her off safely at the parsonage, he reminded her to stop by the surgery in the next day or two so that he might have a last look at her feet, and bid her goodnight.

Poppy sailed inside the parsonage and straight to bed, pleased that her aunt kept early hours and was already asleep.

THE NEXT DAY in conversation she glossed over the details of the concert, returned the half-crown to her aunt, and that afternoon, called at the surgery in town.

The doctor's housekeeper let her in, and she followed the older woman through a corridor, past the room with the large worktable where she had observed Mr. Ingleby's corpse. Repressing a shudder, she was brought to a comfortable study. The room had a small smoky hearth that needed cleaning, many shelves of medical texts, a squat, sturdy black leather bag on the floor next to a large writing desk, where sat Dr. Wilson. He waved hello and bid her sit on a low cushioned seat and remove her boots and cotton stockings while he finished writing a letter.

Away from prying eyes, she felt more comfortable in his presence, even if it felt curiously inappropriate to have a man about to touch her feet.

He took no notice of her moral qualms and pulled up his chair, taking her left foot and resting it on his knee. He lightly felt the foot and examined it, before saying, "It looks very well and has healed nicely, although I should warn you to take care not to walk barefoot on glass again."

"Yes, doctor. And thank you for the ride home last night. I'm sorry to have disrupted your evening," she said.

"Not at all, Miss Morton. I had heard my fill of music for one evening. And what kind of a man would I be if I didn't go around rescuing damsels in distress, eh?" He grinned and lightly removed her foot from his knee, before examining the right foot. Once satisfied with her progress, he scooted his chair back to a more appropriate distance. "I'm glad to see you are in good health and if you'll forgive me for saying so, I know of someone else who will be pleased to hear that you are well."

That shocked Poppy. "I beg your pardon?"

"It always amazes me, the subtle signs of affection that go unnoticed by the young women of today. Haven't you noticed a certain young man's fondness for you?"

Poppy laughed. "Dr. Wilson, you are as bad as my aunt."

"I do enjoy a good gossip, but I promise you that for any man with eyes, it's clear to see. You have captured his attention and I for one like you the better for it. He is a capital fellow."

Poppy glanced at him and began to put her stocking back on. "That is very kind of you to say, but I only admire him as a friend, nothing more. I don't think we are suited to one another."

"I think you are being unkind to yourself. I know you must think the odds of such a union between you to be impossible, what with him being engaged and all but–"

"What? Engaged?" Poppy stared at him. "Who are you talking about?"

"Who are you talking of?" He stared back at her.

There came a sharp knock at the front door of the surgery, and the aged housekeeper went to answer it. Seconds later she announced, "Dr. Wilson, there's a Mrs. Alleyn and Miss Alleyn to see you."

The ladies froze when they saw Dr. Wilson and Poppy pulling on her stockings. Louisa's face flooded with color as she stared at the scene. "Miss Morton, what are you doing here?"

Poppy began to pull on her stiff walking boot. "I…"

"I was examining Miss Morton's feet after she became injured. Thank you for coming, Miss Morton," Dr. Wilson said. Turning to the ladies, he asked, "Now, what seems to be the problem?"

Mrs. Alleyn came forward, ignoring Poppy. "No problem, Doctor, we just wanted to thank you for the extraordinary kindness you showed toward Louisa last night. And to thank you, I wondered if you might like to come for dinner tomorrow evening?"

"It would be my pleasure. What time shall I come by?"

"Six o'clock would be perfect," Mrs. Alleyn said, and Louisa beamed at him.

"Excellent. Til then." He nodded to them.

Louisa shot Poppy a triumphant look and walked away.

Once the Alleyns had gone, Dr. Wilson turned to Poppy, who had just finished lacing up her boot. She asked him, "Doctor, who were you talking about before they came in?"

"I'll tell you if you tell me first, why were you in such a hurry to leave the assembly rooms last night? Did your party actually leave you?" he asked.

She swallowed and rested her hands on her knees, smoothing her dress back over her legs. "Mr. Heyworth heard me talking about him and got annoyed and then his sister went after him. They heard me saying something I'd meant to keep private, and now…" Poppy gripped the folds of her faded blue walking dress and sniffed. "Now I've gone and ruined it, and Miss Heyworth was my close friend. She might have been my only friend."

Dr. Wilson frowned. "I see. Well, that is sad, certainly. But it was not Mr. Heyworth I was speaking of. I meant our own constable, Constable Dyngley."

Poppy glanced at him. "You're joking. He is engaged to Miss Caroline Everly."

"Perhaps. But it would not surprise me if he found a reason to end their engagement."

Poppy blushed. "I'm sure I don't know what you mean."

Dr. Wilson snorted. "Never play cards, Miss Morton. You are a terrible liar."

She rose. "Excuse me, I must be going." She curtseyed and left. But as she walked out of the surgery and blinked in the midday sunshine, her mind went wild. Was Caroline seeing another man? She was certain that the man Caroline had been embracing outside was not Constable Dyngley. If that was true, did she owe it to him as a friend to tell him his fiancée was being unfaithful? Perhaps most pressing of all, did he fancy her?

A shadow passed over her eyes, and Louisa Alleyn stepped into view. Her normally kind brown eyes were flinty, and her pleasant mouth had hardened into a firm line. "Miss Morton, a word."

"Of course." Poppy stood aside as Louisa walked alongside her, although it felt more like a march.

"It has not escaped me that you have been spending time with Dr. Wilson," Louisa said.

"Yes, but only because of my foot."

"And pray, what is wrong with your foot?" Louisa asked.

"I stepped on some broken glass when I was chasing an intruder out of my home. I'm surprised you haven't heard about it."

Louisa blinked. "An intruder? I declare, the lengths you go to in order to get a man's attention. If I didn't know better, I would think that you had fabricated the whole thing."

"Excuse me?" Poppy said.

"I've seen the way you act around men. You're witty and

smart, and everyone around thinks it's so charming. But let me tell you, Miss Everly won't appreciate you sniffing around her man, and I don't like it either."

"I beg your pardon?" Poppy stared.

Louisa was in full tilt. Her face heated with blooms of crimson upon her normally pale cheeks, and her brown eyes flashed. "Your behavior in the company of men is overly familiar and not at all genteel. You act as if you are like one of them, and can solve a crime, when you're nothing but a poor clergyman's niece, with no connections, and a busybody at that."

"Why I never… that is to say I mean, I would never—" Poppy sputtered, struck by Louisa's sharp tongue.

"Miss Alleyn, how uncharitable can you be? First coming after Poppy for her injury and now suggesting she is after your doctor?" Jane Heyworth stepped into view. "The entire world knows that he's besotted with you, so why are you plaguing poor Poppy when all she was doing was having him look after her injuries?"

"Well, what am I supposed to think? Dr Wilson saved me after a fall and then goes riding off with her at night. What excuse did you give your party last night at the assembly rooms for leaving? That's what I want to know," Louisa said.

Jane turned pink.

"And as to her so-called injuries, she could have made it all up." Louisa eyed Poppy.

"I didn't," Poppy said.

"She says she didn't. I believe her. And after all the nice things she's said about you to the good doctor, this is how you thank her?" Jane scoffed.

Louisa's face grew redder and her gaze fell to the ground.

"Now will you excuse us? Poppy and I have secret affairs to discuss." Jane took Poppy by the arm and said over her shoulder, "And believe me, none of it has to do with a doctor."

Louisa stared after them as Jane led Poppy away.

ONCE THEY WERE safely down the main road and away from Louisa's prying eyes and sharp opinions, Poppy said, "Thank you."

"Oh, don't thank me. I've not forgiven you yet for speaking so rudely about Robert at the concert." Jane whirled and tapped Poppy in the shoulder with a gloved finger. "How could you? You hurt him so much. You know he fancies you."

Poppy's face fell. "I didn't mean to. I was just speaking with Miss Everly and then he was right behind me, and she didn't say a word."

"That's hardly better. You're basically saying that if you'd known he was there then you wouldn't have spoken so to his face." Jane frowned, her eyes full of hurt. "I thought we were friends."

"We are."

"And I thought you and Robert had an understanding," Jane said, her gaze burning into Poppy's.

"You are mistaken. There is no understanding."

"Robert was so embarrassed. He thought your words were cruel and unkind. He could hardly bear to look at you after that, and neither could I."

"I'm sorry," Poppy said, "I do like him—"

Jane stopped her with an upheld hand. "Don't perjure yourself more than you have already. Robert and I thought that out of this town of gossips, snobs, and even a murderous baker, you were a voice of sense. I should have known better."

Poppy frowned. True friends were hard to come by. "Miss Heyworth, I swear, I didn't mean your brother any unkindness at the concert. I loved coming with you both, and it was a pleasure to be there, with you. I'm sorry that I hurt Robert. It was unkind, but I never meant to hurt him."

Jane's shoulders slumped and she said, "Walk with me a little?"

Poppy agreed, and the girls trod along the main road in town, past the shops, and then across the road and past some others.

Jane let out a little sigh. "I'm sorry we left you at the assembly rooms last night. It was heartless and if we hadn't been thinking of ourselves and Robert's wounded pride then we would never have abandoned you like that. I'm assuming the doctor escorted you home?"

Poppy nodded.

"After we left, Robert felt guilty about leaving you and came back to look for you, but you'd already gone." She pursed her lips and looked at Poppy. "The fact is that Robert has done this before."

"What do you mean?"

"He loses his heart so easily and gets hurt by young women. He is a kind man, any girl would be lucky to have him—" she glanced at Poppy. "But I am protective of him, especially as he gets hurt so often. When I saw that he fancied you, and I liked you, I thought that maybe… You two might make a go of it."

Poppy gave her a wan smile. "I'm sorry."

Jane said, "I know. I probably should have warned you, but then he was so excited and so keen, especially when he made that pie."

"What?" Poppy stopped. "What pie? Do you mean…Robert made your entry at the competition? The raspberry trifle?"

"Yes. I thought you knew. I can bake, but this time he wanted to do it. He loves his sweets," Jane said. "I admit, I was surprised, but he was so keen. He begged me not to say a word. I suspected it was his passions run away with him again."

"Again?"

Jane had the grace to blush. "He thought he was defending you, I think. Or rather, I think that's how he saw it. You see…" She aimed a kick at a pebble and missed. "I don't know why I'm telling you all this, especially when I'm supposed to be angry with you. I think it's just that I want you to know what he did for you, for your honor."

"My honor?" Poppy repeated.

"Yes. We had called at Mrs. Walker's, as she lives nearby, and has lately come to visit father and give him medicine. She's cheaper than the doctor, you know. Well, when we came for tea, Mr. Ingleby was also there, and he was talking about you and your aunt."

Poppy stiffened. "Oh."

"He called you a born spinster and said your aunt was the rudest, most ungracious woman he'd ever met. He said that he couldn't bear to stay under the same roof as two women who—" Jane paused. "Sorry. Suffice to say, he did not speak well of you both."

"So I gathered." Poppy kicked the pebble into the dusty dirt road.

"Mr. Ingleby had come to see Mrs. Walker because of his pains, and she gave him a rhubarb tea for excessive wind." She grinned. "So once he left, Mrs. Walker rolled her eyes and told us what a horrible man he was."

"Then why would she entertain him?"

"She's a widow. She sells her pills and tinctures and he pays her. If it weren't for the money, she wouldn't open her door to him."

"But your brother..." Poppy prompted.

"Oh yes. Robert asked if she had any laxatives." She giggled. "She said she did and gave him some rhubarb powder. She said if it was truly bad, then to purchase some calcined magnesia from an apothecary."

"Right. So Robert has some digestive problems." Poppy's face burst into a grin and she covered her mouth. "Sorry, I know I shouldn't laugh."

"Oh, I do too. But he doesn't. He didn't buy it for himself," Jane said.

"For your father?"

"No." Jane grinned.

"Your mother?"

"Nope." Jane laughed and whispered, "For Mr. Ingleby."

"No." Poppy's eyes widened.

"He put it in the raspberry trifle, the whole lot of it. Mixed it in the custard layer and dusted it on top. No matter which piece you'd try, you would need the privy later for sure."

Poppy's mouth dropped open.

"So you see, I wouldn't be too harsh on Robert. He was only doing what he thought was best, and he was in his way, defending your honor." Jane shrugged. "I hope you won't think less of him."

POPPY WAS CLEARLY forgiven for her gaffe, for she received a note from Jane to call on her the following afternoon. But when she called at the house, she was met by Robert, who looked unhappy to see her. Avoiding her eye, he told her that Jane was in fact in town.

But as she turned to go, he followed her outside their dwelling and touched his hat. "Forgive me, I would escort you, but I have urgent business to attend to." He hurried away, his face red.

Poppy's shoulders sagged as she watched him go. Clearly, she was not forgiven by the entire Heyworth family.

She sought out Jane in the sweets shop and saw her through the window, chatting amiably with a young man. A smile came to Poppy's face, for it was Colin Barton, the handsome young man that had caught her eye from before, and who had helped them carry the baskets in the garden once Mr. Ingleby had fallen at the picnic. And yet something about him looked odd, but she could not place it.

She walked on to the carpenter's to discuss arrangements for Mr. Ingleby's coffin. His funeral was to be Tuesday, once she had paid the next available minister to conduct the service and hire a gravedigger. Just talking about the details of his internment felt morbid, and as she walked out into the sunlight, the day's colors felt muted, as if she looked out from beneath a veil or shroud.

She began walking down the main road when a familiar face stepped into her line of sight. "Constable," she said with a smile.

"Miss Morton." He bowed.

"How are you getting on in your investigation?" she asked.

"I might ask you the same thing. How is the young lady?"

"I beg your pardon?" she said.

"The young woman who fainted at the concert. I trust she is all right now?"

"Oh, you mean Miss Alleyn. Yes, she is very well."

"I am glad to hear it."

She caught his eye, and he tilted his head. "You know something. What is it?" he asked.

She smiled. "I believe we can cross the Heyworths off our list of suspects."

"And why is that? Tell me you have proof," he said.

"Jane admitted to me that she didn't prepare the raspberry trifle they entered into the contest, her brother did."

"So we need to look into her brother. What's his name?"

"Robert Heyworth. And no, you don't," she relayed the story Jane had told her.

Dyngley steepled his hands and rested the tips of his fingers against his mouth. "Well, it is obvious." He looked her square in the eye. "You are a charmer, Miss Morton."

"What? No." A blush crept up her cheeks and she averted her gaze.

Dyngley laughed. "No doubt about it, you are. Otherwise why else would men be doctoring puddings in your honor? The man clearly thought he would have his revenge on Mr. Ingleby for sullying your good name."

"You are teasing me, Constable." Poppy laughed.

"It is what I do." His dark eyes danced.

"And yet my charms don't work on everyone." She pointed out.

"Oh no? And pray tell, who has defied your charms so far? I shall hunt them out and tell them it is inevitable. It will be only a matter of time before they fall under your spell."

"You make it sound like I am a witch," she said.

"I am sure there are good witches throughout history somewhere. But come now, you artfully deflected my question. Who is the man who has captured your eye?" he teased.

She blushed redder. "I am sure there is no such person."

"You do make for a terrible liar, Miss Morton. I shall endeavor to always play cards against you, for I know I will always win."

She made a wry face at him. "I shall not tell you anything, for I know you will not keep my secrets. You have proven that already."

His smile faded. "What do you mean?"

Her voice grew quiet, and her face felt hot. "When you told Miss Everly about my finding the hidden letters from my mother, in my uncle's study."

"But I didn't. I swear I didn't speak about it," he said.

"But you must have. She knew all about it."

"I tell you I didn't. You must be mistaken. I would not betray your confidence, especially in a private moment like that," he said, all semblance of gaiety gone.

She frowned at him and received an equally unhappy frown in return. She looked into his eyes and said, "I'm not sure I believe you. Caroline told me herself that you had told her."

"I told her no such thing. I would remember if I had shared something private about a friend."

She felt defeated, and her shoulders slumped. She raised her head, looked him in the eye, and said, "Then I don't know what to believe."

"Miss Morton," he started.

"Do excuse me. I see Mr. Jenkins coming and would not keep you." She curtseyed and walked away.

CHAPTER TWENTY

D YNGLEY FELT OUT of sorts. His exchange with Poppy had left him discomfited, and as he watched her walk away, his dark brows knit together in a frown.

He joined Jenkins in the local tavern and relayed what Poppy had shared. Jenkins removed his weathered dark hat and scratched his curly hair. "Say what you want about that girl, she gets results. I'd not spoken to the Heyworths yet."

Dyngley nodded. "That leaves Mrs. Grant and Mrs. Walker to speak with."

Jenkins cleared his throat. "And your fiancée, Constable. Don't forget about her."

"She didn't do it." Dyngley's tone was curt.

"It might look bad if we don't speak to her," Jenkins pointed out.

"From what she tells me, you already did."

Jenkins shrugged, unabashed. "She didn't like me asking questions."

Dyngley scratched the light fuzz on his chin. He needed a shave, but he had more pressing things on his mind. "Keep asking questions. Someone wanted to kill Mr. Ingleby, we just need to know why."

Dyngley turned and walked out of the tavern, blinking in the afternoon sun. He was walking past the local hospital when he ran into Dr. Wilson. "Ah, Doctor." He touched his hat.

"Constable. How goes your investigation?"

"Well enough."

"Hah. By which I'm guessing you mean not well at all," Dr. Wilson surmised.

"Is it obvious?"

"You frown when you're perplexed, and you have a faraway look about you. I've seen that look in a few of my patients when they have a problem they cannot solve. Although normally it's lighter burdens than who killed a parson," he said cheerfully.

Dyngley smiled. He liked Dr. Wilson. The man was young but experienced for his age, with a smart head on his shoulders. "For a man who knows there is a killer in town, you don't seem that bothered by it."

Dr. Wilson shrugged. "It's part of the job. I try to save lives, but people die every day. There's not much I can do about that."

"Who do you think did it?"

The doctor ran a hand along the side of his face. "Someone who either made a mistake, and is too embarrassed to speak up. Or someone who knew exactly what they're doing, and had a bone to pick with Mr. Ingleby. I'll tell you what is odd."

"What's that?"

"When my surgery was broken into, it was when we had Mr. Ingleby's body. Now that his body has gone into cold storage, my surgery hasn't been broken into since." He looked at Dyngley thoughtfully. "Miss Morton's house was broken into as well, but nothing was stolen, was there?"

"Not as far as she or I could tell."

"And have any other homes had intruders?"

"None."

The men looked at each other.

"In your experience, doctor, are surgeries often broken into?" Dyngley asked.

"Sometimes. People can become addicted to laudanum, so I keep my stores of medicines locked away. But whoever broke in didn't take any. As far as I can tell, nothing was stolen. What do you make of that?"

"Perhaps it was children pulling a prank? To see who could get in and see a dead body?" Dyngley suggested.

"I doubt it. Children like to show off, but even the youth of today would have created a mess or stolen my tools." He shook his head. "I don't like it. My housekeeper was out when they broke in, and she swears that she locked the door when she left."

"And you believe her?"

"I do. Why would someone break into my surgery and not take anything?"

"Perhaps to see if they could," Dyngley said. He spotted Caroline crossing the road, about to enter a millinery, and said, "Excuse me."

He crossed the road and entered the shop, his presence announced by a swinging bell attached to the door.

Caroline glanced over and her face lit up. "Dyngley! What are you doing here? I didn't expect to see you. Or are you on a quest for ribbons?"

Dyngley smiled. He liked her instant warmth and cheeky laughter; it's partly what drew him to her in the first place.

Her eyes danced at the sight of him, and he felt her gaze pass over his broad shoulders and thick dark hair, resting on his face.

They were silent for a moment, and then he answered, "I've come to see you. Can we walk a little?"

"But I was just looking at ribbons. Surely we can talk here?" she asked.

Seeing his expression, she said, "Never mind. I'll come back later. Shall we see if there are any Chelsea buns in the shop?" She took his arm and let him lead her outside.

In no time at all, they stood at the glass counter of the sweet shop in town, and Caroline was choosing two Chelsea buns for them. After he paid for the buns and two glasses of lemonade, he brought the drinks over to a high table and stools where Caroline perched. She smiled at him as she tucked into her Chelsea bun, deftly tearing apart the rich round soft pastry with her knife and fork. "What did you want to talk about?"

Dyngley drank his lemonade. He would normally have savored the refreshing tang of the cool drink, but not now. "Did you tell Miss Morton that the intruders found her mother's letters?"

Caroline set down her fork. "Of course. She has asked me to look into her mother's background. It seemed only fair to tell her what I knew."

He frowned and stabbed his fork into his Chelsea bun, the metal utensil screeching across the plate. "Did I tell you that? You should not have told her."

Caroline laughed. "Surely you cannot blame me for commenting on something the three of us already knew? What does it matter?"

"It matters. You shouldn't go telling people about the investigation. It's private," he said.

She lifted her fork again and popped a piece of light fluffy pastry into her mouth. "Mmm. Then perhaps my dear, you shouldn't go telling me the intricate details of your investigations. You know I love hearing these things but it's your own fault."

He stared at her. "I don't remember telling you that fact."

She shrugged. "I can't help it if you've got a poor memory. How was I supposed to know what I should and shouldn't tell her? She's my friend." She pointed out.

"I didn't realize you two were so close."

"You cannot monopolize all of Miss Morton's free time." She smiled and sipped her lemonade.

"I don't. She takes it upon herself to speak with people. It is her way of restoring the neighborhood's faith in herself and her aunt."

Caroline munched on another bite of Chelsea bun, relishing the sweet sultanas in the pastry. "You are so naive. She doesn't give a fig what the neighbors think or say about her and her aunt. It's you she cares about."

Dyngley blinked. "I beg your pardon?"

"It's true, and if you cannot see it then you are blind. Dyngley, that girl has feelings for you. Romantic feelings. It is written all over her face whenever you are near. Did you truly not know?"

"Caroline, you are mistaken. We are just good friends." He stared down at his half-eaten Chelsea bun. His appetite had vanished.

"Dyngley...." She set down her knife and fork and placed a hand on his. "It's all right. I'm not mad."

He looked into her eyes.

She smiled sweetly. "It's a compliment. A young woman admires my fiancé. If I didn't find her utterly ridiculous in her attempts to gain your attention, I might be worried, but the fact of the matter is that I am not threatened by her."

He pulled his hand away. "Caroline..."

"She is the poor niece of a clergyman. She is plain, uncommonly tall, and has no connections. Not even her own mother wished to know her." She smirked. "No self-respecting girl would be threatened by that."

He pushed the offending Chelsea bun away. "I thought you were friends."

"We are. But if she tries to seduce you then she will find my company rather less friendly."

"Caroline," he said, "That is my friend you are talking about."

"And I am your fiancée, or have you forgotten?" Her voice hardened. "I understand you feel sorry for her, but these little encouragements have got to stop. Your loyalty and attention should be to me as your future wife, not some girl wearing a dress two years out of date."

He blinked. "Caroline..."

She smiled prettily and the hardness was gone. "She's my friend too. I am simply letting you know the truth as it stands. I have eyes, you know. I'm not blind to her subtle attempts to gain your approval. It's sweet in a way." Her smile showed far too many teeth. "Now, how is your investigation going? I want to know. Have you found the killer yet?"

"Keep your voice down," he said, looking around.

Caroline's laughter rang out, attracting more than a few looks from those sat nearby. "Come now, Dyngley, everyone knows what you are up to. The entire town knows the man was murdered and that you are looking into it. What's the harm?"

He gave a little sigh and spoke quietly, "I still need to speak with Mrs. Grant about her gooseberry fool. And... Mr. Jenkins wishes to speak with you."

Caroline looked up from her bun. "I dislike him."

"Everyone dislikes him. But he still needs to speak with you."

"Why? I will tell you anything you want to know." She gave him a coy smile.

Dyngley's eyes were unflinching. "We need to prove that you are above suspicion. It would be unseemly for me to ask you your whereabouts at the time of Mr. Ingleby's death. It needs to be Mr. Jenkins. Will you allow him to question you?"

She shifted on her wooden stool and sulked. She pouted prettily, eyed him and speared a final piece of Chelsea bun into her mouth. "Fine, but I don't see what the trouble is. I barely even met the man more than once or twice."

"Please, Caroline."

"All right. I'll do it for you, Dyngley. No one else."

BUT A REPORT from Mr. Jenkins the next day proved uneventful. As Dyngley walked through town, Mr. Jenkins relayed that Caroline had received him and listened to his questions about Mr. Ingleby's death, and behaved most cordially. It had gone downhill from there, however. As Dyngley suspected, Jenkins had put her back up, and she had reacted accordingly. From what Caroline told him later, Jenkins had insinuated that she had killed the clergyman. Caroline had of course refused, demanding proof behind such ludicrous accusations. When Jenkins told her he didn't have any but would be watching her, she told him to leave.

Or at least, that's what Dyngley surmised.

"She threw me out with a bee in my ear, she did," Mr. Jenkins said. "Not my fault. She's got something to hide, that one."

Dyngley shook his head. "For once, could you try questioning someone without them making a complaint afterward?"

Mr. Jenkins grinned at him. "Worried I've hurt her fine sensibilities, eh? She's a tough one, that fiancée of yours. I'd watch out."

"She has nothing to hide. She's my fiancée. She's innocent. You just blunder about without a care of who you're talking to." Dyngley shoved his hands into his pockets.

Mr. Jenkins paused. "For what it's worth, I don't think she did it."

"And what prompted this scintillating discovery?" Dyngley asked, his voice harsh.

"She didn't know much. About baking, I mean. I don't think she bakes at all. I thought every girl was taught how to bake but I don't think she does."

"Not all women do. Many genteel women don't. They have cooks to do that for them," Dyngley pointed out.

"That must be it." Jenkins touched his hat and left.

STILL FUMING, DYNGLEY marched across town to the fine brick house of Mrs. Grant, a wealthy mother of three boys. A maid ushered him into a smart parlor and moved aside one of the boys' toys from a chair as Mrs. Grant bid him sit down. An affable woman, tall with a thick middle, bright blonde hair nicely coiffed and a smart olive-green dress, she received him with such dignity into her sitting room that he could well imagine her at the prow of a ship.

Mrs. Grant said, "Constable. To what to I owe the pleasure?"

Dyngley made polite conversation as tea was called for and Mrs. Grant's sons were shooed outside to play. Once Dyngley had been presented with a steaming cup of black tea, he began, "Mrs. Grant, I wonder if I might ask you about the day of the baking contest."

The middle-aged matron smiled at him and blew on her hot tea, holding a dainty cup in her hands. "Yes?"

"You know that Mr. Ingleby died that afternoon," he said.

"A terrible thing, that. So sad. I heard he became sick after eating one of the puddings. Is that true?"

"It is."

"What a horrid thing to befall that gentleman." She shook her head.

"You didn't attend the contest that day, I believe."

"No, I didn't." She sipped her tea.

"Why not?"

"Constable, a man is dead. Do you need to be asking questions about this sort of thing? I find it distasteful."

"I'm speaking with each of the bakers. You made a raspberry tart, did you not?"

She rose to her feet, the folds of her matronly olive-green house dress wrinkling like creased paper. "Um, yes. Now constable, if you don't mind, I need to speak with my husband."

Dyngley leaned back in his chair, holding the half-full white china teacup on his knee. "It's funny, you see. I have in my notes that you entered a gooseberry fool into the contest. Am I mistaken?"

Mrs. Grant pursed her lips together. "Yes, that's right. I forgot. I bake so many things you see, it's hard to remember."

He glanced at her hands. They were prim and clean, a lady's hands. If she had spent more than a few moments inside a kitchen, he would be surprised. "I quite fancy a gooseberry fool. Could you tell me the ingredients to get?"

She hesitated. "Well, gooseberries, of course. And, um, you'll need to make a sponge and um... The salt and gooseberry leaves."

"Funny, I thought gooseberries grew in brambles, much like blackberries. Did the thorns not hurt your hands?"

"I wear gloves," she smiled thinly, rubbing her hands against her sides.

"You must have a new variety of gooseberries in your garden. The ones I've seen don't have any thorns at all," he said.

"Are you trying to catch me out, Constable?" she asked, her voice tight. "I assure you I have done nothing wrong."

"How well did you know Mr. Ingleby?" he asked, changing tack. "He was a guest here a few times, was he not?"

"He was. He liked to come and read to us sometimes. We are a very religious family." She sat back down and drank more tea.

"It seems to me that Mr. Ingleby was quite popular in the neighborhood," he commented.

Mrs. Grant smiled thinly, her mouth curling into a sneer.

"Did you dislike him?" Dyngley asked.

"Me? No, not at all. He was a wonderful man. So civil." She looked away and patted her hair.

"And yet, I have heard a rumor..." he started.

"Rumor? What rumor?" Her blonde head snapped back toward him.

"I have it on good authority that–"

She cut him off with a hard look. "Let me guess. Mrs. Alleyn has been opening her mouth again. You can't believe anything that woman tells you, honestly."

"I understand Mr. Ingleby was very fond of her cooking."

Mrs. Grant's gaze was flinty. "That does not surprise me. The man could eat any family out of house and home. His appetite knew no restraint. Once when we had finished dinner and my boy Cornelius hadn't eaten all his carrots, Mr. Ingleby asked if he might eat those too." She huffed. "It was scandalous. What an absurd little man."

"Indeed. I gather you were not overly fond of his company after that."

"Well..."

"He did seem rather attentive to the Alleyns. I believe they had hoped he would make their daughter an offer," Dyngley said.

"Louisa?" she snickered softly. "Only if she could bake. But then that is where his true love lies."

"What do you mean?"

She looked down at her tea. "He was at first very charming company but after having dined at everyone's table, he found some more appealing than others. And made it known."

Dyngley asked gently, "Did Mr. Ingleby have a preference for the Alleyns' table?"

"He did." She sniffed. "He would come over here and spend half an hour extolling Mrs. Alleyn's cooking. He would say, 'such glorious tarts' or 'such excellent pudding, so rich', then look down at our offerings and turn up his nose at them. He would actually tell me to put more suet in my pie crust so it could be more like Mrs. Alleyn's."

"You didn't like that, did you?"

"Of course not. He became insufferable. I half wondered if he wanted to drive a bit of competition between us, to see whose cooking was best. My—we would win, so there was no contest. But it was very hard to entertain him after a while. I couldn't face seeing him at the fete, so no, I'm not sorry to see him gone, if that's what you're after."

"And I gather you didn't bake that gooseberry fool either," Dyngley said.

Her cheeks bloomed pink. "Of course I did. Are you accusing me of lying?"

"I'm not accusing you of anything, Mrs. Grant. I'd just like to know how you made that dessert. I don't think you've ever made a gooseberry fool in your life. How about you tell me the truth?"

Her husband lurked in the doorway, a stocky man with a round belly and hands dusted with flour. "Best tell him, Elizabeth. He'll find out soon anyway."

Her shoulders slumped as she looked from one man to another. "Very well." She waited for her husband to clean his hands on a dishtowel before joining them. As Mr. Grant sat beside her, she helped herself to another cup of tea. "The fact is that I was unwell."

"Oh?" Dyngley asked.

"Yes. And it was hot. Too hot and I am liable to faint. So–"

"I prepared the gooseberry fool," Mr. Grant said.

"Edward," she admonished.

"I did," he told Dyngley. "And if you don't believe me then I can show you." He quit the room and returned with a plate of honey cakes. "I made these this morning. What do you think?"

Dyngley bit into one and tasted the sweet crumbly texture mixed with honey. "Delicious."

"Aye, that's what the clergyman thought too." He shot a look at his wife. "I'd just made a batch of oatcakes when he came calling one afternoon. Caught me in the kitchen covered with flour and deduced the whole thing."

Mrs. Grant set aside her tea with a clatter, her face pale.

"There's no shame in it, Elizabeth," her husband told her.

"I agree. Many men enjoy baking," Dyngley said.

Mrs. Grant said, "Excuse me," and left the room.

Dyngley bit into another honey cake. "So Mr. Ingleby found out you were the baker. What did he do?"

"To me, nothing. But he ignored Elizabeth at church. It was strange behavior, as he'd been so cordial the previous week. When she came to talk to him after church, he told her it was unseemly for a woman not to do the cooking, as the kitchen is a woman's domain. Told her she was living a lie and unless she paid him, he was going to tell everyone."

Dyngley blinked. "He was going to blackmail her?"

"Aye. The next week she said she was too sick to go to church, but then later when Mr. Ingleby called, she said she wasn't in. I knew something was wrong. Once he left, she broke down and told me everything. She'd never been so humiliated. She didn't want to go back."

Dyngley set down his teacup. "Why didn't you report this to us?"

"I wanted to tell the man what he could do with himself, but she begged me not to. Said the secret would get out and we'd be laughingstocks. And with the contest coming up, she had agreed to bake something to raise money for the church roof."

"So you made the gooseberry fool."

"Aye." he scratched his chin. "I went to Ingleby the night before the contest and told him what to do with his high and mighty ideas. He's just a replacement clergyman and not a very good one at that. Told him that I, for one, looked forward to Mr. Greene's return and that when he did come back, I'd be telling him all about Mr. Ingleby's rude ways."

"What did he say to that?"

"He laughed at me. Said that he would be sure to write to the reverend himself and tell him not to let liars into his parish."

"You didn't threaten him or fight him?"

"Lord, no. Me with a wife and three boys. Who would provide for them if I was in the jail?" Mr. Grant shook his head. "I did plan to get him back for what he'd done to Elizabeth. I was going to salt the pudding." Mr. Grant's face turned red.

"Salt?"

"It ruins a gooseberry fool. Gooseberries are already tart; they need lots of sugar like rhubarb does." Mr. Grant looked down at the plate of honey cakes and bit savagely into one. "But on the day of the fete, I couldn't do it. I can't bake bad puddings. I just can't do it."

"So you entered the gooseberry fool into the contest."

"Yes. But I did it under my own name, so the secret would get out," Mr. Grant said.

"Or at the very least, people would think that you both are talented bakers," Dyngley said.

"Yes. So what will you do now, Constable? You have found us out."

Dyngley ate another honey cake and sipped his tea. "You didn't salt the gooseberry fool or add anything else to it?"

"No. I mean, anyone could have tampered with the pudding after I left, but I doubt they would. Lady Cameron's footmen were there overseeing everything. You could speak to them, but I doubt they would have seen much. It was busy."

"Thank you." Dyngley set aside his teacup and rose to his feet. "Well, I must be going."

"You'll not be taking us to the jail?" Mrs. Grant peeked out from the doorway to the parlor.

"What for? You've done nothing wrong. I suspect more than half the ladies who entered the contest had their cooks prepare the dishes for them. I see nothing wrong with your husband showing off his cooking skills, and you did nothing to hurt Mr. Ingleby." He bowed. "Good day to you."

CHAPTER TWENTY-ONE

P OPPY'S AUNT WAS feeling tired, so Poppy took on her weekly duty of visiting the sick. She stopped by Dr. Wilson's surgery to say hello, and he said that she might visit the Heyworths, as Mr. Heyworth had suffered from a broken leg and boredom and might do well with some company.

She knocked on the smart door of the house in town and met Jane at the door. "Oh. Miss Morton, what are you doing here? I expected you to call yesterday."

"I did but couldn't find you. I'm here to pay a call on your mother and father. Dr. Wilson said your father suffered from low spirits and thought I might be able to offer some company."

"Alone?"

"My aunt is tired and so I thought I would come alone."

"I see." Jane stepped back. "That's very nice of you, but my father is resting. And now that you are here, I can show you my new enterprise."

"Oh?"

"I was just on my way to the hospital. There's a patient there who is very curious. Do come along and see what you make of him."

Poppy spared a glance for her father and then nodded. The girls walked through town past the jail to the hospital and were ushered through a waiting room, down a corridor, and into a large airy room with a high ceiling and rows of beds. The air felt warm and while the room had beds for twenty, only three patients were there. Being the afternoon, one was a boy laying abed who was being nursed by his mother; another was an old man. And near him lay a young man.

The man had light brown hair, was mildly handsome, with skin still too young to grow a beard, and looked to be just out of university. He lay with blankets up to his chin, looking pale as death.

Jane said in a hushed voice, "No one knows his name. He was brought in from a carriage accident outside town."

Poppy gazed down at his face. "He looks so young."

"I know. And not a penny on him. The doctor said the carriage overturned. It might have been highwaymen."

Poppy blinked. "I didn't think they'd be so far out from London as this. Enfield, maybe. But Hertford?"

"Well, it's one theory. I just can't believe he's still breathing. The doctor said his injuries were very bad. A broken arm and leg, and a nasty head wound. It's a wonder he's still alive." Jane pulled up a chair and sat by his bed. "I talk to him sometimes. I heard once that if you talk to a person while they're in a numb sleep like he is, then it can help them wake up."

"Do you think it's working?" Poppy asked.

"I don't know. I'd like to think so." She spared a glance for the other invalids in the room. "The others have family who come to visit them. That boy over there, his mama brings him hot soup every day."

"You like him, don't you?" Poppy said.

Jane carried on as if she hadn't heard. "But this young man has no one. He has no connections, and he's penniless. Even the clothes he's wearing are from the hospital's own supply." She stifled a tear. "And we don't even know his name, so there's no one to tell his family what's become of him. What if he dies without a name? And no one to care for him?"

Poppy looked down at the young man. He lay so peacefully,

he looked like he might wake up at any moment. "Is there nothing we can do for him?"

"I've already asked. There is nothing we can do but stay and see if he wakes up." Jane pulled a small book from her reticule. "I've been reading him poetry. Sir Walter Scott's *The Lay of the Last Minstrel.*"

At six cantos, that would take anyone a while to read. Poppy smiled. "I think it's wonderful what you're doing. Very kind."

Jane brushed at her eyes. "I don't mind. I just wish he would wake up. At least then we would know his name."

POPPY TOOK HER leave of Jane then and walked outside. Breathing in the late afternoon sunshine, she felt a slight breeze and knew that the sun filled days of August were soon to be left behind. As she walked through town, feeling the warm sunlight on her straw bonnet, she wandered through the farmer's market in the center of town. Birds were drowned out by the sounds of men calling out their wares, offering onions, peas, carrots, potatoes, and farther down the road, a butcher's. The smell of raw meat lingered in the air, and she held her breath as she hurried past. Finally out of the town center and along St. Andrew's Street, she spied a familiar figure ahead and fell into pace not far behind.

Upon hearing her footsteps, Constable Dyngley turned around. "Miss Morton." He bowed.

"Constable." She nodded and caught up with him.

"I am on my way to speak with the last baker on the list, Mrs. Walker," he told her, "I wonder if you would care to join me?"

"It would be my pleasure," she said, then stopped. "But would it be appropriate?"

His mouth twisted into a frown. "You are unaccompanied. Of course, it is not right. I shall speak to her myself and call on you later. Unless of course…" he pursed his lips together. "Mrs. Walker would surely not begrudge us both as visitors if perhaps you were to call on her first, and then I a short while later?"

Poppy couldn't stop the smile tugging at her lips. "Excellent plan."

He flashed her a grin and walked along beside her in companionable silence.

He cleared his throat. "Miss Morton, you should know, while I don't recall telling Miss Everly about finding your mother's letters, I would be doing her a disservice by not taking her at her word. She is my fiancée and a good, honest woman. If she says I told her about the letters, then I believe her."

Poppy looked at him. Something inside her felt hard and tight like a violin string stretched taut and if pulled on a centimeter more, might snap. She did not care for those who lied to her. But what if this was an honest mistake? She so wanted to believe him.

"I did not mean to betray your confidence," he said, meeting her gaze. He removed his hat and ran a hand through his dark brown hair. "I hope you won't think less of me. What I mean to say is, I am too close to this investigation and am not thinking clearly."

"Why not?" she asked.

"Well it concerns you and your aunt, and Miss Everly and my thoughts are in a jumble. I cannot think straight. There are too many bakers who seemed to hold a grudge against Mr. Ingleby and when I think of how he treated you and your aunt, I find I cannot muster up the strength to pursue anyone. From most accounts I hear, his death was a boon to this community, not a tragedy. I am having trouble finding anyone who didn't dislike him." He glanced at her. "I don't think I need to say this, but it is a testament to you and your aunt, that so many of your neighbors came to your defense."

Poppy's smile waned. "I thank you for your concern, Constable."

"Poppy," he started, then looked around. They were alone on the side of the riverbank, well outside of the town center. The only things nearby were leafy green boughs, trees, and bushes, the quiet interrupted by the occasional bird call. He said, "There's no need to be so formal. We are friends, are we not?"

"We used to be. But now that you are engaged, I'm not sure we should be seen alone together." She looked away, eyeing the wild green plants that grew haphazardly along the banks of the River Lea.

He put a hand on her shoulder and she flinched, stepping back. Before his eyes, she lost her balance and tumbled backward, flying off the high riverbank and down into the river below with a splash.

In moments her world was wet. She was instantly cold and breathed in river water that filled her mouth, ears, and nose. She splashed and started to kick her way to the surface, but her walking boots became entangled in weeds, and the weight of her dress, corset, and spencer jacket began to weigh her down. Biting cold water froze her bare skin and she clawed at the floating weeds alongside her for purchase, their silken leaves escaping her grasp. Seconds felt like years as she scrabbled at the water with numb fingers, desperate not to sink any further. The afternoon sunlight glinted above her against the water's surface as she clamped her mouth shut, struggling to breathe. Fear seized her and she kicked powerfully with her feet, her legs fighting against the weight of her dress. Her spencer gripped her upper body like an iron vise as she kicked and tried to swim to the surface.

Then a dark form plunged into the water next to her, sending a surge of bubbles spiraling toward the surface, filling her vision. When they cleared, she met Dyngley's eyes, full of concern, and flinched as he gripped her waist with strong fingers. He stared at her as if to speak some silent message and hooked his arm around her left arm and pulled. He dragged her up toward the surface with powerful strokes, kicking like a fish at the water, disturbing fish and other underwater life.

Poppy tried to help by kicking, but her feet only became tangled in the mass of skirts she wore. Her bonnet, now loose and free from shading her head, now threatened to choke her with its tightly knotted strings that dug into her throat. She could not escape it and struggled as she began to see black spots against her vision.

The surface came ever closer until suddenly she was free. She spewed out a mouthful of river water down her chest as she breathed blessed fresh air into her lungs, and coughed and wheezed.

Dyngley swam with her sputtering and coughing and roughly dug his fingers into her soaking wet spencer, pulling her over to the side of the riverbank. He heaved her onto the bank and shoved her up until she lay against the grass. He climbed up after, dripping wet.

She coughed and sputtered, her sides heaving as she lay on her side, spewing out river water and breathing in fresh air, feeling the weeds and blades of grass sticking to her skin. "You…"

"Are you all right?"

She looked down at herself, sodden and bedraggled, her straw bonnet sitting squashed like a sad muffin on her head, its strings still knotted against her neck. She tugged at the strings and failed, and instead opted to lay down, gasping for breath. Once she spat out as much of the river as she could and wiped her mouth, she took a breath and felt alive again, if a little soaked.

"Miss Morton?" Constable Dyngley asked, "Poppy?"

"Why did you…?" she asked.

"I only meant to be comforting, I did not mean for you to fall into the river," he said.

She glared at him, sat up, and unbuttoned her dripping wet spencer with numb fingers, peeling it off her arms and flinging the offending jacket to the ground. She was soaked to the core and now shivered in the afternoon sun, her white muslin dress clinging to her long limbs.

Dyngley began to remove his coat for her, but she held a hand up and croaked, "No. I am not in need of assistance, thank you very much."

She struggled to undo the knotted tie of her bonnet until Dyngley said, "Let me."

He closed the distance between them and in an instant, sat

mere inches from her, his long fingers deftly undoing the knotted tie. He loosened it and with a satisfied smile, said, "There," and looked up into her eyes.

From this close, she could see the day's stubble on his chin and see tiny rivulets of water dribble down the side of his face. No doubt he could equally easily see the small shape of her nose, her pale skin, and the wet straggles of brown hair that plastered her face and neck. He looked at her, and she swallowed.

"Poppy, I…" he started.

"You have a—" she began.

"What is it?" he asked.

"Here, let me." She reached forward and pulled a damp green vine from his shoulder.

"Thank you," he said abruptly. "Poppy, won't you tell me what is wrong?"

"Nothing. I'm fine. Well, mostly." She looked down at her wet clothes. "You need not trouble yourself any further, I am fine."

He pushed a wet strand of her out of her face. "I don't understand. Why won't you talk to me? I'm not a clairvoyant. I cannot do anything if you don't tell me what is bothering you."

She looked down, taking great interest in the sodden grass of the riverbank.

He removed her ruined straw bonnet and set it on the ground. He swallowed and said, "I have never seen you with your hair long."

Her hands trembled, she dared not meet his eyes. "Constable…"

"Dyngley. Call me Dyngley," he told her.

She closed her eyes then, breathing in his scent, when…

"What is happening here?" Caroline said, standing over them. Her face was livid.

CHAPTER TWENTY-TWO

I T STRUCK DYNGLEY then, that he was perhaps not behaving as an engaged man should. "Caroline," he said, getting to his feet.

"I said, what is going on here?" she demanded.

"Miss Everly," Poppy began, "I fell into the river. Constable Dyngley swam in and rescued me."

"That explains why you two are soaking wet, but not why I find you both in a compromising position. It's indecent," she practically spat. "I am surprised at you, Dyngley, for falling for her charms."

"What?" Dyngley and Poppy said, then looked at each other.

Poppy said, "Miss Everly, I assure you, nothing inappropriate was taking place. My bonnet was stuck and he undid it for me." She blushed.

Caroline snorted. "Do you realize how that sounds? I should have known better than to trust you."

"What do you mean?" Poppy said, getting to her feet, getting tangled in her damp dress that stuck to her boots.

At the sight of her standing up, Caroline's mouth dropped open and she held up a hand before her eyes. "Miss Morton, you are positively indecent. Cover yourself at once. I can see right through your dress."

Dyngley immediately took off his coat and gave it to Poppy, who wrapped it around herself. "Caroline," he began, "I don't know what it is you think you saw, but it's God's honest truth, she fell in. That is why we are both wet. She could have drowned."

"Hah. As if I would believe that. She probably planned the entire thing. It's no surprise considering she's in love with you."

Poppy stiffened. Dyngley didn't make a move. "Caroline, don't be ridiculous. Miss Morton and I are just friends."

"You cannot expect me to believe that, not after what I have just seen. Do friends fix each other's hair and remove their bonnets? You are engaged to me, Dyngley, or have you forgotten?" Caroline asked.

"Miss Everly, I promise you—" Poppy started.

"Oh, don't Miss Everly me, I'm the one who's hurt. I'm such a fool. Here I was coming to see you as my friend, to tell you the latest in my search for your mother, and instead, I find my fiancé in your arms." Her face flushed with anger. "Admit it. You've fancied him all along. How it must have hurt you to see us dancing together. Do you know what Dyngley actually thinks of you?"

"Caroline, stop it," Dyngley began.

"He told me that you were a tall, oafish girl, much like a donkey or a goose with too long a neck. At first, I thought he was trying to reassure me of his affection for me, but now I find you both in the dirt. I see his description of you was accurate; at least you belong there. I always thought clergymen's girls were supposed to be meek and nice, I never thought they would be so fickle, or mercenary. It wasn't enough you had Mr. Heyworth dangling on your arm, now you've moved up in the world, have you?" She kicked a tuft of grass at them, and it landed on Poppy's ruined bonnet.

"Caroline." Dyngley came forward and took her arm.

"No, I've seen enough." She tore her arm out of his hand. "Miss Morton, forget that we were ever friends. I no longer need your services. I'm sorry I ever met you. And you." She faced Constable Dyngley, "You will need to bloody well beg if you want me to still marry you. Because after what I've seen, you seem to be having a crisis of faith."

"Don't say that. You know I—" he started.

"I know that you need money, Dyngley. You're the second son of a titled family who is poor, and my dowry will save your estate. I'm no fool. If you still want that, you'll need to show me you are serious about us and not let a little scheming busybody distract you." She sneered and spat on the ground.

"Caroline, please. It's all in your head. Poppy and I don't love each other, we're just friends."

"Poppy, is it? My, you two are familiar." Caroline seethed.

"I swear, I don't love Miss Morton." His voice rose.

"Hah. You may not love her, but she has not denied it. Go ahead, Miss Morton, tell us that you don't love him." Caroline's eyes flashed.

Poppy opened her mouth and sneezed.

Caroline shook her head.

"I don't love him," Poppy said, wiping her mouth.

Dyngley turned and stared at her.

"I don't believe you." Caroline glared. "You're lying."

"I'm not. I love someone else," Poppy said, sneezing again.

"Who?" Dyngley asked.

Poppy looked away. "That is not for you to know."

Caroline snorted. "I'll leave you two lovers alone. I love your new perfume, Miss Morton. It smells so fishlike." She walked away, stomping onto the dirt road.

Dyngley hurried after her, picking up his hat along the way. But as he ran down the dirt road, he wondered, what if Caroline had said was true. Did Poppy fancy him?

CHAPTER TWENTY-THREE

C HIVALRY WAS TRULY dead, Poppy decided. Not only had she gotten soaked and now smelled horribly of the river, but Caroline had embarrassed her to the core, and she'd ended up lying to her closest friend. Would Dyngley ever trust her again, or would he always look at her and think she fancied him? Could they still be friends after this? She didn't know.

Sopping wet, she hugged Dyngley's coat closer around her, picked up her sodden spencer and bonnet from the ground, and began to trudge home, when she walked by Mrs. Walker's cottage.

Mrs. Walker was an elderly widow living off of her husband's pension from the war. The dusty dirt path leading up to the cottage was well kept and the border of plants around it looked trim and tidy. Mrs. Walker stood outside in a plain dress and apron, tending her plants when she saw Poppy and said, "My dear girl, what happened?"

"I fell in the river."

"Good heavens, you're wet through. Come inside. You'll ruin your dress."

Poppy looked down. The white muslin dress she wore had torn, the hem had frayed and the light pretty embroidered flowers she had sewn were now ugly and damp with thorny threads sticking out. "I think it is too late for that, Mrs. Walker,"

Poppy said.

"Perhaps. You look like you could use a good cup of tea. Would you like to come in? You can sit by the fire and dry off those wet clothes."

"That would be wonderful." Poppy accepted, and followed the older woman into the cottage through a little corridor and into a small but tidy sitting room. The walls were white but adorned with many humble paintings of landscapes and more than one portrait of Captain Walker and his wife in their younger days.

Mrs. Walker bid Poppy strip but was refused. "Oh no, I couldn't possibly," Poppy said, turning red.

"There's no need for decorum, Miss Morton, we are but neighbors, and I have seen you running about the churchyard since you were a child." Mrs. Walker gave her a fond look.

"No, I couldn't. Truly."

"Well in that case, shall we adjourn to the kitchen? It is warmer there and you'll do no harm to the wooden chairs."

"You don't mind?"

"What, and save my sofa cushions from a watermark? You won't have to work hard to convince me. Come, follow me and I'll make tea." Mrs. Walker led her into a humble dining room and adjoining kitchen, and settled about industriously, adding to the fire burning merrily in the hearth and filling a large kettle with water, before hanging it over the fire.

Taking her direction from Mrs. Walker, Poppy sat in one of the hard wooden highbacked chairs across from her at the aged wooden table, with her back close to the fire. She shivered and hugged Dyngley's coat around her.

"That is not your coat, I take it." Mrs. Walker noted.

"No. I fell in the river and Constable Dynglcy saved me."

"Fished you out, did he? A true gentleman, that. But where is he now?"

"He was very kind, but he needed to see his fiancée." Poppy fingered the coat and felt its sodden texture. It smelled like the river but she didn't care. It was his, and he had given it to her out of kindness. She watched as Mrs. Walker prepared two cups of tea.

As the scent of green tea hit her nose, Poppy began to relax in the warm kitchen. She leaned back against the hardback wooden chair and watched as Mrs. Walker set a cup down in front of her. "How are you holding up after all this?"

Poppy blew on her cup of steaming tea. "You mean Mr. Ingleby's parting?"

Mrs. Walker wrinkled her nose at the mention of him. "Yes. Although I am surprised you can speak of him so civilly. He did not treat you with the same courtesy."

Poppy lowered her gaze and sipped her hot tea. "Yes, I heard that. I think he was a troubled man."

"And I think he's better off dead." Mrs. Walker said flatly.

Poppy looked at her hostess. Mrs. Walker often said aloud what she thought, rather than dance around her true meaning with petty niceties and false platitudes about the state of Hertford's roads or the weather. Poppy rather liked that about her, but at the same time was wary.

"There are some people who would mistake your meaning, Mrs. Walker. I am sure you wouldn't wish Mr. Ingleby harm."

"No, of course not." Mrs. Walker's eyes took on a guarded look. "And I agree, he was troubled, but not in the way you think. He often came here, did you know that?"

"No," Poppy admitted, not wanting to betray Jane's confidence.

"Oh, he did. He often showed up at my door, wanting a medicinal drink or cordial to settle his stomach. Flatulence was his problem, you see." Her grin was full of missing teeth.

"I see." Poppy hid a smile by taking another sip of her tea. "Do you often nurse the sick?"

"I can make medicinal cordials and unguents that some find ease their pain," Mrs. Walker said with pride.

"I bet Dr. Wilson would appreciate your help in the surgery."

"I bet he would. He's not come to visit me though, and I have no need of his services. Can suit myself just fine."

"Of course. I'm sorry, I just cannot stop thinking about Mr. Ingleby's death. He might have been unkind, but it is odd, isn't it? That Mr. Ingleby died at the fete. He was so looking forward to it," Poppy said.

Mrs. Walker snorted. "No surprise there. That man loved his puddings. But it's his own fault that's done him in."

"What do you mean?"

"One look at him and it's plain to see. The man eats too much and likes his food rich, not simple. It's no wonder he didn't approve of Mr. Greene's table, begging your pardon. Not rich enough for him. Even when he came here, he wouldn't drink my tea without sugar in it, to take the edge off. I only add sugar in my pies, I told him, not tea. It's enough to give anyone a bellyache."

"You think he had an improper constitution?"

"Aye. There are regimens to help with that, guides to a healthy and long life, but he wouldn't want to hear of it. It's no wonder he died so young. Too much rich food. I dine on plain and simple broth every week, and I'm seventy-three," she said with a gap-toothed smile.

Poppy nodded in understanding. "I'm sure you're right." She looked around the room and finished her tea. "What a comfortable kitchen you have. It's so warm. I feel dry already."

"Mind you come by whenever you feel the least bit poorly. Mr. Ingleby can say what he might but you're a good egg, Miss Morton. You wouldn't harm a fly." Mrs. Walker stood and led Poppy to the door. "That is a shame about the missing church money though. Wish I knew where it had gone to. I gave sixpence toward it."

"That is very good of you." Poppy felt a rush of warmth toward her. "If I hear anything I'll let you know."

"Wouldn't surprise me if that man Ingleby had something to do with its disappearance. Maybe that's why he died." Mrs. Walker scratched her chest.

"I beg your pardon?"

"Mr. Ingleby was a thief. Didn't you know?"

"No. I didn't. Did he steal from you?" Poppy asked.

"Not under my eye, he didn't. But I know the type. A wandering eye for goods, and ones of quality too. He did admire my husband's musket and pistol." Mrs. Walker pointed to them hanging over the fireplace, giving the room a military air. "They would be worth something to the right buyer. But Ingleby wouldn't dare. He'd know what would happen to him if he did."

"And what would that be? "Poppy asked nonchalantly.

"Why I'd—" Mrs. Walker stopped and took a breath, smoothing down imaginary wrinkles in her house apron. "He simply wouldn't get any more of my restorative teas. And I'm a damn sight cheaper than the apothecary or general infirmary."

Now that Poppy stood at the main entrance, the ladies curtseyed to each other, and Poppy bid her adieu. And not a moment too soon, for she had seen something that had disturbed her in Mrs. Walker's kitchen. A little bottle labeled poison, right next to the sugar jar.

CHAPTER TWENTY-FOUR

I N HIS SODDEN state, Dyngley lost sight of Caroline fairly quickly and gave up trying to follow her. Instead, he made his way around the outskirts of town to a residential neighborhood. He walked by children playing in the road and passed by servants who hung up clothes to dry outside and beat rugs while ladies paid calls on neighbors or ran errands. All in all a quiet, tame affair to what he had just witnessed. Did Poppy truly care for someone? Was it himself? Did she have a secret beau?

Dyngley walked down the country lane and approached his own rented lodgings, a small room in a boarding house for men, run by a Mr. Ben Phillips, an elderly widower. Mr. Phillips was a good man and ran a decent household, but he was nosey. No doubt he would have enjoyed knowing that one of his guests was the second son of a Baronet, which was precisely what Dyngley wished to avoid.

Dyngley preferred to keep his life private from those around him, and instead had told his valet to remain at his family's estate in Essex. With his brother as the heir, Dyngley held no hopes that he would inherit anything from his father's passing. With little taste for a military commission and no doting grandfather able to help him enter the law, he pursued a career in the constabulary, much to the distaste of his parents. Their dislike of his chosen profession (that was so distinctly outside of those which were appropriate for a man of a good family like theirs) was perhaps an added incentive for Dyngley to continue, and after a few mishaps and faults along the way, had found he was quite enjoying himself.

What had started out as catching petty thieves and keeping the peace in the taverns of Essex and Cambridgeshire had now taken him to a vacant spot in Hertfordshire.

But now he had the added complication of Caroline and Poppy. Poppy was a friend, nothing more. So why did he think of her each day? And why had Caroline insinuated that she fancied him? That was nonsense. Caroline didn't need to distract them both from the case, it was all he thought about. Well, that and his upcoming marriage to her.

It had been his aging father's wish to see him married off, and soon. Since he had first met Caroline by chance in a London jeweler's shop in Bond Street, it was like meeting a breath of fresh air. On a warm day in late May, he had come on a personal errand, on his way to see his brother Edmund at their social club, when he passed by the jeweler's and remembered a promise he had made to restore a broken pearl necklace.

In a previous case, and the first that had brought him to investigate in Hertford, Dyngley worked with Poppy (Miss Morton, he reminded himself) to find the killer behind the death of a strangled servant. They had found the killer but almost too late, for the blackguard had lured Poppy onto a balcony alone before professing his love for her and then attempted to choke the life out of her when she refused him.

"As if she could marry such a man," he muttered.

Dyngley had come in to save her, but the pearl necklace she had worn, a loan from her aunt for the evening, had not survived the encounter. They were not a wealthy family and Mrs. Greene had seemed so distraught at the loss of her necklace, that Dyngley had promised Poppy he would replace it. But he found himself at a loss at the jewelers, for the broken necklace was a family heirloom and held sentimental value for the ladies. It would not be so easily replaced.

But then he came across a young lady who was returning a jeweled bracelet and couldn't help overhearing her plight. "I tell you it's from a suitor. I don't dare tell you his name, for he would be embarrassed to know I was returning it, but my sister wants nothing to do with him. She would much rather return the piece and tell the man she'd lost it than have to face him again. Please, could you not take it back?"

She was a pretty thing, about twenty years of age, with fashionably coiled auburn hair dangling beneath her bonnet trimmed with silk, with dewy pale skin and a heart-shaped face. When she spoke, it was with purpose, she was no meek miss. He liked that and eyed her with some interest.

The jeweler, a fussy little man, said, "I am not a pawnbroker's miss. There is one a few streets away, I believe. Maybe they can help you."

The girl acquiesced with good grace, and then came across Dyngley. "Oh! Forgive me, I did not realize there was another customer. Excuse me." She paused and looked him up and down. "You look lost."

Within minutes they were talking. She helped him pick out a set of pearls and he escorted her to a reputable pawn shop that paid her handsomely for her unwanted jewelry, especially with a constable present. In the end, after hours of talking and laughing together, he had become so attached to her company, he presented her with the pearl necklace he had bought and begged to see her again. He felt at once enraptured, smitten, and felt for the first time like maybe he had fallen in love.

Until now.

Once he had returned to his lodgings, bathed, shaved, and changed, Dyngley felt restored. He was just tying the laces on his boots when there came a knock on his door.

"Yes?" Dyngley asked.

"A Mrs. Grant to see you, Constable," Mr. Phillips said behind the door.

He looked up. "Thank you, Mr. Phillips, I'll be down in a minute."

He finished tying his boots and spared a glance in the small looking glass. His cravat was slightly crooked and his damp hair needed combing, but he would pass. It was unseemly for a woman to go calling on a single man alone, but this was no ordinary time. Death had come to Hertford, and his world would not feel right again until he had found out who had cut Mr. Ingleby's life short.

He rose, opened the door, and came face to face with Mr. Phillips.

The man had a large gray bushy mustache and when he spoke, he smelled of onions. "I don't need to be telling you, but lady callers aren't allowed. This is a respectable boarding house, not a brothel."

"I am sure she has come on constabulary business, Mr. Phillips," Dyngley said as he hurried down the steps.

Mrs. Grant stood at the entrance of the house, looking very smart in a green walking dress and matching ribbon on her bonnet. She clutched a small reticule in her hands and said, "Forgive me for intruding, Constable, but I need to speak with you. As a matter of urgency."

Dyngley led her into Mr. Phillips' drawing-room but found a few men sitting reading books or the paper. Their arrival instantly gained a few questioning looks, so he turned and said, "Let's go outside."

As he followed Mrs. Grant outdoors and walked a fair distance from the house, she touched her blonde hair and gripped her reticule. "I hate to speak of something so rude. My husband I argued about this you see, and while he thinks I'm daft to say anything, I would want to know. The truth will out, he always says. But how will it come out if no one tells him?"

"Tells who?" Dyngley asked.

"You. So here I am."

"Yes?" he asked.

"To tell you."

This was beginning to sound like a farce. "Tell me what, exactly?"

"I've seen your fiancée." She looked uncomfortable and glanced away.

"Yes, I see her most days."

"No, you don't understand. I've seen her with another man," she whispered, even though there was no one nearby.

Dyngley stiffened. "And just what did you see?"

"Well, she was walking in a very familiar way with another young man. Arm in arm, if you must know."

"Who was the man?"

"I don't know. I've seen him around before. I could point him out to you if you like. When I next see him, that is," she said.

"That is very kind of you but there is no need. You are describing Mr. Barton, Caroline's cousin. He is in town, and she has been staying with him."

"Oh. Her cousin," she repeated, "That makes much more sense. I am glad to have that resolved. I did not mean to trouble you and then there I go making you believe the worst. I am sorry, Constable."

"Think no more of it. It was an honest mistake. I am sure you were acting in what you thought was my best interests," he said.

"Yes. I am. I was. On the subject of that, I meant to ask you about the money."

"What money?"

"Well… Before Mr. Ingleby died, he called on us many times and told us how hard life was for Mrs. Greene and Miss Morton, especially as the good Mr. Greene was trying to pay for the roof repairs himself. I remember it now, as he took one look around our sitting room, which we are very proud of by the way, and said how nice it must be to have such finery when the missus Greene barely had candles."

"Candles?" Dyngley repeated.

"Yes. He said it had come to his attention that they were very mean with their candles, and the reason was that the good reverend would rather squint or read by firelight than waste precious funds on idle frivolities. He said the least we could do as good Christians would be to donate money, for the repair of the church roof."

Dyngley was beginning to have his concerns about this roof. "Yes?"

"Well, we gave him twenty pounds."

Dyngley's eyes widened.

"And now that he is dead, we were wondering what's to become of the money? Not that I mind, of course, we're not hard up. It's just that he pocketed it right away and then not much later he stopped calling so often. So I wondered, I mean, did Miss Morton take it or did Lady Cameron or…"

His eyebrows knit together. "I'm afraid that the money donated for the church roof at the baking contest is gone. It went missing after the fete. In the chaos of Mr. Ingleby's death, it went missing."

Mrs. Grant's hands flew to her mouth. "Oh my."

"But we are looking for it. I assure you, we will find it. Along with whoever killed Mr. Ingleby," he said.

"Of course, you will. Of course. I will ask around and see if anyone knows where it might have gone."

Dyngley bowed and prepared to take his leave of her when she didn't move. "Yes? Was there something else?" he asked.

"Only that we are missing a comb of mine. I wore it at dinner, and it fell out and I put it aside, but then it went missing."

"A comb?"

"It's inlaid with mother of pearl. A gift from my uncle, from his voyage from the West Indies. It's very valuable," she said, "and it's very special to me. It has a tiny ship motif carved into it."

"Have you spoken with the servants?" he asked.

"We have but they all deny it. They've been with us for years, so why would they steal now?" she shrugged.

"I will keep a lookout," he said, eager to get away.

"Oh Constable? One more thing."

He turned back. "Yes?"

"Well, if Miss Everly is just cousins with that man, as you say, then why did I see her kissing him?"

CHAPTER TWENTY-FIVE

P OPPY HAD GONE home, bathed and laundered her clothes, as well as Dyngley's coat. Betsey was an excellent kitchen maid, but as a housemaid she was a bit overstretched. The following day Poppy rose, refreshed, and went to pay a visit to Jane.

As she passed by the old Crosskeys tavern, a familiar peal of womanly laughter stopped her in her tracks. She paused before an alleyway and heard a pair talking.

"Where could it be? He promised it was a lot," a man said, "more than enough to settle his debt to us. Enough to set us up for life."

"And you believed him?" a woman tutted. "I should have known you'd botch this. Leave it to me."

Poppy made to go, then stopped. One of the voices sounded familiar. She cocked her head to listen.

"You hear something?" the man asked.

"No. Probably a cat. You're hearing things that aren't there. Next you'll be saying a ghost found you."

"It weren't no ghost," he muttered, "Girl caught me by surprise, that's all."

"We'll have to try again soon. He's bound to have hidden it somewhere."

"What about your man?"

The woman laughed. "Don't worry about him. He's wrapped

around my little finger. As long as he marries into a fortune, he don't care where I go or what I do."

"Or who you see?" the man asked suggestively.

The sound of amorous kissing hit her ears, and Poppy realized she was trespassing on a courting couple's privacy. She took a deep breath when the man walked out of the alley when she recognized him, or so she thought. He looked familiar somehow, as if she had seen that dark green coat and smart hat before, paired with the same pair of beige trousers. He looked quite jaunty with a walking stick in hand, and his light brown curls showing beneath his top hat.

Poppy wondered who he and his companion were, but then she spied Jane across the road.

"Miss Heyworth," she called and waved.

Was it her imagination, or did Jane look away before recognizing her? She offered Poppy a polite glance of recognition as Poppy successfully avoided carriages and crossed the road to join her.

"Miss Morton," Jane looked warily at Poppy. "I have heard a disturbing report."

"Oh? Do tell me, for I am just on my way into town. I have to pay the carpenter for Mr. Ingleby's coffin."

Jane's polite expression fell. "Oh. That sounds like a dreary business."

"Would you like to accompany me? Then you can tell me all about this report you have heard. Is it about anyone we know?" Poppy asked.

"You could say that, yes."

Together the girls walked through town to the carpenter's workshop, where Poppy paid the man a pound and four shillings. He showed her the finished work. "It's elm, with two pairs of handles," he said proudly.

"It looks very nice." Poppy agreed. "So it's ready for tomorrow then?"

"Yes. I'll have my boys bring it round the cold storage house."

"Thank you," Poppy said.

Jane repressed a shudder as they walked out of the shop. "That place sends a chill through me, I swear."

"You've been reading too many novels. It's only a coffin," Poppy said.

"Never mind about that. Look over there, it's him." Jane pointed.

There across the street strolled Jane's mystery man, Mr. Colin Barton, whom Jane had locked eyes with and fancied from when they first went to the sweets shop. But at the sight of him, Poppy's face fell. This was the same man who had come out of the alley, right down to the ornate topped walking stick, the green coat and top hat. No matter the number of handsome smiles he might offer her friend, Mr. Barton was courting someone else.

"Isn't he dashing? So handsome." Jane watched him walk ahead on some errand. "I wonder where he's going."

Poppy didn't reply.

Jane looked at her. "Miss Morton?"

"Yes?"

"Don't you agree, he is very handsome?"

"Very handsome," Poppy agreed.

"Not so handsome as my brother, but I find his face very pleasing," Jane said and looked at Poppy. "What is it? You know something, don't you?"

"What? No." Poppy shook her head.

"Out with it. It's not like you to be so quiet."

Poppy smiled at that, but it soon faded. "Miss Heyworth, I think he is… um…"

"What? Tell me," Jane said.

"I think he is courting another girl."

Jane stared at her. "You're teasing me."

"I am not."

"You are, and I don't like it. You are trying to test me, to see how much I like him. Well, I tell you now, I like him very much.

And I don't care a fig about what anyone says."

Poppy stiffened and looked away, seeing her unhappy reflection in a shop's window. "That's as may be, but I overheard him talking with a young woman and it seemed like they were courting."

"Who? What young woman?" Jane asked.

"I didn't see her exactly, but I did hear her."

"Then you have no proof. No evidence," Jane said triumphantly, then paused. "Frankly Miss Morton, I'm surprised at you. Or rather, I'm not. I should have known you would be like this."

"What do you mean?" Poppy asked. "I was only trying to help. I thought you would want to know."

Jane frowned at her. "The disturbing report I mentioned? It was about you."

"What? Me?"

"Yes. Miss Everly paid me a call earlier and told me everything. How you took a tumble in the river and pulled that constable in after you, so he would have to rescue you. How when she confronted you about it, you denied having any feelings for the constable at all and instead announced your love for another man, but refused to say who. How you practically threw yourself at her fiancé to try and catch him. I must say I find it all a bit ungrateful, especially when she is only doing you a kindness, and I won't even mention your treatment of my brother."

"I beg your pardon?" Poppy stared at her. "I did fall. But I didn't pull him in after me. It was not so romantic or as devious as you say."

"Then you did do it." Jane paled. "I had hoped to hear you deny it ever happened, but now that I hear you—"

"Nothing happened between us. The constable is a friend, nothing more," Poppy said through gritted teeth. "I was walking too close to the edge of the riverbank, lost my balance and fell in. He dove in after me and helped me ashore. I assure you, nothing untoward happened. It was a rather soggy situation." She smiled at her own wit.

"You laugh about your attempts to capture another girl's fiancé? I cannot believe you. She warned me about you, you know. Miss Everly said that no man was safe with you in town. You might act all meek and innocent, but in truth you're worming your way into men's hearts and toying with their affections."

"And that is what you think of me?" Poppy asked. "Jane, I'm telling you the truth. Will you not take me at my word?"

"How can I, when I hear this disturbing account of your behavior? And then you admit to it, by telling me to stay away from a desirable man. You're as bad as Mr. Ingleby, God rest his soul." She crossed herself.

Poppy's mouth fell open. "Miss Heyworth, I swear to you, I have no devious plans to try and steal other girls' beaus. I only told you because it is the truth; I did hear Mr. Barton laughing with another woman, and it sounded very much like they were courting. If it were me, I would want to know. I was only trying to tell you as a friend."

"A friend? Hah. As if I could stay friends with you after this. You probably have designs on him yourself and that's why you fabricated this stupid story. Well, I don't believe a word of it." Jane laughed and it was mocking.

"I promise you, I have no interest in your young man," Poppy snapped.

"How can I believe that when you encouraged my own brother in his affections? I once thought that Robert might do for you, but now I see I was mistaken. He's too good for a girl like you." Jane seethed. "And you, throwing yourself at that poor constable. Cannot you see he made his choice? He has chosen Miss Everly, who I daresay is much more amiable and honest than you."

"How can you speak of Miss Everly and honesty in the same breath? I thought you two disliked each other," Poppy said, her hands trembling.

"She and I have come to an understanding. We know each

other to be good honest young women, without an unkind bone in our bodies. Miss Louisa Alleyn warned me that you weren't to be trusted, but now I know it to be true. You are after whatever man you can find and haven't a care if he is already engaged. Around you, no man is safe." Jane's eyes flashed.

"Miss Heyworth, I... I thought we were friends." Poppy's voice shook.

"So did I. I'm just sorry I spent so much time worrying about your feelings, instead of sparing a thought for my own." Jane sniffed.

"I do believe we have nothing else to talk about. Good day." Poppy walked away, blinking away tears.

POPPY STUMBLED HOME, miserable. She rubbed at her eyes angrily, brushing the tears away. She would not cry about this. But as she crossed the road to take the path home she bumped into a person. "Oh, excuse me." She looked at the ground, hoping to hide her teary state from beneath her bonnet.

"Watch where yer going. Oh, it's you," a familiar voice said.

Poppy looked up and met the steady gaze of Mr. Jenkins. "Hello."

"Where are you going? Something in your eye?"

"Yes. Some dust, I think." She wiped her eyes again.

"Aye well. I got enough to worry about without you getting in my way," he said.

"I'm sorry," she mumbled.

He stared at her.

"What?" she asked.

"You look like your dog died. Something happen?" his piggish eyes narrowed.

"No. I'm fine." She sniffed.

"Fair enough, it's no difference if you don't want to say. You and everyone else in this town," he said, scratching his chest.

"What do you mean?"

"I've just been called over to the Alleyns, cause Mr. Alleyn is missing a pocket watch. Seems he left it out a few days ago when they were entertaining and now it's gone. He can't remember when he lost it and they've asked the servants and they don't know where it is either."

"Oh. Is it very valuable?"

He nodded. "Gold. A gift from a French cousin. Worth at least ten pounds."

Poppy's eyes widened. That was expensive indeed. "Why did he report it now?"

Mr. Jenkins shrugged. "These people only call us as a last resort. They try to find it and hunt around, then once they do call us it's usually right under their noses."

"Did you find it?"

"No. But I will. I can promise you that." He touched his black hat and said, "Mind you look after yerself, Miss Morton."

"And you, Mr. Jenkins."

They parted ways and she took care walking home, thinking about what she had learnt. She had many things to worry about, and yet a thought niggled in her brain, pushing her forward at greater speed. Something that had occurred to her which she didn't believe, and did not wish to still, but she had to check.

She ran in her haste to get home, her bonnet flapping against her head. As she flung open the front door, she startled her aunt, who called from the sitting room, "Poppy, is that you?"

"Yes." Poppy shut the front door behind her and hurried up the stairs, her boots slapping the wooden steps. She dashed up the top of the stairs and turned right, following the corridor to the far right, to the room they had prepared for Mr. Ingleby. She stopped before it, her hand trembling above the doorknob. She took a breath, twisted it and walked inside.

The room smelled. Discarded plates with the vestiges of crumbs had attracted flies, and more than one glass of wine lay set off to the side of a small writing desk. From the collection of dirty plates and empty glasses, he had been taking food to his room for a while. She took one sniff of a teacup and wrinkled her nose. It smelled like rhubarb, and she could see the leaves collected at the bottom of the cup, staining the white china.

The man was messy, that much was clear, even with his clothes. For one who took such care with his appearance, his bedroom told a different story. Boots and socks lay strewn about the floor, and his trousers, waistcoats, white linen shirts, and cravats were flung haphazardly about the room. One or two hung in a closet, but most of his clothing lay in wadded up piles on the floor, leading from the door to the bed. As she drew closer to it, a noxious smell came from that side of the room.

She walked over to his bed. Like his clothes, the bedding was disturbed, but that didn't surprise her. Below the bed sat a chamber pot that stank. He had not had the presence of mind to put a cloth over it for delicacy, no doubt thinking to hand it to Betsey before he needed it again. As she approached it, she pinched her nose and peered down. The urine in the pot was red with blood.

She stepped back and came to stand by his small writing desk and peered down.

"What are you doing?" Aunt Rachel asked, "Pooh, it stinks in here."

Poppy turned around. "I know. I was looking for something. Anything. I realized that we're burying him tomorrow and we don't know him very well. We have no one to write to, we don't know if he had any family."

"I wrote to Reginald and told him, shortly after Mr. Ingleby died. And it's true, we don't know about any family connections. Is that why you're disturbing his things?"

"It's not like he's coming back for them." Poppy quipped. "And it does smell in here. I think he was sick, aunt. The chamber pot…"

"I have no interest in that man's chamber pot." Aunt Rachel held a finger against her nostrils. "Well. I can't abide such morbid business but if you find any letters from family or anything that might give us a clue, do let me know. Maybe we should bury him with his effects?"

"I doubt it. His family will want them, surely," Poppy said, "Aunt Rachel?"

"Yes?"

"Perhaps you could take this downstairs with you." Poppy held up the fragrant teacup.

"What is that?" Aunt Rachel sniffed its contents. "Oh, it smells like rhubarb. How odd, we don't have any rhubarb tea."

"Miss Heyworth told me that he was taking an herbal tea remedy from Mrs. Walker, on account of his poor constitution."

"Was he? That doesn't surprise me. Very well." Aunt Rachel took the offensive cup and left her.

Poppy examined the papers on the writing desk, but all that was there were a few notes and scattered sermons. She looked over the notes, but nothing seemed out of place, aside from the collection of invitations to dinner he had painstakingly arranged in a little pile at the head of the table. He had liked being a popular dinner companion, she gathered.

She turned, ready to go when her boot caught on something, and she tripped and fell to the floor.

On her hands and knees, she brushed herself off and backed up, standing to look for whatever it was that had caught her boot.

There it was, a floorboard had come loose. She bent to raise it slightly and push its edge back into place, but it wouldn't budge. "That's odd," Poppy said aloud.

She pushed but still the board refused to move. She peered down at it, then lifted it up to see if there was a rock or button lodged beneath it. She tugged and a bit of paper peeked out from beneath. She tugged and pulled, and the floorboard rose with a loud noise, revealing a depression in the space.

"Poppy? What was that sound?" Aunt Rachel's voice carried up the stairs.

"Aunt Rachel? You'd better come up quick."

In moments, Aunt Rachel stood in the doorway. "What is it, child?"

"I think I know why Mr. Ingleby died."

CHAPTER TWENTY-SIX

POPPY STARED AT the collection of trinkets and letters stuffed into the space. There was a gold pocket watch, a pearl comb, her aunt's silver bracelet, coins, and letters. She took it all out and laid the items on the floor.

"My word. What in heaven is all that?" Aunt Rachel asked, looking on from the doorway.

"Your bracelet, Aunt." Poppy held it up to her.

"What was it doing in Mr. Ingleby's room?" she asked.

"I think a better question to ask is what is all this doing here? As far as I can tell, none of it is his."

"Are you sure? Maybe he stowed it away for safekeeping," Aunt Rachel said.

"What use would he have for your bracelet? And why would he keep a gold pocket watch hidden away and not wear it?" Poppy asked.

"That is true. He was rather vain. Maybe it had broken?"

Poppy shook her head. "I doubt it."

"Poppy," her aunt said, "I think that's the missing collection money."

Poppy stared at the little pile of notes and coins with dread. "I think you're right."

"What do we do with it? We can't very well keep it."

"It's for the church, so that's what we'll use it for." Poppy's shoulders fell a bit. "We'd better call the constable."

CONSTABLE DYNGLEY AND his deputy arrived a short while later. Betsey prepared tea while Aunt Rachel greeted them politely in the sitting room. "Constable, Deputy, hello."

The men bowed, the ladies curtseyed, and Poppy kept her eyes fixed on the floor. She could feel the constable's gaze on her as he asked, "What happened?"

"Poppy, you tell him," Aunt Rachel said.

Poppy looked at a fixed point on the constable's chest and then at Mr. Jenkins as she relayed what she had found.

"Show us," Constable Dyngley said.

She led them up the stairs and into Mr. Ingleby's room. She pointed at the floor. "There, that is where I found it. If I hadn't tripped over the loose floorboard, I would never have noticed it."

Constable Dyngley frowned and pinched his nose. "What is that smell?"

Poppy felt a trifle embarrassed. "His chamber pot. I think you'll find there's blood in there."

Mr. Jenkins shot her a bemused look, as Constable Dyngley stepped forward to examine the white porcelain bowl. "So there is. I wonder what Dr. Wilson would make of that." He pushed it away with his boot.

Mr. Jenkins stepped forward and peered at the item, noting the others on the floor. "Look, that's Mr. Alleyn's pocket watch."

Dyngley came forward and picked up the fragile comb, holding its iridescent mother of pearl handle up in the light. "And here, if I'm not mistaken, is Mrs. Grant's missing comb."

"We found my aunt's missing bracelet among the items as well," Poppy said, "and we think the money there is the collection money that went missing from the church."

"Some money went missing?" Dyngley looked at her. "Why did you not report it?"

"We did. I sent you a note about it," Poppy said.

"Aye, I came and looked into it. Didn't find nothing," Mr.

Jenkins said.

"Tell me more," Constable Dyngley said, putting the comb back on the floor.

Poppy crossed her arms beneath her chest. "Weeks ago, the money from the church collection plate went missing. We first thought it had gotten misplaced, and then Mr. Ingleby was sure that one of the altar boys took it, but the boy came and said he didn't–"

"Which boy was this?"

"Geoffrey Sutton."

Mr. Jenkins snorted and said, "I know that boy. He's stolen apples from my mum's orchard before. He's a thief, no doubt about it. Church money though, that's a new one. His mum baked honey cakes for the contest too. And if they've had words with the dead man, that's a motive, Constable."

"Wait a minute, we are sure the boy didn't do it. Geoffrey simply went to a different church, he never saw Mr. Ingleby after that. Besides, the money is here," Poppy said.

"Can you say for certain that the boy never met Mr. Ingleby again?" Constable Dyngley asked. "How do you know that money there is the missing church collection money and not Mr. Ingleby's own funds?"

Jenkins said, "What if it's the baking contest money? Mayhap he took it for safekeeping."

Poppy frowned. "I don't know if it's from his personal funds, but I doubt it. I think we can eliminate the fact that it's the money from the baking contest, as that was in a box. We'd find the box here, surely. Even then, he died and we would have found the box on his person. It wouldn't be here, because he never had a chance to come back here alive after the contest." She sighed. "But this proves Mr. Ingleby was a thief. How else do you explain my aunt's missing bracelet here along with the other missing items?"

Dyngley rubbed the side of his face. "I don't like this. Mr. Jenkins, speak with Mrs. Greene downstairs and make a list of the items found here. Take this." He pulled a small wooden stick from his pocket and a scrap of paper.

"What is that?" Jenkins asked.

"A pencil. It is a new invention, for ease of writing without a quill. It is a new thing in London; I purchased one at a stationer's shop a few months ago."

"How does it work?" Poppy asked.

"It is a stick of graphite which some entrepreneurial soul has fixed within two slim pieces of wood. I have seen other sticks of graphite wrapped with string, but it does leave one's hands messy. Here." He offered it to the deputy, who took it warily with two pudgy fingers.

"Don't see the point. It'll never catch on," Mr. Jenkins said, eyeing it with distaste.

"Go on. I need to have a word with Miss Morton," Constable Dyngley told him.

Mr. Jenkins made for the door when Poppy said, "There is no need, I'll join you downstairs."

"Stay a moment please, Miss Morton." Dyngley's voice was coldly formal.

Mr. Jenkins looked from one to the other, and walked out, leaving them alone.

Dyngley stepped over and shut the door.

"Well?" Poppy asked, uncrossing her arms. She stared at the floor.

"What is wrong with you?" he asked, "Why won't you look at me?"

Her gaze snapped up. "How can I, when the girls of this town are going around saying I'm after you?"

He laughed. "What are you talking about?" He faced her. "What are the gossips saying now?"

"That no man is safe around me. That I have little care for female friendships or engaged couples because I am after any single man in the vicinity." She saw his amused face and said, "Don't laugh."

"I assure you, Miss Morton, I take this information most seriously." He grinned. "Who is talking about you?"

"Your fiancée. Louisa Alleyn. And Jane Heyworth."

"I thought Miss Heyworth was your friend."

"Apparently not," she said glumly.

"And are you after the men of the neighborhood?" he asked.

"No. Of course not. How could you think that?"

"Peace, Miss Morton." He stepped close to her. "I know that you are innocent in this. Anyone who cares to know you will too."

They stood close enough she could smell his aftershave. "Constable, I..." she started.

"How could anyone accuse you of impropriety when they know you love someone else. These are rumors, nothing more. Once these misses are engaged or married, they will trouble you no longer. They will then turn on each other, as gossips always do."

"And what of your fiancée?" she asked.

"What about her?"

"She spoke against me too." Realizing they stood too close for propriety, she backed up a step.

"I will speak with her. She is troubled, after the river incident. I fear she has gotten the idea in her head that we are courting behind her back." He snorted. "You love another man. Who is the lucky fellow? Perhaps if we saw you two together, it might ease her concerns."

"There is no other man," Poppy said, "I lied."

"You did? Oh." he looked at her. "Why?"

"You know why." Her heart thumped in her chest.

He looked at her blankly.

"Because I did not wish to admit that what she said is true, Constable. I do have feelings for you."

CHAPTER TWENTY-SEVEN

C ONSTABLE DYNGLEY STARED at Poppy, his mouth dropping open.

"Poppy!" her aunt called. "Come down, the tea is getting cold."

"Miss Morton…" he began, his dark eyes looking directly into hers.

"Poppy!" her aunt called again.

"I must go. Excuse me." She walked past him and quit the room.

As Dyngley walked downstairs and joined the company, Aunt Rachel handed Poppy a cup of tea, "My goodness Poppy but you are looking rather pink. Have some tea, that will restore you."

Mr. Jenkins glanced at Dyngley in the doorway, then at Poppy. He said, "I'm taking it all down." He waved the pencil in the air. "It's, handy, this. What do you call it again?"

"A pencil. Ladies, we cannot stay. It was very wise of you to call us," Constable Dyngley said.

"Anytime, Constable. Whenever there is a crime, we shall know to call you. Pray, where are you staying, if we have need of you?"

Constable Dyngley glanced at the matron. "You can find me at Mr. Phillips' boarding house, on Castle Street. But there is no need, as I will see you both at the funeral tomorrow."

"Yes." Aunt Rachel looked away. "It is distressing to find we had a thief beneath our roof. Poppy if you recall, I did have my doubts about him at times."

"What I wonder is what happened to the money raised for the church roof at the fete?" Poppy asked.

"What do you mean?" Mr. Jenkins asked.

"Well, the money I found was clearly taken from the church collection plate. But the money raised at the fete would have been much more than a handful of banknotes and shillings. Assuming that Mr. Ingleby took it, where did he hide it, I wonder?" Poppy asked.

"I don't know," Dyngley admitted. "But I think it is possible that he didn't take the baking contest money at all. We would have found it on his person and besides, he was dead by the time people noticed it was missing."

"Then someone else took it," Poppy said, her mouth dropping open. "There's more than one thief."

"Maybe. Let's not jump to conclusions. In any case, you can keep the money you found, or put it wherever you put the collection money each Sunday." He touched his hat. "Do excuse us. We must be going."

DYNGLEY LEFT WITH the missing items stuffed into his coat pockets. Mr. Jenkins followed him soon after and hurried to catch up. Dyngley had long legs but slowed his pace for his deputy.

"Come, we will pay our respects to the families. If you take Mr. Grant's pocket watch back to him, I'll return Mrs. Alleyn's hair comb to her." He mused darkly about what Poppy had said. "And maybe have a word with her daughter, Louisa."

"Don't let that fiancée of yours find out. She'll think you have eyes for another girl…"

"Don't you start," Dyngley said, "I've had enough of the women in my life deciding who I fancy."

"Oho, trouble in paradise? You're not even married yet." Mr. Jenkins snorted.

At a dirty look from Dyngley, Mr. Jenkins cleared his throat. "You going to the funeral?"

"Aren't you?" Dyngley asked.

"No. Why would I?"

"Everyone who is involved in this death will be there. Innocent or not, Mr. Ingleby insulted so many people in this town, I believe it will be a very crowded affair."

"What for? Bit morbid if you ask me," Mr. Jenkins said.

"Some will go for the entertainment; others will want to see him in the ground. And I suspect one person will be very glad to see him buried and gone."

"Who's that?" Jenkins asked.

"Whoever killed him."

THE NEXT DAY was dull with a gray morning light as Dyngley dressed in his darkest clothes, then realized that Poppy still had one of his walking coats. He hurried along in his second darkest coat and was glad of it, for despite being August, there was a nip in the morning air.

He walked along the dirt track that curved around the small graveyard behind St. Andrew's church, and happened to walk behind a young tall woman and another portly one. From their voices, he recognized Poppy and her aunt immediately.

These two wore frocks in drab colors and huddled together as if to ward off a chill. Then as Poppy opened the doors, she stopped.

The church was nearly full.

"Why are there so many people here?" Poppy asked.

"He must have touched many lives," Aunt Rachel said sagely.

"You're in a good humor," Poppy said.

"Am I? I shall have to try better to hide it."

"I don't see why you should. Everyone in town knows we didn't like him."

"But he's dead and not everyone believes it wasn't us who killed him. We'll see a few unhappy faces today I'm sure," Aunt

Rachel said.

Dyngley cleared his throat. "Good morning, ladies."

Poppy whirled around, blushed, and muttered, "Good morning," and walked on ahead.

Aunt Rachel glanced at her quickly retreating figure. "What have you said to my niece, Constable? I have not seen her so disturbed in many weeks."

"Nothing of consequence, Mrs. Greene. I assure you." He followed Mrs. Greene into the church, a fine old building with high oak beams, darkened with age, low wooden pews that creaked and drafty aisles in between.

Sunlight streamed through simple glass windows as Dyngley looked around and noticed all of the families who baked desserts for the contest on the day of Mr. Ingleby's death. Why were they all here?

Soon met by Mr. Jenkins, Dyngley met the long faces and serious gazes of the Suttons, Grants, Alleyns, the Heyworth brother and sister looking like a matched pair in a set of dark blue clothes; Mrs. Walker and even Lady Cameron made an entrance, followed by two footmen. She had a pew all to herself, as was her way. No one dared disturb her.

He stood by the back and watched as she nodded gravely to Poppy and her aunt, a great condescension on her part.

He also saw Caroline enter, who glanced at him and then ignored him, only to look over and see Robert Heyworth glaring at him and then Poppy. Robert murmured something to his sister before watching Poppy and her aunt take their places in the front row.

He walked over to where Caroline sat alone and knowing many in the congregation were watching, stood at the end of the pew. "May I join you?"

Caroline pursed her lips and tilted her head in thought. "Hm, I don't know if it would be proper."

She was toying with him. He muttered, "Move," and stepped into the pew, forcing her to shuffle aside.

"Honestly, Dyngley," she tutted and faced him. "What are you doing?" she whispered.

"Sitting beside my fiancée. Or is that not allowed?"

"I am surprised you would want to, considering your dalliance with Miss Morton," she hissed.

"There is nothing going on between Miss Morton and myself," he said curtly. "And I'll thank you not to speak of her when in conversation with others. You have done her enough harm with your idle gossip."

"Hah." Her harsh laugh echoed in the quiet building. "It is not gossip if it is true."

"There is no truth to it. Honestly, Caroline, what do I have to do to convince you?"

"Run away with me. Let's go to Gretna Greene, tonight."

He laughed at her. Her face, twisted in anger, made him feel better. "Don't be absurd. You'd rather have the world think I have taken advantage of you? I think not. We will wait and marry once it is proper."

"And when will that be? Why do I have to wait while you go around town in the company of that strumpet, under the pretense of investigating Mr. Ingleby's death? For God's sake, Dyngley. What am I supposed to think when that girl throws herself at you? As if the river wasn't enough. That girl is just like her mother."

"What did you say?" he asked. "What about her mother?"

"Wouldn't you like to know?" She smiled snidely.

Mr. Grant turned around in his seat and said, "Ahem. If you would care to lower your voices, the funeral service is about to begin."

Caroline smiled sweetly at him, a picture of innocence, while Dyngley sat back and crossed his arms.

The service began. Perhaps it was a sign of how little the guest minister, Mr. Reed, knew the deceased, or that the man had a ready-made sermon prepared for any untimely death, but he spoke about the arrival of Mr. Ingleby, his great heart and passion for doing good works, that as he was suddenly struck down meant he was taken by the Lord too early.

Dyngley heard sniffs and coughs and looked around. More than one woman held a handkerchief to her eyes to dab at non-existent tears, and Louisa Alleyn looked positively wretched. He made eye contact with the sober-faced Dr. Wilson, who looked on the proceedings with concern.

Dyngley felt his pain. To go to Miss Alleyn's aid would be kind, but would do the doctor no favors. Dr. Wilson's attention to her would no doubt set tongues wagging and build up the hopes of her mother and the matrons of the neighbors that they would wed, not to mention the expectations of Louisa herself. Dyngley knew well the perilous line a man walked when offering even a polite attention to a girl which might offend so many others.

But was he now thinking about Dr. Wilson still, or himself? He had encouraged Poppy in her own investigation of this murder, but at what cost? Now the poor girl had feelings for him. And his fiancée, threatened by his attentions toward her, had now spread false rumors about them both to ruin Poppy's reputation. He would dismiss the allegations with no harm done, but to a penniless girl like Poppy, Caroline's words in the wrong ear could be devastating. It was cruel, and he would have to put a stop to it.

He gripped the wooden pew he sat on and squeezed, sending tension into the hard wooden bench. He whispered, "If you know something about Miss Morton's mother, you should tell her. She has a right to know."

"Oh, I will. When it suits me," Caroline chuckled.

"What did you find?" he asked.

Mr. Grant turned and shushed at them. "Shh."

"I learned that the good Miss Morton is not the meek innocent she pretends to be. Her mother is quite another character indeed. It's no wonder her aunt and uncle adopted her when she has such a mother. I wouldn't want that sort of woman in my family."

"Hold your tongue," he said. "You have spread nasty rumors about that girl, and it's unkind."

She snorted softly. "We'll see."

Mr. Reed shot them a dark look and said, "It is a terrible crime that took Mr. Ingleby from this earth too soon."

At the same moment, a voice hissed, "Not soon enough. His killer is here."

Mr. Reed turned red and stopped talking.

Constable Dyngley said, "Who said that?"

The voice rose again, "I know his killer is here. He told me he thought his life was in danger. And one of you did it."

Louisa Alleyn rose from her seat, her face white and pinched with emotion. She faced the congregation and ignored her family's attempts to quiet her. "Arrest her, Constable! Arrest Miss Poppy Morton."

Beside him, Caroline smiled.

CHAPTER TWENTY-EIGHT

POPPY PALED AS dozens of suspicious faces turned toward her. The congregation was in an uproar. Poppy said, "I didn't do it, I swear."

Her aunt rose and turned back to say, "Shame on you, Miss Alleyn, spreading vicious lies."

"It's not a lie if it's the truth," Louisa shot back. "She has long had it in for Mr. Ingleby. She didn't like what he was saying about her and her aunt, and now she has had her revenge."

"Louisa, stop this at once. You don't know what you're saying." Mrs. Alleyn stood and tried to urge her to sit down.

"No. I won't be silenced. You should all know, Mr. Ingleby and I were… that is to say we… had an understanding. I don't care who knows it. We were sweethearts."

Mrs. Alleyn shook her head. "No, you weren't. Mary, help me," she told her younger daughter.

"Mrs. Alleyn?" Constable Dyngley asked. "This is a very serious allegation."

"It is, and I for one have no appreciation for amateur dramatics," Mr. Reed said, an angry red flush climbing up his neck, in stark contrast to his clerical collar. "Dear lady, your daughter is overcome. Please see her outside."

"Come along, dear," Mrs. Alleyn urged, gently nudging Louisa to move.

"No. I won't budge. Not until that girl is arrested for what she's done. You, Constable, how long will you allow a murderer to walk freely about the town?" Louisa glanced at Caroline and said, "But then perhaps the gossip is true. Miss Morton truly has entranced you with her charms. We all know what a temptress she is."

"Hold your tongue!" Mrs. Alleyn scolded. She looked at the constable. "Forgive her, she is overwrought."

"It is not me she should apologize to," he told her.

Mrs. Alleyn looked at Poppy and swallowed. "Yes, well. Louisa, we are leaving. Right now." She pushed her daughter out of the pew and Louisa stepped out, weeping.

Dr. Wilson stepped in and instantly Louisa collapsed on him, allowing him to guide her outside. Dyngley followed and soon stepped into the morning sunshine, followed by Mr. and Mrs. Alleyn and their daughter Mary, as well as Poppy and her aunt.

Once the church doors closed, Dyngley rounded on Louisa. "Miss Alleyn, what do you have to say for yourself?"

"Me? It is her you should be asking. She is the one who killed him." Louisa glared at Poppy.

Poppy stared back. "I didn't kill him. Why on earth would you think I had anything to do with it?"

"Because you hated him for all the nasty things he said about you. He told me the last time he saw me, that your aunt had threatened him, and knowing how spinsterly you were, he feared for his life," Louisa said tearfully.

"Louisa," her mother chided. "Miss Morton, I am sorry for this. My girl has been under some strain since that man's death, and—"

"His name was Mr. Ingleby, mother. And I know it to be true because I never saw him again, except at the church fete." Louisa wiped away a tear. "I saw him, disqualifying your aunt's pudding at the contest. He must have known you were trying to poison him."

Poppy blinked in disbelief. "And just what did I poison him

with?"

"Well, I don't know. Salt instead of sugar? Rat poison? Anything is possible. And he did taste it before he died."

"I've had about enough of this," Aunt Rachel snapped. "First, I hear nasty rumors flying about my niece and now this. Mrs. Alleyn, have a care for your girl. She seems overwrought and her tongue is flying away with her."

Mrs. Alleyn shot Aunt Rachel a thinly veiled glare. "Mrs. Greene, whatever trouble my daughter has caused is only because your niece has made it possible. She is not the meek miss she claims to be."

"Why, I beg your pardon—"

"I have heard an alarming report of your behavior. But… No. I know Miss Morton to be a sensible girl, and I'm not one to listen to idle gossip. The fact is…" she turned to Louisa, "Mr. Ingleby was not the gentleman you thought him to be. I thought he might do for you and hinted as much, and he laughed in my face."

"What?" Louisa turned pale. "He wouldn't."

"He did. Why do you think he stopped calling around?" Mrs. Alleyn asked her.

"I don't know. I thought it was something you said, or Mary perhaps."

Mary shook her head.

"He was not interested in an alliance with us and stopped calling. It was a relief, to be honest. But I did not think he had led you on so," Mrs. Alleyn said.

"I can't believe you. I don't. He wouldn't be so rude." Louisa frowned.

"He was. And he stole. My missing hair comb turned up in his possession."

"What?" Louisa asked.

"He was a thief, Louisa, and we are better off without him." She glanced at Poppy. "I can see we have caused you such trouble. Come away, girls." She took Louisa by the arm and led her away, leaving Mary to follow.

"What did I miss?" Caroline came outside and shut the church door behind her. "Where are the Alleyns going?"

"Home. Where you should be," Dyngley told her.

"Oh, it sounds like I missed all the fun. What a shame."

"How could you say those things about me?" Poppy asked her. "I thought we were friends."

"Once upon a time, maybe. That ended when you tried to seduce my fiancé in a river." Caroline snapped.

"I did no such thing. I fell. He jumped in to rescue me," Poppy said.

"Exactly. Always so full of answers, always with a fresh excuse. Can anyone blame me if I'm concerned by your actions? Besides, it's not a rumor if it's true," Caroline said.

"You've caused enough trouble for one day, Miss Everly," Dyngley said, "Please."

She smiled at him. "So formal, Dyngley? Very well. I'll go. But I want to let Miss Morton know, first, that I've learned some information about her dear mother."

Aunt Rachel started. "Her mother? I'm afraid, Miss Everly, you are mistaken, Mrs. Morton is dead."

Caroline fixed Mrs. Greene with an even look. "I see deceitfulness runs in the family. Or were you withholding the truth out of kindness? I assure you, your niece deserves none." She smirked. "Miss Morton, your aunt has been lying to you. Your mother is alive and well, and living in London."

"What?" Poppy said, "Truly?"

"Oh yes. As a whore. She's ever so popular."

Poppy paled. "You're lying. You're saying this to hurt me."

"No, dear, but it does make me feel better to tell you the truth you've been so longing to hear. Didn't anyone ever tell you it's not ladylike to toy with other girls' sweethearts?"

"Caroline, that's enough. Go home," Dyngley told her. "You're being spiteful and mean."

"It is no more than she deserves," she told him, and turned to

Poppy. "Goodbye, Miss Morton, I would say I hope you don't follow in your mother's footsteps, but then it wouldn't surprise me if you already had. It would explain a number of things," she simpered and walked away.

Silence reigned for a few seconds before Dr. Wilson cleared his throat. "I had best rejoin the congregation." He touched his hat and went back inside.

Poppy stood like a spirit, frozen in place. She turned to her aunt. "Is this true? Is my mother alive and…"

"It is nonsense, my dear, the girl is simply making up lies to feed to you. Don't believe a word she says," Aunt Rachel said, her eyes wary.

"Then why did I find her letters to my uncle in his study? Why was she sending him correspondence and never to me?" she demanded. "Why did you all pretend my mother was dead? And don't deny it, I found the proof."

Aunt Rachel sighed and her shoulders slumped. "I will tell you everything. But not now. It's not the time nor place for such a discussion."

"Then when?"

"Give Reginald and me the chance to tell you properly, together. Once he gets back. I never approved of the decision to keep this from you and it's high time you learned. Will you wait?"

Poppy let out a breath. "All right."

They walked back into the church, and quietly reclaimed their seats at the front. Poppy felt the others' eyes on them but didn't care. What she wanted to know was, who killed Mr. Ingleby?

CHAPTER TWENTY-NINE

T HE FUNERAL SERVICE was done. Poppy and her aunt made a pact not to speak to anyone but walked out after the coffin was taken to the churchyard and stood by the gravesite. They waited until almost everyone had gone, and then paid the reverend, altar boys, and gravediggers for their work.

By the time they returned home, the front door to the parsonage was open.

Poppy went inside. "Hello? Betsey, it's not wise to leave the door open. Betsey?"

"Where is that girl?" Aunt Rachel asked.

Poppy hung up her coat and bonnet on the coat pegs by the door and walked up the stairs. She let out a little cry. "Betsey."

"What is it? Did you find her?" Aunt Rachel hurried up after her.

Betsey lay unconscious on the landing at the top of the stairs. Her skin was pale, her eyes were shut, and her wispy blonde hair was sticky with blood.

"Oh my lord," Aunt Rachel said, "Move aside, I have more knowledge of nursing than you."

Poppy said, "I'll fetch the doctor." She got to her feet and ran out the door.

She did not know how long it took her, only that she called at the doctor's surgery and it seemed like no time at all had passed.

Dr. Wilson came immediately on his horse and gave her a ride back to the house. She stood by as Dr. Wilson and her aunt administered expert attention to Betsey. Once Betsey was laid out on Mr. Ingleby's bed and her head injury seen to, in a few minutes she came to.

"Oh!" she cried, kicking at the blanket covering her feet.

"Betsey, calm yourself, it's fine. You are safe, girl," Aunt Rachel said.

"No, you don't understand. The man, he was here." Betsey's eyes were wide.

"Who?"

"I don't know. I seen him before I think, but he was in Mr. Greene's study. I surprised him and when he turned around, he shoved me against a wall. He said *where was it* and I didn't know what he meant. He said *the money, where's the baking money* and I screamed. He hit me then and I don't know what happened. Then I woke up here."

Poppy stood back as Dr. Wilson dabbed Betsey's brow with a cool cloth. "Relax. No harm will come to you."

"I'm so sorry, Mrs. Greene, I fear he's robbed you," Betsey babbled.

Aunt Rachel frowned. "None of that. Poppy, go see if anything is disturbed."

POPPY WANDERED BACK into her uncle's office and found everything overturned. Drawers were open, his chair was overturned, papers were scattered on the floor, and it was all too familiar.

But on the floor where they had found Betsey, she spotted something else. Silver flecks of some substance lay on the floor, catching the light.

"That's odd." She dabbed at some of the silver with her finger and returned to Mr. Ingleby's room. "Dr. Wilson, could I have a word?"

She stepped outside of the room, and he followed. "What is

it?" he asked.

She held out her finger. "What do you make of this?"

He peered at it. "It looks like flakes of silver or metal. Paint, perhaps?"

"I found this with the blood on the floor. Could it have come from her attacker?"

"Definitely." He led her back inside the room to Betsey's bedside. "Betsey, did the man strike you with anything?"

"I don't know. But he did have a posh walking stick with him. I remember it had a silver top or pewter. Real nice." She shuddered. "I think he swung it at me and then... I don't recall nothing."

"There you have it, Miss Morton," Dr. Wilson said, "A man with a walking stick. Do you remember anything else, Betsey? What did he look like?"

"I don't know. I can't remember. I didn't get much of a look at him, I was so scared. Tall, I think. Green coat? Or trousers? I'm not sure."

Poppy frowned.

"Unfortunately, that could be any young man. I myself have a green coat," Dr. Wilson echoed Poppy's thoughts. He motioned for Aunt Rachel and Poppy to join him outside the room.

Once away from the vicinity, he said, "That young woman has got a nasty bump on the head, but she'll heal. She may be out of sorts for the next few days. She may feel sick or not remember what happened. Just let her rest, and don't let her back to work for a few days."

There was a knock at the front door, and Poppy went down to answer it. "Oh, hello, Constable."

"Miss Morton," he touched his hat. "I called for the doctor at his surgery and his housekeeper said he rode here. Is everything all right?"

"No. Our maid was attacked by an intruder." She stood aside to let him enter and closed the door after him.

"My God. Is she hurt?" Dyngley asked.

"Yes, she has a head wound. The doctor is seeing to her. Did you need him?"

"I'll join you if I may. What did the intruder want?"

"Money. She found him in my uncle's study."

"How odd."

"At least now we know what he was looking for. Betsey said he demanded to know where the baking money was," Poppy said.

He frowned. "That is serious. Whoever is invading your home thinks that is where the missing money is. And if they've come here a second time, they may come here a third."

Poppy led him upstairs, where he consulted with the doctor in private. She walked into the mess that was her uncle's office and began cleaning up, putting papers into neat piles, arranging ledgers and sermons into organized places on the writing desk. She was just righting his fallen chair when she noted more of the letters from her mother to him and picked it up. This one was dated two months ago.

Reginald,

How good it is to hear of my girl. Please find enclosed the following amount for her upkeep. Do send her and my dear sister all my love. I hope you will give my dear girl leave to visit me soon in London. I long to see her. It's been long enough, hasn't it?

Ever,
Celeste

Poppy turned over the letter, but found no return address on it. She still did not know where her mother was writing from. To find out more she would need to speak to Caroline, as much as it would pain her to do so. Or did she? Could she bargain with her for the information, or pay her? Not that she had any money to do so.

Poppy sat in her uncle's chair, looking at the letter when

Dyngley came in.

"Pardon me for disturbing you, but I didn't want to leave without saying goodbye. The doctor is talking with your aunt downstairs, so I'll be going."

She nodded.

"You should take care and lock the doors, Miss Morton. The thief may try to break in again."

"Oh, wait a minute. Before you go, I've got your coat to return to you. I'll just fetch it."

She walked past him into her room and got the coat, freshly laundered by herself. But as she exited her room, he was already gone.

She hurried down the steps and saw that he was just walking away from the house. The doctor had climbed atop his horse and muttered something to Dyngley, who waved him on.

It began to rain, a light patter of drops that misted in the air. Hurrying out in her dark funeral dress, Poppy advanced toward him and said, "I've got your coat."

"Thank you," he replied, taking it from her.

Their eyes met, and it sent a shiver through her. "Constable, I…" she started.

"Poppy, I thought we'd agreed to call each other by our Christian names, at least in private," he smiled. "Good friends do that, you know."

"And what if I don't want to be good friends?" she asked.

"Why not? Have I offended you?" He stood close to her, his voice quiet.

"No."

"Who else would I solve crimes with?" he asked.

"You have a deputy," she pointed out.

"And if you were a man, I would deputize you. But you're not. You're a woman."

"Exactly." She looked into his eyes.

He looked at her, utterly confused. "What—"

"For God's sake, Dyngley." She stepped forward and kissed him, shocking him to pieces.

CHAPTER THIRTY

P OPPY HAD DONE it. She had gone and in a very unladylike, forward manner, unbefitting a young woman of good family and breeding, had kissed a man.

Their lips met, pressed as softly as the touch of a butterfly, and stopped. She pulled back.

He stared at her, his dark eyes wide. "Poppy, I…"

"There. Now, do you see? I don't want to be good friends." She looked down. "I thought that if I told you how I felt or showed you, then perhaps you would see."

"Poppy," he began, "You must know that you mean a great deal to me."

She swallowed, her heart beating in her throat.

"But I am engaged to Miss Everly. I have made my choice."

"Even after all that she has said about me? She has made me out to be a monster amongst women." She let out a shaky breath. "I should have known."

"No, it's my fault." He removed his hat and ran a hand through his dark hair. "She warned me you felt this way. And God knows I believed her."

"Then you don't care for me at all." She turned her back on him.

He gently took her by the arm to turn around and face him. "You're wrong. I do care. You mean very much to me. I hold you in very high esteem. If I had a sister, I would want her to be just like you. I do not have many female acquaintances with whom I trust, or whom I would call friends. But you are one of them."

Her shoulders slumped. "And that is all we are?"

"That is all we can be," he told her. "No matter how I might…" he swallowed.

She met his gaze then, and her eyes were wet. "I am sorry. I will not continue to press you for sentiments that will only injure us both. Do excuse me."

"Poppy, wait," he said.

She turned away, rain dotting her brown hair, and wiped at her eyes angrily. "I have been a fool. It has been made perfectly clear to me that I am penniless, and even now, have a mother who didn't want me. What hope could I possibly have of measuring up against Miss Everly?"

"Do not speak of yourself so rudely," he told her. "It doesn't suit you."

She snapped, "Why should you care what does or doesn't suit me? It makes no difference what I say or do, you don't care. You're engaged. You said it yourself, you made your choice. If only I had a dowry of ten thousand pounds."

His face darkened. "If you had such a dowry then I should think you very lucky indeed."

"But not worthy of your attention." Her eyes flashed.

"I never said that."

"No. But I have been told that Miss Everly's charms extend to a handsome inheritance of that sum."

"She has many other charms. I will admit that her conduct as of late has been troubled, but I don't think you will hold that against her when she is to be my wife."

She sniffed.

"The fact is Poppy, my family's estate is in such a way, that is the estate was mishandled and my brother, he has been unwell and…"

She looked into his dark eyes then and knew what he was

trying to say. He needed an heiress. A girl with money, who could help his family. Not a penniless girl.

She nodded and drew herself up, pulling her composure over her features like a cloak. "Forgive me. I will not trouble you with such girlish fancies again." She turned toward the road.

"Poppy, don't be daft. It's raining. You'll get soaked through."

"What does it matter? You're only a friend. You don't care." She walked off into the rain.

Poppy walked and walked, not caring that her boots soon became muddy, that she walked without a bonnet or a walking coat, or that Dyngley rode impatiently beside her, then took off at a gallop, his horse's hooves angrily striking the wet muddy ground. She walked until she came into town, and saw Caroline entering into a residence in town, and realized that must be where she lived. But first, she had a stop to make. She knew where she had seen a young man with a green walking coat before. Indeed, she had even danced with him.

She knocked on the door and it was opened by Robert Heyworth. "Hello, Miss Morton." he blushed. "Come in out of the rain. What brings you here?"

"I wanted to speak with you."

"Oh?"

"Yes. I want to know why you broke into my house and attacked my servant."

He stared at her. "You're joking."

"I am not. My maidservant was attacked by an intruder just two hours ago, and she recalls seeing a young man with a green walking coat and a walking stick with a metal top." Her eyebrows rose expectantly.

"And you thought it was me? You are mistaken, Miss Morton. What reason would I have to go parading around your house?"

"I cannot say. But I know you own both those things."

"Once again you are making assumptions without knowing the whole story," he said, annoyed. "I accompanied my sister to Mr. Ingleby's funeral and then we parted ways. She went to visit the hospital and I came here, to look after my father. I have been here ever since. Ask my mother and father if you don't believe me, or one of the servants."

She looked behind him and there was a maid clearing up tea, with the spoons and saucers clattering against the tea tray.

Robert said, "I also have not worn my green coat for a week, as it got a hole in the pocket and the servants haven't patched it up yet. I should also point out that I don't own a walking stick. I'm not an invalid, old, nor carry one for show." He looked at her. "Am I still a criminal in your eyes?"

She turned pink and eyed his dark blue suit, and recognized it from the funeral. "I'm sorry. I...for all the trouble I've caused you, sorry. I'll go."

He said, "Wait a minute."

She paused.

His eyes were kind. "I know what some of the young ladies have been saying about you and I want you to know I never believed it. Not a word of it. I know we may not be close but, I would never think you fickle or inconstant. You are not one to toy with a man's affections."

She smiled. "That is true. If I were to abuse your person, at least you know I would do it to your face."

He offered her a bittersweet smile. "Do you think we might be friends?"

"I would like that."

His smile was genuine then, and almost lit up the entrance in which they stood.

She returned his happy gaze and said, "I must go."

"Miss Morton, wait. I know I have no right, but I worry about your safety, especially if a strange man has broken into your house. It is not safe for a young lady to be going around alone. Might I escort you?"

She saw he was genuinely concerned. "Do not trouble yourself, I will be fine."

She walked on to another door in the center of town and

rapped three times.

In moments, Caroline opened it, her face twisted in a sneer. "Miss Morton? What in God's name are you doing here?"

"I wanted to talk terms with you," Poppy said.

"For Dyngley?"

"For my mother."

CHAPTER THIRTY-ONE

C AROLINE GAVE HER a knowing smile. "Come in, come in."
She stood aside to let Poppy step into the entryway and shut
the door behind her. She led the way into a sitting room that had
seen better days. It was a modern dwelling, which was to say it
was rented accommodation, lightly furnished, with smoke stains
from candles marring the white walls and casting a dirty tinge
about the room. Caroline sat on a striped sofa that was overstuffed and looked serviceable, which had a side table next to it
that bore the traces of a late luncheon. There was a small hearth
and a comfortable looking chair facing the sofa, but Caroline
waggled a finger as Poppy stood in the doorway.

"I would offer you a seat, but I can see you're wet through,
and would rather you not leave a watermark on my cousin's sofa.
Be so good as to stand. Don't be offended, but I'm afraid we keep
a simple household here and that does not extend to offering tea
to guests. I'm sure you understand," she said snidely.

"Of course," Poppy said.

"You haven't been crying, have you? You look horrible. First
your maid, then you. What is this world coming to?" Caroline
asked.

"I assure you I am perfectly fine," Poppy said.

"Well, what is it? What do you want?"

"You said you learnt of my mother. Her whereabouts."

"Oh yes, I did." Caroline gave her a calculating smile.

It pained Poppy to see her looking so pretty as she did it. "I want to know. Where is she?"

"Didn't your own search turn up anything? Or perhaps you spent your time looking to entice a young constable, rather than searching for your mother. I can well understand, you know, Dyngley is quite handsome. Rather dashing."

Poppy was silent.

Caroline said, "You're no fun. Fine. I do know where your mother is living. I can give you her address. But I want something in return."

"What?"

"You are to leave Dyngley alone. Cut off all contact with him."

"But we are friends."

"Not anymore. Not if you want the information I have on your dear Mama. I have it on good authority that your mother is a well-paid whore. You need to decide, Miss Morton, which is it? My fiancé, or your mother?"

Poppy looked down at her wet hands. They were pale and damp, much like her disposition at the moment. Maybe it was better this way. She could pen Dyngley a note and explain. She would miss him of course, but maybe it was for the best.

"Well? I've got things to do, Miss Morton, I can't stand around here all day waiting for you to make a decision," Caroline said.

"Are you that threatened by me? He made his choice. He told me himself," Poppy said, her eyes glassy.

"Hah. Threatened? No. Bothered, yes. You're like a mosquito that won't go away. And if Dyngley and I are to have a happy life together, we can't be bothered with annoying little distractions like you."

Poppy took in a breath. "Do you truly think I was after him that day in the river?"

Caroline smiled. "I don't care what you were doing. What I

saw was clear enough. It doesn't matter what I think, just as long as everyone else knows you are a harlot out to steal other girls' beaus. But then, I suppose like mother, like daughter."

Poppy gritted her teeth. "Enough. Stop spreading lies about me."

"Leave my fiancé alone," Caroline snapped.

"Fine."

"Good. And you'll promise not to talk to him, or say anything? Even if he talks to you?" Caroline stood and walked over to her, until they were face to face.

"I'll walk away."

"Good girl. My, if I had known it would be this easy, I would have brought this news to you before. Very well." She left Poppy standing in the doorway before returning a moment later, holding a slip of paper in her hands. "This is her last known address. I wasn't lying. Your mother *is* a whore and quite a popular one too. I do wish you luck in your search, although I would make an effort not to take after her. Syphilis at age twenty isn't a good look for anyone," she simpered.

"Give it to me." Poppy reached for it, but Caroline plucked it away from her grasp.

"Uh, uh, promise me first. Shake hands on it. You'll not talk to Dyngley anymore. Not even if he asks you."

"I won't. I promise," Poppy said.

"If I hear of one word exchanged between you two, I'll make your life a misery. Your reputation will be ruined. You will be a laughingstock. I will tell everyone I meet that you're the bastard child of a whore. See how well your marriage prospects are then." Caroline placed the slip of paper in her hands. "Good luck, Miss Morton. I do hope we never see each other again."

"The feeling is mutual," Poppy said, marching to the front door of the house.

"Take care, I wouldn't want you to suffer the same bad luck as your maid." Caroline grinned and slammed the door in her face.

CHAPTER THIRTY-TWO

T HE NEXT DAY, Poppy prepared to write a letter. At long last she had her mother's address, but what would she say? What did one say to a woman who had not known her for years? Why had she given her up? Did she not love her?

She stared at the scrap of paper Caroline had given her. There was so much she wanted to ask and to tell. But when she put quill to paper, her hand froze, and she dropped her pen. When she picked it up, her gaze drifted to her uncle's newspaper, when the wanted advertisements caught her eye. There were requests for ladies' maids, kitchen maids, ladies' companions, milliner's shop assistants… A plan formed in her mind. Maybe she could start a new life somewhere in London and figure out a way to approach her mother. Or not.

Having written a few lines, she had a quiet morning at home, where she did little but read her uncle's newspaper for the fourth time, make bread, tend Betsey, and run down to the farmer's market in town for some fresh vegetables and to post her letter. More than once she spotted Dyngley's familiar figure, but turned her head from the sight. She had made a promise, and by her honor, she would keep it. Her heart was already sore, and maybe Caroline was simply doing her a kindness. Either she, wouldn't run the risk.

Poppy walked past the doctor's surgery with a basket full of vegetables and decided to stop by. She knocked on the door and was received by his housekeeper, who ushered her into Dr. Wilson's small sitting room where he received patients.

"Ah, hello, Miss Morton. I was just on my way to the jail. How is your maid?" he asked.

"Very well, doctor. She is improving by the day. I just thought I would pay a social call."

"That's kind of you. You know, now that Mr. Ingleby is buried, I feel like a pall over the town has lifted."

"Oh?"

"Yes. What with the man dead, there was some speculation as to what might have killed him. You recall how we wondered what might have done him in. I consulted my notes, and I don't know why I didn't see it." He tapped his chin.

"Oh?"

"He was being poisoned," Dr. Wilson said.

"But we know that, doctor. We know that one of the puddings at the contest contained arsenic and that's what killed him."

"Ah, yes. But Lady Cameron ate the same pudding and while she ingested a smaller amount, she became sick but did not die. Why? A lady of advanced age like herself might well have had a weaker constitution."

"Indeed," Poppy said.

"Yes, so then it hit me. You mentioned how before the contest, Mr. Ingleby seemed pale and had stomach complaints."

"Yes, I think he had an upset stomach."

Dr. Wilson raised a finger, much like a teacher making a point. "Mr. Ingleby suffered another health complaint, one that he might not wish to be known. Why he did not come to me I don't know, but... You don't have any rhubarb plants in your garden, do you?" Dr. Wilson asked.

"Only plums. But we're looking into getting an apple tree," she said.

"You miss my point. You recall the tea found in his room," he said excitedly, "Constable Dyngley told me, along with your observation of the man's bloody chamber pot."

"Yes. The teacup in his room smelled like rhubarb and I saw the leaves at the bottom of his cup."

"Exactly! Rhubarb tea." Dr. Wilson grinned at her like a prized student. "Which on its own is not dangerous, but the leaves are. Highly toxic in fact, especially if taken in concentrated amounts. If the contents of that cup were as full of rhubarb leaves as Dyngley described, do you know what that means?"

"Someone else was poisoning him," Poppy said, her eyes wide.

"Exactly." He clapped his hands like a cheerful professor.

"Then... whoever was giving him the rhubarb tea—" Poppy started.

"Is the one who killed him. Not the only one, mind you. But the arsenic pudding would have accelerated the toxins already in his body, and the man would have suffered a hasty death."

"My God. You mean to say..."

"Precisely, Miss Morton. Two people killed Mr. Ingleby."

OUTSIDE THE DOCTOR'S surgery, Poppy fretted. She wanted to tell the constable immediately but dared not break her promise to Caroline. Feeling the warmth of the afternoon sun did nothing to lessen her sense of dread, as she walked along Fore Street to the local jail, where she asked to see Mr. Jenkins. Even with the fresh smell of the vegetables in her basket, the moment she was let into the jail, the air itself felt dank and oppressive, and the walls inside the building had few windows, allowing for little sunlight. The result was warm, damp and depressing. Upon answering questions from the magistrate and jailer as to the nature of her request, Mr. Jenkins eventually came out of a locked corridor to see her.

He blinked at the sight of her standing there in his province, surrounded by the dark walls, and said, "Dyngley's not here."

"Good. It's you I came to see, Mr. Jenkins," Poppy said.

"Me? What, you two have a fight or something?"

"No. It's just…" She relayed what Dr Wilson had shared.

Mr. Jenkins removed his dark hat and scratched his head. "Who was giving him rhubarb tea?"

"Probably the same person who baked a rhubarb pudding at the contest," Poppy said.

Jenkins pulled out his list from his pocket and began to look over the names, when Poppy said, "But I don't think it was intentional. It was an accident, if anything. I'm sure of it."

"Sureties ain't proof, girl." He scanned his list. "Aha. We'll see what Mrs. Walker has to say. If she's going around poisoning people, she'll have to pay for it."

"Pay for what?" Dyngley strode into the jail. He stopped at the sight of Poppy and bowed. "Miss Morton."

She curtseyed. "Mr. Jenkins, Mrs. Walker is a harmless old woman," she said, "I am sure she meant no real harm. Do excuse me, I must be going."

Dyngley followed her outside the jail, and it was all she could do not to tell him everything.

"Miss Morton." He touched her arm.

She pulled her arm away and fixed her gaze to the ground.

"What troubles you? We have our killer."

She began walking.

"It's no good defending her, if Mrs. Walker has killed that man, then she deserves a prison sentence," he said harshly.

She whirled around and glared at him. She opened her mouth to speak, then shut it.

"Will you not speak to me?" he asked.

She pursed her lips, turned her back on him, and kept walking.

"Miss Morton?"

She hurried away. She would keep her promise, even if it meant hurting herself.

CHAPTER THIRTY-THREE

L ATER THAT AFTERNOON, after Poppy had returned home, the ladies at the parsonage received a letter from Lady Cameron, inviting them to a ball at Blackgate Park. It was to be a grand affair, and Aunt Rachel received the invitation with pleasure. "How wonderful. No doubt her ladyship means to cheer us all up after that unpleasantness with Mr. Ingleby."

Poppy couldn't rest. Had she sent an innocent woman to the jail? She couldn't rest or relax. She walked from room to room, unhappy. She felt there was nothing to be done but plead the woman's case. She didn't dare go into town for fear of seeing Dyngley, and now that Betsey had improved, there was little need for Poppy to continue running errands for the household. No, she thought to herself, there was little she could do. If only she were a man, she could train as a barrister and plead Mrs. Walker's case in court.

She wrote to Mr. Jenkins, asking him to call on her. When he did come, she encouraged him to take tea with her in the blue sitting room. Aunt Rachel sat by and made small talk while Poppy poured tea, and asked, "What news of Mrs. Walker, Mr. Jenkins?"

He looked ill at ease. He was used to disrupting peaceful settings like this, not partaking in them, and he tugged with one finger at his briskly tied cravat. "It's a funny thing, that. She admitted to it. She said it was true, she'd been poisoning Mr.

Ingleby."

Aunt Rachel dropped her teacup and hot tea spilled all over the floor. "Oh lord, I've spilled the tea. Betsey!" she called, rising from the sofa and heading for the kitchen.

Poppy stared at him, an oatcake halfway to her mouth. "She admitted to it?"

"Yep. Clear-cut case if you ask me." He took one of Betsey's oatcakes and bit into it. "Not much we can do at that point. She'll go to court and all, but she admitted to poisoning him with that rhubarb tea of hers. Right now the jail is full, so she's staying in her home."

Poppy's hand drifted to her mouth. "The poor woman. Is she all right?"

"Right enough. There is one thing that's odd," Mr. Jenkins said.

"What's that?"

"She don't admit to poisoning that pie of hers. You know, the rhubarb tart she made for the baking contest. She says she don't know nothing about where the church money's got to, and we searched her house for arsenic and didn't find any."

"But what about the bottle of poison? I saw she had one in her kitchen."

"Strychnine. She uses it to keep rats from getting in the larder. So that's at least one mystery solved." He finished his oatcake and reached for another. "So either she's lying, or she's telling the truth."

"What do you think?" Poppy asked him.

"Me? Something about her seems honest. I mean, she was slowly killing the man, and there's no saving grace for that. She'll face punishment for sure. But icing her tart with arsenic? I believe what she says." He stood, shedding oatcake crumbs all over the floor. "We've returned the stolen items to the people in town, and they're grateful. I told them you're the one who found them in Mr. Ingleby's personal effects. They know he was a thief."

"That's kind of you."

He reddened and tugged at his cravat again. "Thank you for the tea. Oh, and Miss Morton?"

"Yes?"

"Dyngley thinks you're avoiding him. Are ye?"

Poppy looked at her teacup and took a sip.

"I'll take that as a yes. Good day, Miss Morton." He touched his hat and left as Betsey and Aunt Rachel came back in to clear up the mess.

THE DAY OF the Blackgate ball arrived, and Poppy faced the mirror in her bedroom as Aunt Rachel fussed with her dress. As she glanced in her small looking glass, she saw a pale face, fringed with long brown hair coiled artfully at the nape of her neck. She wore a plain white gown of muslin, trimmed around the small cap sleeves with embroidery. A small white ribbon curved around her waist, another adorned her hair, and with a pair of thin white dancing slippers on her feet, she was ready to go. She had even let her aunt dab a bit of rouge on her cheeks and lips.

Seeing her dour mood, Aunt Rachel said, "Come now, Poppy, cheer up. You'll have a lovely time dancing, and you look a treat. I bet even Constable Dyngley will ask you to dance." She winked.

Poppy tried to smile but failed. Under Caroline's watchful eye she couldn't even talk to the man, much less dance with him.

Unlike her aunt, Poppy cared little for what picture she might present that evening, for she had gained notoriety in the town. Perhaps not as a woman who lusted after single men, but certainly of a girl not to be entirely trusted. It was with that knowledge that Poppy mentally prepared herself for hours of sitting on the sidelines while other young people danced the night away.

THAT EVENING WAS to be no exception, for she stood by with the spinsters and older matrons as her aunt conversed with their neighbors. She drank a glass of wine as footmen circulated around the large ballroom. She watched as Louisa Alleyn danced closely with Dr. Wilson, rather too closely for propriety's sake. In the line with them stepped Mr. and Mrs. Grant, followed by Caroline and Dyngley. At the sight of them, Poppy turned away and came face to face with Robert Heyworth.

"Miss Morton," he said, "may I have this next dance?"

She agreed, set aside her glass of wine and followed him onto the dance floor. As they stood in line for the next set, the musicians struck up a tune and they joined two lines of dancers in a simple country dance. He said, "I have been thinking about your intruder."

"Oh?"

"And it occurred to me that you came to me just shortly after the unfortunate event, is that right?" he asked.

"Yes." She nodded.

"Which is when we were all at the funeral. That means that you can discount me, and anyone else who was there. We couldn't have done it."

Her eyes widened. "So who could it be? Most of the people I suspected were there. Many of them left after the service, but it would have only been a few minutes until we returned to the parsonage."

"If that's true then they would have needed time. It's likely they thought your household would be at the funeral and they wouldn't be disturbed." He took her hand and guided her through the dance.

"Then by your reasoning, Mr. Heyworth, they would have known we would be gone. But many people knew when the funeral service was, it was common knowledge. Anyone could have broken into our home," Poppy said.

"But most of the people in this town aren't murderers. They're not common thieves, they are your neighbors. I know my family is new in town, but who amongst the people here could have a reason to want to break into your house?" he asked.

Her forehead creased in thought. "Whoever did it before."

"Before?" he repeated.

"Yes. They broke in before when we were all asleep. You recall I told you earlier how I disturbed him and hurt my feet trying to chase him away. We didn't know what he wanted before, but we think now he was after the money raised at the fete, for the church roof."

Robert's eyes widened in comprehension.

"Come to think of it, it all makes sense. The doctor's surgery was broken into. Our house, broken into twice," she said.

"Whoever is committing these break-ins is after the money," he said, "But where would it be? Who would have it?"

"I don't know. Certainly not us," she said.

"On the day of the fete, the money disappeared quickly, did it not? Who was there when it went missing?" he asked, touching her hand lightly as they completed more steps of the dance.

"Well, it was Lady Cameron and her footmen, plus myself, my aunt, you and your sister, Miss Everly and Constable Dyngley, and I can't recall who else."

"I can. There was another young man there, in fact, there he is, dancing with my sister."

Poppy followed his gaze. Jane beamed with happiness at being paired with the man she fancied, who in turn gave her a very handsome smile. She only had eyes for him, but there was something about the curl of his smile and the hardness of his eyes that Poppy did not like.

"She seems very happy," Poppy said.

"She does. I have made it my business to learn about that fellow. That is Mr. Colin Barton, Miss Everly's cousin," he told her.

"Her cousin?"

"Yes. I gather he loves to gossip, and is always having tea or escorting Miss Everly around town, when her fiancé isn't available." He shot her an even look. "I told Jane it's nonsense what Miss Everly said about you, you're as sensible a girl as I've ever met."

"Thank you."

The dance ended and they bowed. Poppy joined him for a quadrille and politely refused the allemande, as Jane approached them and asked Robert to fetch her a drink from a footman.

Faced with Jane, Poppy pressed her lips together tightly. She had no wish to start a fight with Jane in public, and their last exchange had been painful.

"Miss Morton." Jane gave a miniscule curtsey.

"Miss Heyworth." Poppy returned the movement.

"How are you finding the dance?"

"Very pleasant. And you?"

"I danced with Mr. Barton, did you see?"

"Yes. You looked very smart together," Poppy said.

Jane flashed her a smile, and her eyes narrowed. "I trust you won't try to warn me away from him again."

Poppy inhaled through her nose. If Jane was just going to be rude, she had other places to be. "Not at all. Do excuse me."

"Miss Morton, wait." Jane put a gloved hand on her arm, stopping her. "I'm sorry."

Poppy looked at her.

"I didn't mean to be uncivil. I was hurt by your advice, and it rankled me to think that my own friend would tell me so."

Poppy gazed into Jane's eyes. She missed her friend. "I was only trying to be honest. I never meant to hurt you."

"Well, as you can see, Mr. Barton is not courting anyone. He is all charm and good humor."

Caroline and Dyngley approached. Jane added, her voice carrying, "And you shall not ruin my mood by telling me otherwise."

Poppy curtseyed and moved away, hurrying to avoid the group. Leaving Jane's smirking form behind her, she approached her aunt and asked, "Have you seen Lady Cameron?"

"Not since the receiving line. Why?"

"I thought I might ask her a question. I'll just have a look for her."

"Don't take long, dear, it is getting overly warm," Aunt Rachel said, fanning herself with a white lace fan.

Poppy made a tour of the grand ballroom, but her aunt was right, it was becoming very warm. From the dozens of expensive candles lighting the room, to the rows of dancers twirling around the floor, it was hard to see who was present. Fortunately for her, her height proved an advantage, and she easily scanned the ballroom. However, she did not see Lady Cameron anywhere. It was strange.

She exited the ballroom and walked to the corridor outside, shutting the door behind her. With the doors closed, it was quieter and easier to think.

Then she heard it. A small cry, coming from upstairs.

She hurried up the grand staircase and looked around. This was an area off-limits for guests, for it held the private bedrooms of Lady Cameron and her houseguests. But then Poppy heard a strangled cry, a thud, and dashed into the corridor.

She walked along the long corridor of rooms, listening at the door of each, when she heard it. A loud thump and a man's voice. Not thinking, she pushed open the nearest bedroom door. "Lady Cameron? I thought I heard a cry–"

There stood Mr. Barton, the silver topped walking stick in his hand, and crumpled on the floor beneath him lay Lady Cameron, her head bathed in blood.

CHAPTER THIRTY-FOUR

"OH MY GOD. What have you done?" Poppy stared at the scene.

Mr. Barton's features twisted in anger. He crossed the room in three easy steps and loomed over her, the blunt handle of his walking stick at her chin. "You're the friend of that girl, Jane."

She swallowed. "I'm Miss Morton."

"Poppy Morton? Such an infamous name." A wicked smile curled at his lips.

"Your cousin doesn't like me, I think." She backed up, hitting the door.

"My cousin?" He laughed. "You think right." He yanked her by the wrist and flung her back inside the room. The stick was in his hand, but he wielded it easily, seeing her eyes go to Lady Cameron. "The old tart had a fall."

Poppy breathed in. "How funny, the music's stopped."

He cocked his head to listen when she screamed.

He jumped, startled, and she elbowed him in the gut. He coughed and bent over double as she used the opportunity to run and fumble for the door's latch. He grabbed at her dress, and she toppled to the floor.

She kicked at him, her slippered foot connecting with his face. He grunted in pain and she scrambled forward. "Help!" she screamed, got to her feet and flung open the door, hitting Mr.

Barton in the shoulder.

Jane was just walking up the stairs when she stopped at the sight. "Poppy? What are you—"

"Get help!" Poppy breathed as Mr. Barton stepped out of the room.

He sneered. "You stupid chit. I'll kill your precious lady. Just see if I don't."

Jane gasped as he snarled, "You didn't see nothing." He gripped Poppy by the arm and slugged her with the butt of the walking stick. Poppy fell to her knees with a grunt. Pain ripped through her lower back.

Jane shrieked and held her hands up to her mouth.

Mr. Barton poked her side lightly with the tip of the stick. He smelled like sour wine, and breathed in her ear, "There now, you're coming with me. One more scream and I'll slit your throat."

He pulled Poppy to her feet by the arm and dragged her back inside the room, shoving her forward. He kicked the door closed. "Stupid girl. Now that one's going to scream the whole house down." He aimed the walking stick's point at her. "Where is it?"

"What?" Poppy asked.

"The money. The goddamn church fete bloody baking money. Hundreds of pounds. Where is it?"

"I don't know. Nobody does. It's gone," she said.

"You're lying." He deftly passed the stick from hand to hand, and unscrewed the top, releasing a nasty looking blade.

Her eyes widened to see that his fancy walking stick was in truth, a swordstick. "I'm not," she said, "I'd tell you if I did." Something about him seemed familiar. "You're the one who broke into my house, aren't you?"

He smirked. "You're not as stupid as you look."

"Why did you go back a second time?"

He shot her a dirty look.

"You killed him, didn't you? Mr. Ingleby. Why?" Poppy asked.

He smirked. "He got his just desserts."

"What did he ever do to you?"

Mr. Barton snorted. "You are dumb. He had you fooled, the lot of you. He wasn't the saint you all thought he was."

"If you're saying he's a thief, I already know. We found the goods he'd hidden."

Mr. Barton scowled. "Then what you found was mine."

"I doubt that. We found stolen items belonging to our neighbors, and the collection plate money that had gone missing."

"What else?"

"That was it. There was nothing else," she said.

His face twisted. "You're lying."

Poppy shook her head.

The sound of voices came from outside and he pointed the blade at her. "Don't push me, girl. Tell me where it is."

"I don't know. I don't have it," she said.

"Who does?" he snarled.

"I don't know."

He sliced at her dress, tearing the pretty fabric a few inches down at the bodice. Poppy's hand flew to her dress, covering her chest for modesty.

He grinned at the sight. "This old bat didn't know anything. Of course she don't, when's she ever had to work a day in her life?"

Poppy glanced at the unconscious form of Lady Cameron, bleeding from her head. "If you leave now, I won't say anything."

"You'd better not. Or else I'll tell Caroline you were throwing yourself at me."

Poppy tensed.

He grinned. "You wouldn't like people to hear that, would you? Good little clergyman's niece, trying to seduce a man in the old trout's bedroom. I bet she's got fifty rooms just like it." He walked toward Lady Cameron.

"Leave her alone!" Poppy looked around for something to throw at him, but all she saw was luxurious bedding on a meticulously made bed.

He stood over Lady Cameron's unconscious form and snatched a jeweled necklace from her neck. He pulled hard and it came free in his hands. He stuffed it in his pocket with a self-satisfied grin.

Poppy lunged and knocked him to the ground. They fell on Lady Cameron, and he punched Poppy in the gut when the door opened.

Poppy gasped as Caroline stepped inside the room.

CHAPTER THIRTY-FIVE

"WHAT IN THE blue blazes do you think you're doing?" Caroline cried.

"Help," Poppy said, struggling with Mr. Barton.

"You harlot, get your hands off him."

"Me?" Poppy said.

"I cannot believe you would stoop so low. First my fiancé and now my cousin? You truly are a light skirt, Miss Morton."

Caroline shut the door and aimed a small pistol at Poppy. "Don't move. Unlike him, I'm not afraid to hurt a girl."

Poppy's mouth dropped open. "You're in this together?"

Caroline threw her head back and laughed, a light peal of sound. "How dumb can you be? Yes, we are together." She shot Mr. Barton a coy smile.

Mr. Barton smirked, got to his feet and walked over to her, putting an arm around Caroline's waist. He pulled her close into a kiss.

Poppy felt reviled. "My God. You're cousins."

Caroline snorted. "We aren't cousins, Miss Morton. That was our story," she said to Mr. Barton, "I told you that would work. This dumb skirt believed it."

He linked hands with Caroline and gave her a leer.

"You were in on this the whole time. Why?" Poppy asked.

Caroline said, "We're a team."

"You mean you're thieves," Poppy said.

Caroline shot her a glare. "We survive. We're the best north of London. We were doing well when we met a new chap, who said he could double our money if we worked with him. So we did the job, but then he double-crossed us and left us without a penny."

Poppy's eyes widened as Mr. Barton sneered, "The dirty stinking bastard never made our rendezvous. I knew we couldn't trust him."

Caroline smiled. "So we tracked him here, to Hertford. It's just a shame what happened to him. But then, I suppose he always did like his food. He was the fattest thief I'd ever met."

"You mean Mr. Ingleby," Poppy said.

"Now you understand. Imagine my surprise when my dear cousin and I attend a country dance, only to find him in plain sight, and masquerading as a clergyman? I laughed out loud when I saw. And I made sure he saw me too."

"That's right. At the dance, I was sure he recognized you," Poppy said.

"We had a little chat at Lady Cameron's picnic." She gave the unconscious hostess a nasty smile. "And told him if he didn't pay up, we'd ruin him. He said he knew about a bigger amount of money. More than we'd dreamed of."

"The money for the church roof. The prize for the baking contest," Poppy realized.

"Exactly. He said it would be hundreds of pounds, all coming to him for safekeeping. He'd give it to us, and we could walk away."

Poppy started. "I can't believe he would do that."

Caroline smirked. "For a man who only said rude things about you, you are surprisingly loyal."

"The entire town trusted him," Poppy said, "I'm just shocked that he thought he could get away with it."

"Oh, I can. But I'm not one to be fooled a second time. He didn't take our warning seriously. You'd think his little accident at the picnic would be a big enough reason not to toy with us, but no." She gave a hearty laugh. "It was all going so well until the baking money disappeared."

Mr. Barton passed his swordstick from hand to hand. "Caroline, you've said enough."

"Tie her up. She won't say anything. Especially when she's got everything to lose. Colin, put the necklace in her hands," Caroline said.

"What? But I wanted it," he started.

"Do it." Caroline trained her pistol with two hands at Poppy. "With any luck, the only thief they'll find here is her, especially when we catch her red-handed."

Poppy looked for a way to get out, but knelt by Lady Cameron.

Caroline cocked the pistol's hammer back. "I wouldn't make any sudden moves, Miss Morton. My hands are getting tired. Wouldn't want it to go off."

Mr. Barton tore some of the bedsheets off the bed and used his walking stick's blade to mutilate the fine silken fabric, cutting it into strips. He tied Poppy's hands behind her back, making sure Lady Cameron's necklace was stuck there too.

"What about Dyngley?" Poppy asked as Mr. Barton tied her ankles together.

Two spots of color rose in Caroline's cheeks. She seethed, "You just couldn't keep your hands off him, could you? I'll ruin you. Just see if I don't. You're finished."

At that moment, Poppy didn't care. "Do you truly love him?"

Caroline glanced at Mr. Barton and said lightly, "Of course not. He's a lovely man. So sweet. So keen to marry me for my money. I have half a mind to go through with it, you know. Marry him, I mean. Just to see what he'd do when he found out I didn't have a farthing to my name. Dyngley is just so damned honorable, he'd be stuck with me."

Mr. Barton grunted and tied Poppy's binds tighter, making her gasp.

"Only teasing," Caroline giggled and lowered her pistol. "Do you know, he was buying a set of pearls the first time we met, and he was so grateful for my help he gave them to me instead. Now I wonder if they were for you. I guess we'll never know." She shot her an even smile and touched the pearls around her neck. "I will always think of you when I wear them."

Mr. Barton said, "Come on, Caroline. Let's get out of here."

Lady Cameron groaned, and Poppy screamed, "Help! Somebody help!"

Mr. Barton punched her head and she fell to the floor. He stood over her and said, "You want more?"

Poppy breathed, and shook her head.

"Do it again and I'll cut you." His blade trailed along her arm.

"Quick, hide. Somebody's coming," Caroline said.

Mr. Barton held Poppy stiff like a captive, while Caroline disappeared from her view.

"Help! Help!" Poppy cried, "We're in here!"

Mr. Barton dragged her back, saying, "What did I tell you?"

The door opened. "There! He's there." Jane squealed. "Look, he's hurt her!"

Men filled the room. Not that Poppy could see, but she assumed so, as she heard many boots strike the floor. She bucked and kicked with her feet, and Mr. Barton slapped her upside the head.

Footmen and Dyngley entered the room and pulled Mr. Barton away, who sputtered with anger. "Get your hands off me! I ain't done nothing wrong. This girl's mad. She's crazed. I caught her stealing and tied her up. Look at her hands, she stole the lady's necklace!"

Jane said hotly, "He's lying. I saw him, he attacked her. I saw the whole thing!"

Mr. Barton served Jane a glare of such force that she stepped back.

"Take him," Dyngley told the men.

Mr. Barton served *him* a black glare and spat on the floor. He told Dyngley what he could do to himself, and Dyngley ordered the footmen to hold Mr. Barton fast and tie his hands. The men grappled briefly but soon separated Mr. Barton from his blade.

Poppy blinked as Dyngley helped her sit up. He asked, "Are you all right?"

"Never mind about me. Lady Cameron is hurt. We need Dr. Wilson." Poppy turned to Lady Cameron lying on the floor. She looked pale and her expertly arranged gray hair was in disarray as a head wound leaked blood over her face and the floor.

Dr. Wilson was sent for and came, and with the help of Lady Cameron's footmen, she was lifted into the bed and tended to. Dr. Wilson pronounced her weak, but alive.

Dyngley removed the necklace and untied Poppy's bonds from her ankles and wrists. "Are you hurt?"

She shook her head, feeling her sore wrists. "He attacked Lady Cameron and threatened to kill me," Poppy said, "They put the necklace in my hands."

Robert entered the room. "Miss Morton? Are you all right? Jane said there was trouble." He stared at her. "What happened?"

"Miss Morton caught Mr. Barton trying to steal from her ladyship," Dyngley said, his eyes narrowed at Robert.

"Heavens. Miss Morton, allow me to take you home," Robert said.

"No, I'm fine, honestly." Her stays felt very tight around her chest as she breathed.

"Miss Morton, your dress," Dr. Wilson said, "what happened?"

Poppy glanced down and her hands flew to her chest. She'd forgotten that Mr. Barton had sliced open the top of her dress. She blushed as the three men glanced at her chest then quickly looked away.

"Did that creature attack you?" Dyngley's face was stormy as he glared at Mr. Barton. "If you have harmed her person, I will–"

"I'm fine," Poppy said, "Just a little worse for wear."

"Here, take my coat," Dyngley said, shrugging out of his suit jacket.

"Allow me," Robert was already removing his coat.

"I insist." Dyngley placed his jacket around Poppy's shoulders, ignoring Robert's dark expression.

Robert and Constable Dyngley exchanged a look, but what it said, Poppy couldn't tell.

Jane said, "Come, Brother. We should attend our Mama. There is nothing for us here."

Watching them go, Poppy said, "Constable, Caroline was involved. She was helping him. She's here."

Dyngley glanced around the room. "You must be seeing things. Miss Everly is not here."

"She was, Constable. She aimed a pistol at me," Poppy said.

He rolled his eyes and shook his head. "I cannot believe the tales you tell. Miss Morton, I have told you before about speaking ill of my fiancée. Miss Everly is a sweet, honest girl and I won't hear any more—"

Mr. Barton laughed out loud. "You're a fool, mate. A bloody fool."

Dyngley's head snapped toward the criminal, as did everyone else's.

"She's played you for a fool. She never wanted you. She only wanted your title. She has no money. She thought you were an easy mark." Mr. Barton smiled.

The blood drained from Dyngley's face. "You are—"

Mr. Barton's mocking laughter filled the room. "You fell for her hard, didn't you? Gave away your heart to her, eh? I pity you."

"You're lying," Constable Dyngley said.

"Am I? You may have your fancy title, but she'll always come running back to me. I'm the only one who could satisfy her." He grinned.

Constable Dyngley's face turned cold and stiff. "Take him away."

Mr. Barton spat on the floor as the two footmen hustled him

out of the room.

Dyngley bowed to Poppy. "I will see that Mr. Barton spends the night in jail. Excuse me. Mr. Jenkins!" he called.

"Here, Constable." Mr. Jenkins appeared in the doorway, holding a struggling Caroline. "I found this one with a gun. She tossed it down the hallway but I caught her before she could run off."

"Dyngley!" Caroline cried, "Help me. This fool almost broke my arm. He's trying to kill me."

"She's lying. She came here to kill us," Poppy said.

Dyngley came forward and helped Caroline to her feet, releasing her from Mr. Jenkins' grasp.

She flung herself into his arms. "I'm so sorry, Dyngley, I couldn't let her get away with hurting all those people," Caroline babbled tearfully, "All because she was jealous."

"Jealous?" Dyngley murmured, holding her hands close.

"Yes. It's why Miss Morton killed the clergyman. She was the killer all along. She found out what nasty things Mr. Ingleby was saying about her, and she went mad. She decided to kill him with a poisoned pie."

"What are you doing here, Caroline?" he asked.

"Me? I came to confront her. I saw she attacked my cousin and ran to get help. I found the gun lying on the floor when your deputy found me. You must believe me, Dyngley. I knew she was guilty all along. I wanted her to confess to her crimes," Caroline said, "I'm so glad you're here. I'm sorry I didn't tell you sooner."

"I'm sorry too." He looked down.

"About what, my love?" Caroline asked.

"I'm sorry I believed you, when you said you loved me." His face hardened, and his grip on her wrists became stiff as iron. "Mr. Jenkins, let's escort Miss Everly down to jail. She'll be in good company there." Dyngley jerked Caroline forward and slipped a strong rope around her wrists, looping it around and tying it tight.

"Dyngley, no! You're making a mistake!" Caroline kicked and

jerked back, but was held fast.

Mr. Jenkins grinned at Poppy as he grabbed Caroline's wrists. "Smart of us to watch you all, wasn't it? Bet you're glad we kept an eye on you women."

Her face mutinous, Caroline spat in Mr. Jenkins' face and shot Poppy a murderous glare as Jenkins took her forcefully from the room. Dyngley gave Poppy a searching look before he followed them a moment later.

Hearing the commotion, Mrs. Sugg entered the room and let out a cry of alarm. "My lady!" She fawned over the older woman, shaking her head. "I never should have drunk that much sherry. I let her out of my sight and look what happens. I'll never forgive myself if something happened to her."

Poppy looked on as Mrs. Sugg sat on Lady Cameron's bed and held her hand. "Will she be all right, doctor?"

"She will. But she needs plenty of rest."

They didn't stay much longer. Once Poppy had been checked for injuries, Dr. Wilson released her into the care of her aunt, who was keen to get home.

As Aunt Rachel flicked the reins on their horse to take them home in the family cart, she listened to Poppy's account of Mr. Barton's attack and said, "My poor girl, what a fright you've had. What I don't understand is, then, who killed Mr. Ingleby?"

"I'm not sure," Poppy said, "But both of them are definitely guilty. Whichever one of them poisoned the pie is anyone's guess."

Poppy sat next to her on the cart and pulled Dyngley's coat closer around her for warmth. It smelled like him, clean and fresh, with a hint of men's eau de toilette. She felt comforted and relieved. Mr. Barton and Caroline had been caught and Lady Cameron saved, and while the business with the baking contest money was not resolved, she felt confident it would either turn up at some point, or it wouldn't. Either way, she felt like a burden had been lifted from her shoulders. She wanted to tell Dyngley everything, but not yet. For now, she just felt free to talk to him again.

THAT NIGHT, POPPY slept fitfully. She dreamed that Caroline had escaped. She tossed and turned and dreamed she was there on the day of the contest all over again, except this time she was tasting the puddings, and Caroline was forcing her to eat a poisoned pie at gunpoint. She ate and chewed and swallowed, feeling sandy arsenic crystals course down her throat and threaten to choke her. "Poppy..." a disembodied voice whispered.

Poppy coughed and spat, and opened her eyes.

There in the dim candlelight of her bedroom stood Caroline and her aunt. Aunt Rachel held a plate with a piece of pie and stared straight ahead as Caroline pressed a pistol against her temple. She grinned. "Hello, Poppy."

CHAPTER THIRTY-SIX

POPPY OPENED HER eyes with a start, and jolted up in bed. Morning sunlight streamed through the windows, blinding her. It had all been a horrid nightmare. She laid back against the pillow and sighed with relief. Her aunt was safe and Caroline was still in jail. No one was in danger. She rose and glanced in her looking-glass. As she suspected, there were dark circles beneath her eyes and she looked weary from poor sleep.

But as she dressed in a simple blue gown and hummed a little tune, her spirits lifted. The sun shone through her window, warming up her bedroom as birds sang outside. She smiled, feeling light in her heart for the first time in weeks.

But the soreness of her wrists bore truth to last night's events. The daytime might be pleasant but her memory of the previous night was most definitely not. A glance down revealed fresh pink lines on her skin from where Mr. Barton had tied her up. She felt a bit sore and bruised from her tussle with him, but relieved at the knowledge that the culprits had been found. And her friendship with Dyngley would be restored, for there on the back of her writing chair hung his smart dinner jacket, looking as dark and steady as his soul.

Caroline and Mr. Barton were safely in jail, and everyone knew of their foul characters, despite Caroline's protests to the contrary. Dyngley hadn't seen proof of her guilt, but Poppy suspected that Mr. Barton would soon disabuse him of any notion of her innocence. Still, Poppy wondered about Dyngley and their friendship. Was she released from her bond now to speak to him? Could she do it in good conscience? And worse, she had kissed him.

How could she look Dyngley in the face after that? But never mind. She would find a way to repair their relationship. Perhaps they could go back to being friends and pretend that the kiss had never happened. The knowledge of her opening her heart to him would fade into a distant memory, and instead, she would cherish him for his loyal friendship, for that was all he could offer her.

She walked down to the center of Hertford and purchased more vegetables from the farmer's market. Their family's vegetable garden was doing well but it still needed some support from the local market, where foodstuffs like potatoes and beans were plentiful. She purchased enough to fill her basket, when her gaze landed on the direction of a side street, where she knew the local jail sat.

Without knowing why, Poppy walked to the jail, bid hello to Mr. Jenkins and the guard, and asked if she might speak with the prisoners.

"Whatever for? They're in there for a reason."

"I'd like to talk to them," Poppy said.

The guard scratched his head. "Which one? That Barton fellow is a mouthy one."

"What about the woman? Miss Everly?"

The guard exchanged a look with Mr. Jenkins, who said, "You can speak with her. I'd leave your basket here though. Sticky fingers, that one. She'll take anything."

Poppy blinked, set aside her basket, and paid the guard a halfpenny to take her to Miss Everly's cell. He led the way down a shadowy corridor that smelled. It was cooler than the outside, but the walls looked cold and damp, and the scent of mold and urine lingered in the air.

Poppy shuddered as the guard led her to a cell that was dark.

He turned to her and said, "Five minutes."

A low laugh sounded as Poppy waited for the guard to leave.

Caroline slowly walked up to the front bars, her face and evening dress from the night before stained with dirt, or worse. Caroline coughed and asked, "To what do I owe the pleasure, Miss Morton? Oh wait, it's not. What do you want?"

"To talk to you," Poppy said.

"Do you have any food? I haven't eaten since yesterday."

"Haven't they fed you?"

"That costs money. In case you haven't noticed, I wasn't carrying many funds the night of the dance," Caroline said.

Poppy peered into the darkness that was the cell, but it was mostly in shadow. A thin trail of light floated from a slit in the wall that let in the outside air. She said, "I'll bring you something to eat. But I'd like you to answer my questions first."

"Fine," Caroline said, "Colin is in jail and it's all because of you. There, happy? Now sod off."

"It's not my fault you're a pair of thieves," Poppy retorted, "Why did you do this?"

Caroline sulked. "You've meddled and ruined all my plans. Dyngley and I were going to get married and now…" Her upper lip curled into a sneer. "My Colin is in jail and it's all your fault. I deserve a little payback, starting with you."

Poppy came forward. "Why?"

"When I get out of here, and I will, believe me, you'll get what's coming to you. You and that nosey aunt of yours."

Poppy rolled her eyes. "I'll believe that when I see it. These empty threats of yours are tiresome."

Caroline's dark brown eyes flashed. "You would do well to listen to me, Miss Morton. My words have influence." She tutted. "I do wonder at you, you know. Your friends and neighbors were all too quick to believe what Ingleby said about you. By the time I started gossiping, they believed every word I said."

Poppy was getting irritated. "Why did you poison Mr. Ingleby?"

"That's not his real name, you know. But he did like his sweets, and arsenic is easy to get. Besides, we warned him. Double-cross us and he'd get what's coming to him. The bastard never saw it coming."

"And what about Constable Dyngley?" Poppy asked. "He knows you are a murderer. Mr. Barton told him."

Caroline's smile fell, then re-emerged. "He'll never believe that. He adores me too much. I'll tell him I was forced to act under Colin's control or else he would kill me. He made me do it. Dyngley would believe anything of his sweet, innocent fiancée. And with you out of the picture, it's not like he would marry a corpse."

Poppy's expression was mutinous. "Miss Everly, you are in a cell."

"Not for long. Dyngley will come and I'll explain everything. He has not come to visit yet but I have every assurance he will. We're engaged to be married," her voice rose, "He'll believe me. It's all one big misunderstanding. I'll be the darling of this town again, just you wait."

Sadness filled Poppy's heart. "Tell me one thing. Why did you hire me?"

"That was Colin's idea. It was the perfect cover. That deputy had already put people's backs up, so all I had to do was say you were looking into the crime too, to prove me innocent, and no one would think any different," Caroline said, "It's such a shame you'll never get to meet your mother. A real whore of the first water, I'm told. So popular with the men."

Poppy's expression hardened. She'd heard enough. "Good-bye, Miss Everly. I hope you never get out."

Caroline flashed her a triumphant smile. "See you soon, Miss Morton. I hope you're hungry."

Chilled to the bone, Poppy hurried away from the cell and down the shadowy corridor. Upon finding the guard and Mr. Jenkins, he said, "What's wrong, Miss Morton? She give you a scare? You look pale."

"I'm fine." She took up her basket of fruit and vegetables. Part of her felt angry for even coming by. She bid the men farewell and stepped out into the fresh air, breathing in the warmth and basking in the sunlight. It was such a far cry from the damp darkness inside the jail. She wanted to run home. But something stopped her. Caroline was a horrid person, to be sure. But she was also hungry. A little Christian charity might not go amiss. Not that Poppy expected to gain anything from it, but she could almost hear her uncle's words of advice in her ears, recommending her to tend the sick, care for the hungry and those in need, no matter who they were. Thinking on Caroline's situation, she thought, *murderers have appetites too.* She knew in her heart that she would never be as good as her uncle, but...

She returned to the jail and passed Mr. Jenkins an apple. "Give this to Miss Everly. She's hungry."

"You really want to feed that woman, after all she's done?" Mr. Jenkins asked.

Poppy nodded. "She deserves our charity. And it's only an apple." But as she turned and walked away she thought, *I hope she chokes on it.*

A WEEK LATER, Poppy walked home from her visit to the town's farmers' market, her stomach growling in protest. At the sight of the sweetshop in town, her stomach had groaned. She wished she had more pocket money; she had forgotten to eat before she'd left and now felt ravenous. But she had hurried back, for an alarming rumor was going around that Miss Everly had escaped jail. She put little stock by it, however, as the local town gossip, Mrs. Markham, took up any rumor she heard and spread it about like wildfire, with little care as to its truth.

Still, Poppy walked home hurriedly, clutching her basket of fruit and vegetables. She approached the parsonage and found a letter on the doorstep. She picked it up and opened the door. "Aunt, there's a letter here in uncle's writing. I wonder if he'll come home soon."

"Oh, Poppy, come in, let me see," her aunt called.

Poppy hung up her coat and bonnet, brought the basket of vegetables to Betsey in the kitchen, and joined her aunt in the blue sitting room. There on a small table sat a freshly baked pie, and Aunt Rachel was just cutting a slice. "You're just in time for pie."

She passed Poppy a plate and Poppy dug in, handing her aunt the letter.

Poppy bit into the slice and swallowed, tasting the tartness of blackberries and flaky golden pastry slide down her tongue. It wasn't a very sweet pie at all.

Her aunt opened the letter and began reading. "Aha! Your uncle is very well, and his brother is much improved. It looks like his calming presence and Hilda's medicines did the trick. He expects to return home within a few days' time." She set the letter down. "Thank goodness."

"That is good news," Poppy said, eating another bite. It tasted sandy and gritty, as if the person had added sand instead of sugar. She swallowed it down and gave her aunt a look. "Um, Aunt?"

"Yes?" Her aunt began cutting herself a slice of pie.

"I've heard a rumor from Mrs. Markham that Miss Everly has escaped from jail."

"Oh, I wouldn't believe all that you hear from her, she was going around telling everyone the other week that I was at death's door, all because I declined her invitation to tea the other week." She munched and shook her head, then spat out a mouthful of the pie. "I don't know how you can eat that. It tastes horrible."

Poppy snorted and ate another mouthful. The pie didn't taste as well as it should, but she felt she should eat some to soothe Betsey's feelings. No doubt their maid was trying a new recipe. "Did you bake it?"

"Me? No." Aunt Rachel pushed the offending plate away. "I wouldn't eat that if I were you."

"Should we tell Betsey that her new recipe is not as good as her others?" Poppy smiled.

"Hmmm? No, Betsey didn't make it."

Poppy cocked her head, eating. "Then where did the pie come from?"

"I don't know. It was sitting on the front step. I assume one of your uncle's parishioners dropped it off. They do that sometimes, you know."

Poppy looked at the empty plate before her. She had been so hungry she had eaten the whole thing. Could her aunt be right?

Her aunt looked at the pie. "Although I don't mind telling you, I would bake a much better pie. And you would too, if you wanted to learn. That cook has mixed sugar with salt, I think. Oh, and it came with a note, addressed to you. Let me see, where is it..."

Poppy turned as her aunt lifted up a small note. Poppy took it and tore it open. It read in a hasty scrawl:

My dear Miss Morton, by the time you read this I will be long gone. With any luck, our paths will not cross again.

Poppy looked up, her hands trembling. "Oh my lord."

"What is it, Poppy? Is it a nice letter?" Aunt Rachel asked.

Poppy shook her head and scanned the last line in horror:

I hope you enjoy my little gift, I baked it especially for you. Eat up.

– C

"My God," Poppy said, tossing the letter aside. Her stomach churned and she felt queasy. "Aunt," Poppy rose. "Don't touch that."

"Poppy, whatever is the matter? You look pale. Are you all right?" Aunt Rachel asked.

Sweat beaded her forehead and Poppy's stomach groaned. She clutched her belly and swayed on her feet.

"Goodness, Poppy." Her aunt stared.

Pushing a sweaty tangle of hair out of her face, Poppy tried remembering what the doctor had said. "Aunt, it's not salt, it's arsen—"

She tumbled to the floor and was violently ill. The last thing she remembered was saying, "Call the doctor...Dyngley..." before she blacked out.

CHAPTER THIRTY-SEVEN

POPPY HAD MISERABLE dreams. In one, she shot Caroline, and her eyes stared at her through a river of blood. In another, Caroline forced her to eat poison, with Jane, Robert and Dyngley urging her on. In a third dream, she witnessed Caroline and Dyngley's wedding, but as they moved to kiss one another, Caroline's head dissolved to that of a skull, rictus grin and all.

Poppy awoke with a start. "Ah!"

"There now, Miss Morton, you are safe," Dr. Wilson said, looking down at her.

Poppy opened her eyes. She was in her bed. "What happened?"

"You ingested a small amount of arsenic," Dr. Wilson told her. He sat by her bedside in a smart black jacket and trousers, with a lightly tied white cravat and shirt. "You collapsed and vomited a lot of it from your system, but I suspect it will be days before you are on the mend. You need rest and quiet."

"What about Miss Everly?"

"I never want to hear that girl's name again," Aunt Rachel sniffed. She sat in a chair nearby, sewing.

"Do you feel up to a bit of reading, Miss Morton?" Dr. Wilson fetched a newspaper.

"I don't mind," Poppy said, sitting up in bed.

"I wonder if you might care to read the *Hertford Gazette*." He opened the paper and turned the pages, handing it to her. "You might find this section interesting." He tapped a column.

Poppy looked at him curiously but shrugged, made herself comfortable and took the paper. She read:

> It has come to this editor's attention that the young Miss Caroline Everly, who appeared to be a charming patron and welcome dinner companion in the county, has been nothing but a figment of our imagination. This comes as a great surprise and disappointment, particularly with the expected nuptials of Miss Everly and local constable Mr. Henry Dyngley to be announced any day now. Unfortunately, this paper regrets to share the unhappy news that due to recent events, their betrothal has come to an end.
>
> For those who were acquainted with the young woman, they may have seen Miss Everly often in the company of her cousin, Mr. Colin Barton. However, these connections will now find themselves mistaken as to the true nature of their intentions. The editor of this paper has been informed that Miss Everly and Mr. Barton are none other than the Enfield Duo, a pair of thieving lovers who charm their way into polite households north of London and steal from their hosts. The pair were recently captured at Lady Cameron's ball, attempting to steal from her ladyship. While they were apprehended by the local constabulary, Miss Everly has escaped the noose, and has fled to locations unknown. Whither she has gone we do not know, but caution all to beware of her pleasing countenance and charming smiles, for the unwary person may well find their goods missing after such an exchange with the pleasant Miss Everly.

Poppy lowered the paper. "Gone? So the rumor is true. Miss Everly has disappeared?"

"She has. It is believed that she charmed one of the guards minding her, and he let her out, believing her to be innocent."

"Hah. That one has as much charm as a crab apple," Aunt Rachel huffed.

Dr Wilson glanced at her aunt before saying, "Mr. Barton is

due to be transported to Newgate Prison in London, where he will await trial," Dr. Wilson said, taking Poppy's wrist to feel for her pulse.

Poppy let out a breath. "Then it is over. They are out of our lives."

"It seems so." He looked at her. "How are you feeling?"

"Well enough. A little sore in the head and in my stomach, but all right. How long was I asleep?"

"You drifted in and out of consciousness for about two days. This is the first time I've seen you lucid." He smiled. "I am glad to see you are in good health, Miss Morton. Or at least, almost on the mend."

"That makes two of us. Might I have some water?"

He poured her a glass from the water jug on her writing desk and handed it to her. She sipped and felt the water course down her throat, but coughed and felt very sore. "It hurts." She handed the glass back to him.

"It will. I will come back later to monitor your progress, but I am pleased to see you are awake." He bowed and said to her aunt, "Send a servant for me if her condition sours."

"I will." Aunt Rachel nodded and returned to her sewing, waiting until he left. She rose and shut the door. "I have received a letter from your uncle, and you have two letters." She took them from the pocket of her white apron and held them up. "You should know that our neighbors are not so unfeeling. Many felt Mr. Ingleby's rudeness was behavior unsuited to a clergyman, and it reached the ears of Lord Ryder."

"Mr. Ingleby's patron?"

"Yes. Apparently Lady Cameron knows the man, at least by association, and sent him a note, asking about Mr. Ingleby's behavior. She mentioned his appearance and penchant for cakes, and the man wrote back to say she was mistaken. The young man he champions is thin, with brown hair and would never dare read aloud a sermon that wasn't his. Isn't that shocking?" Aunt Rachel said.

"My word," Poppy yawned.

"Indeed. Lord Ryder was most confused and wrote to your uncle, who became very disturbed, especially when the poor soul died while as a guest in this house."

Poppy blinked.

"So there you have it. They don't know who Lady Cameron is referring to, but felt it necessary to impugn her report, as it is so contradictory to the man they knew."

"Goodness."

Aunt Rachel smiled. "I have also had a letter from her ladyship, inviting us to tea as soon as you are well. I gather she wants to hear firsthand just what happened. She is a kind woman, but she does love her gossip."

Poppy smiled. "I should be glad to see her."

Aunt Rachel let out a deep breath. "And I wonder if this might be as good a time as any to tell you of your mother."

Poppy tensed.

"Are you sure you wish to know? It is not a happy story."

"Yes."

Aunt Rachel set down her embroidery, then picked it up again. By doing the menial task, it allowed her to avoid Poppy's eye and talk. "I have a sister, Celeste. While I have always been short and round, she has been tall and thin. You take after her, you know. She and I grew up not far from here, in a town called Ironbridge. They have an ironworks, and an iron bridge, and it is not far from Birmingham. Anyway, we grew up poor. Our parents died when we were young, and we were sent to the workhouse. My sister was very pretty, and clever, with a sharp mind like yours. She attracted a man early on as a patron, who offered to take her away. She agreed but only if I too was taken. I worked in the man's house as a servant, and it wasn't until a visiting clergyman noticed me, did he offer me a place in his household as his housekeeper. It wasn't long before we were courting, but as wonderful as Reginald was, my sister lived in sin."

Poppy breathed in. "You mean Miss Everly was right?"

Aunt Rachel stabbed her embroidery pattern. "My sister always was too smart for her own good. She dallied with the wrong man and was cast off. She soon found herself another patron but... She enjoyed it, you see. Living as the pampered woman. A kept woman. Unmarried. A recluse from all good society."

"She was a prostitute," Poppy said.

"No, dear. A mistress. And a very well-paid one. She has dined at finer tables than we ever will and wears dresses worth more than what Reginald makes in a year. But there is a cost to that. It was about a year into her new life when she became with child."

"Me," Poppy said.

"Yes. For whatever reason, the Lord did not bless Reginald and me with children of our own. So when Celeste arrived at our door, it seemed like the best solution for all of us." She met Poppy's eyes, and they were wet. "We took you in and agreed to raise you as our own. Reginald would not admit to being your father when he was not, so he encouraged you to call us Aunt and Uncle. And in return we received a bit of income from your mother."

"How much?" Poppy asked.

"Enough for your upkeep."

"But we live so humbly."

Aunt Rachel's eyes narrowed. "We live a good deal better than some in this neighborhood, so you should count your blessings. But..." She let out a little sigh. "Reginald believes it sets a good example to others, to live modestly and to not exceed one's means. The money we receive from your mother keeps us in candles, clothing, food, and it provides for your dowry."

Poppy's eyes widened. "My dowry?"

"Since your birth, we have set aside money each year for it. It is Reginald's hope that you marry well. Maybe even a clergyman like himself. You would make a wonderful pastor's wife, Poppy."

Poppy swallowed.

"Which brings me to this." Aunt Rachel passed over the two letters to Poppy. "I think I recognize the constable's handwriting on one, but why are you receiving a letter from a London address?"

"I don't know." Poppy took the letters and paused. "Why did you not tell me about my mother all this time? Why did you keep it a secret? You told me she was dead. Why? Did she not want to know me?"

Aunt Rachel flushed. "No. Never that. She loves you. We thought it was better that... No. I will not lie to you. Not anymore. The fact is that Reginald was embarrassed by my sister. She can tease men too much, and can seem either spiteful, wanton or humble as she pleases. Celeste and Reginald have never gotten on. The only way he would accept you into our household is if she paid for your upkeep and did not make contact with you."

"What? Why not?" Poppy asked.

"We thought it was best. We did not want you to be influenced by her wild ways. You are so young and impressionable. What if you turned out like her?"

"From what Miss Everly said, I already have," Poppy pointed out.

"Do not take Miss Everly's teasing to heart. She may have tried to goad you, but I assure you, you are as kind and gentle a soul as if you were my own daughter." Her smile was warm.

"So what now?"

Aunt Rachel set aside her embroidery. "The letters stopped. I do not know why. Sometimes it is every few months, sometimes every month. If you wish to write to her, I will not stop you."

"I would like to," Poppy said, "May I meet her?"

"I'm not sure that would be wise." Aunt Rachel's expression was guarded. "I have already said too much, and Reginald would not be pleased if I let you break your mother's promise to him."

"Please. I'd like to get to know my own mother." Poppy

gripped the bedcovers.

"I will speak to Reginald. But for now, you need your rest. There will be no more talk of mothers or anything else until you are better." Aunt Rachel rose from her seat. "I know we have not been honest with you, but I hope you will not judge us too harshly. We did what we thought was best, which is all that any parent would do."

ONCE AUNT RACHEL had left the room, Poppy let out a little breath. She didn't know what to think. The answer of her mother was solved, to a point. But then what were the letters she had received?

She opened the first. It was from a London address. It read:

Dear Miss Morton,

I read your application with interest. I have been looking for a suitable lady's companion for some time and wonder if you would care to come to London for an interview? I would very much like to meet you. Please call on me on the afternoon of Thursday, September fourth, at two o'clock.

Best wishes,
Miss Beatrice Hayes

Poppy stared at the letter in her hands. It was written in a pretty script, on fine paper, in a delicate hand. Who was this woman? Then she remembered.

She had written to her, applying for a position. She had never imagined her application would actually be considered. What had she to offer, aside from conversation and reading? She had little interest in fashion and had not been educated in drawing, poetry, modern languages or music. She frowned, perhaps this was a bad idea. But then, what if this was the answer toward finding her mother? She had a new path to take, if she wanted. Would she do it? And what about the constable? Now that Caroline had been caught, the mystery was solved.

PUTTING THE LETTER from Miss Hayes aside, she reached for the other letter. She carefully opened the cheap paper and read.

Miss Morton,

I hope you are on the mend. I wanted to let you know that all is at an end between Miss Everly and myself. I only feel foolish that I was so distracted by her charms, that I ignored the sensible advice and sound reasoning you offered me time and again. I hope that you will not think less of me for falling for such an adventuress. I hope you will accept my friendship, as much as I esteem and value yours.

Henry Dyngley

After all this time, Dyngley had finally written to her. Poppy read the letter again, feeling her heart pound in her chest. Perhaps that was all they were to be now. Just good friends. Perhaps that was all she could have from him.

"Miss Morton?" Betsey tapped at the doorway. "Constable Dyngley is here to see you."

CHAPTER THIRTY-EIGHT

Poppy put on a suitable housedress, socks and slippers, and held still while Betsey pulled her hair into a plaited knot at the nape of her neck. She was sick of lying in bed, and it felt good to move around, even if she did feel a bit delicate.

She walked downstairs and met the constable, who stood upon seeing her. "Miss Morton, I did not mean to drag you out of bed."

"It's fine, Constable, I'm glad to have an excuse to get up."

Aunt Rachel said, "Betsey, bring us some tea, will you?"

Poppy entered the blue sitting room and took a seat by her aunt. The small movement from her bed to the downstairs had taxed her, and she felt weak. Sitting on the green overstuffed sofa was a comfort, and she leaned back as Constable Dyngley asked, "How are you feeling?"

"Better. I'm not my full self yet, but Dr. Wilson is optimistic."

"Miss Morton, there is something I wish to speak with you about—" he started, when there came a knock at the front door.

Poppy rose as the constable made his excuses. "Forgive me, I cannot stay. I'll call back later." He touched his hat and left, brushing by Louisa Alleyn and Jane who entered the room.

"Miss Alleyn, Miss Heyworth, hello," Poppy said, rising and then sitting back down. "Do sit. Betsey is just preparing tea."

Louisa and Jane looked uncomfortable, and made small talk

until Aunt Rachel excused herself. "I'll just see where that tea's got to."

Jane and Louisa shared a look, and Louisa said, "We came to talk to you. And to share our commiserations."

"I beg your pardon?"

"That is, we were misled by Miss Everly. She said such nasty things about you and…" Louisa gazed down at her clasped hands. "We believed what she said to be true. When I saw you at the doctor's surgery after I had fainted, I thought you were… you know. Scheming to get him."

Poppy's eyebrows rose. She wanted to call out Louisa on this, but something made her hold her tongue.

"I, too," Jane started, "Thought that you were after the man I fancied. I never imagined Mr. Barton was a thief. I was hurt and angry that you did not care for my brother. And when Miss Everly said you were after her fiancé, and then you warned me off Mr. Barton, it was too much. I couldn't believe what I was hearing and chose to ignore your advice." She stared at the floor. "I misjudged you."

"Thank you," Poppy said.

As welcome as their attempts at apologies were, it hurt her deeply to know that these young women had been quick to think so little of her. She found it easy to forgive but hard to forget, and even with a polite apology, she felt her heart harden against trusting people so easily as friends again.

Part of her desperately wished to have a friend, a real friend whom she could confide in and chat with, but also one who would not jump to conclusions or think the worst of her after hearing some idle gossip.

It seemed like their conversation had reached a natural conclusion, when there was a knock at the door. With Betsey out of earshot, Poppy rose to answer it herself.

There stood a young man, dressed in plain clothes, who looked vaguely familiar.

"Can I help you?" Poppy asked.

The young man said, "Forgive me for calling on you like this, but I wonder if you could help me. I'm on my search for the parsonage and I got lost. Am I at the right place?"

"This is the parsonage, yes. Who are you, sir?"

"My name is Charles Ingleby."

CHAPTER THIRTY-NINE

P OPPY STARED. "I beg your pardon? Did you say you were…"
"Mr. Charles Ingleby. I assist the rector up by Lord Ryder's estate in Foxglove Park. This is the parsonage, is it not? Forgive me but I do believe I am terribly late," he said.

At a loss for words, she brought Mr. Ingleby into the room and sat him down immediately.

"Who was at the door, Poppy?" Aunt Rachel asked, carrying a tea tray.

"Mr. Charles Ingleby," she introduced the man standing behind her.

Aunt Rachel dropped the tea set with a crash. It spilled everywhere, all over the floor.

"Oh my, let me help with that." Mr. Ingleby bent to his hands and knees and took out a small handkerchief to start mopping up the mess.

Aunt Rachel stared at him, and then at Poppy as if she'd seen a ghost. "Mr. Ingleby?"

Mr. Ingleby was a comely youth, with short brown hair and a plain yet honest face. He looked up at her, his knees damp with spilled tea and said, "Yes?"

More tea was sent for and arrived, as he was pressed to tell his tale.

"Some time ago my instructor received a letter from Mr.

Greene, asking for temporary assistance in his parish. I try to help where I can, so I offered to go at once, and it seemed like a satisfactory arrangement. I live in the household of the Reverend Jones, so I am sure he appreciated the time without me." He tugged at his collar and had more tea.

"I hired a post-chaise and met the Euston Flyer, which was coming up from London. On the way there I met a young fellow who was also traveling this way, and we decided to journey together. We shared stories of where we had come from, and I told him how I was off to Hertford to look after the parishioners in Mr. Greene's absence. He seemed most interested in my life, and asked a lot of questions about my study as a clergyman, my family, even my patron, Lord Ryder." He took a sip of tea and said, "I found his attention quite gratifying and very kind. But then we began traveling over some bumpy road and the carriage crashed. I can't remember anything after that."

"You poor soul," Aunt Rachel said.

He offered her a warm smile. "I vaguely remember someone talking to me, but I thought it was an angel or perhaps a dream. It happened quite often to be honest, so I do wonder if it wasn't some kind Christian…"

"It was me," Jane said, "it was me."

He looked at her in surprise. "I know that voice. Was it really you? You were talking to me?"

Jane nodded. "I visited you in hospital and would read to you. I heard from the doctor that sometimes talking can help people recover, even if they're comatose."

He blinked. "I am very grateful. I think it was you who helped bring me back."

She beamed at him, and he colored briefly and looked away.

"So you don't recall anything after that?" Aunt Rachel asked.

"Nothing. Only waking up in a strange bed and finding a doctor and nurse by my side. They said I'd been out of it for weeks." He scratched his head. "The strange thing is all my personal effects are gone. I'm very surprised by this. Has no one come looking for me?"

The people in the room exchanged glances.

"Sir," Poppy began, "your traveling companion. Did he have blond hair?"

Mr. Ingleby looked at her, his brown eyebrows furrowing. "Yes. Light blond hair, I think. What of it?"

"And was he, um... portly?"

"I beg your pardon?" he asked, "What are you suggesting about my traveling companions?"

"Did he like his food? Was he a bit plump?" Poppy asked, ignoring the snickers of Louisa and her aunt.

"He was, now that you mention it. I think so anyway. But what does that have to do with anything? Is he all right?"

"Mr. Ingleby, your traveling companion was a trickster. For weeks now, he has been masquerading as you, and causing trouble in town," Poppy said.

"What? What kind of trouble? What do you mean?" he asked.

Poppy sipped her tea as Aunt Rachel relayed what had happened since the false Mr. Ingleby's arrival.

"My word," the real Mr. Ingleby said, "That is remarkable. And to think, he seemed like such a friendly, inquisitive fellow. Do you honestly think he left me for dead, once the carriage crashed?"

Poppy nodded. "He was a thief, on the run from two other members of a gang. Taking your identity was the perfect cover."

"No, I cannot believe it. But if he did decide to take my name for a time, I can only think it was because he wanted a second chance at a new life." He smiled benevolently at her.

Jane said, "You are too good to think poorly of anyone."

Mr. Ingleby said, "I have you to thank. I do not think I would have awoken so soon if you had not sat by and talked to me. I thought it was an angel, talking to me."

Jane blushed. Mr. Ingleby blushed. Then they blushed at each other and laughed. Poppy exchanged a knowing look with her aunt, who snorted and drank more tea.

As THEY TURNED to go, Poppy rose and felt herself relieved. At least her reputation was restored, and as the ladies made their goodbyes, Aunt Rachel busied herself with getting Mr. Ingleby settled in.

Word of the real Mr. Ingleby spread amongst the town, and over the next few days he made sure to visit each of the families in the neighborhood with Aunt Rachel and Poppy, and in turn was regaled with tales of the imposter. He returned each day quite tired, wrote sermons in his spare time and consulted Aunt Rachel constantly for her opinion, praised the fare of her table, and retired early each night. He did snore dreadfully, but there were worse things to have in one's houseguest, Poppy decided. Peace had finally descended on the household and Poppy felt relieved.

AND YET, SHE had not heard from Constable Dyngley in some days, not since receiving his letter and his brief visit. Fortunately, she, Aunt Rachel, and Mr. Ingleby met Constable Dyngley at Lady Cameron's for dinner, where the real Mr. Ingleby shared his tale, and once again heard the story of his replacement.

Poppy smiled at the constable and joined in the conversation, but never got a moment to speak with him alone. She felt his eyes on her, watching, waiting. For what, she didn't know.

Aunt Rachel was in good form, for she announced, "I have had a letter from Mr. Greene, who says that his brother is much improved. It looks like his calming presence and Hilda's medicines did the trick. He expects to return home within a few days' time."

While the others expressed their well wishes for his swift return, Poppy noted that Mr. Ingleby was the only one who looked disappointed by this news.

After a fine meal of light watercress soup, roast lamb with mint jelly, and sweet biscuits for dessert, Lady Cameron beckoned them all to adjourn to her grand sitting room. Once everyone was seated comfortably, she said, "It has been bothering me, that the fake Mr. Ingleby was so harsh in his treatment of you, Mrs. Greene, particularly during the baking competition."

Aunt Rachel gazed down at her lap. "That's all right, your ladyship."

"No, I think not. His behavior toward you was cruel and unkind and had I not been dazzled by his charms, I think I would have seen through his unchristian ways. That is why I wish to award you the prize for the baking competition."

Aunt Rachel gasped. "Me?"

"Yes." Lady Cameron motioned to her companion, Miss Sugg, who walked to a corner of the room and pulled out a small object from a writing desk drawer.

Poppy leaned forward in her seat. This was it. The prize they had been waiting for. The money that the false Mr. Ingleby had hoped to win, and even wanted to learn how to bake puddings for. What all the competitive bakers in town had hoped to earn, along with the gratification and bragging rights of being the best baker in town.

Poppy's eyes widened as Miss Sugg returned with a small, embroidered cushion, on which was embroidered a large red rosette and underneath it, the words, "Best Pudding."

Aunt Rachel's mouth dropped open as the small cushion was presented to her. "I don't know what to say."

Lady Cameron beamed and said, "It was a very good pudding, you know. Much better than the others. What is your secret?"

"Sugar, your ladyship," Aunt Rachel sputtered, looking down at the embroidered cushion. "Sugar."

"I can see from your expression that you are touched, and I am glad you like it. I made it myself. Your hard work deserves recognition, and it was a job well done." Lady Cameron took a seat. "I expect to see it having pride of place on your sofa when I next visit you for tea."

Poppy laughed out loud. So there never was to be a monetary prize after all, despite what the fake Mr. Ingleby had thought.

Seeing the others looking at her, she clapped, which brought on the others in the room to clap as well.

Aunt Rachel turned bright red and said, "Thank you, your ladyship."

Lady Cameron said, "Now, I wished to speak to you all about another matter. The missing contest money."

"It is a shame it has gone missing," Aunt Rachel said, still gazing at the embroidered cushion in her hands.

"Yes, about that... I know exactly where the money is," Lady Cameron said.

"You do?" Poppy asked.

"Yes. You see, the former Mr. Ingleby was most adamant that he be given the money raised for the church roof, to hold for safekeeping, but something about his forthright manner disturbed me. Perhaps even then I had an inkling of his true nature." Lady Cameron wondered aloud. "In any case, I refused and told him that it would be unseemly for a young clergyman to be walking around with such a large sum of money. What if he were robbed?"

Aunt Rachel and Poppy exchanged a look.

"I want to thank you, Miss Morton, for coming to my rescue. It fills me with dread to think that the thief made his way into my room and was ransacking the place. If it weren't for you, I'm not sure what would have happened. Not to mention saving my necklace. That was a dear keepsake of mine."

Poppy shook her head. "It was no trouble, your ladyship."

Lady Cameron gave her a knowing smile. "Enough of that. Good breeding and manners will get you only so far. I am pleased that I did not tell that man a thing, and thanks to your interruption, he did not steal. Besides, I wasn't lying when I told him I didn't know. I have only learned this morning where the money was." She gazed at them, enjoying the attention. "Do you know a young Geoffrey Sutton?"

Aunt Rachel's eyebrows rose. "Yes. He was an altar boy at our church, before Mr. Ingleby..." She looked away.

"What about Geoffrey?" Poppy asked, "Is he all right?"

"Oh, he's quite well. But today he paid my housekeeper a visit." Lady Cameron smiled and said, "On the day of the church fete, the boy saw many people eye the box of money, and seeing that it was a precious commodity, he lifted it."

"You mean he stole?" Constable Dyngley asked.

"No, he didn't. The boy is not a thief. He took the box for safekeeping. It seems that in all the hubbub when Mr. Ingleby died, Geoffrey took the box of money home. He'd planned to return it the next day, but then when he heard that Mr. Ingleby had died, and rumors spread that the man had been poisoned, Geoffrey didn't know who to trust. So he kept it. His mother was one of the bakers you interviewed, I believe."

"Yes, we know Geoffrey very well. But why didn't he come to us?" Aunt Rachel asked, "Or the constable, or his deputy?"

"I think he was nervous. Mr. Ingleby had come from your household, after all, and from what I gather, the boy's exchanges with Mr. Jenkins in the past have not filled him with trust."

"Why did the boy come to you, Lady Cameron?" Dyngley asked.

"The boy's mother is close friends with my housekeeper. He told his mother what he had done, and they arranged for him to have an audience with me. I think he was relieved to hand the money over. It is a good sum, and one that would have tempted many a lesser Christian to keep it." At her nod, Miss Sugg rose and fetched the box, which she brought over to Poppy.

"My goodness," Poppy said, cracking the box open. "There's banknotes here."

"Yes. Quite enough to fix the church roof, I would say. Although from what I have heard, the roof is not in as dire a condition as Mr. Ingleby made it out to be."

"That is true," Dyngley said, "I inspected it myself."

"What? You mean it was all a lie?" Aunt Rachel's mouth dropped open.

"I suspect the man meant to steal it and run away. But perhaps the money could be used for a different purpose?" Dyngley asked.

"Just what I was thinking," Lady Cameron said, smiling at Aunt Rachel. "Maybe Mr. Greene might find a way to use it upon his return, or Mr. Ingleby here could suggest a use for it?"

"Excellent idea," Mr. Ingleby began, "I think the church windows—"

"However, if I might suggest," Lady Cameron interrupted, "Perhaps you might retire that cart of yours and purchase a carriage instead? I know Mr. Greene believes in modest transport, but I find I have an old carriage I no longer need, and wonder if you might want it? I would, of course, sell it to you for a small sum."

Aunt Rachel's eyes lit up. "How much?"

POPPY, AUNT RACHEL and Mr. Ingleby returned home that evening much contented. Mr. Ingleby had already made subtle suggestions on how the remaining funds could be used to benefit the parish, and Aunt Rachel was yawning when there was a knock at the door.

"I'll answer it," Poppy said, rising.

"Very well," Aunt Rachel said, halfway up the stairs. "But if it is a caller for Mr. Ingleby, tell them to call back tomorrow. He's already gone to bed."

Poppy smiled as her aunt disappeared inside her room. She set a candle down on a nearby side table and opened the front door.

There in the darkness stood Constable Dyngley. "Miss Morton." He bowed, stiff and formal.

"Constable," she began, "Is there something the matter? Why are you here so late?"

"I must speak with you." He stepped inside and shut the door behind him.

"Is everything all right?" she asked.

"No, it is bloody well not all right." He glared at her, his dark eyes boring into hers. "I will not move until you say why you have been avoiding me all this time. For days, I have felt like a leper. What have I done to offend you?"

Poppy stepped back and let out a breath. She could bear it no longer. She had to tell him.

"Miss Everly forbade me to talk to you. It was the only way she would agree to tell me about my mother. She wanted me to break off our connection entirely, and threatened to spread the news about my mother if I didn't agree."

"What news?" he asked.

"My mother is…" She looked at the floor. "She is a kept woman. She lives in London, unmarried, as a—"

"She is a mistress," he said bluntly.

"Yes." Poppy blushed in the candlelight. "I would understand if you no longer wished to speak to me—"

His brows knit into a frown. "Surely you would allow me to make up my own mind about whom I wish to talk to?"

"Yes, of course. I did not mean to offend," she said.

"You did not offend. It is I who have been in the wrong. For too long, I chose to believe Caroline's rude words because I didn't want to believe the alternative. I've been such a fool. I didn't want to think that maybe… I came to you that afternoon to talk to you about it, you see… And then tonight at dinner, I couldn't think of how to broach the subject." He stepped toward her.

"You're the son of a baronet," she said, "Miss Everly alluded to it."

"And you're the daughter of a mistress," he said, confused. "What of it?"

"You never told me," she accused.

"Does it matter?"

"No."

"Then that makes two of us. Dash it, Poppy, I haven't been able to stop thinking about it. Poppy. I must know. Did you mean it? What you said?" He asked, "When you said that you…?" He stepped forward with purpose, pulled her close about the waist, and kissed her.

POPPY FELT ON fire. Her entire body felt alive as if she had been doused in flames and now came out drinking fresh water. If she had been stumbling through the desert, Dyngley was her oasis. His hands caressed her hair as he pulled her toward him tighter, and a note of longing came from her throat. The kiss melted into one, then another, until...

"Ahem." A young man cleared his throat.

Poppy sprang away from the constable like he was a hot coal. Blushing to the tips of her ears, she looked at the floor in embarrassment. Dyngley grunted in annoyance and released Poppy's hand.

Mr. Ingleby faced them, looking tired on the stairs in his long nightgown and sleeping cap. "Forgive me for interrupting, I just wanted a glass of milk. Excuse me."

Poppy waited as Mr. Ingleby left for the kitchen, and she met Dyngley's gaze, her cheeks aflame. She shivered beneath his gaze.

Even in the dim candlelight, his expression was intense, and his dark brown eyes smoldered. "Forgive me. I've wanted to do that for quite some time." He swallowed, bowed courteously, and left, not offering her a second glance or goodbye.

Poppy stood there, her heart beating madly.

When Mr. Ingleby returned with a glass of milk, he found her standing in front of the open door. He coughed gently and said, "Forgive me for interrupting you, Miss Morton. I did not realize you had an understanding with the constable."

"I don't. That is to say, we don't—" She blushed again and shut the door.

"Say no more. I completely understand. I'll not say a word until you give me leave to offer you my congratulations." He tapped his nose and began to climb the stairs, then stopped. "Say, you don't know if Miss Heyworth is, um, available? She was most attentive to me in hospital from what I understand, and I think it would be remiss of me not to repay her kindness. Such a good, charitable soul she has."

"She is not engaged, sir," Poppy said with a small smile.

"Excellent. Then I shall call on her. Perhaps your aunt might bake one of her puddings for me to bring over? If they are as good as her ladyship says, then I have no doubt they will be well-received."

Poppy looked Mr. Ingleby in the eye and laughed. "I am sure she would be delighted, sir. And you can trust there will be no arsenic in her pudding."

The End

Historical Note

It was a pleasure to write this novel, and fun to research arsenic poisoning, as well as foods that were around in the Regency era, like gooseberry fool, rhubarb tart, and honey cakes. It was also fun to learn what foods were not around at the time, and what items (such as tiered cake trays) were not in use. Arsenic was readily available and many households kept it. However, there was also a case where it was mistaken for sugar to be used in sweet lozenges, and ended up killing over two hundred people in Bradford in 1858. The idea of poisoning an obnoxious clergyman who loved his puddings is all mine (and fictional), but the use of arsenic as a poison is completely real.

About the Author

E. L. Johnson writes historical mysteries. A Boston native, she gave up clam chowder and lobster rolls for tea and scones when she moved across the pond to London, where she studied medieval magic at UCL and medieval remedies at Birkbeck College. Now based in Hertfordshire, she is a member of the Hertford Writers' Circle and the founder of the London Seasonal Book Club.

When not writing, Erin spends her days working as a press officer for a royal charity and her evenings as the lead singer of the gothic progressive metal band, Orpheum. She is also an avid Jane Austen fan and has a growing collection of period drama films.

Connect with her on Twitter at twitter.com/ELJohnson888 or on Instagram at instagram.com/ejgoth.